I0735975

THE VALKYRIE SERIES

Dead Radiance

Dead Embers

Dead Chaos

Dead Wrath

Dead Silence

THE HAND OF KALI SERIES

Fire & Shadow

Blood & Gold

Time & Fate

Fury & Virtue

Spirit & Soul

Demigod

THE DARK SIGHT SERIES

Dark Sight

Cursed Sight

Vissarion

Shadow Sight

DEAD RADIANCE

USA TODAY BESTSELLING AUTHOR

TEE AYER

DEAD RADIANCE

A VALKYRIE NOVEL BOOK 1

Cover art by Eduardo Priego
Cover art © Tee Ayer. All rights reserved.
ISBN-13: 978-1-991127-00-6
ISBN-10: 1991127006

DEDICATION

For my grandfather Ram Ayer – a beautiful soul.

PROLOGUE

Hovgården, Sweden, 1993

Each sweep of her soft-bristled brush spanned a frozen eternity. One tender stroke caressed the tiniest remnants of dust particles clean. To an untrained eye, nothing remained but dead earth and detritus, but to the Professor and her student assistants such infinite care proved both frustrating and mesmerizing.

They worked, untiring, unceasing. Shift after dedicated shift, hour after relentless hour they toiled until at last the skeleton emerged from the arms of the dark earth. Another ancient burial site had relinquished its lone occupant.

The archaeologists stepped back against the strutted walls of the grave, stretching cramped muscles, while at their heads onlookers gasped and shuffled closer to the grave. So far, only students, site directors and representatives from the Stockholm

Museum and Preservation Society had gathered at the site. They scrambled for space at the edges of the large tent, which protected the open pit against the elements.

The cracked plastic of the tent shuddered in a rude blast of wind. Geoffrey Halbrook clutched his fedora with one hand, afraid he would lose it to the grasping gust. He craned his balding head, a weak attempt to peer over the shoulders of the people in front of him. They appeared to line up just to keep him out.

"Dr. Halbrook?" A woman's voice wafted from the pit, gritty with irritation and impatience. "Has anyone seen Dr. Halbrook?"

"I am here, Professor Wayne!" Halbrook yelled from behind the wall of shoulders as he pushed his glasses back up his sweat-drenched nose, still gripping his hat. "I would get to you if I were allowed through!"

The wall parted, and Halbrook, annoyed they had kept him out in the first place, shouldered past. He stepped on toes to keep from falling into the pit, and made his way to the rickety wooden stairs at the head of the open gravesite, cramming his metal case and crumpled fedora against his chest.

A rumble of complaints rose from the crowd, surly and vulgar. Halbrook did not care. He had one thing on his mind. Take his samples.

And then get the hell out.

But he stopped dead on the last step, his eyes fixed on the desiccated remains, which lay in the bottom of the grave.

"Remember to breathe," said Professor Wayne, an indulgent grin on her lips.

Halbrook took no offense. He performed what should have been an automatic bodily function.

He breathed.

"Amazing, isn't it?" asked the Professor.

Her smile widened as she welcomed him down, all teeth, auburn curls, and sun-toasted skin. Hardly an attractive face, but at least a welcome one.

Halbrook restrained the urge to look up at the unhappy group behind him. The heat of their words aggravated the heat of the day as he squatted alongside the skeleton and set his case beside him with overt care.

His hands trembled as he scanned the corpse from the skull, intact and immaculate, to the lifeless strands of her rich red hair, to each individual tarsal and meta-tarsal grazing the foot of the grave.

The bones themselves were ordinary enough, merely remains of a person from a life and a time long past. Wayne, Halbrook and the spectators were suitably in awe of them, but it was the bed upon which they lay that would be burned into their memories forever.

Tall, graceful and elegant, the remains lay against the haunting and eerie remnants of a pair of wings too large to belong to a bird. Each feather so real, so well preserved it still glimmered where the light hit it just so. Many of the feathers were so long they reached at least a third of the height of the skeleton itself.

Halbrook's thigh muscles cramped as he crouched over the dried-out husk of what had once been a living, breathing human, so entranced he barely gave his discomfort the slightest attention.

"So? What do you think?" Wayne asked. An expectant smile revealed her perfect teeth.

Halbrook shrugged. "Some sort of headdress?" He spoke the

lie effortlessly. He would rather not look the fool. He would be risking his name and his reputation if he admitted aloud what his instinct screamed this creature looked like to him.

A thing of myth and fable. A creature so remarkable that thousands of years after the myths had died people still half-believed the stories. A Valkyrie or an angel. Judging by the location of this dig, only one option made sense.

A Valkyrie.

Halbrook glanced at Professor Wayne. Her narrowed eyes silently called him a coward. "I'd say this is a Valkyrie, Dr. Halbrook," she said. "Now take your samples and prove me wrong."

The mob sniggered and Halbrook's cheeks reddened. He turned to the remains, not deigning to justify her challenge with an answer. Not deigning to provide the vultures above with more fodder for their jeers. His job was paramount, not bets with some hard-nosed feminist archaeologist with her head in the past and her fingernails filled with dirt.

He reached for his case, snapped the locks and withdrew a scalpel and a syringe. He concentrated, searching for viable flesh, for bone still intact, which could possibly contain living DNA.

Minutes then hours ticked by and soon the sun sank into the hills somewhere in the west. He did not register the flashes of the cameras, the buzz of the media when they arrived and swooped around the tent on the scent of a hot story. Neither was he aware of the dispersion of the unsavory crowd, as the light fled from the graying sky. At last, all his samples taken, labeled and stored within his temperature-controlled case, Dr. Halbrook stood and straightened his trousers and jacket.

Only Wayne had remained behind, still supervising her find. If he didn't know her, it would have been easy to assume she didn't trust him.

"How long?" Professor Wayne possessed the most disconcerting way of examining Halbrook with her honey gaze, as if she could see right through him into his soul. And she needed a timeframe. How long until she could confirm the true identity of the remains as a Valkyrie?

"The actual test procedure will take a few weeks, Professor Wayne. These things take time, as you well know." He raised his voice just the tiniest fragment as she opened her mouth to protest. "You do want accurate results, do you not?"

She nodded, arms crossed, skewering him with her heated stare.

He smashed his hat onto his skull, grabbed his case and marched out of the pit, as well as a man could march up a flight of rickety stairs.

His mind whirled, already planning the details of his experiments and tests before he cleared the last step. Instinct told him what his eyes confirmed. And if his hunch proved true and the skeleton belonged to a Valkyrie, then Halbrook had plans for the precious DNA he carried.

Special plans.

CHAPTER 1

I was cold, like the roses on Joshua's casket, like the muddy dark-brown soil waiting to embrace the lifeless remains of the boy who was my friend.

My fingers curled around the stem of a butter-yellow rose, knuckles tight. I blinked away the liquid burn stabbing my eyelids. I had to get out. Give him the rose. Then get the hell away.

I tried to squeeze past the old woman who guarded my route to the center aisle, glaring. Her stares slithered down my neck as I passed. I shuffled by, careful not to touch her. But she huffed, her shoulders stiff and unimpressed with my rudeness. Her disapproval slid down my back.

I straightened my pencil skirt and short coat, scraped my wet hands on my hips. I knew the cool black silk wouldn't dry my sticky palms, but I did it anyway, needing to do something with my hands other than clutch the dead flower.

The slim heels of my pumps sank deep into wet ground. I jerked them free and swallowed, my throat aching with tears. My best friend would soon be entombed within this sodden mush, to lie beneath Craven forever. Until his flesh fell off his bones and he turned to dust.

A cool hand tapped my shoulder.

"Bryn Halbrook. " She spat my name, each syllable harsh, and dripping venom to match the tiny emerald flecks in her hazel eyes. "You've got some nerve coming here." Cherise Barnes knew she looked good, even in drab funerary garb. She stood, a bony hip jutting out, one foot forward. The Cherise pose.

The last thing I needed was a bitch-match. Not here. I straightened, pulling my jacket closer in the face of this poisonous storm. Her eyes widened as I drew to my full height. Guess Cherise forgot it wasn't easy to intimidate a person who was a full head taller. I stared down at her.

Waiting.

"Perhaps you should leave." She tapped the foot. "Now."

"I *am* leaving, as soon as I pay my respects. *You* are holding me up."

A streak of red colored her cheeks. She avoided my eyes, then addressed my ear. "You shouldn't have come in the first place. You aren't welcome here."

She wasn't backing off and I knew why. Cherise was *The Body* here in Craven. Not the body to die for, though, as most guys didn't need to go that far to sample Cherise. Joshua had belonged to her, and she'd lost him. Lost him to me. Or so she thought.

I brushed past Cherise, had no patience for her any more. I fingered the bandage on my temple, touched the braid tied at my nape so my deep red hair wouldn't tangle in the stitches on my scalp. The slight movement shifted my hair and the wound stung, releasing a flash of memory.

White light, blinding, sears my eyes.
Brighter now. Bright enough to hurt.
Tires squeal, harsh screams rip at my eardrums.

I swallowed a gasp, shoving the memory out of my head.

I had to get a grip.

I'd survived and he hadn't. It didn't matter anymore. The only person who'd supported me had died on me.

I'd known he would die. And I'd done nothing to stop it.

As I neared Joshua's parents, they threw me weak and teary smiles, which made the dam of tears inside my own heart yearn to burst free. Even in their time of grief, they'd been so concerned about me, asking if I'd recovered enough to get out of the hospital, if I'd grieved enough, let it all out.

No one shared their concern, not last week and not today. Claws of ice scraped up and down my back. Again. More accusing stares. Too many eyes. More heads turning. Whispers. I ignored them. Concentrated on anything else but those voices. Cars passing by at the bottom of the hill. People going about their daily lives, neither knowing nor caring that a friend and a son and a brother was about to be consigned to the dead earth of Craven.

Stepping closer to the coffin I sucked in a sob; the hollow in my gut grew harder, more painful, as I stared at the shining black casket.

Roses trailed the ebony lid, droplets of color scattered across its gleaming surface by a careless yet artful hand. Eternity crept by while the box descended into the dark mouth of the grave.

The rainbow of color shivered, slim green stems entangled on the curve of the lid. One rose, bright, blood red, slid off, as the coffin moved deeper and deeper.

Ice sliced through my veins.

Piercing to the bone and to the soul.

Blank, gray afternoon skies shed occasional tears for Joshua O'Connell. The casket lurched, then continued its descent. I gave in. Better give him the rose, a little piece of me to take with him.

I choked on a breath, swallowing a wave of nausea.

Metal shrieks, grating in a lurid embrace. Deafening.
Sparks spit, ozone coats the back of my throat.
Gasoline fumes creep up my nostrils, burning, suffocating.

I stopped at the edge of the gaping wound in the earth. Something felt wrong. Inside the grave, the black box came to rest within deep grasping shadows. Darkness simmered, broken by a line of glimmering, golden light that seeped through the edges of the casket.

He still glowed and I was still helpless.

My fingers uncurled their desperate grip on the rose and it fell, tilting, to drop head first onto the coffin, twirling as it descended into the eerie depths. It hit the lid and shattered. Petals flew in all directions and everywhere yellow scraps of the dismembered flower reflected Joshua's iridescent light.

I turned, eager to flee.

Not possible. Not in heels, which sank into the mushy soil as if the soft earth itself yearned to claim me. Not when mourners had risen from their seats and were lining up to toss soil and tributes onto the casket. I struggled for breath, my heart knocking double, triple time like an angry jackhammer abandoned in my chest.

I steered a path through the crowd. Ignored a young man in the middle row whose skin held the first yellow specks of iridescence. Who was he? Did it even matter who he was? I sighed. It wouldn't be much longer for him anyway. I ignored the woman with the red-rimmed eyes, holding onto his arm. I didn't want to see him patting her pale hand and giving her that watery smile.

Will she be alone, like me, when he's gone? Who will pat her hand then?

Turning away, I kept walking. Didn't want to look anymore. Didn't want to see any more glowing people.

I breached the throng and paused to breathe.

To wait for my erratic heartbeat to slow down.

To forget I left my friend behind, alone in the unforgiving ground.

CHAPTER 2

The first time I'd laid eyes on Joshua, he'd already begun to glow. What a way to kick off week one at Craven's only high school. At the time, I had no idea what the aura meant, and there was no one I could talk to about it.

Not in Craven. Not anywhere.

I was the new kid in town, an outsider. New towns unnerved me. No surprise since I encountered a new town every few months, running the foster circuit, pushed around by funding cuts and just plain burnt-out foster parents who were never real parents anyway. And Craven was no different.

My foster mom, Ms. Patricia Custer, had tried to make me feel welcome, even insisting I call her *Mom*. Her big, broad smile matched her generous hips—tacit proof of her scrumptious cooking. Enormous white teeth in a mouth curved in a permanent smile, even when she scolded.

But if Ms. Custer threw some sunshine onto my life at Craven, then North Wood High epitomized the dark zone. North Wood's warm, redbrick buildings were at odds with the aloofness of the student body, the distant teachers and the near-vicious vice principal.

Arriving just in time for senior orientation didn't help at all. Not as if I would fit in anyway. So I kept a low profile. Steered clear of the popular crowd, the jocks and the smart kids. Mouth shut. Head down. Waste of effort making friends. Even if they stuck around, they ended up turning on you. And if they didn't turn, *you* left.

Two days later, the arrival of an unexpected package disturbed my usual process of new town assimilation. Lawyers handling my father's estate had finally tracked me down. An official-looking letter confirmed it as a much-delayed sixteenth birthday gift. I moved around too much, wouldn't have been easy to find.

I escaped to my room to unwrap the shoebox-size cardboard package. A flat rectangular box, covered in a deep green fabric, lay buried within piles of foam chips. I'd never received mail before.

Giant butterflies fought for space in my stomach and I wondered what the box could possibly contain. I fiddled with a tiny gold wire clasp holding the lid shut tight, jiggling it, careful not to destroy the intricate filigree. At last the clasp gave and I lifted the heavy lid.

Within the box, on a bed of black satin, lay a pendant so exquisite, so entrancing, it stole the breath from my lungs. A warm, ethereal glimmer emanated from the elegant amber teardrop, as wide at its base as a dollar coin and encased by silver filigree lacework.

The gemstone sat in my palm, a little shining sun, warm and tingly and entrancing. The thick leather string should have clashed with the elegance of the silver filigree, yet it meshed. Richness tempered by the earthiness of the raw cord.

I tied it around my neck and stood before the mirror, staring. The pendant sat in the hollow of my throat as if made and measured to fit, and after that day, it never left my neck. Its warmth soothed a little of the loneliness within the heart that beat beneath it.

The comfort of the amber jewel hadn't taken my mind totally off of my new-school blues, but it certainly made things easier in the first few days. I could deal with the sideways glances, the up-and-down inspections, even the solitary lunchtimes.

I managed well enough on my own until I ran into Joshua. Yeah, I *managed*.

Until the day star quarterback Joshua O'Connell radiated the first dustings of gold. Sprinkled on his cheeks, shimmering in the sunlight and growing brighter each time I saw him.

A glow only I could see.

A glow that kept my eyes trained on him throughout our first Biology class together. I stared. And he noticed. He frowned at first, then grinned and winked. I paid little attention to the lesson, distracted by the glow on his skin and the clear warmth in his eyes.

After class I fumbled in my locker until the rather loud sound of a throat being cleared drew my head out of the metal space. Surprised, I looked into the eyes of the glowing boy.

"Hi," he said. His cheery grin hadn't faded. "You must be new. I'm Joshua."

I stared at the hand he'd stuck out, then reluctantly grasped it. My first real welcome. Wow.

At least he didn't assume I was stalker material. We hung out after school that day, and every day. He was safe. Safe because Joshua and I didn't have the whole chemistry thing going on.

Just friends. He wasn't my type; I knew that much even though I hadn't yet defined a personal type, romantic or otherwise. And my height posed a problem. Hardly the best start to a romance, towering over a guy.

So we talked. A lot. I assumed he'd never understand me, but Joshua surprised me. He understood being different. He was beige.

Not quite black enough, not quite white enough; his mom was Indian and his dad one hundred percent Irish, straight off the plane.

He was awesome enough to look at, with all that naturally tanned skin and black, black eyes. The ebony hair made him look all the more bad-boy. Which he totally wasn't.

But it didn't take long before I couldn't bear to be in his company for more than a few minutes at a time. Looking at his ever-brightening face hurt my eyes, bringing on strange, persistent headaches.

Avoiding Joshua rocked the foundations of our friendship. I had hurt him, but he didn't take my sudden aloofness lying down.

He insisted on walking me home one day, ignoring the fact that I was ignoring him. "Why are you avoiding me?" he demanded, a dark scowl wrinkling his good looks. I didn't look at him, just put one foot in front of the other and gritted my jaw against the headache gnawing at my temples.

I couldn't tell him that it hurt to look at him. I couldn't tell him that I had this weird gift. The ability to see strange auras around random people wasn't exactly useful, and I'd learned the hard way to be careful who I told.

I'd seen the glow before. Had seen it since forever. No amount of psychiatrists could make it go away. For some strange reason my father understood and accepted my weird visions. I remained grateful until he was no longer there to stand by me. After that, I never spoke of it again.

Even if I told Joshua he'd never believe me. And I would've been fine staying silent if it hadn't been for Aimee Graham. I'd seen her around school, on and off.

The short, dark-haired girl had glowed and brightened, soon matching Joshua's glowing intensity, until she stopped coming to classes altogether. I'd had no idea what the golden auras meant until she returned to school one fall morning, and the rumors began.

Cancer, they said. Some sort of leukemia that ate away at her body like a wood-borer munching on old furniture. I'd stared at her as she walked by my locker, then looked away, looked anywhere except at the rainbow patchwork headscarf covering her bare scalp.

She shone with such radiance, blazing like a small sun, so bright that my eyes teared. She'd turned and met my gaze. And smiled.

And never smiled at me again.

Aimee had made it back to school for only a single day. The next morning, Mr. Freeman addressed the class, his voice soft and subdued, as if a loud voice would be disrespectful.

Aimee had died during the night.

That day I knew for sure. I'd lost control of my tears then. They fell in huge, mocking drops. I stared at Joshua through those bitter tears, my heart missing beats as I tried to remember to breathe.

I finally knew what the glow meant.

I was a freak and Joshua was going to die.

CHAPTER 3

It started and ended with the Camaro. Joshua's dad messed around with his '85 Camaro in his garage, passing the passion to his eldest, to his wife's utter dismay. One day at school, when I'd finally regained control of my constant urge to either stare or burst into tears, we'd launched into an argument.

"You reek like an engine." I scrunched up my nose. He didn't really reek though. I smiled at the random grease stains, which flecked his jeans and gave him away. "What are you working on?"

He chuckled, ignored the insult. "Camaro Z28," he said with a fluid twist to his head. All challenge, brooking no argument.

"Ha! A Camaro? Now if you'd said Mustang Cobra I'd have been impressed." I stared him down, squashing the laughter that threatened to spoil my macho stance.

Two foster homes ago, I'd had a foster dad much like Joshua's dad. Real speed freak. Loved his Cobra like a child, not that he ever allowed me to ride. Nope, he took his foster responsibility seriously. Fast cars meant danger, so I'd been relegated to watching him work on those gleaming machines.

I never forgot the acid spike of the spirits he used to clean the chrome or the dull tone of the oil when he changed it and droplets spilled on the bare concrete. And when Joshua spoke of his baby, I knew I'd get a ride in it, no matter what. Beneath the banter lay the bet. He eventually gave in. What would it hurt anyway? Just one ride.

WHEN HE CAME to pick me up, Ms. Custer frowned as I sped to the door.

"He coming in then? Or is he gonna let that monster growl outside like a hell hound?"

"Nope, we're going out for a ride."

The frown deepened. "Now, Bryn. I . . ." She paused. She was so going to stop me. I held my breath but the frown smoothed and her eyes crinkled. Wrong. Perhaps she trusted me. "Be careful, and wear your seatbelt."

She followed me out onto the wraparound porch just to be sure, and stood watching while I jumped into the gorgeous red machine, adjusted the strap and fastened the seatbelt as she'd instructed. Joshua had cursed its bum clasp to no end but thankfully the darned thing chose this night to lock loudly. We both sighed.

I curled my arms around my midriff, unsure what to do with them. Folding them in my lap would appear silly, especially when we sat within a growling machine so far from demure as to be ridiculous.

Excitement and nerves warred inside me. Beside me and beneath his leather jacket, Joshua glowed brighter than yesterday. More radiant than last week. My heart stuttered and I forced those thoughts away. How could I change the inevitable? Was it possible that I could influence his life? Prevent his death? Who could I go to? Who could help me?

Nobody.

The best answer I'd come up with.

I was all out of luck and so was Joshua.

A moonless night and a patch of oil were never meant to be friends. Not anywhere and certainly not within the dark embrace of Craven. A black and angry cloud hung over the town, permeating the spirit of the place, hiding behind closed doors and beneath masks of pleasantry. Paranoia? Maybe.

I blamed my jaded opinion on the ache in my heart. The first time I understood that the damned glow was synonymous with death, it happened to be coming from the first friend I'd ever made.

Joshua grinned at me, teeth glinting in the lights from the street-lamps, mischief and self-satisfaction plastered across his face. I'd gotten what I'd wanted. But he'd gotten more. He revved the engine and I could have sworn the hefty laughter coming from the vicinity of the veranda belonged to Ms. Custer. Taking off at a walking pace, we slid along the darkened streets.

I closed my lids, absorbing the throb of the engine through the reconditioned leather, resting them from the ever-present radiance of Joshua. I bore the pain of meeting his eyes, because I longed for one more smile. I had no idea when his laughter would embrace me for the last time, or if the next silly, girlish giggle he gave, when a joke happened to be unconstitutionally funny, would be his last.

We turned onto Main and headed uphill, through the empty streets. Up ahead a pair of lights turned into Main and rode toward us.

Nothing ever happened in Craven. Nothing to get tongues wagging. Not until our night in the Camaro.

The oil patch appeared in the split second between Joshua's gasp and the crunching of metal. The rainbow at its center caught my eye. The shimmering, bland menace of it; a warning too late. A second, meant to be the shortest of moments, was enough. A blink in time filled with Joshua's grimace of fear, filled with hopeless desperation, as he wrenched the wheel against the spin of the car. Filled with the stark horror on the faces of the couple in the other car as we spun toward them.

The crunch of metal.

The barely audible click of my seatbelt as it came undone.

Metal tasted metal.

The two cars crumpled into each other, the force of the impact flinging me across the street. Slamming my body into the light pole outside Joe's Barbershop. Any normal person would have broken in half, spine crushed from the impact of vertebrae to steel pole. Not me.

Coming away from the accident with a head wound, no matter how serious, wasn't enough for Craven. I should have died like Joshua. The couple in the other car was still in the hospital.

But I was still walking.

Still breathing.

They hated me for that.

CHAPTER 4

I skidded out of my memories and walked back alone from the funeral, away from the eyes.

The wind blustered and thin silk was no match for its icy tentacles. My feet dragged me back toward Ms. Custer's, the silent afternoon keeping me company. I was thankful for the solitude. Thankful for the subtle warmth soaking into my body from the amber at my neck.

One block to go. An engine suddenly growled behind me, throbbing closer and closer, raucous laughter raising the hair on my neck. A car tailed me; its honking brought goose bumps to my skin. A bunch of nasty, dumb kids voicing their displeasure at my survival. I kept walking. Exhaled only when they whined past. The driver thrust his arm out the window and raised his middle finger. Strident laughter followed. I flushed, embarrassed, furious at his nerve.

My heart stuttered as the twin red eyes disappeared into the gathering shadows ahead. Sighing, I turned into Elm Wood, seeking the lights of home. Bright lights beckoned in the dusk like so many welcoming flames. The house promised warmth and comfort. A blessed haven in which to hide away.

But only a temporary home. I'd learned not to grow too fond, not to get too comfortable.

Three other kids occupied the loving home of Ms. Custer, laying claim to foster-hood more than I had the right to. All orphans. Simon Harper and Brody Stevens were both ten and cute as a pair of unmatched buttons could be cute. Simon, pale and blond, in contrast to Brody's dark skin and sooty hair. Otherwise, they were the same. Boisterous, cheeky, funny and a handful. Ms. Custer called them "Ebony and Ivory." Most appropriate.

Isabel Martin was elegant, sweet and very, very quiet for a twelve-year-old. But all three accepted me, drew me into their little family despite my discomfort and constant protests.

I let myself into the house, expecting Brody and Simon to be in the living room pretending to do their homework, and Izzy in the kitchen peeling vegetables or laying the large dining table. I craved peace and quiet and knew I wasn't going to get it.

The living room's silence greeted me, while the kitchen simmered with cheerful chatter amidst the clinking of utensils. As I stepped inside the kitchen a second of peace reigned before Brody and Simon spoke over each other, asking how Joshua's brother was doing. Izzy smiled, waiting for her turn to question the life out of me.

Ms. Custer stood at the sink, drying a dish that looked dry to begin with, her smile a faded copy of her usual toothy blessings.

"Come on, kids, get to your chores. Boys, help Izzy set the table please. Use the good dinner service and be careful. Anyone break anything and they'll be scooping horse poop at McGregor's Farm for the whole of spring break."

They groaned and flashed out the door, bickering comfortably as they worked.

"It's dry, you know?" I lifted an eyebrow at the dish.

She huffed, laid it on the table and proceeded to fill it with steaming mashed potatoes. The food should have assaulted my taste buds, but not a particle within me did any sort of dance at the prospect of eating. Not anymore. It'd been weeks since food had last satisfied me and I longed to eat the roast just for the sake of recalling the taste and sensations on my tongue. It would no doubt do no good. These days food equated to tasteless sludge.

"When was the last time you ate a proper meal?" Ms. Custer's eyes narrowed, as if she possessed some kind of inner lie-detecting radar. She had no idea how long it had been and I didn't intend to tell her I survived on air and water these days. Just about anything could get a foster kid moved.

"A proper meal you mean?" I received a curt nod and a further narrowing of her eyes. "Around the time Aimee Graham died."

The truth was the last thing I'd intended but it slipped out of my mouth anyway. The queen of avoidance was also an awful, awful liar.

Ms. Custer nodded. The skin around her eyes softened. "That was three weeks ago, young lady. How are you surviving?" I waited as she yelled for Izzy, who hauled the mashed potatoes to the dining table.

"Not sure," I said. What was wrong with my mouth?

Way to go, Bryn. A secret stash of smartass quips, a thousand snarky responses and you spew out the bald truth?

"Are you eating anything at all?" Concern and fear swam back into her warm brown eyes.

I shook my head. "Food tastes like sawdust. And makes me ill." I gripped the chair in front of me, needing the solid wood to ground me.

"But you don't look like you've survived on nothing. Not skin and bones at all. You *look* fine." Ms. Custer spoke below her breath. Since she didn't seem to expect an answer, I bit my tongue. "Maybe you need to see a counselor?"

My head shook a violent response while inside my mind I screamed, panicked. I drowned in memories.

My mother's voice echoed in my head, harsh with pain. Her accusations. My fear when I figured out what I'd done by admitting I could see the glow.

The visits to the psychiatrist who persisted in his treatment, delving deeper, searching for a reason for the visions. A reason that would match one of his textbook definitions. Even the quiet understanding of my father hadn't made it any better.

"No!" The skin on my knuckles went taut as I gripped harder, terrified I'd lose control. The word barked out, harsher than I'd intended. "I'm sorry, Mom. It's just . . . I've had my fair share of counseling. If anything, they make things worse, not better."

She paused and I just knew she wouldn't let the issue slide. But her next words surprised me. "That's okay, Bryn, honey." Her smile, like the soft pat on my shoulder, was gentle and sweet and enduring. "Did it go well today?" She reached out and gently touched my bandage.

Ms. Custer had intended to come to the funeral but I'd asked her to stay home. Didn't want the kids exposed to more grief. And my sorrow craved solitude. I wasn't sure why, but I knew I'd shatter into a million shards of grief if my little family were with me.

I just nodded. No sense in telling her about Cherise and her malicious machinations. Ms. Custer's face tightened but she let it be.

Tender garlic and herb-roasted chicken and butter-glazed carrots made it safely to the table. I went through the motions, pretending to eat under the stern supervision of my foster mother. Washing up was easier to do and I escaped the kitchen, both dishes and myself in one piece.

A wide veranda hugged the front half of the house, dark and private, especially in the evenings. I surrendered to its comforting embrace. Enjoyed the thrill of having the porch swing to myself, reveled in the enveloping dark night and the sweet scent of Ms. Custer's pink climbing roses. I sat alone, enclosed in my little private world, with just the crickets and cicadas to vie for my attention.

I STAYED HOME, under doctor's orders to take things easy after the accident and the blow to my head. A week dragged by. A week in which I relished the chattering of leaves outside my window, as the wind frolicked through the thick branches of the red maple. A week I wanted to last forever. Not because the end of it meant I'd have to run the North Wood High gauntlet again, but because I'd lost my support. My strength. My only friend who I'd just let die, without doing a thing about it.

The porch swing creaked, and I sighed, loving the silent, fragrant darkness. A fake haven where I remained invisible and the world walked by without knowing I watched. I should have seen Aimee's father walking his dog, trying to maintain a sense of normality after losing his only daughter. Should have seen Anna and Cherise slip into Anna's house and throw vicious stares at our house as if the building itself had taken their hunky quarterback from them. But all I saw were lonely pink petals falling and falling into nothingness.

Until the black and chrome Ducati roared, loud and intrusive as it turned into our driveway.

CHAPTER 5

Biker-dude cut the engine and swung off the machine, his movement like a river of mercury. He strolled to the front door. *Walk* wasn't the most appropriate word for the rolling gait he used to go from bike to door, but it did strange things to my heart and my breath. Deliciously nice things.

I stared from the darkness, half a smile on my lips, one foot on the wooden deck so the swing didn't give me away with a random creak, holding my breath. He thumbed the doorbell and peeled off his helmet. Long black hair dripped over his forehead and caressed his nape. He fluffed the dark mop, not in the vain I-look-so-hot way, but in an unconscious get-out-of-my-face way.

For the first time in my sad and predictably unlucky life, my heart lurched in my chest. All the soppy, mushy stuff was present: lightheartedness, breathless expectation, deep rosy blushes.

Exactly the way girls fell for the male lead in chick flicks or the way the simpering heroines swooned in great romance novels.

I barely heard the porch door squeak open. I even missed Ms. Custer saying, "Oh, it's you. Come in, come in!" He followed her inside and I waited while they talked. Crickets chirped, reminding me to get my head out of the clouds. A steady breeze tugged at the branches of our red oak and cooled my heated cheeks. I didn't dare enter the house. Or leave the veranda.

I peered through the drapes as they talked in the living room. Though I strained to make sense of their conversation I got nothing but muffled sounds. When they shook hands and walked back toward the door, I breathed a sigh of relief. Thank heaven. He was leaving.

Ms. Custer let him out and shut the door behind him. I waited. He took the two porch stairs in a single stride and slung his leg over the bike. Right before he put his helmet on he turned and looked straight at me, through the darkened branches of the climbing rose, which should have hidden me from view.

"It's rude to spy on people, you know?" He softened his words with a smile, teeth glittering even in the fading evening light. The darkness hid the hot red of my cheeks. His deep laughter echoed as he shoved the helmet onto his head. He shut the face-piece of his helmet, cutting off the stomach-tingling sound of his voice, and revved the engine. Silver gleamed at his neck and then he disappeared into the gathering shadows.

I shoved off the swing, sending it into a creaking frenzy. Caught, embarrassed and fuming I'd even done such a thing. I pushed the front door open and barreled into the living room.

Ms. Custer's knitting occupied her generous lap; needles

flashed this way and that, keen on creating her next rainbow-colored scarf. On the TV Hannibal smiled and chewed on his cigar.

"Who was that guy?" I asked, keeping my expression as neutral as possible, hoping the color in my cheeks had faded away.

"Oh, that nice young man is our latest foster." Ms. Custer had fallen for his smile, too. "He'll be moving in tomorrow bright and early."

Fabulous.

Mr. Hot Wheels, who'd made my pathetic heart race, was moving in. Just great. I harnessed my embarrassed rage, ignored the temptation to run upstairs, slam my door shut, throw myself onto my bed and scream into my pillow. Instead, I gazed through the window at the shadows that had swallowed Biker-dude. I still couldn't wipe the stupid half-smile off my face. Guess it would do no harm to have some eye candy around. And though Joshua had qualified as eye candy, he'd been my friend.

Biker-dude didn't look much like *just-friend* material.

Sleep eluded me, and when at last I succumbed, my dreams were hazy, filled with the bright golden gleam of Joshua and Aimee, screeching tires and crunching metal.

And the faint echo of the rev of a motorcycle engine.

CHAPTER 6

Morning rushed in on quicksilver feet, clear and bright and at odds with my musty sentiments. Another school day. Running the gauntlet with Cherise and her friends at North Wood High.

Just great.

Before Joshua, I'd never cared much what other people thought of me. But then Joshua died and I'd survived.

And now Craven deepened its hatred for the interloper, the new girl who'd come into their lovely town bringing darkness, death and destruction.

If I hadn't figured out the true meaning of the glow, I'd have done the same: blame Bryn.

I pushed scrambled eggs and pieces of hash brown around on my plate under Ms. Custer's disapproving gaze. The little yellow globs stuck to the roof of my mouth, while oily bits of fried potato tickled my throat.

I had to choke down the urge to hurl.

Poor Ms. Custer was certain I was eating elsewhere and though I wished I could express my fear that my metabolism was shot to hell, I knew she'd never believe me.

People believed what they wanted.

Foster parents had to believe the child coming to them would be a problem. They preferred the stereotype because they didn't dare to wish for a good kid and end up with a rotten one.

Ms. Custer wasn't the standard out-of-the-box foster parent, but how could anyone believe a person could survive a whole month without food?

Me and my big mouth.

I was simply unable to lie to her. I sighed. She thought I'd lied anyway.

I scraped off my plate when she turned away, then dragged the strap of my bag over my shoulder. Outside, I tucked my chin in against the cool wind and walked fast.

The brisk trip to school cleared my head, refreshing me until I reached the sidewalk in front of the old redbrick structure of the main building.

Huge windowpanes stared out, glassy eyes reflecting the clear blue sky above. The pretty picture did nothing to ease the dread in my gut.

I STEPPED into the gray gloom of the school halls, dull and drab compared to the rich red of the building's facade. Stares tickled the hair at the back of my neck; whispers raised the goose bumps on my skin.

Same old same old, until I received a summons to the vice principal's office during first period English. My feet got me to his office. Reluctantly.

Vice Principal Warren examined me from behind glasses with rims so thick it looked like he had frightful cataracts. Nevertheless he managed to imbue within them sufficient venom to pique my curiosity and awareness.

My heart thumped.

This didn't bode well for my day.

"Miss Halbrook, I want to get a few things straight." His grotesquely misshapen eyes stared.

I waited. Was I supposed to ask him to clarify? Unsure, I decided to go with silence.

Finally, he snorted and said, "It's enough you've managed to influence our young Joshua . . . and now the poor boy is dead. Such a future he had before him. Such a waste." Warren shook his head, the fluorescent light above him throwing his well-oiled hair into starker light, casting strange shadows on the sagging lines in his face. His fingers traced the slippery strands at his neck, fingers coming away slick with the oily residue.

He spent too long scanning my face, a self-satisfied, sinister twist to his lips. I squandered precious seconds wondering if Craven had any links to Salem. I waited, vulnerable prey in the face of Warren's vitriol.

"I hope you will concern yourself with your schoolwork and nothing else, Miss Halbrook." He leaned forward. I ached to back away, but the steel backrest of the chair wouldn't allow it. "I will have none of what you got up to at the funeral with Miss Barnes. The poor girl was upset enough without your insinuating comments."

"Huh? We barely spoke." But I could tell he wouldn't believe me. I gritted my teeth.

My ears rang, great clanging sounds so deafening it was a wonder I registered a word he said, but I did. Damn well heard Cherise's pathetic, successful lies.

I wasn't the most popular kid in the school, but I swallowed a bitter pill sitting in the principal's office, unable to defend myself. It must have been against my constitutional rights in some way, but in Craven things didn't work well for Bryn Halbrook.

"Oh, that reminds me. We have a new student starting today. And since he is from Ms. Custer's care, it seems appropriate for you to shepherd him around instead of any of my other students. It's really, really sad to see there isn't enough being done with kids like you." He sneered, the corner of his lip rising to reveal nicotine-yellowed teeth.

He picked up a sheet of school-issue yellow paper, the ones Craven kept for detention and permission slips.

The oil from his fingers seeped into the paper, spreading, bleeding the ink of the printed words.

"Kids like me?" I tried to keep the bite out of my voice but it didn't matter. Warren listened only to the sound of his own voice.

"Yes, Miss Halbrook. Troubled kids like you fall through the cracks all the time. The system is not perfect, that's quite clear. But I will not, and shall not, allow you to run riot in my school. My school, my rules, Miss Halbrook. One wrong move and you are out."

He slapped the yellow paper on the desk in front of me and motioned for me to leave. I picked the sheet up, careful to avoid the greasy blobs and the smudged ink.

A name ran across the page in bright red ink beside the words *Student Name*.

Aidan Lee.

I read the paper as I walked out of Warren's office, my initial desire to slam the door behind me well and truly forgotten. Now I knew the name of the mysterious biker boy.

"Hi, I'm Aidan."

The subject of my recent conversation and my stupid thoughts now stood up in front of me. He'd been seated at the bank of orange plastic chairs outside Warren's office. I cringed. How long had he been there and how much had he heard?

His smile wavered when I looked at him, my face blank with shock. I stared straight ahead, eyes fastened on the bit of silver at his throat. Three triangles merged in an unusual pattern, gleaming as it hung from a simple black cord.

He cleared his throat, interrupting my scrutiny of his jewelry. I recovered, remembered my manners.

"I'm Bryn Halbrook." I shook his hand. Polite society

dictated it. My eyes remained on the worn leather cuff of his jacket. Anywhere but his adorably tousled locks. The warmth of his palm sent traitorous sparks of electricity firing all the way up my spine.

"Ah yes, my voyeur." His low voice purred against me, then brought me straight out of my electric trance.

"Look, I was out on the porch when you arrived so don't get big-headed," I snapped, tugging my bag tighter on my shoulder, crumpling the disgusting yellow page.

"So why didn't you say something?"

"I wanted to be alone. The last thing I needed was some loud-mouthed jerk disturbing my peace."

"Mmhh. Sorry if I offended you." He raised both hands in defense, a slight scowl wrinkling his forehead. "But I do need you to show me to my first class. I'm pretty sure I can find someone to point me to the next one."

My face bloomed red and this time no darkness or shadows veiled my stupid emotions. "Look, I'm sorry. You are my responsibility for now. And the last thing I need is more flak from Vice Principal Warren. I'll show you around but don't get any ideas. We aren't friends or anything. From tomorrow you are on your own."

I stalked off, and his footsteps thunked on the linoleum behind me. I sighed. He didn't put up a fight, throw a tantrum or sulk. Goody for him.

We went straight to English where we spent all of two minutes before the bell rang. Mr. Levy handed us our homework and shook his head.

Okay, so the principal called me to his office. I wasn't cutting school here. Not doing anything wrong! I bristled in silence, my anger like a little gargoyle, dark and forbidding and so very unpredictable. The reasons for my summons to Vice Principal Warren's office didn't matter. I was guilty as charged, straight to jail, no bail.

The day passed in a gritty blur and the final bell brought an unspeakable relief. Dragging Aidan around all day hadn't been as bad as I'd expected. Most of the time all I did was get him to the class. He was ogled and drooled over plenty by the day's end. Lots of short skirts and close-fitting tees to keep him company.

I gritted my teeth for the umpteenth time. Busy stuffing books into my locker, I jumped when someone appeared right next to me. Cherise almost managed to creep up beside me unnoticed. Only her cloying lavender perfume gave her away, seconds before I would have elbowed her in the face as I turned.

"Seems you have only one thing going for you at the moment, freak." She spoke softly but I caught the sneer right before it turned into a brilliant smile as Aidan closed in.

"Ooh, look who it is," she said as Aidan joined us. "Aidan."

Wow. It is really possible to breathe a name.

"I'll see you on Saturday night then. It's a date." She snuggled closer, running her hand over the dark leather covering his arm.

As those tiny red-tipped fingers ran along Aidan's arm, I clenched my fists. The need to act on those vicious thoughts burned like hot lava. I imagined grabbing her fingers and breaking them off his arm, one at a time.

I blinked away those awful images, horrified. Through the blur of anger, one unfamiliar emotion raised its head, daring me to deny it. One emotion that fairly knocked me on my butt. I had absolutely no claim to Aidan Lee whatsoever.

And yet I was rip-roaringly, green-eyed-glaringly jealous.

WE WALKED HOME IN SILENCE. Me, deep within the maelstrom of my pathetic emotions. Aidan with his nose in his iPad. Some foster kid he was. An iPad for Pete's sake? Okay, so maybe I was somewhat jealous. But who wouldn't be when you spent years with almost nothing? Not even a mom or dad.

Two weeks after my thirteenth birthday, my father had died in a car crash, killed when a drunk driver and an icy winter's night met head on. My father had prepared for the unlikely event of his death, but I would have preferred to have him alive and with me again.

I'd have a bit of my inheritance soon. At the end of the school year, I would receive a small lump sum to allow me to prepare for college. Fees and expenses to be paid directly by the lawyers who executed the estate. Daddy happened to be a bit of a rich dude. Guess genetic scientists made a packet. Still, I'd have to wait until the end of the school year before I could indulge in the luxury of an iPad.

I spent a few seconds wondering about my mother. The mother who'd abandoned me when I was five. Not a birthday card or telephone call since. Where was she right now? Did she ever spend precious moments thinking of me? I doubted it. I may see her as my mother. But she thought I wasn't good enough to stick around for. She'd even refused to take me in after my father's death. All those psychiatrist visits and my childhood tales of people who glowed had probably freaked her out.

I glanced at Aidan again, who managed to keep up the pace without running head first into the black gums dotting the sidewalk.

"What's so interesting?" I tried to break the silence, still thick with the memory and odor of Miss Barnes. The rich lavender scent of her perfume would give even a non-sufferer hay fever. I twitched my nose against a sneeze and waited.

"Nothing much. Just checking the news." Aidan smiled and shut the cover, shoving the tablet into his backpack. Faced with the full impact of his arresting smile I stared, unable to string any words together.

What an idiot.

I was drooling too. It took one sultry stare from Aidan to reduce me to a simpering love-struck mess to rival Cherise and all her handmaidens.

When I didn't respond he asked, "You don't like me much, do you?"

Funny you should say that right when I am busy drooling over you. "You are an anathema." I answered out loud, shaking free of those weak female thoughts.

"Huh?" He grinned, despite his confusion at my words.

"You go against the grain." I bit the words out, hoping to end the conversation.

"Sorry, you're going to have to expand on your train of thought there. I'm completely lost." He shook his head and I wondered if he'd already dismissed me as the fruit-loop of Ms. Custer's little foster house.

"You're not the typical foster kid," I said. "Foster kids don't fit in. Not with the jocks or the science nerds or the popular kids. Nobody likes temporary inmates. But Aidan Lee is unlike any foster kid ever known. He has the popular girls already panting at his heels." A nasty, cold bite laced my words, as if a viper now controlled my voice and swayed in silence, ready to pounce.

Aidan frowned, glancing at my face as we paused to cross a street. "I didn't ask Cherise out, if that's what you mean."

It was exactly what I meant but hell if I was going to admit it. And what did he mean he didn't ask her? I didn't dare to request further clarification. He'd get an even more inflated ego if he knew his new foster sister was vibrating with pure jealousy a foot away from him.

"That's none of my business. And it's not what I meant." I should have bitten my tongue. Maybe then my mouth would've stopped running loose, but things like this usually happened to me. Intention and action didn't always work hand in hand with me. Some sort of rebel I was!

"Well then, please feel free to explain any time this millennium." Aidan grinned but it did nothing to ease the sliver of annoyance and more than slight curiosity lurking in his dark eyes.

"You're here for one day and you're already amassing an entourage. Forgive me for not bowing and scraping along with the rest." What I'd failed to ask was why it was never that easy for me. He'd managed to insinuate himself into the student body with disgusting ease. Within a week, nobody would ever mention he was a foster kid. He'd just be one of the popular kids.

Somewhere within the functioning part of my brain, I knew it was unfair to blame him for my failings at this popularity contest or for his sudden rise to stardom within North Wood High, and I clamped my mouth shut before another snarky comment could emerge.

None of what I said rattled Aidan's serene composure until now. We passed under the cold shade of a huge black gum, whose wide, low branches hid what little sunshine had been warming my head and shoulders. He grabbed my arm, fingers brushing soft skin beneath my woolen jumper. I shivered. The cool shade or the heat where his fingers held on to my arm?

"What is your problem?" The question whispered on my cheek as he pushed me against the trunk. The branches hung low, providing a brief curtain of privacy.

"I don't like you," I stuttered. "That's my problem. So maybe . . . stay away from me."

"Fine." He growled the word.

We were close enough that a breath would bring our lips together. My heart thudded and tumbled within my chest so violently, I was terrified he could hear it. What were we arguing about again? I couldn't recall. I just savored the drug-like heat.

His own heart thudded where his chest lay against my arm. Our breath mingled.

Warm. Enticing.

Rapid.

Neither one of us moved and yet the distance disappeared and Aidan's lips grazed mine. As light as air, a whisper, sending me into a whirlpool of heated emotions. My breath vanished from my lungs, head hot and skin fiery. All this heat was undoubtedly dangerous.

His body pressed close against mine as he deepened the kiss. My traitorous knees were hot jelly and my head molten.

Skin sizzled.

More.

And then a girl's shrill laugh filtered through the low canopy from up the street. The noise, and the reminder that we were in a public place, jolted us out of our interlude. Heat dissipated as we drew apart, dazed and intoxicated with the heat and so many other things I didn't dare admit. Back on earth, I breathed again. What the hell was going on? My hands quivered and I tightened them around the canvas of my bag strap.

Aidan stared at my face.

Dazed. Confused.

Slightly angry.

Angry? Was he angry with me? Well then, why not? I wasn't the most desirable company. It didn't take a genius to figure out if we'd been caught, it would have ruined his little *date* on Saturday night.

I bit back the tears and turned, striding away fast. To get away. But I slowed my pace so no one watching would get curious. Too many rumors followed me around already.

I left him standing half-hidden beneath the tree and walked off without a backward glance.

I slammed the door to my room, dropping my bag on the floor. Faint wisps of the heat and the tingling in my body remained. But my anger hadn't dissipated. No surprise. Aidan was just another social-climbing kid. Too bad he'd lost control and made out with the school leper. I vowed never to entertain a repeat performance. But my traitorous body relived the encounter and a wave of bristling heat swam through me, mind and body.

A knock sounded against the wood panel of my door.

I froze.

I ached to rush to the door and flick the lock. Longed to dive out the window. Anything to avoid looking into Aidan's angry, embarrassed eyes.

Shadows moved at the base of the door. I remained still.

Another soft rap. "Bryn?" he whispered.

A minute went by and the shadows beneath the door hesitated, then disappeared, footsteps retreating down the hall.

I sighed, relieved.

And angry.

Angry he hadn't made more of an effort. How ridiculous. His interests lay elsewhere. Why would he waste any effort on me? Even if we were fostered in the same home, it meant nothing. No obligation, no loyalty.

I shuddered and sank onto the bed, squashing its precisely folded corners. The exhausted muscles in my legs alternated between solid and jelly. My heart hurt from the pounding and my head ached from the constant battle within the confines of my skull.

I hid in my room through dinner. Thankfully, my lack of appetite meant missing dinner was no issue. Anyone else and Ms.

Custer would have screamed blue murder until they got their butts to the dinner table. But she already knew my eating patterns were off. I lay on my bed watching the sky go from pale blue, tinged with orange and reds, to inky midnight blue. At last, when it turned black as pitch, I closed my eyes.

And dreamed of fire and wings.

CHAPTER 7

A crazy haze of strange faces, bronze armor and angry glinting swords muddled my dreams. It didn't make much sense to dream of battles on muddy fields or blood-drenched, dying men. I woke with the pungent copper of fresh blood bathing my nostrils, permeating my lungs.

Such dreams were slow to fade. Despite my desperate morning shower, the odor of blood lingered around me for most of the day. The amber talisman provided weak warmth and bitter comfort.

That day and the next and the next crawled by and I remained as far from Aidan as possible. Leaving home early and arriving late, hiding out in a dark, musty corner of the town library, I pretended to study but all the while I seethed. The weekend drew closer, taunting me, and I seethed some more. What the hell was wrong with me? Aidan had no obligation to me; he was entitled to do his own thing.

But a twinge of guilt still picked at my conscience from time to time. I'd been way out of line, jumping down his throat. I hated his brand of instant popularity, but I'd been unreasonable to hold him responsible for dumb luck. He'd drawn the looks card and the luck card, and neither were his fault. I watched him arrive home late every afternoon, no doubt held back by an eyelash-batting, short-skirt-wearing airhead.

I could hardly blame him for my problems. My own personal bad luck magnet or good luck deflector was in perfect working order. Staying away from him was my safest bet. Besides, people died when they got too close to Bryn Halbrook.

Friday night arrived in all its lonely splendor, and I had the veranda, the swing and the pink rose bush to myself. I read by the fading daylight until the words ran off the pages into the darkness. When Aidan arrived home, I had nowhere to run. Or hide. I just sat there hoping he would head into the house and leave me to the night's silence.

Aidan parked and tipped off his helmet, staring at me through the rose bushes that walled in the porch, protecting it from the open street. He hesitated, then strode toward me, in that special Aidan way of walking, and set the swing in motion with his weight. I gritted my teeth. His thigh seeped heat and discomfort into mine and suddenly the swing, usually large enough for Brody and Simon and me to sit together and swing and sing kiddies' songs, was way too small.

No place to go. Nowhere to wriggle to. I forced my muscles to still themselves, held my breath and waited.

"Hey, stranger." He smiled, tossing his gleaming helmet from hand to hand.

"Hey." I kept my eyes on the roses.

"You got anything on this weekend?"

"Nope. No date in case that's what you're asking." The pathetic words slipped out before I could stop them. What was it about Aidan that forced me to lash out at him?

"Okay then. See you around, if you're around." He moved and his leg shifted against mine and my heart tripped over itself to get the next beat out. In the darkness, I stared at him as he entered the house, tipping me a silent salute. Why was it the one guy who reduced me to a marshmallow mush turned out to be a hotfrickin' biker boy? Thank the stars he hadn't pitched up at school with the bike yet. The whole package was way too much of a crowd pleaser.

I waited half an hour and stole into the house. Friday night was Bingo night at Ms. Custer's friend Molly Barlow's. Brody and Simon were stuck to the Xbox in the family room and Izzy was most likely stuck in her room, her dark head bent over a book.

I sighed. An old movie may be the order of the day.

I passed the dining room with its light blazing, and went to switch it off when I noticed Mr. Popularity, head propped on his hand, eyes pasted to a book, studying hard out. He looked up and my heart tilted. He wore a pair of glasses that should have made him look nerdy but instead just made him all the more sexy.

I growled in silence, threw him a polite smile and forced myself to go in calm silence to my room despite the desperate need to stamp up the stairs and slam my door.

The hours ticked by and I didn't dare sleep, fearful of my

dreams. Near midnight and Ms. Custer's low snores traveled down the passage to my room, despite the closed door. She indulged once a week at her Bingo session. I had no idea what she drank, but knowing my foster mom it would not have been much. She took her responsibility seriously and tried to ensure she set a good example. Coming home punch drunk would not be a good example.

I crept downstairs to the kitchen, hoping I wouldn't run into Aidan. It was pizza night for the kids, unless you were going out. But since I had zero interest in food, the menu had no effect on me. I longed for a soda or whatever sat in the fridge that fizzed.

I fished out a lone soda can, leaned against the sink, popped the tab and swallowed. The bubbles soothed me. I had no desire for water either, but it must have been a psychological thing 'cause I craved the sensation of the bubbles as they coursed down my throat into my stomach.

I sighed. And almost choked when I looked straight into Aidan's eyes as I brought the can down. Damn near jumped out of my skin.

"Crap!" I shrieked then coughed, thankful that none of the fizzy bubbles went down the wrong way. Nothing like choking to death to impress a guy. Not that I was planning to impress anyone anyway.

"Sorry." His bright toothy grin didn't look very sorry at all.

"Shouldn't you be out on the town or something? As opposed to scaring the crap out of me?"

"Nope, got work to do."

"Can't be more than what I have. We're in the same classes, after all."

"I have a part-time research job and I have some collating and writing up to do. Takes tons of time. Sorry if I scared you." He leaned past me to place a mug in the sink. Way too close for comfort.

And he stayed there.

And I wouldn't have had it any other way.

SILENCE SETTLED INTO THE KITCHEN, and only the soft susurration of our breathing and the chugs and clanks of the ancient refrigerator dared to disturb it. Aidan closed what little distance remained between our bodies and placed a hand on either side of me, closing me in but not touching me. Somehow, I don't recall how, air evaporated from my lungs, and we were less than a hair's breadth apart. I wanted more and feared more and desperately ached to get away.

My eyes shifted from his mesmerizing gaze, heat filling my face. I tried to leave the haven of his arms. But he wouldn't allow me to escape. My move to leave bared my neck and he took the opportunity to place his lips at the base of my throat just above the collarbone.

Was it even possible to sigh and moan at the same time? Sure it was; I'd just done that! He ran his warm, soft lips up to my chin and further up to meet my mouth in a heated, heady frenzy. My fingers entwined within his hair, pulling him closer just as his arms encircled me.

This was crazy.

And ridiculous.

And wonderful all at the same time.

Even the knowledge that the guy had a date the next night could not dampen my hunger for more of him.

A low buzzing disturbed us, pulling at the threads of craziness, tugging us back into the real world where death and cheerleaders reigned. Aidan tugged his phone out of his pocket and scanned the message. His jaw hardened and he switched the screen off and tucked it back.

"I've got to run." He planted a quick kiss on my temple and walked to the door. "Oh, and eat something will you? I haven't seen you take a bite all week. It's possible to die without food, you know."

As he left I didn't return his parting grin. I'd seen the message before he so quickly thrust his phone back in his pocket, and I bloody well knew the sender: Cherise. I was numb, head to toe and heart in the middle. The heat in my body gave way to icy needles, which pierced my muscles one stab at a time. In my mind's eye, the backlit text message gleamed:

I need to see you now. It's urgent. I'll be
waiting.

This time the heat filling my head remained as far from romantic as icebergs were from pots of jasmine tea. My chest simmered, a fusion of hurt and anger and self-disgust. How could I have possibly assumed Aidan was interested in me? The freak of North Wood High. No doubt he'd been filled in on all the gory details. We'd hardly spent much time together this week anyway.

Besides, one little text from Cherise and he took off running. Straight into her willing, waiting arms.

Aidan was a player, like most boys.

My fingers gripped the sink edge. I tried to shut out the grumble of his engine as it disappeared down the street.

Stupid.

How could I have been so stupid? Did I lean on him too much because I still hurt from losing Joshua? Or because my heart had twisted itself up in a stupid knot just for him? He may have been a foster kid but he certainly was no different from the rest of the guys in Craven.

I picked up the discarded can of soda, staying my need to fling it across the room. Sure, it would make me feel better, but it would wake Ms. Custer. And the last thing I needed now was company. My heart was breaking and thankfully nobody could hear it crack into a million pathetic pieces.

Moving automatically, I washed the mug he'd left in the sink and placed it on the rack to dry. Switching the light off, I left the kitchen and walked through the dining room to the hall. My fingers reached for the switch to flick the light off when Aidan's pile of books caught my eye.

Stacked neatly at the end of the table, they were old and thick and serious-looking. I inched forward. Breaching his precious privacy was the least of my worries. My heart chilled each time a picture of Cherise and Aidan flashed into my head. She always got what she wanted anyway. How could I change that?

I peered over the stack of books. All the spines followed a common theme. Norse Mythology. Norse Archeology. Thunderbolt of Thor. The Myth of the Valkyrie.

One thick volume lay open, dotted with little Post-it notes, heavily underlined and highlighted. An unusual script leaped off the pages. Incredible. And illegible. Unlike anything I'd ever laid eyes on and yet . . . an air of the familiar permeated the letters on the aged paper. I couldn't read the ancient scribble. It was as familiar to me as a bunch of Egyptian hieroglyphs, but a sense of déjà vu lingered.

I flicked the page, mesmerized by the script, fascinated by the subject. No discovery of the ancient writings of the Norse had captured the imagination of the world yet. Not to my knowledge. But then we learned only the basics of their mythology in school.

Caught within a web of curiosity and fascination I sank into the chair and turned the pages, finding more intricate ancient writings, while in the margins hastily handwritten notes were clear, legible and recent.

I gasped in silence. Aidan was in the midst of translating the writing. Granted, it could have been the work of another brilliant researcher, but he'd just so recently been bent over these very books night after night. Homework perhaps? I shook my head. Nope, this was clearly more than just a class assignment. Must be for that job he'd mentioned. A writing pad sat beside the thick book, random scribblings filling every available space. This definitely counted as serious enough to keep him home the first Friday night of his stay in Craven.

I gritted my teeth. Sure, his commitment was obvious, but dedication to one's work did not guarantee spotless morals and integrity. I studied the letters, more to get my mind off Aidan, and as soon as I began, I forgot him, entranced by the strange letters.

The translations he'd made were easy to follow and soon I strung a few words into sentences. They were just a jumble, requiring further study to guarantee the closest possible translation, but my skin tingled, as if I could sense the real meaning thrumming between the lines, just waiting for me. As if I stood at a sea shore with my toes dipping into the warm waves as they flowed up the wet sand.

A car door slammed somewhere down the street and a bucket of cold reality washed over me. Aidan could return at any moment. The grumbling bike would announce him, but I could be caught. Such was the fortune of Bryn Halbrook.

Still, I turned another page and delved deeper into the translations, holding my breath as page after beautiful page told some misty story of a time long past. Excitement and nerves bubbled within me for Aidan. How amazing would it be to have this accolade?

Another page turned and a painting sprang at me: a Valkyrie, elegant in an ankle-length white dress, draped with chainmail, a deep red cloak, a bronze helmet. At the top right corner, a small etching revealed a much more basic drawing of this creature of myth.

A Valkyrie. The beautiful maiden who rides to Midgard to collect the bodies of Warriors fit to serve in Valhalla, brave and courageous Warriors who would fight for Odin in the Great War of Ragnarok.

The artist had retained only a small part of the Valkyrie's personality though, making more of her voluptuous body than her classical features. A few more pages showed a similar theme. Ancient drawings on which the old painters had modeled their renditions. Painters who'd lived and died at least five hundred years ago.

The next page sent me into shock.

I gasped, all the breath leaving my lungs in one incredible, horrified whoosh. The picture, painted in the style of Da Vinci, all soft hues and natural touches, held my gaze.

The woman stood, spine erect, chin up, a sword extending from her hand as if it were a part of her own body. Flanked by a horse whose white pelt glowed pearlescent. Behind her, a pair of beautiful red-bronze wings rose majestically above her shoulders. The curve of the wings provided a natural frame for a face that stilled the blood in my veins.

Post-its in various colors tagged the yellowed paper; hundreds of notes framed the margins and a name written in red and circled so deeply a small rip ran among the repeated lines of ink.

Brunhilde.

And even if it were not for the coincidence of the name, my ears would have still thrummed with the thunderous beat of my heart as I stared at the painting.

If I didn't know any better I would have sworn it was me.

CHAPTER 8

Aidan didn't come back until the early hours of the morning. So I indulged my curiosity. I snuck back down again to get a second look, wishing I could make a copy of the picture. The best I could do was take a picture with my phone and scurry back to bed in relief.

I fell asleep looking at the screen of my phone and wondering at the mystery of it all.

On my way out of the room the next morning, my reflection stopped me in mid-stride. I leaned close, studying the contours of my face in the mirror. I turned on all the lights to be sure. Traced the lines of my nose and chin. The resemblance was eerie and scary.

I tried not to focus on the face of the Valkyrie, but that meant my mind circled on my Aidan problem.

For days I kept my silence, showing up late for breakfast each morning and sneaking away to my room whenever possible.

On one such sneaking, Aidan's and Ms. Custer 's evening conversation filtered through the closed kitchen door and stopped me in my tracks. I could hear almost every word.

"How was your day, dear," my foster mom asked him. Or had she said "date"?

Aidan mumbled something and I strained my ears. ". . . too busy," he said.

My heart lurched. Aidan, to my amazement, hadn't gone out with Cherise! But I didn't dare hope. Who knew what other plans the happy couple had already made? There were many more Saturday nights to come and if I knew Cherise at all, I knew she never gave up when she wanted a guy.

Aidan spent the evenings and nights poring over his books. And scowling at me when I stalked past him, a cool and indifferent smile pasted on my face.

SUNDAY MORNING HOVERED like a calming mist over Craven. The house creaked and groaned as it warmed in the lukewarm fall sunshine. Ms. Custer had left early for church and the kids were enjoying a lazy morning.

Our foster mom was a deeply religious woman, and often I'd sit on the porch with a book open on my lap, listening to her glorious rich voice render divine church songs. Her voice and her songs had soul.

But with Aidan and my lack of appetite occupying my mind, not even the Divine melody could help ease my worries.

My room offered much needed comfort, as far away from Aidan as possible.

AFTER A LATE BREAKFAST OF PANCAKES, Brody and Simon begged me to take them to the playground, and I relented. The desire for fresh air overpowered avoidance of a certain biker.

The wooden seat of the swing moved back and forth in the filtered sunshine. The boys leaped and hurled themselves from bars manufactured especially for the two human monkeys, giggling with such abandon. A smiled curved at my lips, where in the last week no smile had dared to dwell.

A hollow ache bounced at my temple, a side effect of my turmoil. The image of the Valkyrie twisted and turned over and over in my mind. Who was the woman in the painting? Was it just a coincidence?

The name. The face.

As far as I knew, my parents had no connection with archeology. But the Valkyrie's name was Brunhilde. The root of my birth name of Brynhildr. The painting itself dared me to deny what my eyes knew.

I shivered in icy trepidation.

It didn't help when a large shape moved into my sunlight.

I stiffened and looked away from the two brats to Aidan, who stood staring at the boys as they giggled and squabbled. He turned, his smile congenial, almost conversational, but I rose.

My knees wobbled as I tried to dampen the tiny spurt of joy, which flared on seeing his face this morning. Damn my traitorous emotions.

"Since you're here I can probably head back," I said. "Bring the boys with you." I stepped away.

"When was the last time you ate?" Aidan's words were quiet and serious and I stopped. A cold breeze sent frigid fingers down my collar and I pulled my jacket close. Close against the wind and his scrutiny.

"Why is that any of your business?" I stiffened, ready to flee to the safety of my room if he so much as stepped in my direction.

The smile on his face froze and fell away at my cool response. I should have felt guilty but the words of the text message scrolled across my eyes like a neon sign.

He'd left me in the lurch in mid-conversation. No explanation. And worse were those guilty glances I'd caught ever since that night. Didn't take a rocket scientist to tell he was guilty.

He had no idea I'd read the text message from Cherise. I had no intention of telling him. Why give him the satisfaction of knowing I was burning with embarrassment and jealousy? I'd played the fool and I refused to audition for the part again.

Ever.

A boisterous shout from the boys on the monkey bars gave me an excuse to turn away from him. Not that I needed one. When I glanced back, he shrugged, still staring at my face. "You're not anorexic are you?" He shook his head and answered his own question. "No, no signs of weight loss or dehydration. You don't look like you're starving so where are you getting your nutrition from?"

"Look, it's really none of your business, but I do actually eat. I'm not anorexic, or bulimic, nor do I suffer from any other kind of eating disorder. I eat when I'm hungry and drink when I'm thirsty just like every other person on the planet. So leave me and my food intake alone." Heat filled my cheeks as the lies tripped off my tongue.

I looked away from his face again because my heart always melted when I stared at him. Because I had to acknowledge that deep inside I was thrilled he cared enough to challenge me on my health. Because I hated lying. And because the topic itself scared the crap out of me.

I stared at the romping boys—and cupped my hand to my mouth to stifle a gasp. A sudden chill, icier than the wind, nastier than any winter snap, crept through my blood and froze me to the ground.

Aidan, puzzled, stared at me. "What's wrong?" he said. His jacket rustled as he turned and touched my arm but I didn't move and didn't answer. At my neck, tucked beneath my sweater, the amber talisman burned against my neck. Hot like the tears burning my eyes.

I gasped in silent shock and horror and utter grief.

Brody glowed, a beautiful tender gold.

I SAT ON MY BED, staring at the back of the closed door. A jumble of mismatched hooks were filled with a rainbow of winter scarves and unused bags I'd either grown out of or hated with the tepid passion of teen trend-followers.

It was funny how such bland little details stood out from the fabric of my daily existence now. Things like the rusty doorknob I really should shine someday soon.

And the missing light bulb above my dresser.

And the broken dowel in my chair back that stayed put with masking tape and a prayer.

The clock ticked, a floorboard creaked, the pipes grunted, the TV blared. Everyone shuffled around the house, living the day and waiting for the next one.

But Brody had only a few weeks left of his beautiful life. I'd figured it out. From the first time the glow appeared on a person, it grew steadily brighter.

And as the day of their death neared, the light blazed, brighter and more stunning, until it was so strong it hurt to look at the person.

Thinking of Brody brought another face to me. My eyes prickled as I swam the sea of helplessness and self-pity again. Behind lids shut tight against a wave of aching grief, Joshua smiled his serenely beautiful smile. As if he was trying to comfort me.

My throat twisted on unshed tears. I dared not cry. If I did, I would have to admit Brody was staring his mortality in the face, none the wiser. How did I deal with this?

When I was younger the glows had seemed benign, simply people with a different aura. But it had happened often enough for my father to make the decision to homeschool me, just in case.

After his death, I'd spent short bursts of time in various new places. Long enough to notice a gleaming body but never long enough to find out what happened to them.

I had to wonder though. Was it me? Was it my proximity to these people that caused it? But even as the thought surfaced, I squashed it. I hadn't known Aimee Graham or the man at the funeral with the clingy wife.

If I were to have this pity party, it wouldn't come with stupider and more irrational thoughts. But was it worth it to know people were dying and be unable to do anything about it? Could I even do anything about it?

I stared around the darkening room as the sun fell away from the dull sky and night clawed its way back into the heavens.

No stars smiled down tonight.

Fitting. Glittering lights in a black velvet sky would be all too wrong when the days and minutes and hours were ticking away for my little foster brother.

The amber teardrop gem shimmered at my neck, shedding a tiny light, not large enough to light the room, but well-contained like the bottled gleam of a firefly.

The desire to confide in Aidan was immense, a desperate wind buffeting me toward the edge of a dark and rocky precipice. Visions of doctors and hospitals turned my empty stomach.

I breathed deep to tamp down that nausea. A few more short breaths settled my stomach a little but the tightness in my chest remained.

Perhaps I risked a padded cell but for my sanity, it was worth it. Brody's honey curls and bright sparkling eyes haunted me.

I shivered as his laughter rang out from the living room below.

Deep rolling honest laughter that tugged a smile from behind my wall of grief.

Joshua's death had reduced my confidence to rubble. Forced me to accept that someday soon I would need help. The time was now, had come sooner than I'd thought. Where did I begin? Whom could I trust? I hadn't the vaguest idea.

And it hit me, a frigid reality.

Aidan.

Little Brody's life faded away the brighter the light around him grew. I had to risk it.

CHAPTER 9

Sleep teased at the edges of my consciousness, laughing at my desperate hope to rest. What little time I spent in the Sandman's arms was pilfered away by the dreams. Fleeting images of bloody, half-dead men. A raven rested on a lonely outcropping, one gleaming eye staring at me. The eerie howl of a wolf in the distance shimmied up and down the ridges of my spine. I woke for a few scant seconds, wincing as a stream of moonlight stabbed my sleep-drenched eye.

The rest of my sleep was dreamless.

The week passed in agonizing slow motion, the better to experience the full brunt of my misery and grief. And through the week, Brody's light grew stronger, brighter, more luminescent. More rapidly than Joshua.

I explored the possibility that age could make a difference and it only increased my fear. I'd never be able to forgive myself if

Brody died and I did nothing to save him. I couldn't take that chance.

The decision to reveal the truth to Aidan was way easier than the actual spilling.

Friday night arrived and Aidan ensconced himself among his books at the dining table. I lurked around the house until at least ten, and he was still bent over those books. Ms. Custer did her own bit of lurking too and almost shadowed me.

"Bryn, dear, is something the matter?" Her hand on my shoulder made me jump.

"No, I'm fine." I said. "I was just—"

"Looking like you have nothing to do," she said, interrupting me. "I can always find you something to keep you busy."

Her smile said she was teasing but I preferred not to test her. Mumbling some excuse, I escaped to my room and forced myself to stay put until she forgot about me. I didn't want her to hear when I finally orchestrated the opportunity to speak to Aidan.

In the end I was forced to wait and ambush him on the way to his room two doors down the hall. I headed for my room, leaving my door wide open to watch for Aidan. Minutes passed, and I'd almost given up hope. I had in fact nodded off several times and awakened with a start as my head slipped off my hand and fell toward the desk.

At last, footsteps creaked along the stairs, paused on the landing as he drew abreast of my door. I didn't dare call out to him. That might alert Ms. Custer, and she had strict rules about fraternizing after bedtime. A teenage girl found in a teenage boy's bedroom at night while everyone else was fast asleep was unacceptable behavior. But I followed him anyway.

He quickened his pace toward his room. Head down, he opened his door and turned, closing it behind him. I thought of sticking my foot in the gap but decided against it as I'd bravely padded around barefoot on the cold wooden floorboards. I preferred my feet whole and uninjured, thank you very much. Instead I placed my hand on the door, stalling its movement.

The lack of a click from the door latch alerted him that I was there. He turned and frowned. "What's wrong?" he asked. His tired eyes were red, widening at my sudden appearance after hiding out most of the day.

"I need to speak to you about . . . something." I scanned the passage up and down, nerves spiking.

He hesitated, flicking the darkened room a hesitant glance. He flipped the light switch and nodded me inside to safety. I chose a chair at a small table strewn with papers, books—both school ones and more Norse ones, and a new Mac laptop. More super-technology.

I swallowed. Concentrated on the reason I was risking my hide to be in his room this late. He cleared his throat. Impatient? Or annoyed because I'd ignored him for most of the day and now I barged in on him, demanding his time like some flighty, over-emotional female?

"Do you think it's possible for a person to know when another person is about to die?" My throat convulsed again, struggling with the last few words.

Aidan blinked. "Sure, there have been countless records of people predicting deaths. Even parents and spouses sometimes know when a family member is about to die." As he spoke, his features relaxed.

"So you know much about this stuff?"

He hesitated. "It depends. The whole death-prediction subject is so controversial. There's always an argument both for and against it." He rubbed the back of his head, and yawned.

Sorry to keep you awake.

"Why do you ask?"

"I have this friend. She thinks she can tell when people are about to die." At the last second, I chickened out. Decided it would be safer to broach the subject by gauging how he felt before I shoved a handful of horrible reality down his throat.

"And how can she tell? Are there signs? A feeling or a sensation?" The sleepy haze had disappeared from his face.

I explained how the golden aura appeared, ending with the death of the person, ending my narration with half a sob posing as a hiccup. I swallowed hard, holding back tears that threatened to overcome my composure and my semblance of sanity. "But this time it's different. The brightness increased so quickly. . . ."

Aidan paled, his face tightening into a fearful mask.

"What? What do you know?" I rose and walked to him, holding his arm, forcing myself not to shake the answer out of him.

"How long has she been seeing this glow?"

"Most of her life, really," I said, nerves firing.

"And how many people has she seen with this glow?"

"Too many." I turned to the window, staring out into the darkness. Aidan watched me in the reflection.

"How many have died?"

"Three. Now, four." My mind overflowed with images of Aimee,

Joshua and smiles that still haunted me. But I recalled the man at the funeral. "Two people she knew and one stranger. And now one more close to her. And those are just the deaths she knows about."

"And she's sure it means they are going to die?"

I nodded and my shoulders fell, as if I no longer cared to carry the weight of the world upon them.

"She thinks she's going crazy. She thought it was a premonition but then it happened again with a close friend. Now she has no idea how to handle it." I was super careful as I spoke not to speak as if she was actually me. I hated lying.

He gave me a strange look. "This friend of yours, I haven't seen her at school. You always seemed like a bit of loner."

"What's that supposed to mean?" I snapped.

He hesitated then said, "Nothing, I guess. Can you ask her to come and speak to me?"

"I . . . I don't think so. No, it's just not possible. She won't come."

"Even if it meant I could help her?"

"I could speak to her and . . . be like the middleman."

He scanned my face, a thousand thoughts running across shadowed features, until at last he nodded and said, "Fine, I guess it will have to work for now."

I breathed a silent sigh, still shaking on the inside. "So what myth is it you were talking about?"

"It's information I came across recently. Not a very well-known story."

"From what you've been translating?" I stiffened, regretting the words as soon as they slipped out. Now he knew I'd been nosing around his books. I winced, one eye open to a tiny slit as I waited for the explosion.

Perhaps my stance was amusing, because he laughed, although annoyance still painted his face. "Sorry," I said. "I passed the books on Friday night when you ran out the house like hell-hounds were hankering for a taste of your bacon." Impossible to keep my tone neutral.

And Aidan scowled. "I didn't leave that fast." He snorted.

"Well, whatever Cherise wanted I'm sure she got, so let's get on to my questions now, thanks." I lifted my chin, keen to get off the topic of Cherise's message and desperate to find out more about my cursed premonitions.

A smile bloomed across Aidan's face, and recognition flared within his eyes. "I didn't leave to see a girl. Who did you think it was?"

"It's not my business." My cheeks burned, caught but still betrayed by his choices. "You don't owe me anything." Great time to act like an adult, when I craved an explanation.

"Wait, you thought I went to meet Cherise? What gave you that idea?" He scowled, his brows scrunched up. "You saw my text didn't you?"

"I didn't mean to. Can't help it if I can read upside down," I mumbled.

He shook his head. "I had to meet my boss. The guy I'm doing the research for. The translations . . . ?" His eyebrows raised.

"You don't owe me any explanations." I held my hands up, defending my suspicions and deflecting his reasons. I'd been out of line and all I wanted was for the discussion to end without further embarrassment.

"Yes, I do. I can see why you were angry. I left you so suddenly and the message gave you the wrong idea. I did owe you an explanation. I'm sorry."

Confused by his apology I shook my head. Too late to acknowledge I'd been nosy when our relationship wasn't even a legitimate one. Two kisses, no matter how heated, did not make a relationship.

His warm fingers linked to mine and he pulled me to my feet. "What is it you want, Aidan? I'm not girlfriend material. I'm not an easy one-night stand. What's happening here? Between us?"

"Something you and I can figure out together. And something we don't need to rush. It's nice as it is, don't you agree?"

Our proximity was not conducive to coherent thought. I cleared my throat and asked, "So will you help me find out more about the premonitions?" But my words were more of a heated whisper.

Aidan nodded and his cheek crushed my temple. How did we get this close this fast? I didn't recall either of us moving together. A dance to music only he and I could hear.

Breath mingled, heartbeats tangled. Mine spiked every time our bodies touched. The heat of his fingers entwined with mine scorched my skin, unbearable and incredible. Blood thrummed in my ears, smudged my thoughts. Just wanted him closer.

And, as if he'd heard me, as if he knew just one more step would be a step in the wrong direction, he breathed deep and stepped away. He'd stolen away the warmth and I shivered.

"I think it might be best to keep some distance here. . . ." He wiggled his eyebrows and I giggled softly. "Not sure I can stop myself if you keep getting so close to me all the time."

Cheeky grin.

I smiled. "Can we get back to the topic at hand please?"

"Okay, so who did your friend have the premonition about? Who does she think is going to die?"

My throat closed, rebelling against the thought, the very idea we might be losing Brody soon. My mind refused to form the words but I tried.

"Brody," I said, and the name came out ragged and almost unintelligible.

"Who?" His voice was harsh.

I cleared my throat again and took a deep breath. Why I thought a deep breath would help I didn't know, but it pushed the name past my lips. "It's Brody. Our Brody."

Aidan's face paled. He'd bonded with the two boys so easily. He was so good with the kids, not minding them rushing around the house playing pirates and squabbling about which game to play on Xbox.

"What are we going to do?" I whispered and sank onto the edge of the bed. The mattress sank beside me and Aidan's arm curled me into him. My tears were hot and angry and desperate.

"Do you really believe...her then? That her premonitions are true?" His chin moved in my hair.

"Yes. It's real." I could barely hear my whispered words.

"Then we'll do whatever it takes to find out how it works and how we can stop it from happening. Okay?"

I nodded.

Before I could thank him for his understanding the door flew open and Ms. Custer burst in. "Aidan, help me! It's Brody!"

Ms. Custer stared at us, forehead creased. It didn't look good. Aidan and I, both seated at the foot of his half-made bed, his arm around me, my head on his shoulder and my face wet with tears.

She blinked, swallowed, and then said, "Hurry!" Her eyes snapped down the hall. She turned and raced back to Brody. We would get our telling off soon enough. I swiped at the moisture on my cheeks and eyes, wiping it off on my jeans, and followed Aidan to Brody's room next door.

Our foster mother sat at the edge of the bed, staring at Brody's pale face. Ms. Custer wrung her hands, then placed them in her lap, knuckles whitening. Hands shaking, she reached out to check Brody's pulse.

"He's breathing, but so shallow I almost missed it." I heard the tears gathering at the edge of her heart, pooling, ready to spill over. "He won't wake up."

The lights blazed, yet gray, cold shadows seeped into the room. Simon, who shared the room, stood on the far side of Brody's bed, blue eyes paled to a sad gray, shivering against the gathering cold. He stared at Brody, whose features glowed with a serenity and peace that stabbed molten pokers into my gut.

Aidan's phone beeped as he dialed 911. He spoke fast, his

voice void of emotion. Izzy appeared at the doorway, her eyes widening and then filling with tears and fear as Aidan spoke.

"Ambulance is on its way. Not long now." His gaze, like everyone else's, fastened on Brody. Aidan and I were the only ones already grieving for the little boy. The only ones who knew he would soon be leaving us forever.

This shouldn't be happening.

It was too soon.

The glow, no brighter than yesterday, confused me. My head ached with fear and guilt and confusion.

The paramedics came and left in a blur of urgent and strangely calming activity. Ms. Custer went with Brody. His little body lay prone and vulnerable on the stretcher. I put Simon to bed, snuggling with him, stroking his blonde curls, until his breathing deepened. Creeping out of the bed, I unhooked his fingers from my neck, tucked him in and stemmed the urge to sob aloud.

How will he handle being alone? They made such a troublesome yet adorable pair. Not brothers in blood but in every other way that counted.

I pulled the door until a thin shaft of light from the hall illuminated the room in case Simon awakened and called out for us. He wouldn't be frightened by the dark, and I'd hear him call. I went to check on Izzy but her room was empty. I hurried down to the front room, finding Aidan checking his phone, probably for the eleventy-fifth time. Izzy huddled in Ms. Custer's favorite armchair, clutching a pillow close.

I gave her a weak smile and turned to Aidan. "Any news?" I asked, tugging my cardigan close, hoping for *good* news.

"No, I thought I'd ring Ms. Custer but . . . she doesn't need us annoying her with phone calls."

I stared at Aidan. His eyes were ringed with worry and weariness, but a quiet strength enveloped him, projecting a confidence he didn't possess. I kept my grief at bay, aware too that he might be thinking too much, being too sensible.

And Ms. Custer would never be annoyed if we rang to check on little Brody.

"I will call her." His head shot up. "She would expect us to call her. She's there all alone. She'd need the company a little, I guess."

I dialed and waited for her to pick up. On the final ring, seconds before it went into message, she answered, her voice raspy.

"Hey, it's me."

"Hello, honey." I pictured the teary smile.

"How is he?" It'd been less than an hour, but felt like an eternity.

"Bryn, you have to listen to me, child." She paused, to blow her nose and sniff, the sounds coming through loud and clear.

Right, Bryn, don't go all hysterical on her.

"Okay, tell me what's wrong with him." Pressure built in my chest. Aching, frightening pressure.

"He didn't make it, Bryn." Her voice shook, filled with tears and grief. The first fingers of hysteria slipped around my lungs. I sank onto the floor, leaning against the coffee table, my legs refusing to take me the two steps to the couch.

Aidan rushed to me, crouching beside me, one hand on my shoulder. Izzy rose to her feet, still clutching her pillow.

"What?" I asked, but my voice failed me and the word ended up a disbelieving whisper.

"He's gone, baby." Ms. Custer's tender voice came down the phone to soothe my pain. I loved her more for her generosity of spirit. And I ached to comfort her too. But anger still enclosed my grief in chains of black iron. I didn't ask how she was, if she needed anything. "I'm just signing some papers," she said. "I'll be home soon."

The urge to give in to tears was overwhelming. But I didn't give in, had to be sensible, responsible. I said, "I'll send Aidan for you."

"Good. Thank you, child."

"How did it happen?" There had to be an explanation of how a little boy could die without warning.

"They think it was a heart attack. The doctor said it happens sometimes with undiagnosed heart conditions." She took a deep breath, which rattled down the line. "They'll know for sure after they complete their tests."

CHAPTER 10

Long QT Syndrome, the doctors had said. A fancy name for Brody's death. A reason why his bright light was extinguished. Their words told me nothing, so I checked the internet. It explained about irregular heartbeats in kids that sometimes go undetected. Until one day the patient just dies.

I shed all my tears alone. Izzy huddled in my arms on the porch swing until Aidan and Ms. Custer returned from the hospital. Aidan gently led the distraught old woman up the steps to the front door. She fumbled with the latch. Her hollow eyes made me tremble, made me feel again the emptiness of the house without Brody.

Izzy followed Ms. Custer through the door, grabbing on to her hand. Aidan and I stayed outside on the porch swing, which would never hold the two squabbling boys again. Ms. Custer retreated to the dining room, making calls, preparing for the funeral on Saturday, trying to figure out what would happen next.

"He didn't just die, you know," I said to Aidan, now that Simon couldn't overhear. "I knew he was going to die. I could have told someone."

The swing creaked, laughing at my cowardice.

"And just what were you planning on saying to them? He had no known health issues, Bryn." He faced me, his features masked by gathering gray darkness. He tucked a lock of hair behind my ear, touched my cheek before pulling me closer. "How were you going to convince the doctors? *By the way, Doctor. Brody's going to die. I just don't know how or when or why, but please check him out?*"

Aidan rubbed my arm and turned to stare out into the darkness beyond the porch. Silence owned the next few moments and I mulled over the stark truth of his words. Then he shook his head, speaking so softly it was almost as if he were talking to himself. "No, they would have thought you were insane. Probably committed you. You're a ward of the state, you know. One wrong move and you are dust."

I bristled, despite knowing he was right. My history with psychiatrists would have colored the doctors' judgment. I could never have warned them about Brody or Aimee or anyone, not without risking the best home I'd ever had.

THE DAYS all blended into one indistinguishable week. The day of the funeral arrived and the house was swathed in silence. Poor Izzy couldn't even crack a smile. And yet the sun shone on the fall afternoon, as if blessing us with a burst of golden light to say farewell to our little brother.

I was sick of golden light.

Brody had an open casket, revealing his cute little smiling lips and corkscrew curls. Many well-wishers managed a sad smile when they bid the little boy farewell.

And Brody still shone.

The little boy still radiated lustrous gold so bright it speared my eyes, drawing hot tears. I steeled myself, lowered my head until I regained control. Nobody would know the depth of my anger, the intensity of my guilt. My grief had grown into a solid, black lump in my chest. Fed by anger, and hate. Hatred for myself, anger at myself. Even Aidan's words didn't assuage my guilt.

That night, the dreams made it all worse. For the few hours of sleep I managed to get, every unconscious second was violated by dreams. Dreams of wings flapping, thrusting against my face, lifting my hair. Of muzzles twitching, dark eyes shining, reflecting the white moon. Those eyes bored into me. Knowing eyes. Intelligent, human eyes.

THE WEEK after the funeral crawled by. A week in which every minute was weighed down with my tears and my anger. The dreams worsened and I rarely slept. The house still lay silent most of the time, as if no one dared to have any fun—as if TV, games and laughter would lessen our loss.

I dried the dishes while Aidan stacked them away. Ms. Custer chatted with Simon and Izzy in the living room.

"It's my fault," I said softly.

"It's not."

"I should have done something!" I flung the cloth at the counter and sank into the nearest chair.

Aidan sighed. "Look, Bryn, maybe it doesn't work that way. Maybe sometimes premonitions happen for reasons other than the obvious." He shook his head, eyes narrowed, impaling me with the fiercest stare. "You have to snap out of it."

I got to my feet again and grabbed another dish. He'd never be able to understand what I was going through. Not until he could see the glow and live with the knowledge himself. And that would never happen.

"Stop beating yourself up," he continued. "You see the glow, then the person dies. Each time it's different. You never know when they'll die. So you can't do anything to save them, Bryn." Aidan sighed, his eyes filled with regret and grief. He took a step toward me, hesitated for a moment, then turned abruptly on his heel and left the kitchen.

His parting words chilled me like a plunge into arctic waters: *You see the glow, then they die.* I turned and stared, horrified, after Aidan.

He knew it was me.

THE HOURS TICKED by slower than a sleepwalking snail and I'd wasted enough time moping around, wondering what Aidan was thinking. Time to find out. I padded down to his room, straining to keep the floorboards from creaking beneath my feet.

The clunk of a cabinet drawer downstairs echoed up the stairs. Ms. Custer was still awake. Guess she had her own bad dreams to evade.

We hadn't received our scolding from our foster mom after all. She wasn't faring too well. She'd never lost a child before. And though Social Services understood and hadn't questioned the quality of her care, she still blamed herself.

As if she'd personally caused Brody's death. As if she thought she could have prevented it. Guess we were in pretty much the same boat.

My knuckles tapped the door. Not too loud, as we could still get in trouble. The door whispered open against the pressure of my knock.

"Aidan?" I whispered.

My voice echoed in the empty darkness. I flicked the switch, my heart racing, dread weighing on my bones. Before the bare bulb exposed the room, intuition had already filled me in.

All traces of Aidan were wiped clean. No rumpled bedding spilled across his bed. No computers, electronics or books overflowed the table. His dresser lay bare and his closet hung open to reveal abandoned racks and shelves.

When did he pack? When did he get all his stuff out? And why in the hell would he leave like a stranger, without saying goodbye? As if we'd shared nothing between us. Not the tumultuous heat of those kisses or the shared grief or even my strange and horrible secret. How could he leave me now?

The amber stone seared my throat as if sharing the simmering pain in my gut.

Staggering toward the open window I slumped against the sill, struggling to breathe. Voices filtered to me from the porch below: Aidan and Ms. Custer. "Thank you, and good luck," my foster mom was saying, a sad and oddly hollow timbre to her voice.

I didn't waste a second, just tore out of the room and down the stairs, landing on the last step as the door closed with a soft click.

I didn't think.

Didn't stop.

I just hurtled past Ms. Custer to the door and flung it open. "Bryn, honey. What—" Her voice rose. I ignored her and hurried after Aidan, praying I wasn't too late. On a different level of consciousness, I recognized I was going all crazy, over-obsessed girlfriend on him as he drove out of my life. At this point, I didn't care.

"Aidan!" I called out as I hopped down the porch stairs and skidded to a stop in front of him. "What's going on? Where are you going?"

He reached for his helmet, a weary sadness shadowing his eyes. "I have to leave. My boss wants me back ASAP. Emergency."

"What about school?"

Lame reason, Bryn. There are other schools outside of Craven.

He shrugged, as if school was the least important thing in the world. But the sadness lingered in his eyes. He couldn't hide it.

I ached with too many facets of grief. I felt so profoundly tired. Of losing the people I cared for. Of being alone. Of caring.

Don't you care about me?

The question teetered at the tip of my tongue. Either pride or self-preservation stole my question away. I gritted my teeth, refused to appear a love-stricken teenager begging Aidan to stay.

He swung his leg over the Ducati seat and tugged me close. I didn't want the hug. False comfort when he prepared to desert me. His embrace was a twisted fusion of lies and dreams. But I shared the hug, took every little bit of him I could.

"I'm sorry, Bryn." Above me, warm breath ruffled my hair but the night mocked me. "I have to go."

Then he mounted the bike, tugged the helmet on and tightened the strap. He revved the engine, the sound dragging forth memories of that cool evening when he first rode into my life.

In seconds, he turned onto the street and disappeared into the darkness.

Straight out of my life.

I STOOD IN THE DARK, not bothering to hug myself against the cold, not registering the twitch of drapes across the road. Not caring that Ms. Custer might come out and scold.

The cold night transformed my breath into a ghostly apparition, spreading fading fingers to grasp the softest breeze. My amber talisman burned the skin at my neck as I watched him go.

So many questions he'd left unanswered. What was wrong with me? Why did I see the golden haze? Questions only he knew how to answer. He knew. And he'd left. It wasn't like Aidan at all.

Then it hit me like a bolt out of the deep black sky. How well did I really know Aidan?

He'd barely been with us long enough to call him part of the family, but he'd found little nooks and crannies to immerse himself in. Ms. Custer, her kids and just about the entire population of Craven adored him.

But my knowledge of his past was nonexistent. We'd spent a lot of time together and yet I had no idea where he came from, or what his family had been like. He'd never spoken of his last foster family, never discussed himself at all.

The frigid fingers groping at my heart had nothing to do with the winter cold.

Who was Aidan Lee?

I TIPTOED into the house and held my breath as I shut the door. Then winced when Ms. Custer called out. Entering the living room, I pulled a rug from a small pile near the door and sank onto the couch. Another of her favorite old black-and-white movies flickered on the small screen.

"What did he say?" I asked, staring at Marilyn as her dress floated on a cheeky gust of air.

Her voice crackled and she cleared her throat before she spoke. "That he had to leave. That he was being transferred to another foster home and the circumstances were unusual. It wasn't my place to ask, honey." She nodded in silence, taking Aidan's words as gospel.

"He didn't say why?" I asked.

Marilyn pouted.

Ms. Custer shook her head.

"Or where?"

"Bryn, honey, I think he meant to leave and not be found. So whatever plan you're hatching in that pretty little head of yours . . . forget it." Her eyes were sad as she took my chin in her hands and drew me into her soft embrace. "Your heart will heal, child. First love is always the hardest."

But her smile failed to soothe me. She knew mere words would not help me. I was desperate for her to call Social Services, the police, anyone who could help us to find him.

But in that dark place where I knew I couldn't help the poor people who glowed, in that same dark corner of my soul lived the truth.

Aidan did not mean to be found.

We watched Miss Monroe entrance her beau, in a sad and comfortable silence, until the credits rolled and my discreet tears dried.

THE LAST OF the credits and the onset of Ms. Custer's soft snores gave me a reason to slip upstairs. The stairs creaked in the eerie, middle-of-the-night way they always do when the house settles and warmth creeps out of the wood.

I passed my room and stood in Aidan's doorway. He'd left, despite knowing how much I needed him, and that nobody else could help me. I dared not risk my secret with anyone.

I was completely alone.

I blinked as my eyes stung. I just wanted to go back to my room and close the door on Aidan and his chapter in my life. But as I turned to leave, the light from the bare window caught and reflected on an object beneath the bed. I froze, ears straining for Ms. Custer's footsteps.

Releasing my breath, I tiptoed into the room. I crouched, reaching splayed fingers between the wall and the bed, and retrieved a thick, leather-bound book. It shifted in my hand, fragile and ready to fall apart if I so much as breathed on it.

Holding it with infinite care I traced the edge of the cover, lifting it slowly, unable to curb my curiosity. The floorboard on the second stair creaked and I snuck back into my room in a flash.

Ms. Custer had enough to worry about. I'd only be adding to her worries if she thought I wasn't handling Aidan's departure well, if she found me moping in his empty room.

I eased the door closed with seconds to spare. Ms. Custer paused outside, her shadow slipping in across the floorboards. Then she sighed softly and plodded to her room.

Tears singed my eyes and I rested my forehead on the door, among the multitude of hanging scarves. How long I'd waited to have a mother care for me that way.

Little things like these, when people cared enough to share your pain—these were moments to treasure.

In our grief for Brody, in our communal, familial pain, we

helped each other heal. But my ache for Aidan was my own pain, borne alone, and it would remain alone.

I sank onto the bed and flicked the lamp on. The book and its intricately carved leather binding weaved its spell around me.

I opened it, allowing the book to fall open naturally to a well-used page.

To the painting of the Valkyrie called Brunhilde.

This time more notes filled the margins, and one particular newly printed phrase jumped out, boldly written and circled again in red ink.

Brunhilde - Bright Warrior = Bryn.

CHAPTER 11

My hands quivered. Shock, anger and disbelief warred within my head. The sounds of clanging metal reverberated in my ears and I attributed it to the depth of my fury.

Crap! What had possessed Aidan to attach my name to the stunning Valkyrie? They were figures of myth for heaven's sake. Beautiful, strong women, but just figments of the imagination of an ancient race. Nobody believed such stories were true anymore.

I breathed deep, counted to ten and hoped it would help to reduce the rapid beat of my heart to a steadier pace. I needed facts to help ease the turmoil in my head. Neither Bryn nor Brynhildr were common names. I had a crazy father who might have loved the long-dead legend. Who knew why he chose the name?

I shook my head. Aidan was blowing the coincidence way out of proportion. I ran my finger along the sharp edge of the aged paper, traced the circular grooves Aidan's red pen had carved into the thick paper. The Valkyrie's face drew my gaze, a painted magnetic force, entrancing me.

Uncanny.

Shivers trailed down my spine. The majestic warrior maiden stood confident, bronze chainmail gleaming, her strong chin tilted upward as if in defiance of . . . who? Her god or her father?

She resembled me to the finest detail, even the way my ears curved, and the proportion of my eyes. My twin stared back at me from a painting dating more than five centuries ago. More than uncanny. Downright creepy.

What did Aidan know? And why was he studying this book at all? What kind of cosmic coincidence caused a boy researching Valkyries to pitch up on my doorstep with a painting of a Valkyrie bearing not only my name but my face?

SLEEP ELUDED ME. The book, hidden beneath rumpled clothing in my dresser, whispered. Taunted. So I got up and read until sunrise, despite the niggling feeling that I was privy to priceless information, the feeling that I shouldn't turn another page, that I wasn't meant to have the book at all. All that, overshadowed by that face.

That eerily familiar face.

The temptation to cut school teased at the edges of my conscience, but sanity prevailed. We were all Ms. Custer's kids and my actions would hurt her reputation within the town. Vice

Principal Warren waited with vicious eagerness for my first wrong move and I refused to give him the satisfaction.

I hid the book deep within my closet and trudged off to school.

Each minute of the day crawled by, a caravan of tortoise-seconds. The red second-hand on the wall clocks ticked closer and closer to three. As home time drew closer, the snide comments and knowing looks of the other students no longer penetrated my conscious thought.

At last I escaped, racing home, my mind already rifling through the enticing pages of Aidan's book. I dashed into my room and locked myself in, spending the next few hours poring over the book in much the same way as Aidan had. I read until my head drooped and my eyelids grew too heavy to keep them open a minute longer.

Although I'd slept in small, uncomfortable fits, judging from my strange and fantastic dreams I'd had a fair bit of shuteye. In my dreams the pages swirled to dust as I turned them, and the book glowed like the light of the iridescent living dead. The book burst into flames while the painted Bryn cackled at my despair.

I heeded the message within the dreams. I took extra care with the fragile leather cover whose spine was so worn it threatened to fall apart each time I opened it. Now I understood why Aidan had chosen the expansive dining table for his work. My little study desk was not cooperating and I struggled to get comfortable. But I didn't take the book downstairs. Best not to advertise that I had Aidan's book in my possession.

Many of the pages were written in the strange ancient writing Aidan had been translating. Widely spaced and in overlarge print, much of the beautiful, original writing had faded, ink stolen by the unscrupulous fingers of time. In contrast, sloppy handwritten notes desecrated a multitude of pages, made by bold and sometimes inconsiderate scholars. Brighter and more enduring writing covered the remainder of the pages. Saddened by the violation, I prayed it was just a copy.

I massaged the stricken muscles at my neck and flipped toward the back of the book. A handful of papers shifted out of place. For one terrifying moment, I feared I'd pulled away a whole section from its binding. Then I sighed. A stack of letters, notes and other random things like newspaper articles and copies of photographs had come loose. Taking extra care, I picked through them.

A gasp of surprise escaped my lips. I froze. The sound was way too loud. My eyes flicked to the locked door and I tensed, holding my breath as I waited. Minutes later I expelled a stale breath, at last certain that no one had heard me. I turned back to my discovery: a writing tablet filled with translations tucked in with the rest of the odd collection.

The tablet gripped my attention and curiosity, promising unlimited help in learning the strange script. I'd never had the patience to learn languages, always scraping by with a C or D, but this language came so easily to me. The words held a magnetism not unlike the beautiful and mysterious face of the Valkyrie Brunhilde.

The more I read, the more I understood the script. Before long, I found myself correcting Aidan's scribbled translations, uncovering the story of the Valkyries who served the All-Father Odin in Valhalla. I yawned and rubbed my eyes as the ancient words blended together in a blur. As much as I wished I could continue through the night, I had to get to bed. I barely got much sleep these days anyway and I had to admit I needed some rest.

But the pile of papers still beckoned.

Skimming through just one last time, I dislodged an old newspaper article, which fluttered to the table. I handled it with tender care, and when it crinkled and crackled, I ground to a halt, deathly afraid it would crumble into a pile of dust within my fingers. Searching through my desk drawer, I withdrew a plastic sleeve and slid the article inside. Protected by the plastic, it was less fragile now, less chance that I would destroy it. I lifted it to the light and tried to read the fading type.

Dated eighteen years previously, it stated:

> *The historic town of Hovgårten, Sweden, was a hive of activity this week with what can only be described as the most incredible discovery in Norwegian and Swedish Archaeological history. On revealing its contents the graveside drew the attention of the international press as well as eminent archaeologists from around the world. Although initially suspected to be the remains of a "real" Valkyrie, it has been verified that the skeleton belonged to a warrior princess whose burial was befitting that of the ancient mythological Valkyries.*
>
> *Dr. Elisabeth Wayne, the overseeing archaeologist for the dig site was quoted as saying: "Although we are disappointed that the remains do not actually belong to a real Valkyrie, we are left with a beautiful*

specimen and with ancient relics which will enrich the Norwegian and Swedish Archaeological Society."

When asked to confirm the origin of the wings which were also found within the burial site, Dr. Wayne stated that eminent genetic scientist Dr. Geoffrey Halbrook, on loan to NWAS for the duration of this dig, has confirmed the DNA tests have been unable to verify the exact avian species it belongs to. Dr. Wayne believes they most likely belong to some form of ancient and extinct condor.

All items unearthed from the site will be sent to the British Museum for cataloging and preservation. Dr. Wayne and her team are preparing for a large public unveiling of the remains of the warrior princess once all necessary testing and cataloging has been completed.

Blood thrummed in my ears and I forced myself to read the article again, this time slower, going over the words and the name over and over again in case I'd misunderstood it, or was hallucinating, or going crazy.

At last, certain I'd read right, I sat back with a whole new set of questions.

Because eminent genetic scientist Dr. Geoffrey Halbrook was my father.

A SHEAF of papers accompanied the article, fastened together with a rusted bulldog clip. The large-typed heading proclaimed the document as a ***"DNA Analysis Report."*** The pages were filled with scientific code and references, little of which I could understand except what was typed or written in plain English. These margins too were filled with writing. Notes made by three separate writers.

The first set of notes said:

Full DNA testing performed, partial match to human genetic code with minor anomalies. Possibility: Valkyrie DNA present. DNA is viable for further testing and ??

A second stated:

Genetic anomalies confirmed as Valkyrie—no match to any known registered DNA within the international database, across and within all living species. The request forms and receipt-logs confirm Halbrook requested additional samples to be provided.
Question: What was Halbrook's intention for the use of the additional DNA?

Then:

Confirmation from database—Mrs. Irene Halbrook admitted for private IVF procedure. Attended by Dr Halbrook. Suspicious? Could Dr. Halbrook have used the DNA to create a clone or a mutated embryo and implanted it into his wife? Further information required:

Mother's progress during pregnancy and birth, including all blood analysis.

Infant's blood analysis.

Find infant for further testing.

The last set of writing belonged to Aidan.

Halbrook killed in car accident. Not suspicious but unable to confirm. Daughter found through Social Services records. Remained in the United States under state care. Current foster—Custer, Town of Craven. Daughter's name = Brynhildr. Unusual? Risky for Halbrook. Signs of abnormality—none. Dementia—none, although records show regular psychiatric care provided from age 5.

Then a break in the notes. And finally:

Recommendation to terminate—Negative.

MY LUNGS STRUGGLED FOR AIR; my body for breath and sanity. I wound a scarf around my neck, grabbed a thick coat and fled down the stairs and outside into the fresh, biting air. I breathed and it hurt. Blinked and it stung. Tears singed my eyes as tepid liquid hit frigid cold air.

My sneakers whacked the sidewalk. I moved, unsure, uncaring where my feet led me.

A million agonizing thoughts haunted me. My head burned with treachery and betrayal and lies which had lain in my past, gathering the dust of my ignorance. I was a product of IVF? It didn't make sense. If my parents had gone to such an extent just to conceive a child, why would my mother have abandoned me so quickly? Just because I saw glowing people? I didn't think so. What mother would run from her child just because they were seeing a psychiatrist?

Could Aidan have left the book as a warning? Had he known I'd search his room? Did it even matter right now? Nothing could make the lies easier to accept. Or make me hate him any less.

The article swam before my eyes, though even the memory of it blurred behind the veil of tears. My father's involvement in archeology had been a surprise. Archeology unmistakably connected to the name of a certain warrior maiden turned Valkyrie.

I might have appreciated the name more had I been aware of its origins. Aware of its true meaning. Ugh! Who was I kidding? I still disliked my name. Still wouldn't allow the general public to know it. It brought to mind images of plump women, horned helmets, and braids of bright red hair splayed across generous bosoms.

No. I still hated my name.

But my name was the least of my concerns right now. What had my father been up to, tampering with DNA from an ancient skeleton?

The handwritten notes on the DNA reports, filled with vague facts and wild innuendo, raised questions. My father's notes aside, whoever had written before Aidan had fanned a fire of suspicion. Who was the person who viewed my father's activities with such mistrust?

Aside from my father and the mysterious note-maker, it was Aidan's part in this whole fiasco which crawled deep into my heart and festered as I walked. Was his intention to come to Craven to befriend me? To find me and study me? If so, it meant he'd lied from day one with those sexy smiles and hot kisses. The hurt deepened as I recalled the startled expression in Aidan's eyes when he'd first kissed me. Why take our relationship to a personal level when I was no more than a genetic monstrosity?

Anger blinded me. He'd had control of his emotions. He'd damn well known what he'd gotten into. I'd been the total fool, manipulated from the moment he arrived, who'd fallen for his quirky smile, his knee-melting charm and his cool biker-dude personality.

But they were all lies. Beautiful, torturous lies.

Who was Aidan Lee then? And why the hell would he expect to "terminate" me? I wasn't dangerous, for heaven's sake—not that I knew of anyway. Judging by my inability to help the people I knew were dying, I didn't seem much use to anyone either.

I could have stewed all night, but the high-pitched keen of whistling broke into the depths of my thoughts. Up ahead, a bunch of jocks horsed around. One of them sneered at me and pointed, his shoulders stiff and straight. His friends turned their heads in my direction and stared. Just my luck to run into a bunch of North Wood jerks with far too much time on their hands after school. On the prowl for something to do and they'd found me.

I recognized the park around me, where I'd sat on the swings watching the boys at play in happier days. Where I'd first seen Brody glow.

The little green patch, dotted with kids' play equipment, nestled within a stand of russet black gums and river birches whose leaves had begun to carpet the ground at their trunks. The trees lined a paved pathway, little signboards announcing the names of each variety of tree.

The pebbled pathway led to a small bubbling stream and was a popular walking spot. But on a gray afternoon at dusk the path was empty of laughter and barking and safety.

The boys spread out and paced toward me, the gathering shadows hiding their eyes, hiding their intentions. A quick glance behind me confirmed I was alone with no one close, no one who could help. Not even the failing light could hide the stark reality.

I was surrounded.

CHAPTER 12

They circled, eyes gleaming, cruel. They didn't resemble boys. The feral expressions on their faces said it all: I was meat and they were hungry.

I rocked on the balls of my feet, waiting, unsure what would happen if I ran. They were fast. Running track at school had blessed me with stamina, and I was strong too. But no match for these beefy linebackers who bulked up in the gym every day.

Three to one. Those could have been good odds if I were a trained martial artist, but I was never much of a contact fighter. Too afraid I'd get hit, I'd close my eyes during sparring and get hit anyway every time.

My luck pretty much sucked for the self-defense tricks we'd been taught too. No keys with which to jab at eyes. No heels to grind into insteps. No mace to spray.

I retreated, a few steps at a time.

By the time I'd figured out what they were up to it was too late. They'd forced me down the path into the shadowy cover of the trees.

"All alone with no biker-boy to protect you? Big mistake," one of them snarled, his voice dripping revulsion.

Pete. My memory came up empty for a surname. Who really cared, when jocks were jocks anyway?

"Hey guys, how about some freak meat?" He grinned at his friends, short dreadlocks quivering like spitting vipers.

The others grunted, a rabid pack of wolves, just following the leader. Man reduced to mere animal by his basest need: desire for dominance. Or perhaps it was just plain boredom, nothing deeper, from boys who always got their way because they were popular and sporty. Boys adored by all the girls at North Wood. All the girls besides the freak, that is.

I turned my head and fear dug jagged nails into my gut. One of the boys, the red-headed, freckle-faced Chuckie, caught my eye. He smiled. Reassuring me, as if this were just a game, and they'd soon get bored and run off to clean up for dinner. Not likely.

The third guy smashed the last bit of his Snickers bar into his mouth, flicking the paper into the trees. He wiped his mouth off, hands quivering, eyes searching the path, sweat dotting his forehead.

"Nice girls don't take walks in the park alone, do they, freak?" asked Pete, a predatory glint in his eye. "Hey boys, the freak's not a nice girl. What say we have a little fun with her?"

Laughter rang out, cruel laughter, dangerous laughter. My heart thudded in my chest as fear flooded my veins; my muscles threatened to tighten up on me.

The blow came out of nowhere; granite knuckles slammed into my cheek, bone glancing off bone in the breath of a moment. Distracted by Snickers, I'd missed when Pete closed the distance enough to land the punch. I hit dirt, too shocked to do much else besides throw my hands out to soften my landing. I moaned; lightning streaks of pain forked through my arms and side.

The encounter with the ground also jarred my cheek. My eyes watered and for a few seconds Pete was a smudgy yellow and red blur. I blinked rapidly to clear them of the watery haze, to clear my head of the fury. Anger wouldn't help me at all. Consciousness, awareness were my tools.

I struggled to rise but Pete landed a kick to my gut that crushed the breath out of my lungs. Had I eaten lunch like a normal person, the meal would have been spewed across the leaves by now. My breath rasped and twisted, anticipating smashed ribs, or diabolical internal pain. But the mild ache of Pete's sucker punch was all that remained.

I was aware of Pete's teeth, impossibly white; he could have been in a toothpaste commercial.

Laughter echoed around me. These were regular guys who would someday have families and respectable jobs. Yet they assaulted innocent girls. Beat them up like they were sacks of grain. From their confidence, this wasn't their first attack. Were they seasoned bullies who beat their victims to a pulp? Or seasoned rapists?

Officially livid, I forgot about Aidan's betrayal and my father's secrets and concentrated on my fury, figuring I'd use it rather than try to squelch it. I boosted myself off the path again, this time standing firm, planting my feet into the ground, solid as the rooted trunks of the river birches leaning in overhead. My amulet bounced, smacking my collarbone with a spiking blast of pain.

This was sure as hell the best time ever for my namesake to lend me some of her prowess.

Pete led his team, rushing at me, filled with confidence that the freak would fall again. He raised a muscle-bound arm and swung it at my jaw. The blow never landed.

At the last second, I rammed my fist into his abdomen, knocking the air out of him, hoping I damaged his precious six-pack. Pete fell flat onto his back. Breath left his lungs in a whoosh and he seemed oblivious to the snickering from his buddies. The stunned colors of surprise mottled his face, steadily reddening with violent, visceral anger.

Pete, the linebacker, had just been trounced by a girl.

He growled as he rose and although I was tempted to punch him out in mid-rise it was risky. His buddies, though amused at their leader's predicament, weren't regarding me with approval either. The odds were still against me.

I'd just obliterated my luck by making Pete look like a chump. But surely somewhere within his pounding anger and hot desire for vengeance lay a little niggle of doubt. The tiniest question of whether he'd kicked a rattler in its head.

On his feet again, he hitched up his trousers and circled me. I shifted my feet, whipped my head, eyes darting from left to right and back again. Fear seared my blood every time I had to turn my back to one of the boys. Pete lunged and I scrambled back, straight into Chuckie's arms. He held me down so Pete the hero could punch a girl. What a guy.

Pete landed a solid punch in my belly.

I bent over, feigning breathlessness, allowing him to get closer. Within my reach.

Then I kicked.

The vicious smile on his face turned into a dark twist of purest agony. I may have destroyed his ability to father children, and to pee.

I had absolutely no qualms with that. If it meant reducing the chance of Pete attempting to rape some other innocent girl, I was happy with that.

Around me, Chuckie's arms loosened. Pete writhed on the ground, weeping like a girl. I turned and punched Chuckie straight in the gut. This time I did hear an ominous snap. He crumpled to the ground, mewling in pain, joining Pete. Two down, one to go.

Snickers stared at his friends. Incredulity flushed his face, which was still creased with nervous concern. I shared his disbelief, stunned that I'd wiped the floor with them. I should have been exhausted from the beatings, from fighting back. Instead, adrenaline pulsed through me. Liquid lightning returned energy to my trembling limbs.

If only I could have used one of those fabulous roundhouse kicks to floor him. Instead, I bided my time, waiting for him to get closer. I dodged the first blow and punched him in the face. My knuckles came away stained with blood and chocolate.

He held his face, staring in confused surprise. Then turned and fled.

Violent spasms pulsed through my hands, forcing me to squeeze them together to ease the shaking. I surveyed the scene, then glanced at Snickers' fast disappearing back. *Time to get outta here, Bryn.* I jumped over Pete as he sprawled on the ground, hands cupping his crotch as if the action would somehow soothe his savage agony.

"Next time, take a second before you decide to pick on innocent girls. These days you never know which one of your victims will turn around and beat you to a pulp," I said. "Oh, and I won't tell anyone you and your friends got beat up by a girl. I won't tell if you don't. Okay, Pete?"

I waited, then prodded his thigh with my sneaker.

He yelped, though I'd barely touched him. "Yes, yes! I won't tell anyone, okay!"

Then I turned and ran as if the hounds of hell were breathing down my neck. Somewhere behind me, a single word squawked like a half-strangled bird from the darkness of the trees.

"Bitch!"

Ah well. Everyone is entitled to their own opinion.

From this day forward, I'd need eyes in the back of my head. They might keep silent in school but they'd soon want payback. Pete would want vengeance for himself and for his manhood.

Safe in my room again, I seized the thick volume; the need to erase Pete's assault possessed me with demonic force. I attacked the translations, scribbling word after word, filling pages with the ancient script.

A motorcycle roared along the street and jerked me out of my frenetic trance. I tensed, listening, wondering if it would turn into our drive. I relaxed only when it passed the house and rumbled into the distance. From the dark sky outside the window it was clear that the whole evening had gone by.

I turned to the painting of the Valkyrie Brunhilde, searching for something to translate. The first paragraph told the myth of how Valkyries appeared as swans and how the men who loved them hid their swan-skins to keep them in their human form. Strange story. I smiled, having never felt in the least bit swan-like.

The second paragraph had the hairs on my head standing to attention. The script mentioned the Glow of Courage, sometimes call the Glow of Bravery: the golden aura that identifies a Warrior to a Valkyrie.

My heart thumped a wild tattoo. So that was why Aidan hadn't been surprised when I mentioned the glow! Why couldn't he have just told me about it and put me out of my misery? Granted, knowing I was a Valkyrie probably wouldn't have solved my problems, but at least I would have had something to identify with.

I sighed and studied the book again, hoping to find clues left behind by my father or Aidan or the other mysterious note-maker. Everywhere I hit dead ends. The crumbling article, now safe in its plastic sleeve, would have helped had the newspaper not shut down eight years ago. The leather-bound volume contained no markings to confirm its origins or its author. The internet had no mysterious volumes of books, lost, discovered or missing.

I rubbed dry eyes, prodded my sore neck, scraped my fingers through my hair and repeated those actions all through the night. Before long, I was familiar with every website containing information on Valkyries.

So far, I had avoided the inevitable. A strange reluctance held me back from typing in my father's name. It felt blasphemous, as if the very act was an acceptance of his guilt. As if Aidan and the mystery accuser were justified in their belief.

I gritted my teeth. I knew nothing would come of it, but I had to try. I typed.

The screen filled with multiple links. Geoffrey Halbrook was a prizewinning angler from Maine, an excited winner of a Dolly Parton lookalike contest, a birdwatcher from the Bayou whose latest book featured a CD filled with bird-call imitations in crystal clarity, and an old wheelchair-bound jazz musician with a toothless grin, ice-white hair and sooty skin.

I tapped in the word geneticist, and waited.

Bingo.

The screen filled again with newspaper articles and other sites directing to articles in medical and genetic science journals. I pulled up the medical sites and found that most required registration before providing access. For those that asked for annual fees paid by credit card or PayPal I drew a resounding blank.

Working the sites I managed to access, I trolled through article after article written by eminent genetic scientist and researcher Dr. Geoffrey Halbrook. He sounded like a smart guy. Granted, I couldn't understand half the medical-speak though I did manage to get the gist of most of them.

My eyes complained that it was late; the clock agreed, blinking 3:23 a.m. I promised myself just one more article before I crashed. The last one was co-written and I blearily brought it up, yawning widely through cupped fingers.

I choked and spluttered on the second yawn.

The article proclaimed a collaboration between Dr. Geoffrey Halbrook and Dr. Stephen Lee.

BLOOD THRUMMED THROUGH MY EARDRUMS, drowning out the world.

Stephen Lee.

Aidan Lee.

As assumptions went it was a short, easy leap. Was Aidan related to this geneticist? A colleague of my father? From the contents of the book it seemed they were far more than just colleagues.

They were rivals.

I read every page again in case I'd missed something. Dr. Lee disapproved of my father's experiments and research, and his alleged use of DNA belonging to an ancient skeleton. For good reason, given my uncanny resemblance to the Valkyrie Brunhilde, the glow of soon-to-be-dead people and my unusual strength of late. Dr. Lee's suspicions may not have been far off the mark.

The only thing was I didn't want any of it to be true—especially the part where Aidan was probably the son of my father's rival, sent here to investigate me and estimate whether I needed "termination."

I hurt, deeper than I'd ever experienced grief or pain before. In this huge game, I was a pawn.

Manipulated. Used. Dispensable.

In black despair, I shut the computer down, no longer able to keep my eyes open, but sleep didn't come. I lay in the bed in darkness, eyes shut but body and mind on overdrive. Aidan's betrayal and desertion cut deep.

I quaked with anger at him. Our entire "relationship" was one multifaceted sham. To think I'd allowed him to get so close, closer than I'd ever allowed anyone else to get. The only reason I would ever want to see him again would be to tell him exactly how despicable I thought he was.

I rolled over and curled the blanket tight around me. Bigger issues brewed here than the minuscule problem of my shattered heart. Finding out the truth about who and what I was loomed at the top of my list of things to do. Well before piecing my heart back together.

But what could I do? Where did I start? I didn't have friends to turn to and I didn't want to burden Ms. Custer with problems that were never hers to begin with.

I fell asleep when the dark night sky bled into a dusky gray, only for my sleep to be riddled with dreams of Aidan surrounded by a golden glow that predicted his death.

CHAPTER 13

Days stretched into weeks, and the end of November blew in on a frigid wind. I took to using Izzy's bike to get to school, preferring to get there and back with as much speed as possible.

Hiding from Pete and his henchmen had taken a toll on me. I was grateful that Ms Custer had taken my revelation so well. I'd begged her not to go to the police, and watched as she laughed when I told her how I'd trounced my attackers. I prayed the day would come when those thugs forgot the pain I'd put them through. But I was in for a long wait. Pride healed slower than wounds. In the meantime I chose the safest, quickest route home.

When school let out for Thanksgiving break I sped home, weaving through the smaller back streets and skidding to a stop at our back door. I hoped to escape upstairs unseen, choosing to sneak into the house through the back way. Food was still a sore topic with poor Ms. Custer, a subject I avoided like a vampire did garlic. I didn't want to be responsible for hurting her.

I waited a few seconds in the kitchen, listening. The coast was clear. But just as the door to the dining room shifted beneath my fingers, ready to swing open, the sound of Ms. Custer's voice skittered down the hall. The nervous tremor and icy disdain in her words broadcast an unmistakable warning. Ms. Custer didn't have the constitution to be nervous. Something was wrong.

"I told you twice already, she ran away," she said, her voice edgy, as if hovering between frustration and tears.

"Why would she run away?" said a deeper voice, more authoritative, more official. "Is there something about your care that made her unhappy?"

I didn't appreciate the insinuation. Seemed he was going for intimidation. I didn't plan on allowing it. I gritted my teeth and took a step forward.

"My Bryn had her poor heart broken." An uncharacteristic chill in Ms. Custer's voice stopped me from barging right into the living room. She spoke with a harshness and an undertone of accusation, as if she had aimed the statement at another person in the room. "Then, to make matters worse, she was attacked by a group of boys from the school."

A third person spoke. "What? What happened? Is she okay?" The familiar voice rang in my ears. An unwelcome dizziness accosted my head. My hip nudged the pine table in the middle of the kitchen as I backed into it.

The last voice I thought I'd ever hear again.

Aidan.

Ms. Custer answered him curtly. "Young man, that's simply none of your business." The heat of pure anger blazed in my foster mom's voice and I gave a silent cheer for her. Not only because she was backing me up, but because she had the guts to tell Aidan off in front of those threatening, official-sounding people.

The first man spoke again. "Miss Custer, I would appreciate it if you could answer Mr. Lee's question. This is an official investigation, and if Miss Halbrook is in any danger or has been injured in any way it would be best for us to know the extent of her injuries."

"She's fine. She kicked their butts and sent them packing."

"Sounds like Bryn." I stiffened as Aidan's voice echoed again, only this time a trail of rage ripped at my gut.

How dare you sound pleased or proud of me? How dare you come back here looking for me, and bringing your government goon, too?

"I've answered enough of your questions. What more do you want from me, then?" asked Ms. Custer. Behind the impatience in her voice lay an inch of steel. "You've already turned my place upside down for that book when it simply isn't here. You've seen for yourselves Bryn isn't here. So why are you still here?"

"Because I simply do not believe you. You see, I think you will cover for her given the chance. I think you could very well be lying to us. You say she ran. Why does her room not look like she's taken off for a long time, or for good? All her stuff is still there, isn't it?"

"Oh, so when you decide to run away, I take it you stop to pack your hairdryer and your high heel pumps. No, Mr. Worthington. Bryn ran because her heart was broken. She ran because she was hurt and alone and probably in shock too. I'm sorry she wasn't here for you to arrest her for stealing a book, which I'm sure she wouldn't have taken in the first place." Bitterness laced her words, along with a hefty dose of anger. "If you're done I need my tea. You've wasted enough of my time."

Panic flitted through me. I couldn't run out the back door. It would close too loudly and then Ms. Custer would be in tons of trouble. Slipping into the broom closet at the far end of the kitchen, I pulled the door, leaving it slightly ajar. I couldn't risk the click of the latch giving me away. Already they were filing into the kitchen after her, as if Ms. Custer meant to abscond with the teabags.

She gave my hiding place a quick stare, then went straight to the kettle and filled it at the sink. With the kettle starting its boil, she pulled out a cup and a little plate and prepared her tea.

"Please excuse me if I don't offer you my hospitality, Mr. Worthington." She threw him a tepid smile.

He smiled back, baring his teeth. He seemed unfamiliar with the human act of smiling. Tall, stocky, FBI issue. Aidan stood on the other side of the kitchen table, facing the broom closet head on. Damn.

Ms. Custer fished a teabag out of the plastic container and discreetly dug her fingernail into it as she dropped it into her cup. In a blink the surface of the table was strewn with fine tea leaves.

"Now see what you made me do!" she cried.

Worthington smirked, unaffected. Aidan frowned, his gaze flicking to Ms. Custer's harried face.

She stalked to the broom closet, bent in and grabbed the little dust pan and brush. She shut the door firmly. Darkness wove bands of shadows around me, blinding me. I listened as my foster mom's hand scraped spilled leaves into the dustpan. The pedal bin clanged as she tipped the contents of the pan into it.

Footsteps drew closer and I pressed myself against the wall, hugging my bag tight against me. Inside the bag, the very book these louts were after poked me in the ribs. The door opened and Ms. Custer returned the dustpan to its place, never once glancing in my direction.

When she shut the door again, the darkness of the closet wasn't as bad. My eyes adjusted slowly. I strained my ears, catching the running of water as she washed her hands, the tinkling of the spoon against the cup as she mixed her tea. I knew she would head out to the living room to enjoy her cup. Surely Worthington and Aidan would follow. I reached for the doorknob. Then Aidan spoke. My hand tightened on the knob, strained until my knuckles shone white even inside the shadowed closet.

"I told you. You're wasting your time," he said to Worthington. "She doesn't have the book. I must have misplaced it somewhere else."

"Your father wants the book, Mr. Lee. That means we have to find it. Besides, we've been ordered to terminate Miss Halbrook. And despite your reservations, we will do as we are ordered."

Aidan scoffed. "I doubt one little girl could possibly be a serious threat to a man as powerful as my father."

"Nevertheless, we have our orders," said Worthington, his voice cutting. "You were supposed to come here, get the lay of the land, and return with the information. The only reason you were sent here was because you could fit in. But you can't do a single thing right. Your father is not impressed."

"My father is never impressed, Worthington. Haven't you realized that yet?" I stiffened in the darkness. I could just picture the sneer marring Aidan's lips. "But you see, there's one difference between you and me," he continued. "I don't get paid to be impressed. I don't owe my father anything."

Worthington remained silent. I wondered if he stared at Aidan in disdain or ground his teeth in frustration at the upstart son of his boss.

Aidan sighed. "How much longer do you want to wait here? She would have been here by now if she was coming home at all."

"Perhaps the old woman was right," Worthington conceded. "Anywhere else she used to go to if she didn't come straight home?"

"The Craven Town Library," Aidan answered.

"Fine. Let's wrap it up here, then check the library. I'll have Martinez get in touch with the local police to put an APB out on Miss Halbrook. Suspected theft, possession of a weapon."

"Is that really necessary?" Aidan's voice flooded with alarm. As did my entire body. Things were not panning out well at all. These creeps were supposed to find nothing and leave. Not get the police involved in a statewide girl-hunt. Who were they? More to the point, who the hell was Aidan?

"We need that book back. We wouldn't be here if it hadn't been for your carelessness."

Aidan's hand slapped the kitchen countertop. "Don't kid yourself. You would definitely be here. My father would still want her terminated whether we find the book or not."

Worthington spoke, his voice dangerously soft. "Keep your voice down. The old lady's not deaf. Let's go. We can come back and keep an eye on the place. If she really has run away, then the old woman is safe. If I find she's been lying to cover for the mutant, then she goes too."

My heart iced over. I'd endangered Ms. Custer. The small closet closed in on me and I struggled for air, praying they would leave the kitchen so I could escape this cloying space.

The kitchen door swung and their voices receded into the hall. I turned the handle, inching it open as silently as possible, and stepped out into the empty kitchen.

All clear.

I pulled the back door open and snuck out, keeping an ear out for Aidan's goons, so afraid they'd heard me and would have me surrounded in the next second. My heart thudded as I crept around the corner.

During my sojourn in the broom closet, the sky had darkened, and shadows had taken control of the streets. I rounded the corner of the house to observe them as they left. Only then would I reenter the house.

Worthington and another man—Martinez, I presumed—left the porch. Aidan followed, a dejected slope to his shoulders. He turned and stared at the house, at my room's window, his face filled with sadness and longing. As he stepped into the dark car he scanned the garden and looked in my direction.

He couldn't see me where I crouched, encased in shadows. A violent longing stirred inside me, filling my eyes with heated tears, spicing my blood with need, spurring me to step forward.

What was I going to do? I wasn't exactly sure. Maybe all I wanted was for Aidan to know I was safe and well.

I never found out.

I took a step toward Aidan, but made it no further.

I flailed, losing my grip on my satchel as I fell forward.

A sudden gust of wind buffeted me.

The rough breeze whipped around me, throwing my hair into my face and away again. My nostrils flared as a spike of ozone assaulted my senses. A tiny tornado threatened to consume me and I flailed, then fell forward, shoved by the wild momentum of the rushing air.

My muscles tingled, twisted as if pulled through the wash cycle from hell. My vision blurred and Aidan and his thugs were smudges across the yard.

Then a strong arm grabbed me around my waist and someone spoke in my ear. The last thing I heard was, "You do not want to do that. We have to go. Now!"

CHAPTER 14

I came to with a soft groan, taking stock quietly. Whoever had shoved me to the ground hadn't intended to hurt me. My body, and all its parts, seemed to be in good working order, though my heart still thumped, wild as a cornered bear.

What had just happened?

Who had knocked me unconscious? And who did that voice belong to?

It had to be Aidan and his goons who'd taken me down. Maybe they'd shot me with some kind of FBI dart-weapon thing and I was now locked away in a cell in a dark basement, at a secret location, awaiting my death.

But that didn't make any sense. They'd made it clear they wanted to kill me. From the way they'd spoken, they would've been happy to shoot me on sight.

Aidan must have stepped up and convinced them to keep me alive. Even so, I wouldn't be the most grateful captive. This entire, awful mess was all his damned fault. I was still reeling from the shock of his presence in our house, still mad at the way that Worthington thug had pushed poor Ms. Custer around.

And she was not the "poor Ms. Custer" type. She'd put up a fight at any rate. Protected me. Lied for me. Told me with her actions and her eyes to leave.

Run.

Hide.

I blinked back tears, so grateful to my foster mom. I had to thank her. As soon as I got some feeling back into my limp muscles.

With any luck, I'd fainted and was still lying in the garden, tucked away beneath the dead hydrangeas at the corner of the house. I focused my thoughts, listening. No trees whispered, no wind blew. No icy breeze scraped my cheek, no cold hard ground lay beneath my warm body.

Instead, soft, luxurious fur caressed my skin. A fire crackled happily nearby, spitting occasional sparks, its cozy warmth toasted my cheeks. I cracked open an eye, confirmed I was alone, then sat up slowly.

Groaning again, I placed my hand on the spinning top attached to my neck that masqueraded as my head. I waited until it stopped its hurdy-gurdy motion and swallowed hard.

Bile coated the back of my tongue, though I couldn't recall throwing up. I held on to my stomach, moaned, then gasped.

A soft white fabric covered my midriff, along with the rest of my torso. The garment reminded me of my peasant blouse hanging in my closet at Ms. Custer's house. The dress, long enough to reach my ankles, fell in soft, silky gathers.

My heart thundered in my chest. Then I shivered. I'd been undressed while I was unconscious. I probed my hip and gave a shuddering sigh. I still wore my underwear, thank heaven, but my bra had disappeared along with my jeans, polo, jacket and scarf.

Not that I needed warm clothes right now.

Fear swam through me as I grabbed at my neck. Then I relaxed a bit. My amber pendant remained tied around my neck. At least they hadn't taken it.

I sat still, disinclined to test the steadiness of my legs, just happy to be conscious. Awake so strangers couldn't dress and undress me without my consent. My eyes adjusted to the dim light, and I scanned the strange room.

Walls of unpainted pine surrounded a space as large as my room at Ms. Custer's house. Above my head were bare log-beams lacing their way across a high stud ceiling.

The fire crackled and I studied the open stone fireplace. The darned thing was large enough to roast a whole person in. I changed track, refusing to follow that train of thought.

I decided to try opening the door, and if it opened, finding a way out of here. Pushing away the thick fur covers, I rose to my feet, testing each limb one at a time.

I'd made it halfway to the door when it opened and a girl walked in. I froze, staring straight into a pair of clear gray eyes. Eyes a perfect match to the silvery-gray wings rising behind her shoulders.

Wings that drew my memory back to Aidan's book and Brunhilde, the Valkyrie. The gray-eyed girl's bronzed chainmail armor, her confident posture, all said that she was the one thing I knew was downright impossible.

A Valkyrie.

I couldn't decide if I was astonished or horrified. Even the possible horror of my creation in a petri dish hadn't floored me the way this dark-haired, winged girl did. Her beauty, grace and power left me dumbstruck. Held me in a trance.

"I see you are awake. I was beginning to worry." Her voice was a honeyed wine, soothing and tender.

I clamped my mouth shut and frowned.

She said, "The first time can be hard on the body."

"First time?" I wondered if she was talking about my fall. But she didn't enlighten me any further. And her next words made no sense.

"The . . . what would you call it?" She thought for a while. "Ah, yes, teleportation."

Teleportation? Are you serious?

I stared at her, annoyed and angry. "What do you want with me?"

She tucked a stray ebony lock of hair behind her ear, and the firelight glinted on the band at her wrist. A dainty filigree clasp locked the hinged band in place while intricate triple swirls snaked across the face of the dull gold-edged silver.

"You are special," she said. "I was told where to find you and instructed to bring you here. Safely. I am sorry if I scared you, but I did not want you to get hurt. Those men would have hurt you."

"Not all of them," I blurted out. I managed to defend Aidan despite the distraction of the entrancing bracelet, but deep down I sensed I didn't entirely believe that. Would he have hurt me if he'd been forced to?

And suddenly my knees shook, threatening to fold and take me straight to the ground. She grabbed hold of me, helped me move closer to the bed and waited while I sank onto the blankets.

Satisfied, she perched at the foot of the bed. "You were in very grave danger. It was my job to bring you here safely. I had to wait outside the house while those men talked and talked. I was glad when you finally left the house." She grinned.

Did she really expect me to believe such nonsense? She'd just admitted she'd abducted me. I figured I'd play along for now. "What do you want with me? Why have you brought me here? And where exactly is *here*?"

Her bright gray eyes sparkled as she laughed, little pink spots appearing on her cheekbones. "Oh, you are going to be fun. That is good. You will pull through faster than some of the other new ones."

"Pull through what?" My heart kicked in my chest.

Just a horrible hallucination, Bryn. Nothing to worry about. Probably just a side effect of some newfangled drug meant to force the victim into a state of total delusion.

Or was my mind rebelling and turning against me?

"Never mind that for now. Shall we get you ready? You will find out in a few minutes anyway, and besides, I do not have permission to spoil the surprise." She winked, then rose and walked to a bench beside the fire, bringing with her an armful of bronzed chainmail similar to her own. "Come, you have to dress. We must not keep them waiting."

She spread the armor open. It was fashioned into a single coat-like garment, which opened at the back. Odd, but I said nothing, merely poked my hands through the arms, waiting as she pulled and tugged at straps and buckles behind me.

I glanced at the door, longing to make a run for it, but the armor was deceptively heavy and I wasn't confident I would be quick on my feet. And my captor seemed too strong to knock out in one blow.

Ropy muscles knotted her upper arms, and sinewy calves peeped from slits in the hem of her dress. I didn't stand a chance.

I craned my head to get a view of the back of the armor. My back was bare from neck to waist. Strange.

"Come now. We have to hurry." She rushed me with both her command and the urgency of her tone.

A trickle of fear ran through me. Was I about to follow her to my death in some sort of arena? Or maybe a crazy gladiator fight-to-the-death reality show? Everything was too surreal yet a traitorous part of my consciousness screamed it was real. I should really find out more about this place if I was going to try to get the hell out of here.

"What's your name?" I demanded, the confidence in my voice sounding way too weak to my ears.

She glanced at me, impatient with my question which no doubt would delay us further. But when she saw my face her expression softened. My fear, my trepidation, were both clear in my eyes.

"Oh, I should have introduced myself when I arrived, but I do not meet new people very often, so I rarely get many opportunities to dust off my manners. My name is Sigrun. You are Brynhildr, yes?"

It was a statement, not a question. I didn't answer. She nodded, then led the way out of the room. I followed, tracing the warm curve of my amber stone, planning, plotting.

"Where are we, anyway?" I asked.

"Oh. Yes. That is the best part." She smiled broadly. "We are in the marvelous city of Asgard."

CHAPTER 15

Asgard!

When Sigrun uttered those words, my jaw dropped and I stumbled, certain that I was caught within a fantastical dream. Maybe I'd been reading far too much of Aidan's abandoned book of translations because this wasn't possible. Not possible at all.

My feet slowed their pace, and I soon stopped moving altogether. Needing to breathe, needing to think. Needing to be back home, thanking Ms. Custer for being such a wonderful protector, such a wonderful mother.

I didn't want to be here in this strange place, with a strange girl telling tall tales of magical locations in unknown lands that simply should not exist. Asgard was a darned myth told by ancient peoples to explain the way the world was.

Asgard couldn't possibly be real.

Could it?

Up ahead, the girl glanced over her shoulder and hurried back to me. "Yes. I brought you here, to Asgard, from your world, Earth, or as we call it, Midgard. But we have to be going. I am sorry." She spoke with a kind sweetness that lightened my mood slightly. "I know this must be hard for you, but all will be explained soon and I promise you will feel much, much better."

Midgard. Yes. A vague memory from basic Norse Mythology.

Sigrun tucked her arm into mine, and with a gentle tug she set a rapid pace through darkened passages lit by a scattering of flickering torches. I allowed her to pull me along, grateful for the human comfort of her body beside mine. The entire building was pleasantly warmed so even my bare feet could handle the stone floors.

We hurried through passageways, broken here and there by large archways opening into more passages. The arches, rimmed with intricate carvings, were strikingly similar to the ones drawn in Aidan's leather volume. I slowed, drawn to the lines of almost familiar script, but Sigrun tugged at my elbow. And I allowed her to pull me away. If I'd had time I would've been able to decipher much of it.

The density of the air heightened my awareness. I assumed we neared our destination as Sigrun slowed her pace.

"Just a few rules before we enter." Her voice was soft as she drew to a halt before a magnificent, enormous doorway. A small knot of anxiety twisted again in my stomach. What awaited me beyond that gigantic door? She turned to me, taking both my hands in hers. "Do not speak unless you are directly questioned. Keep your eyes lowered, or at least your chin. You may look upon our Lord, but do not affect an attitude of defiance. Our Lord does not appreciate insolence."

Sigrun held me by the shoulder. "Everything will be fine. Do not be afraid."

"So who is this Lord you are talking about?"

"Oh, our lord is the Lord of All Things, the Blessed One. The Wielder of Power, the Great Warrior."

When she paused, I frowned, hoping she would reveal the All-Powerful One's name. I asked, "So? Who is he?"

"You will find out soon enough, Brynhildr." With those words, she gave me a little shove, sending me through the arch and into the bright, warm cavernous hall.

The way she spoke my name sounded strange to my ears, as if I were really hearing it for the first time. As if it had a new specialness imbued within each syllable.

With a tiny sigh, I walked into the welcoming brightness of the magnificent hall. When I looked upward, I stopped and stared, entranced by the height and beauty of the ceiling.

Yikes! How would the artisans have gotten up so high? The ceiling was sixty to seventy feet at its highest point, but like the Sistine Chapel it curved, joined by six separate beams carved with entwined branch-like figures.

I squinted to make out the finer details of the carvings, which resembled those on the six monstrous pillars that seemed to hang from the ceiling. Each pillar was thicker than the body of a large man, and intricately etched with serpentine creatures and tree-branch curves. My eyes blurred from the confusion of trying to figure out what the carvings were.

Entranced by the architecture of the ceiling and pillars, I'd forgotten I was meant to meet Sigrun's powerful Lord. Her low hiss brought me back to my senses and propelled me further into the hall.

I walked toward the back of the Great Hall and silenced a gasp at the magnificence of the thrones. A matched pair sat on a raised stone dais. Here too, hypnotic carvings edged the entire dais, beautiful and entrancing. Music echoed around the room, and a strange tune floated by, as if it rang out from a long-forgotten memory.

The thrones, carved from a gray-white marble, were beyond amazing. Legs and armrests were normal, carved again with the curving, serpentine design, while the seat itself provided sufficient space to sit five hefty men. The backrests both rose at least eighteen feet in the air.

Stunning!

A hunched old man occupied one of the marble thrones, gnarled fingers curling around a dark hand-carved cane.

Sigrun had claimed this was Asgard. If I had my mythology straight, the god she spoke of must be the Great Odin, the ruler of Asgard, husband to Frigga and father of the famous Thor, god of war.

But surely she must have been mistaken. This ancient man hardly resembled a king. Neither did he resemble what the modern depiction of the Great Odin would be.

To start with, he was small, human-sized actually. I'd expected Odin to appear as Zeus did, gigantic even. His fingers were twisted and arthritic. His flowing gray hair was topped with a large floppy hat, which shadowed almost half of a face so wrinkled it seemed impossible for the man to still be alive. To me, he looked at least a hundred years old.

Garbed in a dark cloak, he was far from my mental image of the Great Odin. Even his eyes were gray, a silvery, smoky gray. One of his eyes. The other eye hid within the shadow of the hat. I strained to part the shadows with my eyes, to confirm the possibility. That single visible eye compelled me toward him, and my feet moved of their own volition.

I frowned and tried to pull back, but soon found I was standing before the old geezer, my head tilted to get a better look at him up on the dais. With a start, I remembered Sigrun's reminder not to look straight at him. I lowered my eyes in case this rickety old man really was the powerful Odin.

A great rumble of laughter echoed around the empty hall, so loud that fine specks of dust fell from the ceilings. I doubted the tiny old guy had barked such a powerful laugh, but I dared not look up.

Movement around me drew my furtive glances. Women, both young and old, filed into the hall and gathered around me. As much as my stomach turned like a windmill, stirring slight rushes of fear, an instinct assured me their presence was neither threatening nor dangerous. Just supportive.

Many smiled as I made eye contact and I sighed, releasing the twisted muscles in my gut. Perhaps it would be okay after all. If this was all in my mind, and I'd just gone seriously cuckoo, then what the heck, I might as well enjoy the ride while I was here.

"Come closer, child." The voice boomed, tinged with amusement. My head shot up, enticed by the happiness in his voice, expecting a benevolent smile on the old man's face.

I gasped.

The old man had vanished and in his place sat a twelve-foot-tall giant of a man, decked out in glorious golden armor and a magnificent helmet, which emitted sporadic bursts of living flame.

I stared open-mouthed at the all-powerful Odin.

Though Sigrun's warning reverberated in my head, it was impossible not to stare. He was, well . . . beautiful. Incredibly, amazingly beautiful. For an old guy. But he shimmered with a golden glow similar to the haze I always saw when a person was soon to be dead.

Instinctive dread filled my bones until it was clear that this glow was different, in tone and in . . . vibration. I wasn't sure how I could know this from a mere feeling but I did, and I accepted it.

His armor was made of the same red bronze material as the one I now wore, only not chainmail. Odin's was fashioned in a more masculine manner, worked by the smith to fit the shape of his body. Beneath the armor, his blood-red shift ended mid-thigh, revealing solid, muscular thighs and calves. This god worked out major.

A sooty raven sat on his left shoulder, large head tilted to one side as if aware of what was happening and waiting for the next episode of Bryn's Introduction to Odin and Asgard. Its knowing eyes gleamed obsidian, its feathers so black it was as if a little spot of nothing hovered over the god's shoulder.

The only thing missing from the scene was Odin's famous winged helmet, but from the headdress he wore it was easy to understand how historians may have misinterpreted it as a helmet with wings. Rounded, it hugged the top of his head, curving down on each side to his sideburns. Fine gold and silver motifs covered its gleaming surface, inscribed on small square panels, which formed an arc across the top of the helmet. Down the center lay a carved golden serpent-like creature whose head settled above Odin's eyebrows. The helmet was a thing of absolute beauty.

Odin watched my face, one eye hidden beneath a leather patch, the other still sparkling gray, the color of storm clouds and lightning. I stared, unable to help myself. My eyes darted first to the strange raven, then back to the old man, who was a real, honest-to-goodness, in-the-flesh, larger-than-life god.

If this was a dream, boy did I have a cool imagination. And if this were real . . . I didn't want to contemplate that right now. I was happy to play along, as long as I didn't have to analyze things too much. I had to hold on to my sanity for as long as I could.

"Do not be afraid, Brynhildr." The words rumbled around the hall like roiling storm clouds.

A sharp elbow stabbed me in the back. Sigrun stood behind me, urging me forward. "Kneel before our Lord, Brynhildr," she whispered. "Before he gets impatient and strikes you dead with a lightning bolt."

"Now, Sigrun, there is no need to frighten the girl." His voice boomed, but he smiled. Maybe he wasn't such a bad guy after all. But I'd just found out he had super hearing. I prayed he couldn't read minds too.

I stepped forward, my heart thudding in my chest as I knelt on one knee, terrified the weight of the armor would tip me over or pull me straight to the ground.

"Now, Brynhildr, you are no doubt in the dark about what is going to happen today."

I nodded, hesitating at first as I wasn't sure whether a nod indicated I knew or didn't know what was happening. His expression didn't harden, so I must have given the correct response. Good. Nobody would want to piss off this big guy, least of all me.

"This is what we call the Rites of the Valkyrie." His smile was benevolent but he showed no sign of giving further explanation.

I stiffened. I'd forgotten about the Valkyries. I'd recognized Sigrun as one of Odin's warrior maidens, but really, truly accepting that she was a Valkyrie was easier when I'd believed this was just a dream.

Now that I'd begun to slowly accept that Odin and Asgard might be real, everything changed. What were the Rites of the Valkyrie, and how did I qualify to experience them? Even if my father was guilty of manipulating Valkyrie DNA and implanting it into my embryo, I'd be a mutant. A freak. Not the real deal. And I'd only be half-Valkyrie anyway. The rest of my DNA would be thanks to Geoffrey and Irene Halbrook.

Odin squinted his one eye as if he could hear my thoughts. "It is time to stop denying what you are, my dear. Now rise and drink of the Mead. It will prepare you." He waved a hand and I struggled to my feet. With the unfamiliar weight of the armor, it proved a challenge. But I managed to stand upright without falling flat on my face and making myself a total fool in the presence of Odin himself.

"Come, Sigrun." He beckoned.

She moved to my side and peered past me. A young girl walked over. Her long brown hair tumbled unchecked to her waist. She was dressed in a garment similar to mine, only hers was made of stiff brown fabric and covered by a large apron.

She presented us with a wooden tray, which held a single goblet. As goblets went this one would rival the Holy Grail itself. Pure gleaming gold, encrusted with dozens of precious rubies, sapphires and emeralds, the goblet proclaimed its heavenly origins. A band of entwined carvings ran around the rim of the cup, glimmering in the light.

Sigrun raised the cup to me and said, "Take it in your hands but with care. It is heavier than it looks."

I held tight and waited as she transferred the goblet into my hand. It really was heavy. I held on, fingers gripped around the golden stem, staring at the shimmering liquid in the bowl.

Beautiful.

Although gold was not my favorite color, seeing as golden people tended to die on me, the Mead had a special, magical quality of its own. It glimmered, enticing me to take a sip. But I waited. Somehow I knew that once I drank, there would be no turning back.

"Drink, Brynhildr, Valkyrie. Warrior of Valhalla. Maiden of Odin." His beautiful voice thundered around me like an invisible arm, buffeting yet comforting as I drank.

I sighed in pure ecstasy after I swallowed my first sip. I'd waited all my life to savor this wondrous drink. I blinked, recalling weeks gone by, in which no hunger touched my belly, no thirst parched my throat. And now, for the first time, I truly tasted and enjoyed something. If only Ms. Custer could see me now. I felt refreshed, revived. As if all hunger was sated in one impossibly glorious sip.

I shut my eyes as I swallowed the Mead. A wonderful warmth filled me, spreading throughout my limbs until my entire body glowed with beautiful heat.

When I opened my eyes, the glow had spread beyond the insides of my body. A stab of fear ran through me.

Like Joshua and Aimee and poor, dead Brody, my entire body glowed with a golden light.

CHAPTER 16

I struggled to breathe, gasping, almost sobbing. Lifted my hands and stared, turning them over and around. As far as I was concerned, any golden glow equaled death.

I shivered with fear.

My hands quaked and spots of bright light shone behind my eyes. I could feel the swirling abyss of madness at the edge of my mind.

Though I longed for release, I strained to keep it at bay, desperate to remain conscious. Who knew what might happen, considering the last time I lay unconscious some unknown person had absconded with my underwear and clothes.

"Brynhildr, Warrior of Valhalla." Odin's voice brought me back to my senses. "Do not be afraid. It is the nature of the Mead. The nectar of the Heavens will imbue your body and your mind with the strength you will need."

Strength I'd need? What for?

I was terrified of that golden glow, but Odin's words were ominous. What was really going on here? My eyes swept the room. Each woman and girl looked on, their faces serene and expectant. Calm, prepared.

They knew. Even that darned raven knew. And they were unconcerned. I doubted I looked as unruffled as they did. But their lack of concern was strangely calming. What was the worst that could happen if none of them were alarmed enough to raise an eyebrow?

"Are you ready, Brynhildr?" Odin asked, an eternal patience in the timbre of his voice, his eye gleaming with patience and assurance.

Ready for what?

This was beginning to sound worse and worse. I could only stare, which Odin seemed to take as acknowledgment on my part. Given the choice I would have turned and run. But even that three-second daydream reminded me I had no idea where I was, how I could escape, or even which way to run if I ever managed to escape from the hall.

I nodded.

Odin nodded too, a short, sharp, no nonsense shake of his head. A rustle of movement and the other women drew closer around me, forming a supportive semicircle.

"You will be fine. Just breathe through it. And try not to be too afraid. It will all be over quickly enough." Sigrun squeezed my hand, her eyes sparkling as she gave me a quick hug and kissed my cheek.

I succumbed to the elation of sisterhood with this girl I'd met such a short time ago. Something I'd never had the pleasure of experiencing. Izzy was too young, and foster homes weren't the best places to make friends. Constantly moving around, from home to home and school to school, didn't help either. Most kids didn't bother with friendships that were likely to last all of three weeks.

But our connection lasted for the shortest instant as she withdrew to take her place with the rest of the women. A stab of fear replaced my rising emotions as warmth overwhelmed my body, swirling around limbs and torso. The heat was too intense.

Too intense to bear.

White-hot irons of pain branded my skin from inside my body. A horrible fire burned within me, demanding release through my very bones.

I gasped and cried out, falling heavily, and even when my bare knees hit the floor with stunning pain it didn't matter. Not in the face of the unadulterated agony in my shoulders.

Living fire burned in my back and I felt movement in my shoulder bones. I shivered, grossed out by the strange crawling sensation beneath my skin. Hysterical laughter burbled inside me. In my moment of pure agony my first thought was how weird it felt.

Sigrun had said to breathe but remembering was the most difficult thing I'd done since walking away from that accident, knowing Joshua was gone forever. I concentrated on taking in a breath and releasing it, one at a time. Beads of perspiration flared on my skin, from the pain and my efforts.

Time stood still as fire raced through me, throbbing and

pulsing in time with the horrendous beating of my heart. I was so enthralled within the fire that I didn't hear the music at first.

A haunting melody wafted through the hall, breaking through the barrier of my pain only when the voices of the other women joined in.

It was the wind singing through the trees, the waves crashing against the shore. A mother's lullaby to a sleeping babe. Both soothing and energizing, it gave me a pleasant serenity, releasing my pent up breath and relaxing my stricken muscles.

Although I seldom took painkillers, seldom took ill in fact, I now longed for a quick, chemical release from the white-hot agony. But no relief came. And finally, when all I could do was blink through the slow torture, the nature of the pain changed.

For an instant I thought I was free, but this new agony was far beyond anything I'd experienced since first sipping the Mead. A scream erupted from my lungs, louder and louder, unlike any sound I'd ever made. And that scream, pulled from deep within my belly, was the catalyst.

A burst of pure searing pain exploded from both my shoulders. In a rush of dizzying agony and bright light, an unfamiliar weight settled at my shoulders and tilted me backward as I shivered on my knees.

The white shift beneath the chainmail stuck to me in soggy clumps while sweat dripped from my forehead and neck. I tilted forward to compensate for the new weight at my back, afraid I'd fall backward if I remained straight up. Hands gripped my arms and drew me with gentle care to my feet. Held on until my legs ceased pretending they were lumps of wobbly goo.

The soft melody continued, weaving threads of comfort

around me. Sigrun held onto my arm and a rush of air touched my cheek. I turned and stared at her, exhausted and very frightened. I glanced around and saw that every woman in the room now had wings at her back, outstretched, fluttering on an invisible breeze.

But it wasn't Sigrun's or anyone else's wings which had caused the rush of air so close to me. The weight on my shoulders moved and I turned my head, taking in the sight of a pair of my own stunningly beautiful red-bronze wings, which shivered and fluttered.

I gasped at the beauteous sight. And fainted.

My respite in the land of unconscious bliss was welcome and relieving. Sleep felt wonderful. I wriggled and stretched like a lazy cat. My eyes were shut tight. *It's just a dream, Bryn. Open your eyes and you'll be back in your bedroom at Ms. Custer's house, with this having been an amazing, scary, pain-filled dream.*

But even while I spent time gnawing at the thought, a part of my consciousness registered the warm crackling of the fire and the comfortable caress of the wool underneath me.

I sighed and cracked an eye open.

Still the same room. The same fire. So it might be real after all. Unless it was like those strange dreams I sometimes had when I would wake with a start, try to shake off the dream, and go back to sleep only to fall straight back into the same dream.

I wriggled, then stretched my tight, sleep-drenched limbs and groaned as my muscles screamed from the torture. But it was not only my arms and legs that rebelled. A heavy constant weight at my back also pulled against my shoulders, which was agonizing all on its own.

Everything came rushing back to me. Sigrun. Asgard. Odin. The golden Mead and the warrior women and my initiation as a Valkyrie.

The wings.

I laughed aloud. This ridiculous dream was going way too far now. It had to stop. Soon, or I'd go stark raving mad. Pushing off the covers, I came to my feet in a rush of pulsing muscles and fluttering wings.

A feather floated past. It swirled and twirled on an eddy of air, as if an invisible tornado spun in slow motion, pulling the feather around and around in a silent dance. Soon it slowed and floated back and forth until it reached the floor in a soft silent sweep.

I couldn't hold back the tears. How long had I been gone from Craven? How long had I been unconscious before Sigrun awakened me the first time, and how many days had I slept after the Initiation?

I shivered. And the wings at my back quivered in answer, understanding and reflecting my fear.

The low fire gave out no warmth and I had no idea how to bring it to life. What sheltered, spoiled lives we lived in our modern age. Lights and central heating, computers and cars. I bet Asgard had no internet available. Or cell phone reception.

My phone! In the pocket of my jeans. I'd have to ask Sigrun for it, if she appeared again. I was beginning to accept this wasn't much of a dream. I got to my feet and scanned the stark room for something to wrap around my chilled body. The white dress looked pretty, but it didn't keep out the growing cold.

My only source of warmth was the amber pendant, still safely tied at my neck, still glowing like a miniature sun. I understood then what a deep sense of security the small jewel gave me.

I tugged the covers and stared at them, fascinated and slightly repulsed. Real animal pelts, not factory spun fake-mink like the one I had back home. I shivered again, and the desire to be warm overrode my revulsion. I drew the fur around me and rose to my feet.

The cold floor bit at my bare feet but I was determined to exercise my cramped muscles. I walked across the length and breadth of the room, pausing to lunge and stretch my thigh and calf muscles. Not quite yoga, but good enough.

I tilted forward to compensate for the bulk of the wings, and rounded my shoulders. Slow and easy does it. Amazing. It wasn't as difficult as I'd expected. My shoulders now possessed a natural strength to bear the weight of the wings. They still felt weird to me and I avoided looking at them. I concentrated on exercising the muscles in my back, neck and shoulders, to ease the tightness and soreness, to get my mind off where I was and how hopeless it seemed to return home.

At last, with some stiffness out of my legs and shoulders, I felt human again.

Human. A sharp stabbing pain wrenched through my heart. But I was not human. Wings were not human. I was more of a monster and freak than ever. Cherise had called me a freak. If she saw me now, what would she say? Mutant? Monster?

The abyss began to call me to the precipice. Loud. Insistent. I gritted my teeth, feeling the solidity, the reality of the pressure, and tried to focus on the here and now.

I felt a little more limber now, able to walk better, and I shuffled to the door, still unused to the weight of the wings. But, as if on cue, it opened and Sigrun glided into the room along with a rush of cold air. Shivering, I tugged the fur closer.

"Oh good. You are awake." She smiled.

A smile that warmed me inside out. I remembered that she'd been a friend to me. She'd helped me through the Initiation just by standing beside me. But it didn't mean she'd been entirely honest with me either.

A doubtful frown replaced my answering smile, but Sigrun just shook her head.

"I know you must be upset with me for not telling you what was going to happen, but those are Odin's rules. I really would have told you if I had been allowed," she said, bringing a large wooden tray to a stool by the fire.

She dragged the stool toward my bed and said, "Sit and eat. You need the strength. I will get the fire going again." She gave a delicate shiver and turned to tend the fire, throwing a few more logs onto it until it blazed happily, giving off the most welcoming toasty warmth.

I stared at the food. A goblet of gleaming Mead. A plate of bread, still warm and slathered with melting butter. A handful of blood-red cherries and a small bowl of honey. The Mead whispered, and though I worried about the deliciously addictive effect it might have on me, my traitorous tongue was already tracing my lips.

Naked thirst knifed my belly and my throat ached, parched, as if I'd roamed a desert for weeks. My body shivered and I gave in, reaching for the goblet, ready to gulp the contents of the goblet down.

"Do not drink the Mead too quickly, Brynhildr. Slow sips will be much better for you, or your stomach may rebel." She smiled as she raised her palms to the fire.

I folded my quaking fingers around the cup. "Call me Bryn, okay?" I still disliked the old name, and all it implied. I was annoyed that everyone kept using my full name, assuming I'd be happy with it.

Sigrun frowned, confused for a moment. Then her eyes brightened. "Ah, yes. Bryn is a shortened form of Brynhildr. Yes, the modern human proclivity for shortening names. If it makes you feel more comfortable then I shall call you Bryn. Now drink and eat and rest."

I sipped the divine liquid and it took all my strength not to swallow everything in one go. The drink was liquid cotton candy and honey straight from the comb. Sweet and warm and delicious.

"I don't think I could go back to sleep. I feel fine, actually." My eyes darted to the door, and despite the gorgeous drink, I longed to leave this claustrophobic room. Fresh air sounded wonderful, even if it was cold fresh air. "I need to get out of here for a while."

"Oh, there will be plenty of time to explore and learn about Asgard. But your recuperation is terribly important, Bryn. Not only for your own health. It is important to Odin and the Valkyries too. It is not often we receive a new Valkyrie into our fold. And besides, you need to get strong and prepare for the goddess to arrive. I am sure she is as excited to know that the child of the legendary Brunhilde has joined us in Asgard."

Content to drink my Mead, I listened to Sigrun's excited ramblings with only half an ear. Not until I'd dripped the last dregs into my mouth did the meaning of her last words register. Child of who? I coughed, sputtered. "Goddess?" I asked.

"Oh, Freya. She is our goddess. The leader of the Warrior Valkyries. She will lead us into the battle Ragnarok when it comes." Sigrun looked away, but not before fear flitted across her usually cheerful features. She even wrung her hands as she fell silent.

I wanted to ask her about Brunhilde, and what Ragnarok was and when did she think this battle would arrive, but my head began to swim, the room tilting at odd angles. The Mead must have been drugged. I struggled to keep my eyes open. But it was much more comfortable when I closed them and the world stopped spinning.

I gave in to the lure of sleep, and crawled under the covers. It was rude to ignore poor Sigrun, but I didn't get a chance to thank her for her help and kindness. As I slipped into the warmth of sleep, I recalled Sigrun's face, the worry and concern in her eyes as she looked at the amber jewel hanging at my throat.

CHAPTER 17

The fog of sleep evaporated, and I tensed as new sounds intruded on my lethargy. Fabric swooshed and rustled, and soft footsteps whispered across the floor. I cracked open an eyelid. A young serving girl, her dark hair braided to frame a plump, cheerful face, stopped in front of the fire and glanced over to me as I stirred. I sighed in relief and yawned, my hammering heart slowly returning to a normal plod.

"Hi. Who are you?" I asked, propping myself up onto my elbow, with the fur still wrapped tightly around me.

"My name is Turi. I am your maidservant. Like one of your human lady's maids." She nodded with vigor, but kept the rest of her body oddly still. She seemed skittish, as if she'd be out of the room in a flash if I so much as moved toward her, so I stayed in the bed. I didn't have the heart to tell her we didn't have lady's maids anymore.

She'd brought a clean dress, white again, and another tray of food. I'd been too sleepy to touch the bread and honey, a gift from Sigrun, but this pie-like creation looked more inviting. I found myself hungry for the first time in such a long time. I tried to recall what my last meal had been but came up blank. It must have been something like Ms. Custer's fried chicken and mashed potatoes, or maybe her unforgettable spaghetti Bolognese.

My tummy squealed and Turi giggled behind her hands. "You must eat. I have brought you clean clothes. And you may like to change out of your rumpled clothing too." She nodded at my creased dress.

What I would have preferred was a bath. I already reeked. I'd dripped sweat like a wet sponge during my Initiation and still felt grimy and unclean. My fingers trailed through the oily tendrils of my hair. Eww!

"I so need a bath," I said, winkling my nose.

"Oh, Sigrun will take you to the Bathhouse when she gets back from her training. She should be here after you have broken your fast."

She was nodding again. Slightly annoying now. But I didn't want to be mean by telling her to lower the flames on her happiness fire. I nodded and smiled even though my muscles hurt. I just wanted her to leave so I could dig into that magnificent looking sweet pie.

She gave a quick, hesitant curtsy and turned to leave, closing the door softly behind her.

I stared open-mouthed at the closed door, all thoughts of food gone from my mind. The girl had seemed normal enough. Until she'd turned away from me.

If Turi had surprised me with her kindness and happy glow, she'd surprised me even more with the long, pale swishing tail, which sprouted from her lower back and followed her out the door.

Strange things had been happening to me. And they just kept getting stranger.

WITH MY MIND still on the swishing tail, I pulled the tray onto my lap and ate. Delicious. Flaky. Asgard had a master pastry chef hidden away in their kitchens. Since my arrival in this dream world, my taste buds had actually begun to function again. I was relieved, as I'd missed the comfort that food gave me.

If only Ms. Custer could see me now, she'd be very relieved. My poor foster mom. I wondered what she would be doing right now. Would she be looking for me? Or would she have assumed I'd taken the warning and gone into hiding after witnessing Aidan and his goons in her kitchen?

Who could've known Aidan would be mixed up with those horrible types? Ms. Custer had been fond of him. Trusted him from the start, and she'd be blaming herself for putting me and the other foster kids in danger. If only I'd had time to tell her about Aidan's reasons for being in Craven. And about the real freak I'd turned out to be. If only. . . .

This dream-nightmare seemed more real, more concrete to me now than ever. And it terrified me. If I admitted this Asgard hallucination was even one percent real it would mean I'd lose my grip on whatever reality I still retained.

Lost in thought, I barely noticed Sigrun's arrival. I even missed a significant portion of her conversation as she chattered on, smiling, blabbing away about baths and bathhouses.

"Hey, hold on. What's a Bathhouse?" I asked, hoping to get a decent answer before she rattled on again.

Sigrun blushed. "It is the place we go to bathe, get clean. You know, to remove dirt and bad odors from your body."

"I know what bathing is," I snapped. Her smile fell at the sharpness in my tone, and a dozen guilty pangs stabbed at my conscience. "I'm sorry, I just meant . . . I wanted to know what the Bathhouse was. I've never heard of one before."

Puzzled, she bit her lip and said, "Oh. Then where do you clean yourself?"

"It's called a shower." She frowned harder, so I explained. "It's a small space, like a box, and it has water pouring from a tube up above you, and that's how you wash, in the falling water."

"Oh yes, a waterfall in a box. But how do you relax while you bathe?"

It was my turn to frown. "Relax? Oh, when I want to relax I use a bathtub."

"So you have another means of bathing besides the waterfall box?"

"Yes, it's a bath, actually, but it's in a small private room." She nodded. "So this Bathhouse," I said, "does it have small baths or large ones?"

"Oh no, it is one large bath. We all bathe together."

"Together?" I asked.

She nodded again and smiled at the squeak in my voice.

Stranger and stranger. Did anyone ever bathe in public groups anymore? I'd read about Roman public baths and that was strange enough, though I suppose any school locker room would be similar in a way. Some girls showered together and others preferred the privacy of the cubicles. North Wood hadn't had the open stalls like a few of the schools I'd been to. Just the cubicles. You had to be pretty confident in your body, even brazen, to shower where everyone could see you. At least, that's what I believed.

"Okay, let's go see your Bathhouse."

"Do not forget your clothing and your sandals, Bryn," she sang out as she left the room.

I grabbed the leather footwear and slipped my feet into them, winding the soft leather strips around and around my ankles and calves until nothing remained to trip me up. My clean white dress in hand, I trotted after her, curious to see what this Bathhouse was all about.

I caught up with Sigrun and found she had company. Another Valkyrie stood with her, tapping her toe, a frown marring her beautiful, pale skin. Blonde hair, bright blue eyes—she was the epitome of Nordic beauty. Even the ivory feathers of her majestic wings screamed pure beauty, right down to the shimmering silver ends of the feathers.

The bright orange of her dress added a surprising elegance and style; on a stunner like her, I bet no color would dare to not look good. Only the hard gray glint in her blue eyes marred the beauty. And just like a flawed diamond, she lost a bit of her luster when she smiled. A cold and shadowed smile, so very far from beautiful.

"If you are about ready, could we please go?" she asked.

Her voice was mellifluent, a clear, bright singing voice, dulled with the edge of impatience, which seeped out as she spoke. Her wings fluttered and her eyes skimmed over me, head to toe and back again. They stopped at my neck, narrowing coldly as she stared at the pendant. She gestured down the hallway with an irritated flick of her hand and walked away, shoulders stiff and dismissive.

"Sorry," I said. The apology slipped out. Why was I apologizing to Her Haughtiness anyway? I hadn't asked her to wait for me. But I shut my mouth. She was Sigrun's friend and I'd hate to cause trouble for her.

"Pshaw! We will not be late, Bryn. Of course, there is no rush. Astrid is just impatient as always." Sigrun brushed off the other girl's annoyance and started walking.

I followed while the two talked about new *oolfer* and *fenrees*, whatever they were. I decided to wait to ask Sigrun my questions later, in private. Astrid put me on edge. The kind of on edge that rubbed me the wrong way, real bad. I didn't trust myself to shut my mouth if she pushed too far.

My wings shivered at my back, a warm bronze-red that reflected the cool light of the day. I still wasn't sure I could control their fluttering, as they seemed intrinsically linked to my emotions and quivered and shifted in tandem to my anger or my fear.

We left the monstrous hallways and exited the building. I glanced back and staggered, almost tripping over my sandaled feet. Even the flash of fear that the weight of my wings would tip me over as I lost my balance didn't detract from my sheer awe.

Gray stone archways and turrets towered impossibly far above us. The building was more than magnificent. It rose high, carved right out of the solid rock of the mountain all the way up to the highest peaks, with some parapets disappearing into the clouds. It was an elegant mess, rocky castles, marble palaces and natural stone beauty melding together to create a masterpiece befitting the god Odin.

I gaped at the entrance. An archway the height of six men housed two impossibly large stone doors. Then I recalled the actual size of Odin himself when he wasn't in the form of an ancient man. The carved doors were thrown open now, but closed they would be impenetrable.

A grunt of annoyance, a flutter of wings and an impatient sigh broke through my thoughts.

"Be nice, Astrid. Remember how you felt the first time you saw the castle of Odin. We have all been entranced before." A hint of steel lay behind the happy words, but Sigrun's own wings remained perfectly still. And I smiled. *Good for you, my friend Sigrun.* Seemed she wasn't all cotton candy and apple pie, after all.

I turned and walked toward the girls, who now waited beside a hillock at the side of the castle wall. Approaching from the rear, all I saw was one set of astonishingly beautiful off-white wings and a pair of blue-gray wings the exact shade of soft steel.

We hurried round the hill and down into a little valley, hidden by trees and rocks twice the size of the average human. The gurgling of water reached our ears. I sped up in anticipation. And was completely surprised.

A pool, five times larger than your average Olympic-sized pool, covered the entire floor of the valley. It formed a large oval and was constructed of a deep blue marble material veined with gold and silver that sparkled and glittered in the weak sunshine.

"So, everyone bathes together, hey?" I had to ask. Me and my big mouth. I'd tried to sound nonchalant and sophisticated about it, but my nerves must have shown through.

"Have you never been to a Bathhouse like ours?" Astrid asked, and I was forced to shake my head in response. "Oh, you will get used to it. Do not worry, Brynhildr."

She tipped her chin, and stared down her nose at me. As if daring me to meet my fear head on and challenge her. Then she tugged the ties at her neck and waist. Her dress slid off her body and fell to her feet in a marigold pool. She raised one eyebrow and sauntered to the edge of the water, slipping in until she stood neck deep, her wings submerged along with her.

Funny how I'd assumed they would float.

She turned and met my eyes. If she'd expected me to bury my mortified head in the sand like an embarrassed ostrich she was sorely mistaken. I squared my shoulders and returned her gaze. Her features tightened, hiding her disappointment. Inside I whooped. Then wondered when it had become so important to me to get one over on another girl. At North Wood, I'd never had time to waste moping over people who didn't like me.

A soft giggle broke my trance. Sigrun smiled and took my hand, guiding me to a small alcove carved from the same gold- and silver-veined rock. We sat on a beautiful stone seat and I was pleasantly surprised to find the seat was warm. Talk about under-butt heating.

"Astrid is a bit of an exhibitionist. She has a flair for the dramatic. Do not allow yourself to worry about her. She is too comfortable in her own skin for her own good." Sigrun's smile fell for a second. "She has her fair share of problems. Perhaps her pride is merely her way of making the best of the good things she still possesses."

"Yeah, I can understand that." I nodded.

I snuck a few furtive glances at Astrid, who'd joined a group of three other Valkyries, bathing on the opposite curve of the pool. She'd stripped in front of me, hoping to shock me. I was still surprised I'd taken it so well. Nudity was not my forte. But I hadn't fainted from the shock of seeing so much naked flesh. Though I wouldn't deny that it helped when all the women here had wings that covered their backs from shoulder to calf.

Honestly, my body had never been a source of appreciation for me. I had boobs where boobs were meant to go, same went for butt and legs and other body parts. I knew my cup size so I could shop for the right bra, went to the beach in summer and was familiar enough with a bikini. But total nudity?

"You can go in with your dress, you know." Sigrun winked. "It is what I always do."

Startled, I stared at her. Wow! Talk about a mind reader!

"Come in and stop staring like that."

Sigrun bent and untied her leather sandals and walked to the edge of the water. She stepped in slowly and I followed, savoring the blissful warmth as my body luxuriated in the welcome heat.

Small steps scalloped the edges of the entire pool, each one curved and long enough to seat three people. I settled on the seat, warm water rushing around me, soaking my dress and massaging my arms and legs.

Behind the seat, hot water rushed at me from little pipes set into the wall. I turned to inspect the holes.

"That is where the water enters the pool," Sigrun explained. "There are geysers up on the hill, and the water is directed down in hundreds of little pipes. All the pipes join the pool at the edges so the water mixes evenly and nobody gets burned." Sigrun ducked lower to pull off her dress, which she flung to the alcove where we'd sat. A sodden maroon mess splatted to the floor, like a pool of coagulated blood. We both laughed. "Now it is your turn. You have to get naked to get clean."

I followed her lead and tugged and pulled until my wet dress came off at last. It soon joined Sigrun's with another inelegant splat. I sank into the water, relieved as the heat enveloped me.

The weight of my waterlogged wings drew me down and I was thankful for the inbuilt seats hidden below the surface.

"Look at these, Bryn. Here." Sigrun showed me the pipes. "Some of the pipes are closed. If a bather wants warmer water she can open them to let the hotter water in. The different geysers have different water temperatures and each bather can adjust to their liking. The only thing you cannot get is a cold bath."

Sigrun waded to the point of the crescent, leaving me to marvel at the technology. At the point sat two marble bowls glistening with water. She reached in and retrieved soap from one and a sponge from another. "You can take these and wash in privacy on the other side."

Relieved, I grabbed the soap and sponge and waded to the

other curved space to bathe. The soap smelled heavenly, a delicious creation made from crushed rose-petals. I used it to lather my oily hair as well, as I was unable to find Asgard's brand of shampoo and conditioner in the marble bowl. As I rinsed, whole rose-petals floated around me and away on the current.

A few minutes later, feeling refreshed, I returned to join Sigrun and commented on the ingenuity of the pool.

"Oh yes, and you will see that dirty water from every bathing area is directed away, to flow down and out of the large pool. There is always running water and everyone knows where the cleaner water is. It's the middle and the sides."

"Amazing."

"We used the natural resources of Asgard. No modern technology in the Bathing Pools at all."

"So you have access to modern technology from here?" I asked, still fumbling with the idea that this place existed in the modern day and age.

"Oh, yes. Some of the new Valkyries are more modern than us Old Ones. And the newer Warriors bring their knowledge too. And Odin is a pretty smart one himself." Sigrun grinned and tapped her head.

With Odin's ferocity and intelligence, I didn't doubt his ability to mesh modern technology with ancient simplicity.

We fell into a comfortable silence until I caught Sigrun studying my amber pendant again, an expression of worry haunting her face.

"What's the matter? Is there something about my pendant that bothers you?" I asked, but she just shook her head and averted her eyes. "Come on, Sigrun, I've seen you stare at it before and you have this strange look in your eyes. You're beginning to scare me."

Sigrun sighed. "I am very afraid of your necklace. If it is what I think it is, then you may soon have bigger problems."

"Well, what is it?"

"I think it may be part of Brisingamen." She paused as if expecting me to know what she meant, but I raised my shoulders in an I-dunno gesture. So she continued: "Brisingamen is also known as the Circle of Suns. It is a necklace of incomparable amber and it belongs to the goddess Freya."

"But my father gave this necklace to me."

"Do you know where he found it?"

I shook my head, though I suspected where the necklace may have come from.

"If it was found in Brunhilde's grave, it means that she had fulfilled her quest for the goddess Freya and found Brisingamen for her. But Brunhilde never returned it to the goddess." Sigrun's eyes clouded. "Freya may take that as a sign that Brunhilde had become greedy and kept the necklace for herself."

"Well, I'd say nobody can assume that. And maybe this isn't the necklace at all." I stroked the warmth of the amber.

"No, the necklace is made up of nine individual amber stones, set in filigreed gold and diamonds. The main jewel, which sits at the front of the throat, is the largest of all. The amber seems to communicate with itself. It glows when the other pieces are nearby. The necklace glitters and shines, like a circle of tiny suns." Sigrun shook her head. "That pendant must be part of Brisingamen, and it is best you keep it hidden in case I am right."

I nodded, filled with a strange icy coldness that fought against the warmth of the water around me. Odin, Valkyries, Freya and now Brisingamen! Naked, soaking in the hot waters from the geysers of Asgard, reality smacked me upside the head.

There was no use in denying it any longer, no use in pretending this was all just a dream.

I really was in Asgard.

CHAPTER 18

We dried off and left the Bathhouse.

"I take it the men and women bathe separately?"

"Yes, of course they do." Sigrun's grin glittered with mischief. "Both bathing areas are at opposite ends of the castle grounds. It prevents the naughty ones from watching us."

"Peeping Toms?" I giggled softly as weariness pulled at my senses. "I guess boys will be boys wherever they are."

"And Odin has his own private Bathhouse, which the other gods share when they visit him."

I listened with half an ear. The muscles in my arms and legs felt like warm Jell-O. I was clean and fresh and way too relaxed. I'd even forgotten the weight of my wings.

The intricacy of the pool's construction still awed me. Just walking by the water's edge was calming, as all around us waterfalls splashed and wavelets crashed against the pool's edges.

Despite the cold weather, the grass beyond the Bath was a lush green, and in the distance, gigantic snowcapped mountains rose, forming a natural barrier around the valley. The sky was a weak blue, and it promised more cold.

I glanced at Sigrun. It felt great to walk alongside someone without the need to make polite conversation, but curiosity compelled me to interrupt the comfortable silence. "Where are we, Sigrun?"

"I told you. Asgard. The beautiful city of Asgard, seat of Odin, home of Valhalla." Her eyes shone with pride. She loved her city, no doubt about it.

"No, no. I mean, our location in the world?" The weather seemed similar to back home, so I assumed we were somewhere in the Northern Hemisphere. I hadn't been in Asgard long enough to observe the time of sunset or anything that would let me know how far north we were, or any information to help me find a way home.

"You are not thinking of running away from Asgard, are you?" She stopped in her tracks, frowning, and faced me. Her wings fluttered, emphasizing her consternation. She gripped my arm with a ferocity I'd never have expected from such a mild-mannered girl. "You cannot try to leave yet. You are here to fulfill your purpose, and you have so much more to learn."

I gently pulled my arm free. I didn't want her to worry. And perhaps she would be in serious trouble if her charge ran away. So I lied. "No, don't worry. I have no intention of running away. Things here are far too interesting."

And she still had so much to tell me. What was this purpose I was meant to fulfill? Why couldn't they be clear from the start? But I didn't want her to be suspicious, to stop trusting me with information. So I smiled.

She scrutinized my face as if my features would reveal my lie. Then she nodded and let go of my arm. "Good. Then come. I have something else to show you today." She tucked her arm into mine.

I wanted to rub my arm where her vice-like grip had dug into my flesh, but I steeled myself against such a show of weakness. The pain ebbed. Together we walked over another hill, farther away from the castle.

Grunts and groans and the sounds of scuffling disturbed my enjoyment of the scenic view. Horses whinnied and chuffed somewhere beyond the hill, and a strange yipping filled the air. Dogs?

I assumed it was a dog hunt.

Yeah, I assumed.

Until I rounded the corner and almost fell on my butt in shock.

A handful of strange horses, along with wolves the size of the horses, were walking, prancing and running as if going through some kind of training. My jaw dropped and I stared in awe.

Sleipnir. A magnificent eight-legged horse. Reading about one and imagining what it would look like was an entirely different experience from actually seeing a Sleipnir in the flesh. And in this case not just one, but at least a dozen. I would have thought any land creature with that many legs would look clumsy and overburdened. But the Sleipnir displayed both the grace and the elegance of an Arabian stallion.

Wow.

THEY WERE SIMPLY MAGNIFICENT. Of varying dark colors, they were solidly muscled and moved with a liquid grace. Despite the mud and solid clumps of soil mixed with upturned sods of grass, the Sleipnir seemed to have magically avoided the mess and came away clean and gleaming.

The wolves, on the other hand, weren't that fortunate. Their mud-splattered, matted pelts gave them the look of your average drenched dog at bath time. I blinked many times, expecting the scene to disappear once I opened my eyes again.

Unbelievable.

"Come." Sigrun pulled my arm.

My gaze strayed behind me, back to the fascinating sight, but the pressure of Sigrun's grip on my arm forced me to move. I followed with a wistful sigh, walking along a stone wall until I stood at the open gate.

"Why did they leave the gate open? Won't the animals escape?" I regretted the question as soon as I'd asked it. Sigrun's face darkened at the word *animals*, and I knew I'd insulted her in some way. "I'm sorry. I . . ."

I wasn't exactly sure what I should say to make her feel better, nor did I understand what I'd said to offend her, but an apology seemed appropriate.

She brushed it off, though her face still retained a stiffness I'd never seen before. She said, "Do not worry about it. You have much to learn and we cannot get angry at you when you have no idea what you are saying."

Her gaze returned to the field where a rather large man stood near the fence, watching the melee within the grounds. As we approached, he turned and I swallowed, trying really hard not to faint.

He was not a man. Where his head should have been was the head of a wolf. A large, black-haired, toothy, scary wolf. At first I thought he was merely a bipedal wolf, but when he turned and waved at Sigrun he used a perfectly normal human hand. I desperately wanted to ask Sigrun what was going on and who this creature was, but it was too late. We were standing right beside him now, and all I wanted to do was to turn and make a run for it. My knees shivered, my wings fluttered in fear and my heart thumped faster than a freight train.

He smiled at Sigrun and glanced at me, curiosity gleaming within intelligent eyes.

Sigrun smiled back and blushed as she made introductions. "Fenrir, this is Brynhildr, our newest Valkyrie." The rosy color in her cheeks and the way her eyes widened made me wonder if my new friend had a crush on this monster. "Bryn, this is Fenrir, the General of the Ulfr Army," she said.

We shook hands and I managed not to grimace as my palm met his. Normal skin to normal skin. What had I expected? Oh yeah, claws and fur. I forced myself to meet his eyes and smile. Ms. Custer would be so proud of my impeccable manners. He smiled back with a toothy, still-scary grin.

But his eyes dropped to gaze at the amber jewel, which I hadn't been able to hide yet. His eyes lingered there. My father's gift attracted a constant stream of attention wherever I went.

A crash among the heaving bodies in the field drew his attention away. Relieved, I watched him lope back into the thick of bodies to attend to whatever mess the wolves and horses had created.

For the first time I recognized men among the animals. Men, dressed in reddish bronze chainmail similar to mine, who glowed a dull gold. Not the bright, blinding gold of Joshua or Brody, but a muted, angelic aura.

"What is this place, Sigrun?" Concern and unease stirred in my gut. "And what is this 'Ulfr' army?"

Sigrun had forgotten me in her silent adoration of Fenrir. She blinked, as if coming out a dream, and turned to me. "Oh, yes. The Ulfr are the wolves of Valhalla. They are the mounts of the Valkyries."

"But I thought Valkyries rode horses."

"A common Western misconception. We never ride Midgard horses, and only the highest ranked Valkyries are ever allowed the use of the Sleipnir." She nodded at the eight-legged horses prancing and dancing around the field. "They are the mounts of Odin. And gifted to the best of the Valkyrie Army. Most Valkyries travel with their Ulfr, but it is seen as far more acceptable for beautiful winged women to ride powerful horses than mangy wolves. Hence the modern perception." The anger in her voice was clear. It appeared that the modern telling of the ancient Norse legends did not sit well here in Asgard.

"Then why doesn't someone set them straight?" I asked. "Appear on a wolf and let the world know they are wrong."

Sigrun opened her mouth to answer, but a deeper voice spoke first. "Because Odin does not believe it is necessary to pander to the modern cultural need for beauty and acceptability," said Fenrir as he returned to the fence.

I sucked in a harsh breath. Looking up at him, I now knew why Sigrun was half in love with this man-beast. He approached us, his furred pelt and snout gone. Replaced by long dark hair that tugged at my tummy with its painful resemblance to Aidan's beautiful curls. He had the looks of a dark Adonis, only his eyes were a steel gray. A gray that matched, strangely enough, the beautiful metallic gray of Sigrun's feathers.

Fenrir was Asgard's answer to the werewolf.

ONE OF THE men marched over, eyes gleaming as his shoulders heaved beneath glittering mail. His skin shimmered as if the low flame of a candle flickered inside him. Spattered with mud, and marked with purpling bruises, he strode toward us, his brow furrowed in frustration. He gave us a nod, then pulled Fenrir aside to have what seemed like a fairly heated discussion.

I tapped Sigrun's elbow to get her attention. "And him? What is he? Why does he have that glow?"

I hadn't yet discussed my visions with Sigrun. Hadn't yet been confident enough to bare my fears and worries to my new friend. Even in a city that shouldn't exist, even when a pair of wings grew out of my back and even when I'd just been eyeball to eyeball with a real live wolf-man, what guarantee did I have that I wasn't imagining it all or going completely off my rocker?

She turned and looked at me. "Have you seen the aura before?"

My throat closed and all I could do was nod.

"When did it begin?" she asked, eagerness bright on her face.

"Ever since I was a little girl, actually. But it changed recently." When she waited in silence, I continued. "I started seeing the auras of people who ended up dead." The bleakness in my voice pretty much matched the way my heart felt when I thought of my inability to help those poor people.

"Then you are ready," she said firmly.

"Ready for what?"

"Ready for Retrieval," she replied.

I was getting impatient. All this cryptic implication annoyed the hell out of me. "Sigrun, can you just be straight with me, please. What is this glow? What does it mean? And what in heaven's name is Retrieval?"

She grinned and said, "The aura is only seen in a true Warrior. A Warrior worthy of the halls of Valhalla. A Warrior worthy of fighting for Odin. A Valkyrie looks for the people who glow and collects those people after they die. That is Retrieval."

"Oh yes, I remember. Valkyries collect the dead. . . ." I trailed off as I turned the facts over in my head. "But there were girls as well. I thought Valkyries collected only the bodies of great Warriors."

"Another misconception. Odin needs powerful Warriors to fight for him. He never would have demanded his Warriors be only men. Our women fight too; just look at all our Valkyries. They are just as strong as the men." Sigrun shook her head. "I think too many of the professors who think they know all about our history are men. You need some women to explain some of this to your men."

"You are probably more right than you realize." I smiled. Strange how spot-on this Valkyrie was in spite of being stuck here in Asgard, safe from the rolling machine of technology.

But now my thoughts turned to Aimee, driven to her death by a cancer so vicious it had eaten her alive. "What if someone dies of a disease?" I asked. "One of the girls was ill, really ill. She died of cancer."

"Then she would still come to Valhalla to fight. Her illness is of no consequence, as it ailed her while she was alive. All the Warriors come to Valhalla in their afterlife. Even if they had a limb removed, they would get it back." She nodded as I raised my eyebrows. "Yes, it is true. Although we retrieve the mortal remains, we are also retrieving the soul and the spirit. Both spirit and soul help to heal the body, and bring back both strength and power."

We continued walking, and I turned Sigrun's words over in my head. It made a funny sort of sense. But what about Brody?

"Sigrun." I touched her arm and turned her to me. "There was a little boy, about ten years old, who had the glow around him? What does that mean?"

"Oh. That means his Valkyrie never had the opportunity to retrieve him in his previous life. With every Warrior, if for some reason Retrieval does not occur within three moons of the day of death, the soul moves on to the next life. When that happens we just wait until we have the opportunity, probably within the first few years of the Warrior's life. Usually such a Warrior will have a very short life."

"But what happens when you retrieve him? He's just a little boy. How can a small child be a Warrior in a battle?" I shook my head. It all sounded way too bizarre.

"He does not come to Valhalla in that form. He will revert to the form in which his soul lived in his previous life. The soul knows what shape and size would be appropriate for Valhalla. You see, the soul is intelligent. It knows what the Warrior needs. It is because of the soul that the body regenerates lost limbs, purges disease and strengthens itself for battle."

I had to admit it made sense, a sort of fantastical sense.

What I had to try to digest was that Brody was a Warrior of Valhalla, one of the chosen. He was now Odin's soldier and he would soon be here in Valhalla. Along with my other friends who'd glowed with such a painfully beautiful light, and then died.

My heart quickened, and I grabbed a fence post to steady myself. I would see Brody and Joshua and Aimee again.

CHAPTER 19

Sigrun kept me so busy, I didn't get much of a chance to think about my friends from Craven. Once she got over her surprise that I could already see the golden auras of the Warriors, she whisked me off the training field.

Before we left, she threw Fenrir a parting command to be ready to instruct me during the Valkyries' training session the next morning. Fenrir, eyebrows raised in surprise, just nodded.

We returned to the castle and made our way to a huge hall filled with long tables. The tables in the large warm space slowly filled with small groups of people. My stomach growled, loud enough for me to look around in embarrassment. But the desperate level of my hunger went unnoticed in the bustling hall.

The aroma of cooked meat wafted through the room and twisted my stomach with incredible yearning. Sigrun pointed me to two empty seats and disappeared toward a trio of huge hearths.

Monstrous pots hung over crackling flames, huge bouts of steam rising from them.

Beside them, spitted beef and smaller cuts of meat roasted above the flames, dripping juices, which spat merrily in the heat of the coals.

Sigrun negotiated the tricky route, dodging around other Valkyries and Warriors, and managed to return safely to our table, bearing two wooden platters filled with meat and bowls of steaming, stewed vegetables.

She grabbed the seat beside me. "Here you go. Your first real meal in Asgard. Enjoy."

Then she proceeded to eat with a fierce gusto terribly unfitting for such a demure and ladylike girl.

I hid a smile, savoring the rich juiciness of the meat and the tenderly cooked vegetables. And then, as if some magical mind-reader had cast his eye over me, a serving girl placed a goblet at my side.

She disappeared before I could thank her. I swallowed, half-hoping it was the delicious Mead, but the liquid tasted more like a stale beer. Despite my disappointment, I drank deeply, grateful as it slid down my parched throat and quenched my thirst.

"So what's next on the agenda for me?" I asked between mouthfuls of the tender beef.

Sigrun swallowed a bite and said, "Training with Fenrir first thing in the morning."

"That's nice of him," I murmured, not too sure I liked the idea of being trained by the man who was a beast. Or was it the beast who was a man?

"No, the Valkyries and Warriors train through the day,"

Sigrun said. "Sometimes we train together but mostly we work within our regiments. Fenrir moves within the fields, going where he is needed. And tomorrow Fenrir will concentrate on you. All the new Valkyries get additional training to get them prepared. And you do have a lot to learn."

Cheerful dinnertime conversation rose and fell around us. The sound of camaraderie. I wondered how many of those around me had lived for hundreds of years. Wondered what it was like to live forever doing the same thing every day.

"So that's the timetable? Training, lunch, more training, bathe, then dinner?" It seemed like nothing much happened here besides fighter training, if that was the routine of the day.

Sigrun shook her head. "Not at all. Some days there are Retrievals. Other days we have sparring matches with the Warriors. If you belong to a scout team then you will leave Asgard for short periods of time." She drained her goblet.

"No time to rest then?"

"We do not require time to rest. Valkyries and Warriors have strength. It is the nature of who we are and what we do. We live very long lives. We have been gifted with the strength to endure the battles, to endure the passing of time." Sigrun scanned my face, her features thoughtful, as if she were choosing her words carefully. "Have you felt your need for food diminish in the last few weeks?"

I nodded.

"Water?"

I nodded again, wondering where she was going with this line of questions.

"Sleep?"

"Yeah, now that you mention sleep, I haven't been sleeping much these days. I can actually get by on a couple of hours." I shook my head.

Why hadn't I noticed this before? Perhaps I'd been so absorbed with the golden auras, and Joshua's death. My ridiculous sham of a romance with Aidan. Brody.

"But I slept like a baby after my wings appeared."

I'd barely been able to keep my eyes open after the torture of the Rites of the Valkyrie.

"That was the power of Mead," Sigrun responded between mouthfuls.

"So what exactly is this Mead? I remember reading that it was a drink of the gods."

"Yes, the Mead is the drink of the gods, the Milk of Strength. The goat Heidrun produces the Mead, which keeps the Warriors, the *einherjar*, strong."

"Ayn what?" I frowned.

"*Einherjar*. It is the Norse word for Warrior or fighter." Sigrun laughed and shook her head at my confusion. "The Mead regenerates the Warriors after a battle or after training. It heals wounds, soothes muscles, relaxes. It is why the Warriors on the field do not fear being wounded."

"I would've thought they wouldn't fear mere flesh wounds since they were dead anyway."

"No, you must not think that at all. The *einherjar* and the Valkyries are all very much alive. The Warriors who have been retrieved have been given life again. The beautiful glow they possess means their death will not be final."

"Won't that make them zombies?" I smiled behind my goblet, before draining it.

"Zombies? What is this thing you call zombies." Little furrows wrinkled Sigrun's forehead.

"They are people who have been dead but are brought back to life," I said. Sigrun nodded, so I continued. "They usually look horrible, with dead, half-decomposed bodies, and go around killing people."

I gave Sigrun the standard Thriller Zombie stance complete with raised arms and flared fingers. Her expression stayed blank. She didn't seem amused or impressed with my reenactment.

In fact, she didn't even crack a smile. Just looked at me as if I were a demented creature best put out of its misery.

"You have some strange beliefs in this *modern* world of yours." Sigrun shook her head sadly. "The scout teams go out into Midgard and bring back stories of your world. To be honest, I have never wanted to visit your world simply because of your strange beliefs. I believe I may have been right in my choice."

"I'm sorry, I was just teasing." I touched her arm, hoping to coax a smile, and I was relieved when she offered a tiny one.

"Never mind that. How do you feel today? I hope we have not taxed you too much."

"Oh, I feel fine," I said. "Really good, actually. And I want to thank you for being so nice to me."

Her smile was gracious.

As I turned back to my plate, the hairs on my neck lifted. Someone was watching us. Watching me. I raised my eyes slightly and caught Astrid staring at me, three tables over.

From this distance I couldn't hear her words, but her

expression made it easy enough to make out her feelings. Why did she dislike me?

She caught my eye across the tables and lifted her goblet, sending me a toast. I returned the gesture for propriety's sake only, despite her frigid stare. Beside me, Sigrun stiffened.

She'd seen it too.

I wondered if she'd noticed Astrid's eyes remain on my neck. The girl she sat with stared at it too. Perhaps it was wise for me to lengthen the cord so the gem hid beneath my armor. I wasn't enjoying the attention the jewel kept receiving.

"What's her problem?" I asked. The nervous, quivering rustle of my wings reminded me they were actually there, that they existed.

"She is afraid of you. She feels threatened now that you are back."

"Back? I'm not back. I haven't been here before, Sigrun."

"But that is just the thing. You have been here before." Sigrun grasped my arm, "You were here a long time ago, Brynhildr. And Astrid still feels you took her lover from her."

I almost choked on a mouthful of butter-soft meat, glad when I managed to swallow it down instead of ejecting it across the table. "So, she has it in for me because some Valkyrie who lived here hundreds of years ago stole her boyfriend?" I laughed. This sounded so like high school.

"Not just some Valkyrie. It was you." Sigrun spoke in earnest, leaning closer. "Gunnar was her first love, but then he met you and you two fell deeply in love. A love that was incomparable. They overcame so many obstacles to ensure their love survived.

Their love is a message we all hold dear. That love can conquer all."

"But I was created in a lab, Sigrun. My father stole DNA from the dig site that uncovered Brunhilde's remains. And he merged those DNA strands with mine. It can't mean I'm Brunhilde. Or even a reincarnation of her."

"That is just what it does mean. Your human father created an easy route for you to live again, and your soul and spirit took that route. He made it possible."

Invisible fingers squeezed all the breath out of my lungs. What Sigrun was trying so say was inconceivable. Me, the reincarnation of the Warrior Princess Brunhilde?

It didn't make any sense at all.

I awakened from a dreamless sleep. Not a common occurrence in recent months. I stiffened, sitting up in the bed, remembering that since my arrival in Asgard I'd been dream-free. No dreams of armor-clad, bloody men, or ravens or howling wolves.

I snorted. No reason to dream when the dreams were now my reality.

Turi arrived soon after with a tray of hot coffee and pastries. The coffee was way too weak and milky for me but I drank it anyway.

Gratitude and thirst were eager bedfellows. I savored the

buttery, flaky flavors of the pastries and stretched the sleep from my body while the fire warmed my toes.

Turi hustled around the room. "I have brought your armor," she said. "And Sigrun says for you to dress and go down to the training field as soon as you have broken your fast." She nodded vigorously and turned to tend the fire, flicking her strange cow-tail.

I made a mental note to ask Sigrun about Turi and her strange tail. I'd intended to do just that yesterday, but after the encounters with Astrid and Fenrir, and with all the new information Sigrun had heaped on me, I'd forgotten all about it.

Until now.

Lost in thought, I didn't hear Turi grasp the clinking chainmail and bring it over to me until she said, "Here you go, I will hold it for you and help you get into it."

She lifted the armor in her hands as if it weighed nothing. I stared in awe. I knew very well how heavy the armor was, and it looked like this particular set had additional chainmail for the upper arms, and a double breastplate too.

My stomach twisted as I wondered exactly what was in store for me on the field that required additional armor. Fenrir didn't seem like the kind of trainer who held back. In fact, he scared me, and I wasn't sure I even wanted to be trained by him.

Surely someone else could do the job.

I decided to ask Sigrun when I got to the field. For now, I tried not to think about it and quietly slipped my arms into the armor, allowing Turi to make quick work of tying the buckles and belts at my back.

The weight of the armor settled onto my body, but it took

mere seconds for my torso and limbs to adjust to the feel of the metal.

As if the chain armor had learned the pattern and shape of my body, learned the curves and crevices, and now lay warm and gleaming against me.

It was much like my wings. They'd become so much a part of me that I only remembered their presence when a stray feather floated off, or a random breeze rustled through them and set them in motion.

Or, of course, when I was upset or afraid. But the last time that happened was at the dining table when Astrid stared daggers at me.

The only other time I was ever truly conscious of the wings was when they forced my upper body to support their considerable weight.

Like now. As I sat on the stool, just bending forward to tie the laces on my lower leg armor threatened to topple me forward.

Turi giggled. "Wait. I shall help you. We really do not want you falling onto your head." She knelt before me and reached for the laces.

I sat back, blood rushing from my head as I watched her finish the job with deft fingers, probably in one-tenth of the time it would have taken me. I was still pretty useless, still had so much to learn about the city and my purpose here.

"Thank you," I said softly, grateful for her kindness and her help.

"No need to thank. It is my job." There she went with that nodding again, accompanied by a bright smile and a slight rustle at her skirts.

I bristled slightly; her subservient manner didn't sit well with me. "Yes, there is a need to thank you."

She shrugged, then stood behind me, tugging at my hair and running a brush through my tousled locks. My hair had been left to dry after bathing at the glorious pool. I'd forgotten all about drying and styling it, with my fearful fascination with Fenrir the great wolf-man.

So it was now a mess of knots. Turi made quick work of them and was soon brushing the length of my hair in long strokes.

She came around, gave her handiwork an assessing glance, one hand on her hip, the other still wielding the brush. Satisfied, she turned back to the large chair and retrieved another bronzed piece that glinted in the firelight.

I inhaled a gasp of appreciation at what she held aloft: an incredible helmet. It was rounded, clearly meant to hug my skull. Turi placed the headpiece over my hair, adjusting it until she was happy. The weight of it was not at all as alien and uncomfortable as I'd expected it to be.

It totally felt like it belonged.

"Come and look at yourself." Turi inclined her head, urging me to a corner of the room where the strangest thing I had yet seen in Asgard confronted me: a full-length, factory-made wall mirror.

I blinked, not at my reflection but at this bizarre piece of modern furniture smack dab in the middle of a room that otherwise looked as if it had last been decorated in Viking times.

Then I saw my reflection and forgot all about the mirror. I gawked at the beautiful creation I now wore as if I was born to wear it. It curved gently around my skull, riding low all the way down my forehead.

Intricate knots, reminiscent of the pillars and walls in Odin's Great Hall, decorated the forehead piece. The helmet curved around both my eyes, two little scallops just revealing my eyebrows. Though it covered most of my upper face, it wasn't restrictive at all.

I stared, my attention drawn next to the pair of wings on the sides of the helmet. Gilded wings, meant to provide further protection, curved around and down my cheeks and accented my face.

Ingenious, and beautiful. Each wing carved so intricately and so accurately that I half expected them to flutter and quiver against my cheeks.

"There, it is a perfect fit." Turi rubbed her hands together, smiling with glee.

"How did they know my size?" I marveled at the immense skill of the craftsmen who'd worked on my armor and now on this incredible helmet. It looked much like an artifact, like it belonged in a museum, not like part of your regular training uniform.

"Oh, because this helmet is yours, Brunhilde." There she went nodding again.

I frowned, staring at the gleaming headpiece. "This isn't mine." The girl was clearly off her rocker. Spaced out.

"Of course it is. The helmet, the armor. They belong to you. We have kept them safe for you, Brunhilde. We knew you would return to us and now, at last, you have come home." She clasped her hands together, her eyes shining in delight as she stared at me.

The awe in her eyes creeped me out. That, and the fact she

insisted on calling me Brunhilde. I turned to leave, still slightly off balance both from the weight of the new armor and the weight of new possibilities.

"Wait, there is one last thing." Turi dusted out a cloak and came around to rest it on my shoulders. Made of heavy wool, weaved so beautifully, it felt like cashmere wherever it caressed my bare skin. "It is cold outside, and the armor will absorb the cold too quickly. The cloak will keep you warm until you get to the training fields."

The last thing Turi did was pull the hood over my beautiful helmet and nod happily. Her job done, she left, taking with her the cheerful smile and her strange cow's tail. I stared at the closed door. Could it be?

First Sigrun had gone on about how I was the reincarnation of the real Brunhilde. And now Turi was also convinced I was this ancient Valkyrie?

Could I really be the Warrior Princess Brunhilde reborn?

CHAPTER 20

The morning light cast a bleary net across the sky, with no hint of sunny skies or rain clouds. I shivered as I walked the route to the training fields, pulling the warm cloak around me, grateful to Turi for her thoughtfulness. But my mind whirled with images of the training fields, and with anxiety. I was unsure if it was the cold or the prospect of seeing Fenrir again that caused the tremors. I marched on.

Plodding along dejectedly was not an option. Not with the burden of the chainmail armor, which was downright painful if I so much as bent forward. And not with the headpiece either. I'd strapped the helmet securely beneath my chin, but what if it tipped off my head and fell into the muddy pathway? It would be criminal to drop such a gorgeous thing into the muck.

I sighed. Life had changed so drastically for me. Ms. Custer's face flashed before my eyes. She would approve, I think, of the way I'd taken the shock of the whole Valkyrie revelation. Of having to forfeit the only family I'd ever known to do a job I had no idea how to do.

Right now, I needed her, badly. To tell me everything was going to be okay, that this was all not just a figment of my all-too-vivid imagination. I guess I longed for just plain old comfort, and although Sigrun was amazing, everything else here had been larger than life and easy to disbelieve.

I managed to get to the training fields without making any wrong turns. The fields were sparsely dotted with gleaming bodies, already warming up with light sparring. Weapons glinted in the dull morning light. Two bodies broke away from the sparring pairs and approached me. My heart thudded beneath the chainmail.

Sigrun and Fenrir stood in front of me. Two pairs of eyes evaluating me.

"I see what you mean, Sigrun." Fenrir's voice was low, and his face was fully human, thank the stars. I didn't think I could handle him all fur and snout this early in the morning.

"What do you mean?" I asked in turn. Why had they been talking about me?

"Sigrun mentioned your likeness to my old friend Brunhilde." Fenrir studied me, helmet to sandaled feet, his eyes pausing again at my neck. I was unable to find a longer string or a good hiding place for it, so I had to wear it. I'd tucked it into the neckline of my dress, but it moved as I moved. "And she was right," Fenrir continued. "You bear such a striking resemblance to her that if I were to introduce you as her, most people would be easily fooled."

"Fenrir, do you think it is reincarnation? Like Kara?" With a tangible excitement, Sigrun's eyes went from my face to Fenrir's and back to me.

"Who is Kara?" I asked.

"Kara was a Valkyrie who came back in a third lifetime," Sigrun replied, a little too enthusiastically.

"Sigrun, just because Kara's story was similar to other Valkyries' before and after her, it does not guarantee she was reincarnated. That is just a romantic story. In reality, star-crossed lovers happen all over the world and all through time." Fenrir shook his head, half to himself and half to Sigrun. He gazed across the field a moment, as if gathering his thoughts, then said, "But that is not to say Bryn is not the reincarnation of Brunhilde. As you said, her father meddled with the DNA, which in all likelihood guaranteed she would have a way back into the living world."

Fenrir circled me as if I were a horse or a cow on an auction block. "Yes, I can see why you are convinced, Sigrun. Hair, eyes, height, build. All the same."

I fumed in silence, not overly fond of being examined like a piece of meat. "Can you two stop talking about me as if I'm not here?"

Both looked at me, startled.

"I am so sorry if we were rude, Bryn." Naturally, it was Sigrun who apologized. "Perhaps it would be better to get on with the training. Fenrir, she is all yours."

She set off for the field of sparring Valkyries, leaving me alone with Wolf-Man. I removed my cloak, tossed it over the rock wall, which fenced in the training field, and averted my eyes. Wolves had great hearing, didn't they? I hoped he wouldn't hear the overly rapid thumping of my heart.

"Why do you fear me?"

I stared at him, shocked. He'd practically read my mind.

"I can smell your fear. What is it you are afraid of?" His voice was soft, non-threatening, and when his eyes met mine, they were almost kind. His gaze flicked back to my pendant for the briefest of seconds. Then he looked at me.

Nothing I was thinking at that moment would've been appropriate to reveal to Fenrir. Like I was going to tell him I'd been brought up with the myth of werewolves, read fiction and watched countless movies on the comfortable assumption that creatures like him didn't exist. It really didn't do much for a girl's confidence to find that a murderous, bloodthirsty creature of fable was a living, breathing, talking creature.

He took my silence as proof of my fear and said, "You do need to relax. I do not eat Valkyries or women or humans. Even if I thought little girls would make a tasty snack, it would be forbidden within the boundaries of Asgard. So you are safe for now."

He grinned, and suddenly I wondered what it was about him that had made me so afraid. *What a beautiful man.* Well built, like Aidan, with perfect, classic, rugged features. An honest blend of grit and gorgeous. Oh yeah, it was the memory of seeing Fenrir all tricked out in his oh-so-furry wolfy form that still jittered my blood.

But I couldn't help the smile that cracked my lips. A werewolf with a sense of humor. Nice. I nodded, not trusting my voice. He inclined his head and led me a few paces into the field.

"Do you know anything about hand to hand combat?"

I shook my head.

"Sword fighting?"

I shook my head again.

"Very well, no experience only means no bad habits to unlearn." He raised an eyebrow and I smiled. I assumed it meant we would get on well enough.

And we did. He demonstrated a few hand-to-hand combat moves, blocking, defense and offensive grips. We practiced for what seemed liked hours. At last, with the sun high in the sky, and my arms and torso aching from both the successful blows and the ones that failed, he let me off the hook.

I looked around. A few Valkyries milled about in groups, eating. Lunchtime? I felt bad that I'd monopolized his time so much, that he hadn't left my side.

"You have done surprisingly well, Bryn," he said. I bristled, almost expecting him to credit my talent to my supposed reincarnation. "You are strong, fast and smart. A deadly enough combination. Tomorrow we will try the sword. Tonight, get some rest."

With that, he turned on his heel and left the field. Only when he disappeared beyond the fence did I allow my tense muscles to loosen. Fenrir was an enigma. I'd spent the whole morning in his company and hadn't managed to get one word out of him that wasn't training-related. Granted, we were here to train, but this entire place was so alien to me that it would've helped for us to get better acquainted.

Footsteps drew my attention and I turned, smiling, expecting Sigrun.

But Astrid strode toward me instead. I had to force myself to keep the smile on my face. Astrid's own tight smile matched the insincerity of mine. What did she have against me? The real Brunhilde may have stolen her lover, but what did that have to do with me?

"I see you have a natural talent for fighting," she said, but it didn't sound like a compliment. Still, I nodded and smiled wider.

"Since you have progressed so well today, you will be needing a sword." Astrid grasped the sword at her side, holding it flat on her hands, offering it to me. The weapon glinted in the sunshine, silvery-gold. Despite the innocence of her gesture, a silent voice screamed inside me to be very careful.

"Astrid, what a lovely thought, but I think Sigrun is already finding me a sword." My arms remained at my sides as we battled a silent war. Her eyes glinted, anger flooding bright blue irises with a dark pool of violet.

She lifted the sword a notch. "Oh no, I insist. Would you turn a gesture of friendship down?" The challenge in her voice tempted me to take the sword and fling the weapon into the mud. I tamped the urge, wary of insulting a fellow Valkyrie. Especially since she was a seasoned warrior and I had barely even begun training.

A tense silence stretched between us, ready to snap at any moment. Then Sigrun's shout broke the impasse. "Astrid, behave yourself and stop teasing Bryn," she said.

She trotted toward us, a cheery expression pasted across her face, but I'd been friends with her long enough to know that her smile was fake. It was more of a grimace than a token of cheer.

Astrid's offer clearly had set Sigrun on edge, but she was trying really hard to hide her worry. Or was it fear?

Astrid relaxed her grip on the sword's hilt. "Oh, Sigrun, you love spoiling my fun. My dear, you really are taking your duties as guide and mentor far too seriously. Let the new girl make her own friends." Her words cut deep. I wondered, just for the briefest second, if Sigrun was only my friend out of duty.

Sigrun grasped my arm and led me toward the wall. "Come, Bryn, we have to get you changed and rested. Tomorrow is a big day for you."

I grabbed my cloak as we went. Too hot and bothered after my sparring session and especially after my little tet-a-tet with my non-friend Astrid, I kept the cloak folded over my arm.

"What is her problem?" I whispered, even though we were well out of earshot. "She tried to give me her sword. Is that something you guys do here? Share weapons?"

Sigrun's eyes widened in shock and dismay. "I suspected that was what she was doing, but I could not be sure from where I stood. I should have known. But I did not think she would go this far. I am sorry; I should really have been paying closer attention to your safety."

A trill of fear sped through me. Now my life was in danger? "What do you mean my safety? All she did was offer me her sword. She said she knew I'd be needing one."

"And why did you not take it?" Sigrun stopped her brisk pace and turned, hands on her hips, waiting for her answer.

"Er . . . I'm not exactly sure. I guess I just had a bad feeling about it."

"That is what I would call smart. If you do not listen to your instinct, I would call you stupid." Sigrun smiled again, pride leaching a glow into her cheeks.

"Why? Why was I right to refuse her offer?"

"Because each Valkyrie has a sword that is made for her. And only for her. No other person, living or dead, can touch the sword, let alone wield it in practice or battle."

I scoffed and resisted the urge to roll my eyes. "So, what, does it have a magical power or something?"

"No. It has a deadly power. When the sword is cast, a few drops of the Valkyries' blood are mixed in with the molten metal. The sword itself then holds the blood of the Valkyrie who will use it in battle. I am not sure if it is Asgard or Valhalla or the smith or faith, but it has always been this way. The sword will kill any person who touches it who does not possess the blood which runs within it."

"Wow. How does it kill?" I asked softly.

"The sword emits a poison which seeps into the skin of the person. It does not take long for the victim to die."

My heart thumped as I processed what Astrid had tried to do.

The bitch had just tried to kill me.

CHAPTER 21

My face, twisted with worry, anger and a dash of fear, must have been a dead giveaway to my inner turmoil. Sigrun sighed. "Come. Don't worry about her," she said. "She has been bearing a centuries-old grudge. And ever since Mimir—are you familiar with Mimir?"

I shook my head.

"Very well. I will explain. Come, we can walk to the sword-smith and talk at the same time."

Sigrun strode ahead, and for the first time it took very little effort to keep up with her. I'd been gaining in strength and stamina during the last few days. Good. A plan was forming in my mind, to learn as much as possible and find a way out of this place. Part of me still held some hope of seeing Brody and Joshua, and satisfying myself that they were okay. But the rest of me was extremely keen to get the hell out of here.

I followed, and listened. Mimir, Odin's maternal uncle. An oracle. During a great war, which Sigrun described at length and to which I didn't pay much attention, Mimir was beheaded and Odin discovered the body. Retrieving the head, Odin returned with it to Asgard. To this day Mimir provides him with the most important predictions.

Sigrun glanced back, as if to make sure I was listening. Then she said something that did get my full attention: "A long while back, after Brunhilde's death, Mimir told Odin that Brunhilde shall return to us when we most needed her. Odin assumed it meant she would return at the time of Ragnarok. And this is why Fenrir and I are convinced you are her. And so is Astrid. But she has vengeance on her mind." Sigrun tutted sadly.

"So I'll be looking over my shoulder twenty-four seven from now on?"

She shook her head. "No. Not over your shoulder. Astrid will approach you directly. Valkyries are not allowed to fight amongst each other. It is Odin's Law. Besides, Freya will not approve, and our leader's wrath is worse than Odin's."

I wondered why, when Odin was King around here. But I held my tongue. We skirted a well-trodden road, gouged by wheel-tracks, with little mud-pools scattered within the valleys they made. It didn't take long before we reached a small village. Tiny wooden homes, with a few longhouses sprinkled in among them. The sounds were an assault on my ears. Clanging, banging, metal on metal. Not deafening, but loud enough that I had to raise my voice to be heard.

"Where are we going?" I asked, almost yelling.

Sigrun hollered back, "Not far. The next building up here." She walked up to the wide entrance.

I stepped into the dark interior and blinked repeatedly. Heat lapped at my face, eking out the last drops of moisture from my skin. A monstrous fire blazed in the single, brick-lined hearth, about half the size of my bedroom back home. Flames danced and burning wood crackled.

We were enveloped by noise. The rhythmic pounding of hammers on metal sounded almost musical in note and frequency.

A figure ambled toward us, a monstrous threatening shape made worse by clinging shadows. What little daylight managed to creep into the choking dark heat fell onto a cheery face, with rosy Santa-like cheeks and sparkling blue eyes. Bushy red eyebrows and a shock of carrot hair finished the picture. I liked him at once. He reminded me of Hagar the Horrible, only without the horned helmet.

"Ha ha, look what we have here!" he boomed. Then he grabbed Sigrun in a bone-squishing hug until she squealed for her freedom.

Sigrun laughed as her feet touched the ground. "We are here for a sword. For Bryn." The smithy turned to me and smiled again. But the cheerful grin lost its sparkle as he stared at my face. "Bryn, this is Njall."

He turned to Sigrun and I could almost hear the unspoken words flowing between them, despite her calm expression and bland smile. Here we go again. Even Njall the smithy thought I looked like the famous Brunhilde.

He peered at me for a moment and said, "Good, then. Come on over here. I think I may have just the thing."

He thumped his way to a back shelf, overloaded with boxes and piles of metal, layered in dust and shadows. If he claimed the corner hadn't seen sunlight in centuries, I'd believe it. He clanked and fumbled his way along the shelf until at last, after much grunting and puffing, he withdrew a long wooden box. Dust and cobwebs traced the grooves of the intricate carvings on the lid and all four sides of the box.

The beauty of the wooden box alone was enthralling, but a strange heat twisted in my gut. Njall brought the box to a table strewn with tools and odds and ends of metal. With one meaty arm, he swept them all onto the floor. Sigrun and I both winced, looking at each other surreptitiously, trying not to laugh. For all his size and seemingly careless treatment of his property, Njall placed the box onto the table with infinite care.

We both commandeered a shoulder and leaned over as Njall opened the lid to reveal its contents. Lined with a deep purple silken fabric, it held a magnificent sword and a matching scabbard. A low, entrancing hum reverberated around the room and sank deep into my bones, reaching the very pit of my stomach. A musical sound that I couldn't attribute to the other men pounding away with their hammers.

Njall and Sigrun stepped away from the table, leaving me to inspect the sword. I breathed softly, as if the mere expulsion of my breath would cause this incredible treasure to disappear into thin air. I dared not touch it yet. Just lovingly traced the beautiful carvings on the hilt and the scabbard with admiring eyes.

The silver blade gleamed, etched with the intertwined carvings from Odin's Hall and the designs on my armor and helmet. By now, I'd gotten so used to seeing the patterns that I'd stopped wondering what they meant. As if on autopilot, my hands reached out to trace the carvings on the sword when Sigrun cried, "No, Bryn. Wait."

I turned to her, annoyed. She'd broken the magical hold the sword seemed to have weaved around me. "What's wrong?"

Sigrun ignored me and spoke to Njall. "Are you sure it is safe?"

"Well, if you know for sure she is either Brunhilde herself or her child, then she will be safe." Njall eyes darted from the sword back to me.

A twitch of fear crawled across his face so quick I almost missed it. But I didn't. That was the problem. Astrid had offered me her own sword, hoping I would take it. If I had, I'd have died. What if Brunhilde's sword did the same thing to me? I certainly wasn't convinced the sword belonged to me just because my crazy father liked to play with ancient DNA instead of poker or Scrabble.

I stepped back, despite the almost overpowering urge to take the sword. The ancient weapon seemed to cast some kind of strange enchantment over me. The sooner I put some distance between myself and the sword, the better.

"Sigrun. I want to leave. Please." My voice was low, soft, as I gritted my teeth against the pull of the sword's song.

"We can leave if you wish, but we will have to come back again today." Sigrun's response was firm. "Fenrir said you will be training with a sword tomorrow morning, so you will have to have a sword by then. You do not want to anger him."

Anger blasted me with biting heat. Why should I care what Fenrir wanted, or what would or would not anger him? I didn't owe him anything. A longing for home spiked through me, and yet a strange sense of rightness also filled me. Confused, I didn't voice my anger or my doubt.

"Can't Njall just make another sword for me?" I asked, looking over at him.

The big man nodded.

"But we must know if this sword is meant for you," said Sigrun.

"Why do we need to know? Why is it so darned important?" My head blazed with angry heat as I turned to stare at the gleaming weapon. "Why can't you just leave me to be me?"

"I would love to do that, Bryn. But people like Astrid will not. They will not let go until they win. Or until you show them who you are."

"And by showing them, you actually mean I must show them I'm Brunhilde?" I asked coldly. I detested this whole game we were playing. Now I had to prove I was someone else before I could be safe.

"If that is what it takes, perhaps that is what you need to do." The voice of Fenrir filtered into the room.

Somehow, I wasn't surprised he was there. Everything that had happened since I arrived in Asgard had been a whole bunch of unbelievable wrapped in a shiny layer of impossible.

Fenrir's words didn't require a response. I had to make a decision, right now: walk right out, go back to my room and refuse to pander to all these ridiculous demands they were making of me. Or accept it, own it.

Only the knowledge that my friends were here somewhere stopped me from turning my back on Fenrir, turning my back on all of it. I held on to what little hope I had of seeing them again.

But anger still boiled in my gut. I hated being pushed into a corner, having no choice in anything. Resentment simmered somewhere inside me, somewhere deep and dark but hard to ignore. Resentment toward Sigrun, for pulling me out of my real-world dilemma. And Odin, for forcing wings on me without even bothering to tell me what would happen. And Astrid, for trying to kill me for vengeance against a person who'd lived and died centuries ago. And now three pairs of eyes bore down on me, waiting for me to accept the weapon that would be my downfall.

If there had been sufficient space between myself and the table, I would have stomped to it. I really wanted to give in to some kind of childish tantrum. I had far too many responsibilities for my liking. Whatever happened to being a plain old teenager where the worst thing in life was a zit, with unpopularity a close second?

I rolled my shoulders and stepped to the table.

"So if I lift this and I'm not Brunhilde, then I die? Right?"

"No. I do not think so," said Fenrir. "If Brunhilde's blood flows weakly within your veins you will merely become ill and weak for a while. You will recover, so you do not need to fear. You can only be afraid if you do not have any of her blood at all. Then you will die. We know that it was Brunhilde's remains uncovered eighteen years ago in Hovgården. And we know that your DNA structure contains her DNA too, or you would not have transformed so easily."

Easy? You mean that horrifically painful, mind-blowingly

agonizing experience I had in front of Odin and the gathered Valkyries could have been worse?

I shuddered and asked, "So what would've happened if I really didn't have her DNA in me at all? Would I still have become a Valkyrie?"

"No. You would have died. The Mead and the pain would have killed you." Fenrir kept his voice flat, so matter of fact about the possibility of my death. "The only way you would have survived is to receive the Anointing of the Valkyrie. It is a rite in which Odin chooses the woman who will become a Valkyrie. The process is different from what you experienced."

I wanted to gasp for breath, but I pushed the hysteria away, using my anger to claw it back out of my throat. I turned and met Sigrun's apologetic, sad eyes. I should have been angry with her, but she'd been my constant companion, teacher and friend. And her bright cheer had helped me get through this strange transition. Seeing her eyes flat and her smile gone hit me hard.

"So I survived that test, and you think I'll survive this one too." I glared at the sword while I spoke to Fenrir.

"Yes."

I waited a moment, but he said no more.

Well, I suppose one can't argue in the face of such confidence.

I tugged the box closer and flitted my fingers over the seductive silk. The sword gleamed and glittered in the dancing firelight. I ignored the scabbard and slipped my fingers beneath the cool metal. I'd expected the sword to be heavy, but it felt as if it were a mere extension to my hand.

"It's so light. And really well balanced."

Three pent-up breaths released behind me. Fenrir broke the

silence first. "It is your own strength that bears the sword. In fact, the sword itself is really heavy, even for a master sword-smith like Njall."

Frowning, I remembered that Njall had grunted with effort as he released the box onto the table. I glanced at Njall, who nodded vigorously, meeting my gaze with glowing pride.

"I guess I'm not dead yet." I faced the three of them, holding the sword flat on my palms. "So . . ."

I didn't need to hear their answer. The fact that I was still alive, still healthy after touching the sword, meant one thing and one thing only.

I really was the Great Valkyrie Brunhilde.

CHAPTER 22

Fenrir had this strange idea that my survival after touching Brunhilde's sword meant I now possessed all the knowledge, power and skill she'd had when she'd been alive. So the ferocity of his training session the next morning didn't surprise me.

I struggled to catch my breath. We sparred alone on the empty field, and Fenrir kept me too busy to ask where everyone else had gone. Despite the inordinate amount of energy and strength I'd been awarded with since receiving my wings, Fenrir's onslaught of thrusts, parries and jabs left me pretty winded. Bruises purpled my arms below the armor, and my ribs ached from a stray shot he'd landed.

"Now rest. I will be back." He patted my shoulder and walked off.

Did that mean he was satisfied with my performance? Fat

chance. I sat on the low wall of stones, drawing the breath back into my lungs, waiting for my thunderous heartbeat to return to something like normal. My stomach burned for lack of breakfast. My pre-training nerves had ruined my appetite, and Turi had hurried away after leaving my tray of fruits and breads. So there'd been no one to force or cajole me to break my fast.

I regretted it now, as my stomach complained. Fenrir returned, a round shield in one hand, large enough to cover him from mid-thigh to chin, and painted with snaking, twisting emblems. He tossed it to me, giving me a split second to think about how to catch this much-too-large Frisbee.

I snatched it from the air, holding onto opposite ends of the circle of wood. I'd heard the thwack-thwack of metal meeting wood during yesterday's and today's practices and now it made sense. Despite the shield's heavy, bulky appearance, it was light and easy to move around.

"Let us try some defensive moves."

Fenrir lowered his body, bending his knees to find his center of gravity. I'd learned to do that during yesterday's practice, after falling a good few times on my rear end. He swung his blade at me, and I deflected the shot easily. But although my instinctive reaction with the shield was a success, a wave of energy from the blow reverberated through the shield and all the way into my arm, right to my bones.

Did I just hear my teeth rattle?

We battled until my arm muscles ached and my hair clung to my face and neck in soggy clumps. At last, he called the end of the session. "You have the basics now. From tomorrow you will spar and practice with the rest of the Valkyries. As you get stronger and more skilled, you will progress to sparring with the Warriors."

Interesting.

I battled against stiffening muscles and limped toward the fence. The other Valkyries filed into the field from another practice area beyond the stone wall, and chatted as they moved around, collecting cloaks and cleaning muddy swords and shields. Fen walked off toward the chattering group.

My ears still rang from the thwack of Fenrir's sword on my shield, so I didn't hear the Valkyrie approach until her voice startled me. "Sigrun says it will not be long before you can go on a Retrieval." Her voice held a bitter edge, and I knew it was Astrid before I turned. The nerve of her, especially after trying to kill me just yesterday! Her eyes rested on the amber pendant. Eyes filled with venom and a strange satisfaction.

"I guess it's up to Fenrir to decide if I'm ready," I replied.

She laughed, her eyes cold and mocking. "No, Brynhildr. It is up to Odin to *decide* when you are ready." She trailed her eyes up and down my body, from helmet to flushed cheeks, armor to bruises. "I am not so sure you are good enough to qualify. Not yet."

I wished I'd just kept my mouth shut. I'd just given her the means and opportunity to mock my lack of knowledge of the correct procedure. I almost sighed with relief when Fenrir strode back and interrupted us. Almost.

"She is ready for a Retrieval. Perhaps not for full battle, but Retrievals are simple enough," Fenrir growled, reminding me who and what he really was.

"But does she not need an Ulfr?"

"She will need one, but we have not had sufficient time to find Bryn a suitable Ulfr partner," Fenrir replied, the tension in his voice coming off him in waves. When did I develop the ability to read his moods? "Therefore I will be Bryn's Ulfr for this Retrieval."

Astrid laughed. A bitter, cackling sound that hurt my ears. She gestured toward a bruise on my arm. "This is what you call 'ready for Retrieval'? I see we have lowered our standards. I think I shall be speaking to Freya about this fiasco. I wonder what she will say."

She turned her back on us and stormed off before either Fenrir or I could answer her.

"So when *do* I get my Ulfr?" I raised a questioning brow.

Fenrir drew his eyes from Astrid's retreating back, clearly distracted. "A Valkyrie rides to Retrieval with a wolf. And they are meant to be a hunting pair. Since we haven't reached that stage of your training, I will substitute for your Ulfr until we get you paired up with one. Of course, Odin may feel you are not ready yet anyway, so let us wait until he makes a decision."

"And what did she mean about Freya?" I threw a dark glare at the disappearing figure of Astrid.

"The goddess Freya is due to arrive in Asgard soon. She comes to collect her share of the Warriors you gather."

"That doesn't sound fair. How does Odin feel about that?"

Fenrir laughed. "It is their agreement. They are both readying their armies for the Great War. And Freya is the General of the Valkyrie regiment as well. The agreement was they would both share the Warriors equally. Every three moons Freya arrives to meet with Odin. Sometimes there is a family gathering with all the gods. But in the end, half the new batch of Warriors will leave with Freya."

"When is she meant to arrive?"

"In a fortnight, on the night of the full moon. Let us hope your Retrieval is completed soon, for then you can concentrate on practicing your skills on the field. Freya has no patience for those who do not work hard and work as a team."

"When do you think Odin will decide?" I asked.

"Be ready this night after the evening meal. I will speak to Odin now, and if he requests your presence it will be after the meal is over." With that, Fenrir walked away without even a farewell. It would be a while before I got used to his surliness.

I'D MISSED Sigrun that morning on the fields, but dared not ask where she was. I didn't want to appear too reliant on her. She didn't make it to the Bathhouse either, but I spotted her as I entered the dining hall. She'd kept a place for me. I sat, smiled at the meal she'd already fetched for me, then wolfed down fresh baked bread and succulent meat.

"Odin will see you after dinner." Sigrun drew closer to whisper the words into my ear. Startled, I opened my mouth to reply. But she shushed me. This wasn't something to be discussed where we could be overheard.

The rest of the meal passed uneventfully. Astrid stayed away but sent a volley of dagger-like stares at me, which I ignored. I refused to allow her to get to me. It was as if I'd escaped Cherise and North Wood High only to be faced with the same problems, just with different faces.

Sigrun walked me to the Great Hall and promised to wait for me.

I SLIPPED into the expansive space, which could easily have housed the entire school of North Wood High. At the dais, I knelt. Odin sat on his throne in silence. His presence, his power, wound around me, an almost palpable thing. Remembering Sigrun's words of caution at lunch, I kept my head bowed. Silence enveloped me as I waited.

"Rise, Brynhildr." I swallowed my sigh of relief and stood. "Fenrir has told me many good things about your progress, child. He thinks you are ready for a Retrieval. And I agree."

"Thank you, my Lord."

"And you will be happy for Fenrir to be your Ulfr?" When I nodded, he said, "Then it is done. We will speak to the scouts and decide on a location."

Happiness rose within me, filling me with hope. I would be returning to the world I'd been born in. Would I be able to take a small detour to see Ms. Custer? Did I dare make such a personal request to the all-powerful Odin? "I, um . . . would it . . . ?" I stumbled over my words.

"Come, Brynhildr, there is no need to be afraid to speak." This new voice was soft, like warm honey on my skin. In fact, I could smell and taste the sweetness as her voice echoed around the hall. Frigga sat beside her husband. I could have sworn she hadn't been there when I'd arrived.

I bowed, extremely ashamed of my rudeness. She was a goddess for heaven's sake, and I'd just disrespected her. "I'm so sorry, my Lady. Please forgive me."

Odin laughed, and I risked a glance upward. His single eye twinkled with mirth. "Oh, do not apologize, child. My wife is fond of appearing within the hall amidst a conversation."

"Dear, leave the child alone and let her speak," said Frigga.

"As you wish, my fair wife," Odin replied, a cheeky grin on his face.

"I was taken from my home without telling my . . . mother that I was safe and well." I hesitated, unsure if I was overstepping any boundaries or pushing my luck by making such an audacious request. "Could I return to see her and say goodbye? Just to let her know I am well and not in any danger."

Frigga nodded her dark head, but Odin remained silent. "I think it is possible. What say you, husband?" She looked at the silent god, who merely grunted.

I waited, fingers crossed at my back.

After what seemed like ages, he said, "Very well, Brynhildr. And do not forget this boon. It is not something I grant often."

"Thank you, my Lord." I was so grateful, I didn't think to ask how this would go down.

He waved me off and I retreated slowly, filled with the pleasure of such thrilling news. I'd been granted the one wish I'd had since I arrived.

I was going back home to see my foster mom.

I LEFT THE HALL, still slightly shocked my request had even been entertained. And more than happy it'd been approved.

"How did it go?" Sigrun whispered urgently as we headed for our rooms.

"Odin approved my Retrieval. But he didn't say when or where."

I said nothing to Sigrun about my bold request, thinking I'd better keep it to myself for now. I hadn't thought to clarify the hows and whens of meeting Ms. Custer, so decided it would be safer to wait until I knew where the Retrieval would take place.

The whole concept of Retrieval fascinated me. Keen to know more, I asked Sigrun, "What happens now?"

"Well, the scouts will tell Fenrir the general locations of the next batch of Warriors. Then he will gather a group of Valkyries and go to fetch them."

"How do they know where to go?"

"The scouts are Valkyries who visit Midgard for periods of time. They travel through countries looking for the ones who glow. In the old days, it used to be easy. Valor was more common among man. It was not difficult to pass through a battlefield after the fighting was done and just pick up the courageous dead. Today, valor and courage are hard to find. People are fickle, angry, resentful and selfish. It stops them from having courage and fighting for something larger than oneself."

I considered her words. Such sentiments would send social networks spinning with bitter responses. Nobody liked to have their failings pointed out, but Sigrun was right. In many respects, people had become more fickle, less likely to take a stand for what they believed in.

"Okay," I said, "so once they know who the Warriors are the scouts come to Asgard, reveal their locations and the Valkyries go to fetch them. How is it done? Do we bring them back to life?"

"No. We just carry them to Valhalla. Once the bodies arrive there, they recover with the Mead and regain their strength. When they are ready they begin to train and await Freya's visit."

"And when do you think we'll have the next Retrieval?" I was eager to get on with my mission.

"I suspect it will be soon. Fenrir is preparing and I think the scouts came back today." I wondered if that was the reason Fenrir had been so adamant that I was ready for a Retrieval. Because he knew the Valkyries would be going again soon? Sigrun continued, "You do need to get some rest. Your first Retrieval will not be easy."

I stopped at my door and was about to enter when I remembered Turi. "Sigrun, wait."

"Mmhh?" She paused and turned. Firelight flickered from the torches dotting the passageway. Cold fingers of night air crept through the halls and my warm room beckoned.

"Turi? My . . . helper?" I couldn't bring myself to say the words *maid* or *servant*. "What is she?"

"What do you mean?"

"Sigrun, she has a tail!" My voice pitched a little too high.

"Oh, yes. I should have told you earlier." She smiled and shook her head. "Turi is a Huldra, a forest sprite. On Earth they are full of mischief, but the ones who make it to Asgard are happy to serve Odin."

"Are they servants?"

"Yes and no. They work because they want to. We cannot make them do anything. And we cannot stop their naughty ways either."

I frowned. "What do you mean?"

Sigrun blushed, trying to find the right words. "Huldra are . . . they . . . they like the men."

"Ah, I see." I suppressed a giggle. For all her years of life, Sigrun was still shy. She nodded farewell. "Goodnight," I said.

That night I was too anxious to sleep. I tossed and turned, searching in vain for a comfortable position, what with the wings constantly getting in the way. The fire crackled noisily and threw leaping shadows along the wall. Even the furs on the bed were too warm. I stared off into the dark corners. There were too many questions of how I would fit my visit in with the Retrieval.

THE NEXT MORNING, Fenrir collected all the Valkyries and confirmed Sigrun's suspicions. The scouts had arrived the previous night, providing the location of at least twenty-five Warriors. Fenrir didn't waste any time, quickly naming those Valkyries who would go and herding them off to the deserted dining hall to discuss the details.

A thrill ran through me when he called my name. He left Astrid off the list, which sent sparks of satisfaction and relief through me. Her scowl and cold sneer proclaimed her feelings, but nobody paid her any attention.

In the dining hall I sat with Sigrun, listening to Fenrir read from a list of international locations. Dartmoor, Cape Town, Brisbane, Bangladesh, Toulouse. I'd never actually thought about where Asgard's Warriors would come from, but the multinational list came as a surprise.

Only when the name Craven came up did I pay closer attention. Fen's process was to call out the name of the town, the name of the dead Warrior and then the name of the Valkyrie assigned to that Retrieval. I wasn't surprised when he named Aimee Graham, Joshua O'Connell and Brody Stevens. What was strange was how he allocated four Valkyries to the town and not three. I just assumed I was along for the ride, as he didn't link me with any of the other dead Warriors. My shoulders sagged with disappointment, but I still felt thankful I'd get to go.

A surge of emotion swept through me. Three people who'd meant so much to me would soon be in Asgard. With me. I'd barely known Aimee, but she'd played a significant part in my understanding of what the glow meant. Now they would all get a second chance.

We were scheduled to head out as soon as all the Valkyries and Ulfr gathered their stuff together. As everyone was already dressed for the battlefield in full training gear, we followed Fenrir to the palace.

At first, I thought he was leading us to Odin's Hall, but he soon took a passage before the hall and entered a different room. A large, open fire occupied the center of the room, throwing comforting warmth around us. The number of people who'd arrived startled me. Each Valkyrie paired off with one other man or woman, leaving only me and Fenrir unmatched.

Slowly, each pair held hands and flicked out of existence.

Just like that. A blink and they were gone.

Very soon, Fenrir and I were the last two left.

"Do not be nervous," he said. "Clear your mind and think of Craven or a person in the town you want to see. We shall be in Craven before you know it." A smile laced Fen's voice and at once I understood. Perhaps I wasn't allocated a Warrior because of my request to Odin and Frigga.

I felt the slight twist of disappointment, but I shook it off. I was going to see my foster mom, which was the only thing that mattered.

CHAPTER 23

No strange burst of light or sparks of fire or thunderclaps heralded our arrival in Craven. One moment we were beside the great fire in Asgard and the next, Fenrir and I appeared beside Sigrun and the rest of the Craven contingent.

Apart from a few short seconds of mild nausea, I remained unaffected. I recognized the area. An abandoned stretch of land behind the Craven Cemetery. Appropriate.

The Valkyries' chain armor gleamed in the murky light of a distant lamp, one of those fake lamps along the curved pathway that bisected the cemetery, made to look old but lit by a modern electric bulb.

The Ulfr, still in full human form, were resplendent in red-bronze body armor.

We made a magnificent sight, but nobody would be able to see us. We came in the night, to retrieve our charges. We would leave in the darkness too, unbeknownst to parents and friends and family of the deceased.

People who would never know the glory of what their sons and daughters would soon become. Once life was breathed into the chosen Warriors, they would rise to fight for Odin and Freya, to win the Great War and save the world from eternal destruction.

Craven itself hardly looked worthy of such greatness. It was just as unremarkable as always. The only difference from when I left was the weather. It was colder now; a blustery wind chased around the last of the autumn leaves.

The sky hung low, dark and heavy, promising snow. I eyed the other Valkyries and their Ulfr, wishing I could go with them to see my friends saved.

A glance over the fence and a stone angel caught my eye, watching like a sentinel over a child's grave. It sent a little shudder crawling down my spine. What would the procedure be? Would they dig up the caskets and remove the bodies? I shivered; the thought of it was detestable.

And wrong. Did the end really justify the means of Retrieval?

The others moved away, disappearing through the darkness of the trees, their minds already concentrating on the task they faced.

For the briefest second, the Ulfr shimmered, shadows veiling them, until they resembled wolves. I blinked, and they were gone before I could get a second look.

In the very next breath, a symphony of howls ripped the silent night air apart, and I shivered despite my warm cloak.

Beside me, Fen's eyes glittered in the bland light. I hadn't yet seen an Ulfr up close and personal, but I knew they were responsible for those blood-chilling howls. And Fen's blood was answering to the call of his kin.

"Fenrir?" I would have placed an arm on his shoulder if he hadn't moved away. Not the smartest thing to do. He shook his arms out, as if the simple action would clear the calling from his blood.

"Come. We do not have much time." Back to business.

We hurried through the darkened streets, arriving at Ms. Custer's house with preternatural speed. At the front door, Fenrir paused and said, "Go. I will stand guard. I'll warn you if there is danger or if we run out of time." Arms folded, he leaned against the wall beside the bell, beyond the circle of brightness from the porch light.

The shadows swallowed him. I squinted to try to see him.

"Go!"

I jumped at his whispered growl, redirected my attention to the door.

White paint peeled from the deeper grooves of the paneling. It still needed a new coat of paint, but I had always liked it just the way it was. It had character. My fingers brushed the frame and released a small cloud of paint flecks, and I smiled.

More character.

I peered through the drapes beside the door. The lights were on inside, but it was quiet. My heart thumped against my ribs as I stabbed the bell, hoping I wouldn't scare the living daylights out of Ms. Custer with my Valkyrie getup.

Looking down to smooth the chainmail along my neckline, I gasped. My armor and headpiece were gone, replaced by the jeans and jacket I'd worn when I'd last stood outside this house.

To the eye, I looked like an ordinary teenager. But when I touched my clothing, my fingers brushed armor.

A grunt came from the shadows. "It is an illusion. You do not want to frighten your mother do you?"

I didn't answer because at that moment the door opened, and it would've frightened my foster mom if she found me on the veranda having a conversation with the cold night air.

I'm not sure how I'd expected Ms. Custer to react, but the bear hug she pulled me into was enough to make me want to sob into her shoulder. Her warm, comforting body smelled of fabric softener and fried chicken and home.

She held me as if she thought I'd disappear again if she let go. When she finally released me, her eyes were filled with tears and her cheeks were moist. And I found I'd shared her tears.

Mine were perhaps more along the vein of self-pity, though.

"Come inside, baby. Before anyone sees you," Ms. Custer whispered.

She hustled me inside, her eyes darting up and down the street as she shut the door. Dragging the drapes closed, she pulled me onto the couch beside her, her hands wrapping around mine again. The house was silent; only the kettle hummed in the kitchen.

"What happened, child? Where'd you go? I knew you'd leave but you didn't say goodbye and then Aidan called last week to say he'd come see me and that he was worried about me and you and so sorry about what happened. But he never came and I haven't heard from him since his call. Have you been with Aidan?"

Ms. Custer stopped talking so suddenly I thought she would

burst into tears again, and I hated myself for hurting her, for worrying her.

Above all, I hated Aidan for giving her false hope and for making her wait and not turning up.

Damn that guy. He'd won all our hearts, and what does he do in the end? Fling our hearts back into our faces without so much as a goodbye.

"I'm so sorry, Mom. I would've contacted you if I could have."

"I know, honey. You must have been worried our phones were tapped or something." She looked over her shoulder as if expecting one of Aidan's goons to be standing there.

My heart sank. All this craziness had made her suspicious, made her lose the comfort and security in her life. I ached to find a way to make all of this go away.

To give her back the luxury of certainty. I couldn't change the past, but I did know one way to make her feel better.

I gripped her warm fingers in mine. "I have something to tell you and I don't have much time," I said.

Then I paused, staring at our entwined fingers, hers tanned brown and mine pale. Hers still comforting and supporting. Mine still thin and needing her. I hesitated, not sure how to proceed.

"What is it, child?" She leaned closer to me, trying to see my face.

"I didn't run away. I was taken."

Her cheeks darkened, her fingers squeezing hard. "I knew it. Those goddamned thugs. I should have known it was them." Ms. Custer launched herself out of the couch, giving vent to her anger the best way she knew how. By pacing.

"No. No, it wasn't them. . . ." I rose to my feet. The pacing had touched something inside me. The hysteria I'd tamped down all these days now welled up inside my brain. "In fact, it's something entirely different," I told her. "I don't think you'll believe me, but I'll tell you anyway, and you can feel free to kick me out if you wish. But I hope you don't."

I smiled as she paused in her pacing, and our eyes met. I prayed this was the right decision and I was not about to jeopardize our safety. "I was taken away, to a place that shouldn't even exist. I'm not sure how to tell you this." Again I paused. Telling her about Asgard was difficult. To be honest I still barely believed it myself.

"Take it by the horns, child. Deep breath and get it out." She sat me back down and squashed me in a half embrace.

"You know how you spoke to me about my eating habits, and you thought I was eating somewhere else?"

She nodded, concern flaring in her eyes. "You're anorexic. I knew it!"

"No. I'm not anorexic, but at the time I didn't know what it was. It wasn't only the eating. I hadn't been drinking much either, or sleeping much at all. And I was getting stronger. But now I know why. My body was changing, adapting."

My hands trembled as I told Ms. Custer how I'd been seeing the auras around people since I was a little kid. I skimmed over my run-ins with the psychiatrist and explained how I realized Joshua was going to die after I'd seen the glow on Aimee.

"When I saw Brody glow I couldn't take it, I told Aidan about it. He said he'd help but . . ." My voice trailed off. The less said about Aidan, the better. "When I disappeared I was taken to this place . . . and I became something else."

Ms. Custer pursed her lips. "Stop this ridiculous nonsense, child. Next you're gonna say you're a vampire or something." She and I both knew she was joking but a smidgen of fear glinted in her eyes. It tripped up my courage.

What if she thought I'd just gone crazy?

I laughed, tamping down my fear. "No. Not a vampire. I'm a Valkyrie."

Her arm fell away and she just stared at my face, her mouth half-open. My heart plunged. I contemplated taking it all back, pretending I'd just been kidding all along. But I couldn't back out now.

Taking a deep breath I said, "I was taken to Asgard. That's where I got my wings. I've been training, and when I knew I'd be coming to Craven, I asked if I could see you. It's why I don't have much time."

Would I even need more time? The look on her face said she was more likely to toss me out on my behind than believe me.

"I know it's hard to believe," I said. Then I remembered Fen hiding in the shadows. Before I'd figured out a plan I was on my feet and pulling the door open, whispering to the shadows, "Fenrir, how do I show her my wings?"

Fen growled. "You want to do *what*? Have you lost your senses?"

"Is somebody out there, Bryn?" Ms. Custer's voice floated to me. Although concerned, she still gave me privacy.

"How?" I whispered insistently through gritted teeth.

"Just believe."

"What?" That was the most ridiculous thing I'd heard.

"Tell her and she will see," Fenrir said. "And be quick. We still have your Retrieval to complete."

I stared at the shadows. What Retrieval? He hadn't read out a name. I opened my mouth to ask him about it, then clenched it shut. Time to think about that later. Ms. Custer was waiting inside.

I shut the door but didn't return to the living room. By the door was probably the best place to be in case she came at me with her broom. Best place to make a quick getaway.

"Bryn?" Her footsteps padded across the floor and she squinted at me.

"Mom, I'm a Valkyrie," I said. "From the Norse legends. The women with the wings who take the dead Warriors to Valhalla. Look at me. Closely." I stared at her, willing her to see me in my true form.

Not knowing if it would work at all.

When her eyes widened, darkening from rich brown to deep black, I suspected trouble. She stepped closer, and then the door was at my back. Maybe this had not been such a good idea.

"Oh my Lord. Oh my Lord," she whispered over and over, almost under her breath, like a prayer. Her eyes ran over me, head to toe then toe to head and back again.

She reached out and touched my chest where the chain armor lay curved to my body. Her fingers traced the threaded links.

She gaped at the armor, the helmet, my face. When her eyes rounded even further, I knew she'd seen my wings. She gasped and whispered. "Let me see." I turned around, allowing her to examine them. They fluttered in tandem with my nerves.

"Now you see?" I said. "This is what I've been trying to tell you. It's what Aidan knew, too." I turned back to face her.

"Is that why they were looking for you? Did he tell them?" Her eyes hardened, still harboring a deep hatred for the thugs.

"No, I don't think so. But he *was* sent here to find me." His betrayal still tore at my heart. "The book they were looking for had a bunch of information on my father and the experiments he was involved in."

"Experiments?" Ms. Custer's eyebrows shot up.

"About eighteen years ago a burial site was uncovered in Sweden. When they examined the grave, they found wings like mine, something they were unable to explain. Some of the archaeologists swore they'd found a Valkyrie and took samples of the DNA to verify it. My father was the head geneticist. He performed the DNA tests and told them it was normal human DNA."

"And he lied?"

"Yes. He knew what he had. My mother was on the clinic list for IVF, and he spliced the DNA with her fertilized embryos. The Valkyrie DNA took over. When I was taken to Asgard, I had to go through a process, like a transformation, where my wings grew. I wouldn't have received my wings at all if I weren't a real Valkyrie."

"So who took you to . . . Asgard?"

"A Valkyrie who was sent to fetch me." I smiled, needing to reassure her that everything was okay. "Her name is Sigrun. I wish you could meet her, but she's busy, on a mission right now. There's something else I wanted to tell you. It's Brody."

"What about him? Did they take him? Oh heavens, they took

him?" Grief filled her face again. Instantly she looked twenty years older, the lines of her face deeper, more pronounced.

"Yes, they did take him. The golden aura was a sign, telling me I was looking at a Warrior of Valhalla. Only a Valkyrie can see the golden glows. He's safe and well, and he'll live forever as a Warrior in Valhalla."

I didn't want to tell her about Freya and her demands or the impending war. It didn't seem fair to heap sadness on her when she'd been given good news.

Her little smile confirmed I'd made the right decision.

"Will you see him?" She searched my eyes, desperate for an affirmative answer.

"I'll try my best." And I meant it. One of the first things I planned to do when I returned to Asgard was to find Brody.

"Good. You must give him our love. Will you come back and visit?" She patted my hand. She seemed to sense that my time was up. Thankfully, I wouldn't have to drag myself away.

"I'm not sure," I said, shaking my head, deep sadness moistening my eyes. "Just one thing. If Aidan ever calls you or visits, tell him I'm gone forever. Just make sure he never comes back. I wish he'd never come here in the first place."

"Perhaps it was fate?" Ms. Custer said, but I knew she was only being kind.

"No. He was sent here to check if I was a Valkyrie." I grimaced. "Our fathers were partners at a genetic science center. His dad wanted to eliminate me. Aidan told him I wasn't a Valkyrie. That the experiment had been a failure. But none of them know what they're in for."

Poor Ms. Custer. So much for her to process. The dazed look

in her eyes told me I'd overwhelmed her. But she threw her shoulders back and drew me into her arms, wings, armor and all.

"You go, honey. Do what you have to, and be safe."

Our farewell was quick, and I got the sense she would head upstairs to her bedroom and have a good cry. I sighed.

At least she knew that Brody and I were safe.

I stepped through the doorway and waited for the lock to click.

"Let's go," I said to the shadows.

CHAPTER 24

We walked into the dark night. Behind us, the lights went out in Ms. Custer's house. I held back heated tears, unsure if I'd ever see her or Izzy or Simon again. My foster family had been ripped asunder, and I stood helpless in the middle of the turmoil.

Looking back, maybe for the last time, I studied the porch and the swing, trying to etch them into my memory. Trying to ensure I'd never forget where I came from. Where I'd sat hidden behind the rose bush, eating up Aidan with my eyes the day he rode into my life. The stairs I'd raced down that day he'd thought he could just walk straight out of my life without so much as a goodbye. The bush at the corner of the property behind which I'd hidden to watch Aidan and his goons leave, before I'd been whisked away to a place I'd never dreamed existed. To an unbelievable life.

I yanked my eyes away.

Goodbye, Mom.

Sometimes I wanted to just give it up, to just go back home, but Asgard made so much sense and gave me a fantastic reason to exist. For the first time, I had a real purpose in life. Maybe I did have something to thank my father for.

Fen and I passed under the large oak at the foot of the driveway. A movement caught my eye; a curtain swayed in one of the windows across the street. Some things never changed in this neighborhood. Nosy neighbors.

I glanced at Fen, relieved he blended into the shadows. His presence would definitely cause a stir on this quiet street. Hopefully I hadn't been seen either.

I had to trot to keep up with Fenrir as he strode ahead. "What did you mean by my Retrieval?" I asked.

"That is the reason you have come to Craven, Brynhildr. The reason you are here at all."

"You called out everyone else's names and then told them who they would be retrieving. But you didn't give me a name."

He didn't even bother to slow down, just walked on, crossing the street, expecting me to run just to catch his words. "So you thought you did not have a Retrieval to complete?"

"I guess." Now I felt foolish. "So do we have a name?"

"Wait. Some patience will do you good." Fen sounded strange, his voice tight and emotionless.

The darkness lay thick and oily around us. Pointless examining his face for clues as to what was bugging him. Even if I waited for the clouds to move and reveal the moonlight, it would probably be of no use. Fenrir was too good at hiding his emotions.

Despite the darkness, I recognized my surroundings. We

passed the park where Aidan had sat on the swing beside me and watched Brody. The wind shoved through the trees and the two lonely swings swayed back and forth. Strange and eerie.

We drew closer to the pathway where Pete and his friends had attacked me. My heart clanged in my chest, imprisoned in a steel cage with the memories of my near disastrous experience. I tried to think about something else. Like why were we here, and where were we going? Fen had refused to answer my questions. He continued walking into the trees and along the path until we neared the stream.

He left the pathway and ducked into the thick brush. I followed, still curious, and a bit concerned. And maybe a little annoyed with the whole cloak and dagger suspense act. Where were we going? I didn't ask him though. He'd just ignore me.

Cold air bit at my bare skin, probing beneath the cloak, as we walked upstream toward a smaller, disused bridge. The footbridge had been cordoned off and the split and rotten wood clearly needed to be repaired before some kid broke his neck playing on it.

Dark, waterlogged planks hung from the remains of the bridge, a half-dozen attached by a single nail, like a line of ragged bats holding on for dear life.

Beneath the run-down bridge, fallen wood and beer bottles littered the banks of the stream. Splits of wood, probably hacked off by kids messing around and testing their courage, lay on the rocks in the water, along with a dense thicket of chocolate wrappers and chips packets.

Fenrir stopped at the stream's edge and waited. He gazed at me, then looked toward the bridge. What was he waiting for? Was there something here I was supposed to see? My heart knocked against my ribs and a sense of foreboding chilled my skin.

The water gurgled and curved around its obstructions and continued downstream until it was forced to curve again. Something dark and solid, like a tree root, jutted partway across the water. No, not a root.

A booted foot.

My heart thudded to a stop. At first, I assumed it was some homeless guy with courage and valor that awaited his one-way trip to Valhalla. But the clothing he wore was too new. Maybe an out-of-towner, going for a walk, had used the footbridge by accident, only to fall off it?

No. If he fell, he'd have been closer to the bridge itself. He lay at least ten feet away from the shadows cast by the ruined wooden monstrosity. More likely, he'd been thrown off the edge of the broken bridge or rolled down the bank.

One foot soaked in the running water, while the other was propped at an odd angle, higher up the bank. Maybe a broken leg. His upper body lay in shadows, hidden by bushes and weeds. I shivered. What would we see? A mangled skull from a gunshot wound, or a perforated chest from a stabbing? Or maybe just a guy, drunk and unconscious, unable to move his broken leg.

One hand lay beside him, outstretched as if he welcomed the night and the moonlight. The fingers were pale, grayed. That solved the drunk and unconscious question. Just one glance at the hand confirmed he was dead.

The rest of his abdomen was encased in a black leather jacket, worn, yet something a confident young guy would pull off well enough. The smoothed leather looked familiar. A lot of boys loved the look, but an icy, ominous fear scrabbled down my spine. I darted a look at Fenrir, but his expression told me nothing.

Despite the sickly sweet odor wafting from the body, I almost ran to him, thrusting the bushes aside. Fenrir didn't follow. I didn't notice. The moon hid behind dense cloud cover. I shoved the bushes aside to reveal the man's face.

That the clouds chose that particular moment to part and reveal the gruesome face of death was ironic and cruel.

The glare of the moonlight was abrasive and cold. It lit up the ridges of his eyebrows, the jut of his classic cheekbone. His face was a marble bust, his body drained of blood and life while I'd received my wings and attained a certain salvation.

While I'd pined for him and hated him in alternate ferocity.

Cold seeped into my veins as I registered that his death could never have been an accident. Not with the bullet hole marring the perfect smoothness of his forehead.

I stared through dry eyes at his face, bloodless and filled with death.

Aidan's face.

CHAPTER 25

The cold cut at me. It stole the breath from my lungs. It scraped the tears from my eyes. It ripped the life from my heart. The cold killed me. I stared, unmoving, at Aidan's alabaster face and stony cheeks. A pale Adonis, carved from night and darkness. His eyelashes curled, provocative even in death.

I sank slowly to my knees. Not caring about the cold, slippery muck on the banks. Not caring that I knelt with one foot touching the frigid water. The stream gurgled on, unaware that it tasted mortality as it passed. Mortality and sorrow.

It somehow seemed right that I sat here, one foot steeped in freezing water, as if I shared in his crossing. Stood with him in an in-between world where he waited for the next stage of his journey.

The moon lay his body bare for my eyes. His milky white

hand rested against the black muddy sand. Lifeless. Not warm like when he'd caressed my cheek, not soft like when he'd held my head and kissed me with a ferocity so unlike his gentle embrace. And here, as I sat swaddled by cold and death and moonlight, everything in me cried for him.

Trees creaked around me, groaning against the grasping hands of an icy wind. Fen moved at my back, his cloak rustling against the brush. He'd been silent, watching and waiting. Mourning a loved one should be a private thing. But I was glad for his presence. Because Fenrir meant life where Aidan's remains whispered death. Fenrir meant hope and trust, while Aidan was betrayal.

Even in death, I couldn't forgive him. I'd forced him out of my head and out of my heart. But I still hurt, somewhere beyond the pain and the tears, a place touched by Aidan. Touched for the briefest moment. A place that remembered him. And waited for him.

"Bryn?" Fen's voice was low, soft.

I met his eyes. Sympathy creased the edges. An apology. "Why didn't you tell me it was him?" I asked, needing to hear what I already knew.

"At first I did not believe it was appropriate to give you such news with all the other teams around. And then you were concentrating on what to tell your mother." He hunkered down beside me, his voice still so soft it made me think of a rug, cradling me in its tender warmth. Was his quiet tone out of respect for the departed or empathy for my pain? I didn't know. "And then it was too late and it seemed best to let you see him yourself."

Fenrir flicked his gaze away, toward the corpse. Toward the empty shell of Aidan. His corpse still glowed. I registered the aura gradually, as if my vision was blurred, fuzzy. I had to peel back the layers of what I saw, look beyond the body and beyond my grief and anger and longing.

Aidan's aura was not as blindingly bright as Joshua's or Aimee's on the days they died. His brightness had faded, a yellow gleaming where it should have been an eye-piercing golden sheen.

"Why is the glow so weak?" I asked Fen. "Isn't he Warrior material then?" My question was laced with bitterness, which surprised me. My emotions churned with a complex mix of resentment, anger, relief and hope. Aidan's death made me bitter. Not hard to understand.

"He has been exposed to the elements since his death. From the looks of the body and the glow, I would say he has been dead a week." Fenrir looked upward, staring at the moon, then at Aidan's lifeless body. "But the light fades with every passing moon. He had a while yet for Retrieval."

Shock sliced through me, icy blades as cold as December. A week. That meant someone had done this to Aidan the day I'd last seen him at Ms. Custer's house. The day Sigrun had taken me to Asgard.

"But I never saw him glow. I would've noticed if he'd glowed like Joshua and Brody." My voice quavered.

"I believe that his death came early. That perhaps it was not his time. Perhaps he only started to glow after you last saw him." Fen nodded. "That would certainly explain why his glow is so weak."

"So now what?" I tried to keep my voice devoid of emotion,

tried to put on a professional mask. I think I failed. Fenrir's eyes, when he looked up at me, were still a mess of pity.

"Now you carry him in your arms, and we take him to Valhalla," he said.

"That's it? I lift him up and abracadabra we go to Valhalla?"

"Did you want it to be more complicated than that?"

A wolf howled beyond the tree line. I was about to ask if it was one of our Ulfr when Fenrir raised his hand, silencing me so firmly that I clamped my mouth closed.

A dog barked. Loud and ferocious. Fen glanced up the bank, back the way we came. Somewhere within the brush the dog scrambled and scratched, its high-pitched barks scraping at my eardrums.

A latent growl erupted beside me. I turned to Fenrir and froze. Even the blood in my veins stilled. I remembered why I'd feared this man from the first moment I'd laid eyes on him. He still stood tall, in human form, not a hair's breadth from me, bristling at the danger he tasted somewhere in the darkness.

A snout protruded from the low bushes. Moonlight painted a tiny pool of silver on the animal's wet nose. The Labrador came closer. Its whole head now poked from the brush.

Fenrir growled, a primal vibration at the back of his throat that spoke of blood and teeth and mindless fear. And every hair on my body rose in silent salute. I remained frozen, watching the ferociously curious dog and the vibrating wolf-man at my arm.

The Labrador emerged from the bush, eager to prove his worth. He growled, but he was no match for Fen, either in ferocity or intent. Fen replied, dialing up the volume and the threat. Ozone tinged the air around us, along with the musty odor of animal fur. I shivered. Hoping he wouldn't change.

The dog yipped. Off in the distance, his master called from the night again, a hollow yell edged with irritation. "Rex, heel! Rex, you stupid dog, heel!"

Sound traveled strangely on frigid night air. We couldn't count on how far away he was. And we had to get out of the park. With Aidan.

"Fen," I whispered. I risked touching his arm, carefully, fully aware he might turn on me just for the disturbance alone, but I was already on the balls of my feet, on the brink of taking flight, just in case.

But he didn't twitch. He was too busy staring down the dog. I watched in amazement as the animal ceased its yipping. Fen's eyes glowed a golden yellow, eerily similar to the auras of the Warriors. It made me think of butter and the gunky ooze that seeped from the Warriors' wounds as they healed deep injuries. Comforting and revolting, in a rather large hairy package.

Rex shivered on skinny legs, eyes twitching this way and that, as if unable to decide whether to fight or flee from this man who growled like a rabid pack animal. Rex bared his teeth, and Fenrir stepped forward. The dog proved the coward of the day, tucking its tail and turning to flee. Fenrir ripped out another growl, and the dog whined and disappeared into the darkness.

A shudder ran down Fenrir's body. He closed his lupine eyes, collecting himself. When he opened them they were nice and human again. Fen scowled at me. "Come, bring him and let us leave. There is far too much danger here."

I didn't hesitate. Didn't consider the decaying flesh or the possibility of piles of writhing maggots feasting within Aidan's corpse. I knelt and grabbed the open lapels of his jacket and lifted his torso up, just enough to allow me to slide a hand behind his back. The leather was soaked, soft and pulpy beneath my bare flesh. Rain and mud and blood had converged here in the darkness of Craven's most unpopular scenic outlook.

I slid my other hand beneath his knees and rose. Expecting the weight of a man, I tilted, way off balance, and stepped wide to find my new center of gravity. It was much the same as carrying a child. His body sagged against mine, the sweet reek of decaying flesh enveloping me. Holding my breath did nothing to help, as I could taste the sickly sweetness of him on my tongue. I shuddered.

And that was what brought on my first tear. I couldn't bear to touch this body. My skin crawled, reacting to the coldness of his skin. His hand lay on his chest, fingers still slightly curled, as if beckoning me to get closer. His body shimmered, refracted. Distorted by my unshed tears.

"Brynhildr."

I looked up, startled.

"We must go."

Beyond the bank, drawing closer, a man's voice shouted. "Rex, you dumb mutt, where did you go? Heel, boy, right now, goddamn it!" I'd been so wrapped up in self-pity and disgust, not a sound had pierced my sickly sweet haze.

"Ready?" Fenrir asked.

I nodded, unable to bear my burden with pride, refusing to bear it with sorrow. I figured I would treat it as a job. Forget who he was, forget the old sexy scent of him, the roughness of his unshaved beard against my skin. The taste of him. Forget Aidan.

As I concentrated on forgetting the boy who'd stolen my heart with one hand and stabbed it with his knife of betrayal with the other, Fen drew closer. Close enough that we breathed the same air.

Then, just as the shouting man broke through the bushes and stumbled down the little bank, we winked out of existence.

The last thing I heard was the man's words. "What the hell?"

CHAPTER 26

I blinked and we were back. The heat of the fire pierced my frozen skin, sending fiery needles of pain into me. I thought I'd been cold when we first arrived in Craven, but kneeling in cold wet sludge and holding a body the temperature of a Slushy made me feel as if I were standing inside an Arctic iceberg.

I wanted to drop my burden but my hands remained closed around him. Frozen, clutching skin and bones, unable to let go.

"Come, everyone. To Valhalla," said Fenrir.

I blinked again and the rest of the teams took shape before my eyes, like something out of Dante's inferno. The Valkyries all bore their burdens in a macabre picture of death. A death procession, only this time the dead would receive the breath of life again.

The teams walked out of the room, ghastly shadows dancing on the walls around us. How fitting the background of fire was to this caravan of cadavers.

My feet moved, and I was thankful. At this point I wasn't

capable of much more than automatic response. I followed with Fen at my side, not even caring that I hadn't the faintest idea where Valhalla actually was.

THE PROCESSION TRAVELED IN SILENCE. The muted slap of leather soles on stone echoed along the passages, torches flickering as if sighing happily to see the Warriors pass.

We left Odin's castle and paced the bricked roadway, past the Warriors' Bathhouse.

The night sky flickered with strange green and blue lights, waving and undulating above us in an eerie hazy dance. Unbearably beautiful.

On a hill overlooking the roadway sat a Longhouse. The highest point of its roof reached half the height of Odin's grand palace, making it the second tallest structure in all of Asgard. Despite its monstrously large size, Valhalla's unremarkable architecture rendered it a plain and simple wooden hall, a practical one, a fitting home for the Warriors.

The only thing that had a claim to beauty here was the Glasir tree, standing just outside the hall. Monstrous branches spread out from a trunk so wide it would take ten men to measure around it fingertip to fingertip. The branches hung heavy with leaves of varying shades of gold, from plain and pale to a dark red-bronze. No matter the color, the leaves twinkled in the fading light.

The gigantic tree shone so bright that I squinted as we

approached, like the rest of the Valkyries. We hobbled up the hill, blinded by the golden tree. The Ulfr, though, had no problems. They strode beside the Valkyries, gazing up at the tree, an expression of reverence on their faces.

All this I registered at the edge of my consciousness. My energy was focused on my burden. I tried to imagine how I would feel when Aidan rose again as a Warrior. The hurt of his betrayal still burned, a glowing coal reminding me of the white-hot pain I'd suffered.

But even that pain was buried deep down. Was it shock? I'd heard that people in shock were numb to sensation. The body's way of protecting the victim against further pain. I didn't want to be numb. I wanted to scream at the top of my lungs that none of this should ever have happened.

I should be back home, kissing Aidan in all his hot and sexy and living glory, in the kitchen between study sessions. I should be walking Brody and Simon to the park and swinging on one of the swings to pass the time, while they laughed and giggled and screeched their way through an hour of play.

But life didn't seem to like me much. Not enough anyway. Not enough to give me back the little bit of normalcy and happiness I'd once enjoyed. It had been so brief I'd begun to forget, as if it were a dream of cotton candy. The taste so sweet and delicious, the sensation so ethereal as it melted on my tongue. But my waking moments were erasing the memory. I could no longer see the bright pink color, nor could I smell the pungent richness of hot spun sugar. Or remember the taste. The delicate sweetness as it traced the tongue and melted like tiny butterfly kisses.

I shed another tear because I'd lost my sweet moments.

I barely registered the weight of my burden anymore. Until I passed the tree of gold. It shone and sparkled, shedding its light on everyone within its shadow, transforming every dark and haunted shadow, every pale and dead face into a shimmering vision.

Aidan's face was no longer an alabaster statue. Now it glowed as if the brightest light lay within him. From the moment I'd seen his lifeless face, at the side of that ignorant stream in the middle of Craven's cold darkness, I'd known he would return. He would walk and talk and laugh again. Perhaps the knowledge had stayed my tears, but now, just before I had to hand him over, before I had to leave him in Valhalla, I was filled with so many emotions. I was torn. Torn in a million directions.

Was this right? Shouldn't he have been allowed to live? Wasn't this barbaric, bringing the dead back to life? How would he feel about this intrusion into his choices? Should he have just been left to rot away in the loneliness of Craven? Left to nature to eat at his flesh and peel him away until all that remained was a skeleton. A mere shadow of his life and spirit.

No. I swept those thoughts from me as I concentrated on carrying the weight of his body into the hall. I gasped softly. Aidan's weight! Between arriving at Asgard and carrying Aidan up the hill to Valhalla, his mortal remains had gained considerable heft. So much that the muscles in my arms now strained and burned. Around me, the other Valkyries breathed heavily, all feeling and bearing this new, impossible weight.

I staggered through the wide open doors, looking for a place to lay down my burden. Along the middle of the Longhouse were tables and seats for dining. At one end, targets decorated the outer walls, presumably for archery practice.

On my right, a row of beds filled a small infirmary. I headed to the nearest bed. A man appeared beside me. A Warrior, perhaps. One who appeared eager to tend to the new Warriors. I bent to lay Aidan upon the clean sheets, sinking to my knees, every last sap of energy drained from my body. I was afraid I had no energy left to stand, so I just sat there, watching.

The Warrior barked orders and people shuffled around. His words sounded odd. Distorted, mangled words. As if I were underwater trying to make out his garbled voice. My cloak fluttered as a young girl swept past me. A bushy red tail peeked out from beneath her skirt. Another Huldra.

"Perhaps we should leave," Fen said. I'd forgotten all about him, but he'd remained at my side the entire time. The anxious way he looked at me spoke volumes about his concern. I nodded and rose, my legs a wobbly mess of nerves. We left the hall.

Outside, Sigrun waited beneath the golden tree.

I turned to thank Fen, but he walked on without a nod or a goodbye, leaving me alone with Sigrun. Fen. I wondered when I'd begun to think of him as Fen rather than Fenrir. When had I developed a relationship that allowed me to shorten his name as if we'd been friends for years?

I shook my head and smiled at Sigrun. But no smile greeted me today. And that made me sad. On top of the horrid things I'd seen and done today, Sigrun's smile would have been my safety net.

I tucked my arm into hers, seeking the warmth of her hand and the warmth from the golden shade of the tree.

"It is okay," she said. "The first time is always difficult. It will be easier the next time."

I glanced at her face. She had no idea what I'd just been through; she thought this was a standard, first-time Retrieval. I doubted that every Valkyrie got to bring the boy she loved to Valhalla.

"Is something wrong Bryn?"

"My Retrieval was someone I knew. Knew very well."

"Oh, Bryn." Sigrun patted my shoulder to comfort me. "I am sorry. That is not supposed to happen. I will speak to Fenrir about this. The Valkyries are not meant to bring back those they knew in their lifetimes. The emotional weight is far too taxing."

"No, Sigrun, please. Don't speak to Fen about it." I touched her arm, a tiny part of me afraid she'd go flying at his fast-disappearing back to give him a solid telling off. "I know why he gave me the Retrieval."

"But Bryn, he really should not have done that."

"It's okay. Aidan was the boy I once loved, and I think Fen knew about it. And I'm thankful he let me bring Aidan instead of some other Valkyrie. He also gave me time to know what had happened to him."

"I am so sorry," she said softly. "That must have been hard."

"It was . . . okay. It's not important anyway."

"What do you mean it is not important? He was important to you." Sigrun wore that righteous look on her face, the one that reminded me she would go to war and give up her life for me if required.

"Was," I said. "He was important to me. But not anymore. Not since he betrayed me. Since he lied and almost got me killed."

"I see. I am so sorry, Bryn." She didn't probe any further, though she barely knew any of the story. Her consideration made me want to burst into tears, but I swallowed hard. I decided to tell her soon, maybe in the next few days when we were alone. To break the silence, I asked, "Who did you bring back?"

"Brody Stevens."

I sighed, relieved. Sigrun was the perfect one to bring our little boy back. I should have paid closer attention when Fen read out the names of the Valkyries connected with the Craven kids. I was just so focused on seeing Ms. Custer. "That's good. Thank you."

"So you knew him, too?" Sigrun frowned. "I suppose you would have known many of the people we brought back from your old town."

I nodded. "I knew them all. It was only Aimee that I didn't get to know very well. Joshua was my best friend, and Brody was my little foster brother. And Aidan . . . well, I told you about him."

Sigrun stared at me, aghast. "I am so very sorry that you had to be present for that."

"It's really okay, Sigrun. I'm happy I knew. Happy they'll get a second chance too."

She hugged me, and I took what I could from the embrace. Strength, support, affection. They were getting a second chance, all of them, and I was happy for them.

I wanted to see Brody, to assure myself he was fine, curious as to what was going to happen to him. Wanted to run back into the hall, but a glance at the door showed it was shut tight. Suddenly all my energy drained out of my body.

I took a deep breath and stared up at the sky. The hazy green and purple lights still flickered, brighter and more entrancing than before. I stared mesmerized by the magical beauty of it. "What is it?" I asked Sigrun.

She tilted her head, staring into the heavens with me. "Your people call it the aurora borealis. It can only be seen in the far Northern Hemisphere. To Valhalla it is the song of the Warriors written in the sky."

"So Asgard is located in the polar north?"

"Yes. Well, somewhere near the Northern Pole, though I am not too sure exactly where."

"The lights are stronger now. Brighter than when we arrived."

Sigrun smiled. "It is a sign that the Warriors are regaining their strength. Some people believe the spirits of the Warriors perform this sacred dance in the night skies. That it marks the journey of a Warrior's soul from death to new life to *einherjar*. The lights fade away once all the new Warriors are well and ready for training."

"It's beautiful."

A gasp of shock from Sigrun disturbed my appreciation of the undulating aqua and green colors. I tilted my head and looked up in the direction of her entranced gaze.

Above me, a leaf had fallen free from the branch. It glittered as it swayed in a wide arc, fluttering on the air, arcing back and forth as if some invisible puppeteer swung it to a rhythm we couldn't hear. We watched in silent wonder as the single golden leaf slowed in its descent and landed on my shoulder. I craned my neck to see it, almost afraid to touch it. I had this image in my head of the fragile leaf shattering into a cloud of golden dust when I touched it.

"Go on, take it," Sigrun urged.

I picked it up between two fingers. It really was a leaf, not a carved piece of gold. The great golden Rowan tree had given me one of her leaves.

"Wow!" was all I could muster.

"Oh my, you are so very, very lucky, Bryn. I am so jealous." Sigrun laughed, not sounding in the least jealous.

"Why lucky?" I asked. The tree must shed its leaves at some point."

"This Rowan is special. No season affects it. No leaves fall from it unless Glasir wishes it. We believe Glasir will only give you a leaf if you are important or special."

"So I'm now special?" I grinned.

"You always were anyway, Bryn. This just confirms it."

"You mean because of Brunhilde?" I tried and failed to keep the bitterness from my voice.

"Yes and no. You are special in your own right, too. I barely knew Brunhilde when she lived. But I know you. And I admire you, Bryn. Not for your incarnation. Merely for who you are as a person. Right here and right now."

Her words made me feel better. They were like drops of water to my parched soul, after having heard so much about this wondrous Valkyrie who was the real me.

I twisted the leaf between my fingers. "So what's the purpose of this leaf then?"

"What do you mean, purpose?" Her forehead wrinkled.

"Does it do anything? What's so special about having it?"

Sigrun frowned. "Does everything have to have a purpose? Can you not see the beauty of something just because it exists? Just because it is beautiful?"

I frowned back. I'd just sounded so petty, so materialistic. When had I become this self-centered person? Or had I always been this way? I didn't like it much. The leaf gleamed and my frown vanished.

A leaf for a leaf's sake. I could live with that.

For a timeless moment we admired the leaf. Very Zen, if you're allowed to Zen in the land of Odin. I would have remained entranced for who knows how long, if not for the footsteps.

Heavy boots pounded across the ground. A Warrior hurtled toward us, only stopping because Sigrun hailed him. "What is the matter?" she called out.

"Freya." He struggled for enough breath to push the word out of his mouth. After sucking in three deep breaths, he added, "She is coming. I have to tell them." Then he sprinted away to tell his brothers inside Valhalla.

"When will she arrive?" Sigrun yelled.

He didn't stop. His last words, shouted over his shoulder, floated to us as the door closed behind him.

"In two days."

CHAPTER 27

The whole of Asgard boiled and buzzed. If Freya was as powerful and imposing as Odin, then I could understand the frenetic tone of the hustle and bustle.

Even Turi rushed into my room after dinner to grab my armor. "It needs a double polish to elicit double the shine!" she said, an excited tremor in her voice. I didn't doubt the girl believed her words. But I paid little attention to her as she breezed in and out of the room. My mind tumbled thoughts of Brody and Joshua and Aidan together. I focused on finding a way to either get into Valhalla or get information on the condition of my friends.

THE NEXT MORNING, our training focused on working with the Ulfr. The whole thing seemed a bit back to front since I'd already been out with Fenrir yesterday, but I choked back my opinion. The upside was the welcome absence of Astrid. Even Sigrun commented on how much calmer and more relaxed the training session was.

I wasn't prepared for the transformations of the Ulfr though. Fenrir paired each one of us off with an Ulfr, and though they were still in human form, the glint in their yellowed eyes hinted that we were in for much more than hand-to-hand sparring. My blood still ran cold with the memory of Fenrir's half-transformation on the day we first met.

The Ulfr, as humans, were a magnificent race. A raw beauty shadowed the harsh, rugged lines of their faces and though you would think such craggy facial structures would be misplaced on the females, you would have been way off the mark. They were beautiful, both male and female. Beautiful and strong. And dangerous. No doubt the best backup a girl could ask for, but still dangerous.

My partner was a woman named Mika. She was tall, muscular. Dark hair held back in a neat ponytail. Exotic Asian eyes. We sparred, exchanging blows and defensive moves to warm up. We were well matched in strength and agility. And although my mind wasn't entirely focused on the task, my body made up for my lack of attention.

When Fenrir growled, the reverberation of his animal call sank into my bones, bringing dread with it. I knew what would happen next. The Ulfr heeded his instruction. Brows flattened, cheekbones flared and canines lengthened. I didn't want to look at Mika but my gaze settled on her face. Her eyes were a deeper yellow and despite the distinct changes to her bone structure, she still retained the look of a human.

I sighed, relieved.

"I see you are not afraid of me," Mika said, her words slightly distorted by her protruding teeth.

I resisted the urge to step back. "I wouldn't expect you to be here to harm me. Aren't we fighting on the same side?"

"Well, technically we are not on the same side," she said. "But truthfully, we all know why we are here. And it is serious. So we take our training seriously too."

A little shocked by her admission, I blurted out, "What do you mean we aren't on the same side?"

She raised a brow and studied me. "The stories tell us that Fenrir will defeat the great god Odin at Ragnarok," she said. "Fenrir does not agree, and has offered to help to train the Warriors of Odin and Freya. All your regiments will know our techniques in case the stories are true."

"So it's a sort of a suicide mission?"

"Something like that, but not quite. Fenrir does not want Odin to lose. Whether it is to Fenrir or to the frost giants. Our master would rather be the loser, as he will never raise arms against his own master. This is the best way to ensure it."

I nodded, appreciating what she meant. Fenrir was an honorable man. Wolf.

We continued sparring. The lack of armor meant more bruises, but freedom from the heavy weight of the bronze meant more strength and stamina. The day passed in a snap, as time sped up to compensate for our hard work.

Later I joined Sigrun at the pool to soak away the bruises and muscle aches. I suspected the water possessed some kind of magical rejuvenating quality, as my injuries healed super-fast, bruises faded away within twenty-four hours and muscles were soothed before bedtime. Easy to understand how the job of a Valkyrie could be fulfilling and comfortable despite stretching through centuries.

"How can a Valkyrie be killed?" I asked, sinking into the welcoming embrace of the heated water.

She blinked at me. "Why? Are you planning to get rid of Astrid?" Sigrun's smile was broad, and we both laughed.

"Of course not. How did Brunhilde die?"

"She chose to marry for love. At that time a Valkyrie removed herself from Asgard if she chose to marry."

"Why?" Seemed a bit sexist to me. A woman had as much right to a career as a man, and I couldn't see the Brunhilde everyone spoke about as being subservient.

"Because it was the belief at that time that the duty of the woman as a wife is all-encompassing. That it is not possible for a woman to be a wife and mother and still fulfill roles outside of her marital home."

I frowned. "And I hope that's changed," I said dryly.

"Yes, it has changed. A long time ago. Frigga had become tired of losing Valkyries because of the old rule. She said that as the wife of Odin, she had certain wifely obligations but as the Goddess of the Clouds and Sunshine, Fertility and Marriage, she had other duties to perform. She argued with Odin that if she left her goddess duties just because she had an obligation to him as a wife, what would happen to the world? He then insisted she was capable of performing both tasks perfectly well without sacrificing the other. Frigga won the debate and the freedom for the Valkyries to choose to marry if they wished."

"Go Frigga!" I whooped and slapped at the water.

"Yes, we are most grateful for her strategy." Sigrun sighed happily and reached across to turn the hotter pipes on. Soon we were perspiring from the heated water, though reluctant to leave its steaming embrace.

"What happens when Freya arrives?" I asked.

"A procession and dinner. The next morning we have a mass meeting, presenting the Warriors. Then Freya chooses."

"What does she base her choice on?"

"Freya is a war goddess. Naturally, she wants the best Warriors but she is not allowed to tip the scales. Balance is important, especially when all she is creating is another regiment within the same army. But Freya is a demanding general. So she is fussy. It is good that Frigga helps with the choosing."

"Frigga?"

"Yes, she is a seer. Not a full oracle, but she senses the nature of a creature. Their deepest desires. Their dreams. Using her knowledge, she will advise Freya."

"Wouldn't that be a sort of conflict of interest?" When Sigrun frowned in confusion, I explained. "Frigga is Odin's wife. Wouldn't she choose the best Warriors for Odin anyway?"

"But you see, it is not a competition. Each regiment must be weighted equally, with the same number of strong and wily Warriors as the next. Nobody wants to belong to the regiment that loses the war. Nor would you want to lead that regiment."

It made a lot of sense, the way the gods worked. I rose from the waters and toweled myself dry, glad now that I'd washed my hair since there would be an official procession. "So, with the procession I take it our training will be canceled?"

Sigrun reached for her clothes. "It depends on Fenrir," she said. "We will meet at the training field, along with all the other Warriors and Ulfr. Fenrir will organize the regiments, both new and old, and prepare us. The new Warriors will be placed at the front of the procession, to allow Freya to observe them."

My stomach twisted as my mind strayed to Aidan and the rest of the kids from Craven. They were in for some grueling training before Freya came around again. I promised myself I'd find a way to get to them, even though Valhalla was totally off limits so far. Maybe Sigrun could help.

"Sigrun, is there any way I could see Joshua and Brody and Aidan?"

Sigrun stopped walking. Clearly, my request didn't sit comfortably with my friend. "You know it is not allowed. Valhalla is where the Warriors recover. Where their life is returned to them. You cannot go intruding on something meant to be an almost sacred activity."

"I just need to know they're all right. How long before I can speak to them?" I hadn't realized how afraid I was until I asked the question. The four kids from Craven were my only link to a real home. Despite the sour taste Aidan left in my mouth, he was still a link to Ms. Custer. "And what about Aimee?"

I'd wondered where they would have sent her. "Aimee? Oh, that would be the girl who was retrieved from your town? She will be in Valhalla."

"But I thought Valhalla was for men only?"

"Did you learn that from your modern history books too?" Sigrun asked dryly.

"Well, it's what I was taught." I bristled slightly. Could I help it if the historians of our time had misinterpreted the real facts of history?

"So in your armies, do they have both men and women who fight for their country?"

"Yes, of course. Women have the same rights as men do."

"Well then, why should Asgard be any different?" Sigrun admonished me with a smug smile.

So Aimee would be with the boys. At least she wouldn't be alone. There was a slight comfort in that. "Is there any way you can get me in to see them before tomorrow?" I was desperate to speak to them, to tell them I was here with them.

Sigrun frowned, but I knew that expression. She disapproved of my request, but understood and sympathized. I hoped it meant she would come up with a plan to help me.

A long moment passed in which I wondered if she had decided it was too risky. Finally, she spoke. "I have an idea. Be ready after dinner. I shall come to fetch you from your room." A sudden, mischievous grin revealed her clear enjoyment of the exercise in breaking the rules.

As USUAL, dinner was delicious and Astrid's absence made it even more pleasurable. We weren't the only ones who noticed.

Sigrun and I both heard Astrid's name mentioned during the meal.

Once back in my room I spent a few minutes marveling at the unbelievably high shine that Turi had managed to coax from the already shimmering armor.

Then I paced the length of the room.

With every passing minute, my heart beat faster and the flip-flops in my stomach bordered on nauseating. When Sigrun knocked on the door at last, I was one step away from screaming my impatience.

I grabbed my cloak and slipped silently with her down the large high-ceilinged passageways. What was the purpose of the height? Had giants once roamed these halls? Or was it a statement? Maybe the height indicated the majesty of the Lord whose house it was.

The entire castle was a magnificent architectural monster. Built into the side of a granite mountain face, the structure dwarfed the mountain, so the natural ridge was no longer visible. Tall spires rose into the clouds, with some turrets encased in cloud cover almost all year round.

We walked the path to Valhalla in the dark, sticking to the low walls beside the roads. The night was silent, cold and dark without the moon. I didn't dare ask any questions. We were too far along to turn back, but my gratitude to Sigrun for even considering my request was enough. I owed her big time.

We gave Glasir a wide birth, staying as far out of her brightness as possible. As I steered clear of the entrancing tree, I traced the outline of the leaf she'd given me. Njall had been kind enough to drill a small hole into the end of the leaf, allowing me to thread it onto the thin leather thong already holding the amber stone. It now lay against my chest like a charm, protecting me.

Sigrun chose a path that bordered the outside of the hall, all the way to the back. It was a long way, only because the hall was so monstrously large. Of course, it had to be, since it housed every Warrior ever brought to Valhalla in the history of time.

We came to another set of doors. Sigrun leaned close and knocked lightly. Three short soft taps. The door opened in silence and a face popped through the small opening. The short red-haired girl smiled in relief, beckoning with one crooked finger for us to follow her inside.

The kitchen was bright and warm and we waited while the girl checked the door.

Leaning close I asked, "What's happening? Who was the girl?"

"She is sister to the Huldra who attends me. They have worked all around Valhalla, know the place entirely too well."

"It was nice of her to help us out."

"I have known her a long, long time," Sigrun said, a happy warmth in her voice.

The Huldra returned, her eyes bright and her face cheerful. "There are clothes inside the cold room." She pointed to a little door behind Sigrun.

Once in the room we changed into the clothing laid out for us. I stared at the two fake tails, which sat on the bench. Pointing to them, I asked, "What are we supposed to do with these?"

"Wear them silly. Here, I will show you." Sigrun grabbed one of the bright red tails and showed me the leather string tied to the stump of it. This she tied around her waist. She slid the tail into her skirt, dropping it onto the floor behind her. It fell through the bulky petticoats and peeked out from the bottom of the skirt. It looked perfect. Even her wings were gone, hidden by Sigrun's glamor. I still wasn't all that sure I knew how to use the whole glamor thing. No doubt she would fix my wings too. I hoped. She opened her neatly tied braids, spreading her wavy hair out behind her, letting it fall down her back. "Now I am ready. Come on. What are you waiting for?"

I took one last look at my foxtail as it peeked from under my skirt. One peek behind me to confirm my wings were invisible. And crossed my fingers. Fox tail or not, this had better work. Or we would both be in deep doody.

CHAPTER 28

I hurried after her to the kitchens, and soon we both stood ready to serve.

"Thank you, Lifa," Sigrun said to the Huldra. "Now how do we get to them?"

Lifa nodded at the question and gestured toward the table occupying the center of the room. Three trays sat there, loaded with goblets and small bowls filled with strange gelatinous goop. Certainly looked like sick people's food.

"We take one tray each, and take it to each *einherjar*," Lifa said. "You will get your chance to speak to them when you serve them. Do not be too long, but there is no real danger of being caught. Almost everyone has retired to their rooms for the night, and the few Warriors still in the hall will leave soon enough. Now follow me."

She picked up a tray, held it at her hip and left the room. We followed, mimicking her confidence and her style of bearing the tray. It was easier than I expected. The hall stretched endlessly before us, empty except for a few warriors gathered together in small groups, and the little infirmary set up by the entrance. We neared the rows of beds where the two dozen warriors lay. Some looked in good nick while others appeared frail, still holding on to death.

Aimee sat up in her cot, talking to another warrior in the bed beside her. Joshua and Aidan were flat on their back, both conscious but silent. Brody was nowhere to be seen. I stiffened. His absence scared me, increased my desire to see him and convince myself that he was okay.

Aidan, one arm on his chest, stared off into space. His forehead was smooth where the bullet wound had so recently gored it open. I swallowed, aware he might not want to see me. Aware he might be as confused as I'd been my first day here.

Soon we were lowering the trays onto a stand of tables beside the beds. Sigrun began to hand out her goblets and bowls to a group of Warriors a few beds away, and Lifa took the far end.

I grabbed a share of the food and drink and walked to Aidan's bed. I hadn't intended to see him first, but my feet pulled me toward him. The hall was warm, and unlike our dining hall, a multitude of fires burned along the walls, throwing off a constant, pleasant warmth. The faint odor of food and the low murmur of conversation drifted toward us.

I tilted my head forward, allowing my hair to hide my face as I knelt beside the low pallet. He turned, expressionless. Until he saw my face. For an instant his eyes lit up, as if joyful and bright, then the joy fled, replaced by a self-deprecating smile. Of course, the tail! He thought he was just imagining it was me.

"Hello, Aidan," I said, taking his hand and placing the goblet into it. I had to ensure it looked like I was performing the task of one of the Huldra. Behind me, my wings shivered, hidden within the folds of Sigrun's glamor.

"Bryn?" He sat up slowly, balancing the goblet carefully as he moved, not taking his eyes off my face. "Is it really you?"

I nodded. "Keep your voice low. I'm not really allowed to see you until you are better."

"What happened to me?" He fingered his forehead where the bullet had entered his skull. "My head . . . I know I hurt my head. It's still sore to touch, right here. I thought I was dreaming."

He looked bewildered, confused, and I was tempted to sit beside him and hold him in my arms. But I couldn't. Not just because it would reveal our real purpose here, pretending to be Huldras, but because I couldn't trust myself to get close to him. I was supposed to be angry with him.

"You called Ms. Custer," I said, thinking it would jog his memory if I gave him some of the details.

"Oh yes. Something happened at her place after you disappeared. I wanted to apologize to her, to make sure she knew it wasn't my doing. She was so angry, like she thought I'd had something to do with your disappearance." Aidan's shoulders drooped. He held his head in his hands as if it was too heavy for his shoulders to manage the weight.

"What happened?" I asked.

"I'm not too clear on that. I went to Craven. I remember hiding out in the bushes outside Ms. Custer's house. Waiting for the right moment to go inside. I recall the blow to my head, then nothing." He pressed his temples. "Wish I could remember what happened after that. Next thing I knew I was waking up here. Even this place seems like a dream, not to mention the fantastic stories they've been telling us. As if we would believe their crap. Probably a government experiment and they've turned us into zombies or something."

"You should believe it. It's all true." I watched him shake his head, conscious of the reasons I was here. "You were killed," I said. "Whoever knocked you out outside Ms. Custer's house dumped you at the reserve. That's where we found you."

"We? You mean you found me?" He stared at my face, shock mixed with sorrow.

"Yes. I was just doing my job, so don't get all excited about it." I placed the bowl in his hand. "I have to go. I need to speak to the others and I don't have much time."

A quick glance at Sigrun revealed she was almost halfway done passing out her food. Looking back, I found Aidan staring at me, a multitude of expressions flitting across his face. I much preferred his unconscious face, where his feelings were not constantly trying to manipulate me.

I grabbed another drink and bowl and knelt beside Joshua. He'd heard the whole conversation, probably more than just the words we were saying. He turned and looked at me, his eyes scanning my face. His smile was tender, like a comfy rug just wanting to keep me warm. He sat up, taking the drink and bowl from me. "Hello, Bryn. Are you okay?"

His voice was soft and I ached inside. So kind, so considerate even in a place that shouldn't exist, faced with a reality he should question, yet he thought of me first.

"Yes. I'm fine," I said. "And you? Are you getting better?

Stronger?" He nodded, so I asked a question that didn't have a yes or no answer. "How do you feel about all of this?"

He winked. "Better than being dead."

I looked around, catching sight of Aimee at the next bed. I'd barely known her. Now I wondered what she must think to see Joshua and me here in Valhalla.

I fetched her food and drink, which she took with a smile. "You here too?" she asked.

"Shocker isn't it? And I'm supposed to be the troublemaker."

"Well, you don't live your life by the rules of people who think they know better. That's definitely a good thing. This whole Valhalla thing . . . it's strange. I never knew you could have female Warriors. The stories were always about men."

"Yeah, and some stories only ever said that our purpose was to bring the big strong Warriors their Mead. Ha! There's more to our job than the world would dare to imagine." I laughed softly, still aware there were other Warriors around.

"You're a Valkyrie?" she asked.

I nodded. "Yeah, and I was as surprised as you are. I wish I could stay and talk but I don't have much time."

She nodded, giving me a weak smile.

Still one more person to find. "Where's Brody?" I asked.

"He's been taken to another room. Apparently he needs a different kind of care. I thought that was strange too, but . . ."

I nodded, understanding things were different with Brody. At Aimee's frown, I quickly explained Brody's incarnation and that he would revert to his previous body to allow him to fight as a Warrior. I was deeply disappointed that I hadn't spoken to him. Would he recall this life? Or would he regress to the memories of his previous life, before his foster life, before Ms. Custer and I had ever known him?

Amie nodded, but from her confused expression I knew the concept was slightly confusing.

I glanced behind me to check if anyone had noticed me lingering here. Huldras didn't loiter. "Did you speak to him at all?" I whispered.

"Yeah, he woke up a few times, seemed confused. He asked for Ms. Custer and for you. I'm sorry, Bryn. I told him who was here, but I had no idea you were here too."

Tears singed my eyes for the lonely little boy who didn't know I was here for him. "Did they say where they were taking him?" In answer, Aimee shook her head. Her jaw tensed and her eyes were moist. I didn't want to press further, refused to make her feel guilt for something she had no power over.

As I rose, Aidan turned and met my eyes. Just one look brought everything back. Those first heated kisses, the comfort and warmth of his arms. The magic of knowing someone cared for me enough to give up his all-important nightlife. But with the wave of love and longing came the frigid reality of his betrayal.

He'd come to Craven with the intention of seeking me out. Of befriending me to confirm I was a Valkyrie. He'd known all along. Picked at the layers of who I was. He'd used me, then brought his goons around to scare Ms. Custer.

"Bryn." Joshua's voice penetrated the fog of hurt and anger. "Are you okay?"

I just nodded. Still staring at Aidan who'd seen my longing and my pain and anger. Aidan stared back, bewildered. He had no idea how much I knew of his maneuvering into my life.

"Bryn, can we talk?" he said. And I refused to answer. Lifa had already taken all the trays away, and Sigrun now entered the kitchen behind her. I shook my head, not sure I was ready to face him alone, not able to trust myself to control my anger.

"It's time I left." I smiled at Aimee and Joshua, wishing I could hug them and say goodbye. "I have no idea when I'll be able to come and see you again. Sigrun took a huge chance bringing me here and I don't want to risk getting her in trouble. And with the procession tomorrow and the Choosing the next day, another visit won't be possible until at least two days from now."

"What procession?" Joshua asked.

"Freya will arrive tomorrow morning and there will be a procession through Asgard. She'll be choosing her share of the Warriors for her own regiments."

"Will she take us too?" asked Aimee, her forehead crumpled.

"No. I don't think so. You've only just arrived. With no training and so little strength, you're not likely to be true Warrior material. No offense." All three smiled though I avoided Aidan's eyes. "I really have to go now. I will try to come again later in the week."

I turned to leave. Behind me the bed creaked and Aidan let out a soft groan. Just the thought that he meant to follow me set my heart racing. Quickening my steps, I rushed to the kitchen entrance that was guarded by one of the many thick pillars spaced out within the room. Fat enough for two of Njall to hide behind without being seen, it shielded the entrance to the kitchen, dousing the rowdiness that must emanate from a busy kitchen in the midst of meal preparations.

Aidan caught my hand as I reached for the kitchen door. As if on cue, the door opened and Sigrun popped her head around it to look for me. Her face was urgent when she saw me, then changed when she caught sight of Aidan's fingers entwined with mine.

"I will wait out back for you." She winked and shut the door.

I turned to Aidan and tried to tug my fingers free. Instead, he held on tight and grasped the back of my head with his free hand.

"What's wrong? Why are you so angry with me?" His eyes swept along my face as if he would find an answer somewhere in my dead eyes or in the thin line of my mouth.

"You know very well what's wrong. You and your lies! I can't take any more of them." My voice broke and tears filled my eyes. It was his touch. His body so close to mine that was my undoing.

"Please, tell me what I did to make you look at me like that." He placed his forehead on mine and as he spoke, his breath mingled with mine.

"I read the book you left behind."

He stiffened but remained where he was. "Then you know I tried to protect you."

"But you came to Craven for the express reason of infiltrating my life, discovering if I really was a Valkyrie. Everything was a lie." My voice shook. It was so hard to breathe and talk and be in the same personal space as Aidan. Thinking of all the reasons I should hate him was becoming more and more difficult.

"True. I can't deny why I came. But once I got to know you I realized how wrong everything was. No way was I going to put you in any danger, even if my father hated what your father had done. It wasn't fair to you." Aidan shook his head. "I wish I could change everything. Go back to the beginning."

"And what about what you did to poor Ms. Custer? You lied

to her. From the moment you first walked into our house you lied to everyone."

"Not about everything," he said softly. His thumb traced my cheek. "Not about everything."

"Whatever happened between us was part of your lies, Aidan. There's nothing left."

As I whispered those words I knew I lied. The way my heart flipped inside my chest and the speed of my breath was beginning to distract me. Behind my emotional attachment to Aidan was anger, and a chasm of granite pain. But deeper than the betrayal my heart simmered with longing.

"That is a lie and you know it." He leaned closer, and his lips caught mine. Heat enveloped us, ripping my anger loose, tearing apart any barricades I'd built between us in the past weeks. His hands were hot on my skin, his thumb now tenderly tracing the curved of my collarbone. We were both lost in each other.

A mindless, breathless sense of belonging overwhelmed me, reminded me why I'd sought out Aidan in the first place, why this leather-clad, bad-boy biker had crawled beneath my skin and why I'd never been able to get him out. He'd filled the emptiness inside me. All those places that craved little emotional fillings like attention and admiration, love and loyalty. At my shoulder, and under the glamor, both my wings fluttered, sharing the solar flare that ran right through my body.

I stiffened. The motion of my wings brought me back to my senses. Along with the curious sensation of being watched. Somewhere close by I felt the almost silent susurration of breathing. And perhaps it was my enhanced Valkyrie senses but the dull throb of a third heartbeat filtered to my ears. A calm and steady beat that said the owner was neither afraid nor nervous at being caught.

I pushed Aidan away, needing air, needing to dissipate the heat between us. Needing not to be caught in such a compromising situation. But Aidan was lost in the headiness of passion. I wasn't sure if it was his need for me or the sapping of his strength by his resurrection, but he refused to let go. Tears filled my eyes as I returned the embrace, despite the suspected voyeur.

This was no longer passion. It was a deeper need too, and I couldn't bear to deny him what I also longed for. The connection to another human.

A shadow flitted by at the edge of my vision. I strained to make out any features, barely catching any details. Just that it was another girl. With fair hair and glittering eyes. I couldn't be absolutely certain, as I was unable to see wings to verify it, but some instinct told me I was in real trouble.

Astrid had just witnessed me making out with Aidan.

CHAPTER 29

I donned my armor the next morning with an undeniable sense of dread. All I could think about was what Astrid planned to do. She really had the dirt on me now.

Turi fluttered about the room, filled with excitement for me. "Your very first procession since your arrival at Asgard!" she said in a sing-song voice. I barely heard her. Memories of last night shadowed my thoughts.

I'd left Aidan standing in the dark and fled through the kitchen. By the time I reached Sigrun I'd decided I wouldn't tell her about Astrid. Guilt ripped me up but I didn't want her to stress over being caught. I was really hoping Astrid hadn't seen Sigrun around Valhalla. I'd rather go down alone than take my friend with me.

At the training field, the news wasn't good. "The procession is delayed until after lunch," Fenrir announced. Unhappy murmurs rumbled through the gathered Valkyries. Fen growled. "In the meantime, we will practice our sword techniques."

Thankfully, my brand new ancient sword was strapped to my waist, its bright gleam hidden inside the intricately patterned scabbard. It wouldn't be my first time raising the great sword of Brunhilde, but I felt a multitude of butterflies doing the rumba in my tummy. Fenrir set us out on the field, keeping me to one side. Satisfied with the rest of the groups, he positioned himself before me. I mimicked his stance.

He drew his sword from his side with a smooth and silent flourish. The perfect approach to a smooth kill. When I did the same, it had a completely different effect. As I slid the sword from its scabbard, it sang. The metal slid out of its casing, ringing like a soft bell.

Every Valkyrie on the field slowed to a dead halt and turned to stare at me. Astrid's face whitened with rage. A small cluster of women whispered and Brunhilde's name floated to me. Sigrun sent me an encouraging smile, but Astrid's expression sent chills through my very bones.

Fenrir tried to keep a straight face, but it was so easy to see he was incredibly amused. By what, I was unsure. Was he enjoying my discomfort or Astrid's anger or the Valkyries' surprise? But his eyes were only on me.

"Pay them no mind." He stepped forward and launched into a series of intricate moves, which I copied well enough, secretly glad I hadn't made a fool of myself.

The other Valkyries slowly returned to their own sparring practices, but I continued to feel Astrid's gaze.

At last Fenrir stood back and assessed me. He nodded. "Okay. We need to get you partnered up and practicing those moves." He turned to scan the gathering of women, a contemplative scowl on his face.

Unfortunately, Astrid chose that particular moment to cut her opponent's weapon from her hand. The sword, thin and silvery, so pale it was almost white, swirled like a boomerang and landed at Fen's feet. Was it some quirk of fate that the bad girls always get what they want? Always. They get the guys and the money and they always get their own way.

Suitably impressed with her display, Fen crooked a finger at Astrid and she glided over. The smile she gave him was certainly no teacher-student one. He ignored the seductive glance and said, "You two, pair off and practice. Oh. And Astrid?" She looked at Fen, eyes wide and innocent. "No funny business. This is practice and nothing else."

As soon as she turned to face me, I knew I was in trouble. The smile that teased her pouting lips disappeared, murdered into a straight, tight line. Her eyes glittered like gems, cold, hard and empty. She bent her knees, bobbing on them to settle into her gravity center.

I did the same, holding out my sword, easing its weight into my arm as if it were merely an extension of my body. The sword, despite its heavy appearance, was incredibly light and easy to use. I swung it, making large figure eights around my body like I'd seen in many a martial arts movie. And the threatening move kept Astrid at bay until I was ready.

We circled each other, her bright blue eyes narrowed, darkened, a sea portent of a coming storm. Astrid didn't scare me, though. Her intentions worried me, but I felt no fear. The knowledge boosted my strength. She thrust, her sword glinting in the morning brightness. I blocked with the flat of my blade, the impact sending vibrations through the bones of my arm.

Astrid shook out her arm, clearly affected by the impact as much as I'd been. She stepped a pace back, as if biding her time, but I had no intention of allowing her to rest up. I thrust upward, and around, landing a blow on the armor on her forearm. The clang echoed the silent crow of achievement ringing inside me. A rustle of approval went through the group.

We were the day's entertainment. Shadows moved at the corners of my eyes. The entire class of Valkyries gathered around us. I felt the support and encouragement from many of them and it bolstered my confidence further. The only problem was that it strengthened Astrid's anger, too.

Her eyes darted around us, from one face to the next. Her pale skin, so milky white and perfect, was now marred by red splotches of anger. She tossed her sword from hand to hand, hunching over, watching me with thinned eyes, while an air of menace grew around her, thick and sour. At her back her ivory wings fluttered, mirror to her rage.

I tried to calm my nerves, breathe my heart back into its normal rhythm. I was ready. Bring it on. And she did. Thrusts and parries galore. Astrid went a bit mad for a while. I could have sworn she growled her unhappiness when I landed the second blow to her torso.

Damn Fen for standing and observing as if we were an interesting science experiment. What the hell did he want? Bryn shish kabob? The woman only got furiouser by the minute. She delivered a blow to my chest that almost stopped my thudding heart.

Astrid smiled. "What is the matter, novice? You do need to pay attention. It shan't be my fault when you get stabbed in the chest."

Er. A little help here, Fen? This woman wants my blood!

But he made no move. Apparently the safety of my skin was not high priority. At least Sigrun seemed concerned, eying Fen out with a threatening stare.

I gritted my teeth, trying to forget the pain of each individual breath. The chainmail had protected me from grievous injury but I had no idea what was going on beneath the metal. Bruises galore, most likely. I concentrated on watching Astrid. Her eyes, her body, her stance. I tried to predict what her next move would be.

She charged again, grunting on the follow-through, putting all her strength behind the blow. Bilious fear rose in my throat. She really meant to hurt me. I watched the thrust, waited for just the right moment and dodged the sword, leaning back so far that I almost fell over. The momentum of the blow, with all her energy and body weight behind it, pulled Astrid along in a wide arc. One that made it easy for me to swing my sword at her calf and trip her onto her rear end.

She landed with a thud, splattering mud onto both our armor. Just as a precaution, I slipped my sword beneath her chin as she gasped for breath. Better to have her down and out than trying to cut me off at the legs. Cheers and applause went up around us, and Fen stepped into the circle. Finally.

"So, there you see a lesson on how not to fight. Do not let your emotions control your movements. Channel them into your actions." He patted my shoulder. "Good job, Bryn. Astrid, I expected more from you than getting whipped by a novice."

He turned and left the field. But not before I caught the slight smile that lifted the corner of his mouth. Behind him, a steaming Astrid stared daggers at his departing back as she hauled herself to her feet. Fen had nothing to fear from Astrid though. Me, on the other hand . . . when she turned on me, her eyes glittered, narrowed. She shoved her face close to mine. "Do not get too happy, little novice. You might need to hone those skills before too long. The life of a certain person may just depend on it."

Any doubts that it had been Astrid whom I had seen the previous night dissolved. I swallowed my fear, refusing to let her see me emotionally weak. I just knew she was talking about Aidan. And she confirmed it when she whispered, "You should have chosen a better spot to get cozy with your lover. Hopefully you have said your goodbyes."

She left me as soon as Sigrun arrived. Left me gulping for air as fear drowned all thought and feeling in me. Sigrun gave me a worried look but said nothing. I paid little attention to my friend. I closed my eyes and saw again my embrace with Aidan in the shadow of the carved pillar. And saw the flash of light hair. What bad luck to run into Astrid, of all people. What had she been doing in Valhalla? It was just as forbidden for her to enter the hall as it was for me.

And what did she mean? I wanted to run after her and beat the information out of her. But common sense prevailed. She'd never give in to me, even if I did beat her to a pulp.

But something didn't sit right. Why was Astrid so desperate to get rid of me, to demean me? Could it all be just her own anger and envy toward Brunhilde? Or was there more than just Astrid's personal vendetta working against me?

Whatever she had planned for me right now had everything to do with Aidan.

WITH MY MIND stuck on Astrid and her intentions, I missed most of the procession. It had been unimpressive to begin with. Nothing like Mardi Gras or the Fourth of July. Just a bunch of Warriors in polished armor leading the procession, with Freya on her mount bringing up the rear. Her dark hair and smoky eyes swept over everyone.

The most impressive thing in the entire procession wasn't Freya's blinding beauty but that of her incredibly beautiful dress, made of finely meshed golden chain armor. I found myself trying hard not to stare, in case she caught me and thought my attention was for her and not the garment she wore. The entire battalion of Valkyries filed in and marched behind Freya. By some fortunate turn of events, I was positioned just to the right of the Sleipnir she rode, the best place to admire her golden robes.

We reached the castle where the new Warriors were led into Odin's Hall along with the Valkyries. Sigrun and I exchanged looks of surprise. The Warriors we'd retrieved just days before were also gathered within the hall. I was relieved to see that, though they looked tired, they were in good health. From the looks of it, they would commence their training soon.

Freya walked up to the dais where another throne now sat beside Frigga's. She seated herself with sheer grace, her expression so serene and demure it was hard to imagine she was capable of being the passionate Warrior that she was.

"This seems to be all wrong," Sigrun hissed beside me.

"What's wrong?'

"Firstly, Freya is never late. Secondly, the untrained Warriors are never presented to her. She only ever wants to see the trained *einherjar*."

Sigrun's discomfort put me on edge. I scanned the hall for Astrid. She was easy to spot. I glimpsed familiar wings and armor, and her position at Freya's side didn't surprise me. I hadn't yet met the goddess Freya in person, but already I wasn't entirely sure I'd be a fan. Not when she gave privileges to the likes of Astrid.

I waited with the rest of the audience, though not with the same bated breath as the rest of them.

"Goddess Freya, your people are gathered here to welcome you home for the Choosing." Odin's voice boomed around the Hall. He inclined his head to his wife. "The goddess Frigga is ready to aid your choice."

The two women conferred, and so began the Choosing. The gathered Warriors were inspected and discussed, with Frigga frequently leaning over to comment. Soon Freya had amassed her half of the Warriors, who stood ready and proud before the dais.

Then Freya rose and walked off the dais toward her regiment. In a well-orchestrated move, the Warriors lowered themselves onto their left knees and awaited their leader's blessing. Once done, she moved toward the Valkyries assembled on the other side, giving us the once over.

When she paused before me, the amber pendent at my neck grew warm. So warm that it burned a cold fire against my skin.

Freya stared, her eyes drawn to pendant. When her gaze rose to meet mine, I shivered. Her eyes were now the same amber shade as the gem around my neck.

"What is your name, child?" Her voice was soft and gentle, with no trace of menace or anger behind it.

"Bryn Halbrook." I felt slightly off balance, unsure if I should curse or bow or refer to her as Majesty or ma'am.

"Well, Brynhildr, it seems you possess something that belongs to me." Freya's eyes sparkled, glimmerings of gold gathered at the corners.

"I'm not sure what you mean." I was more shocked than defensive.

"We will discuss this later, my dear. I will call for you." I met her cold eyes and tamped down a shudder. Somewhere within the depths of her eyes lay a frigid soul. Those glowing golden teardrops in her eyes were nothing but cold gold. With those words, she swept away, back to the dais.

She remained standing, clearly not done with her speech.

"It would be remiss of me not to thank those who have helped to care for and train my Warriors," she said. "To the Valkyries, my strong women warriors. And to Fenrir and his remarkable team, for honing them into powerful and strong soldiers who can help defend the House of Odin." A resounding cheer went up, from Warriors old and new, Freya's and Odin's. And from the Valkyries too.

"And this brings me to a decision that I have made just this morning. I usually only make the Choosing from the trained Warriors. But sometimes, I see a Warrior who is so worthy that it really does not matter if he is not fully healed or fully trained. It does not happen often, but today there is one Warrior whom I want. With the All-Father's blessing, of course."

Odin nodded, forehead creased, no doubt curious about what Freya was up to. He didn't seem to think anything untoward was going on as he granted her request. Freya turned to the audience, silencing the whispered questions buzzing around like a little swarm of curious bees. "The Warrior I have chosen is so new to Valhalla that he is still recovering, so I will go to him."

Sigrun shuffled beside me. Was this another one of Freya's departures? I met Sigrun's eyes and raised a questioning brow. She gave a slight shrug, but her eyes held concern. Sigrun suspected something was amiss. And I couldn't deny that my own heart was slamming against my breastbone.

Freya didn't walk. She glided. The trailing ends of her long gilded dress glittered in the torchlight. Her cheeks shimmered where golden dust covered the skin, and her face remained regal, untouched. She paused before the small rank of Warriors, looking straight at Joshua, who didn't flinch. He just held his ground with his chin confidently forward. But the little vein at his temple, hidden by a curl of his hair, told me he would not be fainting from excitement if she chose him.

She didn't. Freya moved on to Aimee. I hadn't realized until then how tall Aimee actually was. In fact, she was taller than Joshua, standing upright and strong. Stronger than I'd ever known her to be. Aimee had been sick since before I arrived in Craven. I honestly didn't think I'd ever seen Aimee's complexion as anything but a pale and pasty white, or her eyes anything besides huge and almost popping out of her head.

She'd always been weak and incredibly thin, the cancer

virtually eating her from inside out. But now she stood strong, her eyes like a smoldering fire, her stance saying don't-mess-with-me. She too remained calm during Freya's inspection, no indication at all of how she felt about being taken so soon. When Freya nodded and moved on, Aimee released a pent up breath. So she had been stressing after all.

When Freya stopped before Aidan, a familiar creeping sensation trailed down my back. I turned to Astrid, still standing beside Freya's empty seat in mute silence. Just in time to catch a venomous, yet triumphant, sneer from her before she masked her emotions.

I stopped breathing and the thumping in my chest threatened to break a rib. Freya smiled at Aidan and raised her hand. Which he took and bowed over to kiss. Great, where did he learn gallantry? Freya smiled at his tousled head bowed over her hand.

When he rose, she grasped his arm and said, "You, Aidan Lee, are my chosen Warrior."

CHAPTER 30

I wanted to faint and cry and scream all at the same time. I didn't understand exactly what Freya's Warriors did, where they went or what interaction they would have with their fellows in Asgard. But the moment she stood before him and smiled that smile of pure seduction, I knew Aidan was doomed.

The ceremony drew to a close as Freya and her Warriors, including Aidan, left the Hall in what should have been a pretty upbeat procession. To me it was nothing more than a death march.

"Well, at least he didn't much look like he was disturbed by her choice. In fact, he looked pretty entranced by her," I said to Sigrun, unable to hide my bitterness.

She patted my shoulder. "That is the power of Freya. She entrances men with her eyes, seduces them with their own dreams."

"Take it you don't have much love for her?"

"Well, she is my *boss*, as you say. But she always has her own agenda."

"So what's her agenda now? Why'd she take Aidan?"

"From the looks of it Aidan has nothing that Freya needs. Except you."

I looked up from nervously picking at a cuticle. "Me? She's using Aidan against me?"

"So it appears." Sigrun frowned. "But how would she even have known there was any connection between you two?"

"Er . . . I should have told you, but I didn't want to worry you. Don't look so suspicious. When you left me with Aidan in Valhalla, he kissed me."

"He kissed you? So what? Did you kiss him back?" She leaned closer. I couldn't believe she wanted details at a time like this.

"Of course I did," I said. "It's not like we haven't kissed before. He's my boyfriend. Was. My boyfriend. Sort of. I mean, we were together, in love. Anyway, I think someone saw us?"

"What? But we were so careful. Who saw you?"

"I can't be entirely certain, but it looked like Astrid. Or rather, my gut tells me it was her. It was just a suspicion until Freya chose Aidan. That's just way too coincidental." Not to mention the look of supreme satisfaction on Astrid's face.

"So that is what she meant on the field this morning."

"You heard that?"

"Yes, I heard, but I did not understand. You know what it is like to only hear part of the conversation."

"Yup." I sure did; I sighed inwardly, thinking of the time I'd eavesdropped on Aidan and Ms. Custer. "So, what now? What are we supposed to do?"

Worry crept into Sigrun's eyes. "Freya told you she wanted to talk to you. She will call you to her before she leaves."

"So I'm just supposed to sit around and wait?"

"Yes. You can try to order a goddess around if you wish. Personally I would look out for my own neck first. Then my heart."

I DIDN'T HAVE TOO long to wait. Just a night of tossing and turning. When Turi brought breakfast the next morning, it came with a little message. A small scroll lay next to a goblet of Mead. At my questioning look Turi said, "The Mead is for your injuries from your training yesterday, and the message is from the goddess Freya."

"But I wasn't hurt. . . ." Turi was bustling about pretending not to hear me at all.

I downed the Mead. Not only for its rejuvenating sweetness, but for the little rush of peace that came with each swallow. Who would have thought of peace and tranquility as a drug? Just imagine what would happen if some Earthly genius figured out how to make Mead. Instant euphoria. All medical cures would be incidental and gratis. Sure.

I stared at the roll of paper. Did I truly want to read her message? I wasn't sure what Freya was up to. At last, I steeled myself and grasped the scroll with two fingers, my blood thrumming in my head. I smoothed the paper open and read a request for my attendance, after breakfast, in Odin's Hall. That was it. Not even a signature. Only the golden edges of the paper implied that Freya might be the sender.

Right. Still no idea what Her Haughtiness wanted. Guess I'd find out soon enough. I finished breakfast and dressed alone. Turi had snuck out quietly before I'd opened the note. Perhaps it was better I was alone anyway. I wasn't the best company right now. Filled with anger and frustration. I wasn't sure what I'd do or say.

I'd thought, for a short while, that I'd begun to make my own choices, to live my life the way I wanted to. Being a Valkyrie meant the ability to help people. Even if I was just a nicer looking, living version of Charon, the boatman of the river Styx.

But had I really ever had control of my choices, swept along on the tide of this unbelievable fantastical world? I wished it were all a dream. Here again, I was hooked; Freya was just reeling in her catch. What would she want from me?

I CHARGED INTO THE HALL, my eyes darting around for my summoner.

"If you are looking for your lover, my dear, he is not here." Freya's voice was a silken thread, weaving around me.

I walked to the dais, bristling. "He is not my *lover*!"

"Mere semantics, my dear." Freya smiled and beckoned me toward the dais. "Come closer, child. I will not bite."

Well, I'm not so sure about that.

I moved forward and met the eyes of the goddess. Well, I would have looked her in the eye if her attention hadn't been on my neck. The pendant glimmered brightly. Strange. That was the second time it had done that. The first time was only yesterday, when Freya came to speak to the Valkyries.

Now, with her eyes trained on the jewel, I steeled myself against a shiver. She dragged her gaze away and said, "I think my choice of Aidan as one of my Chosen does not make you very happy."

I shrugged, not wanting to let her know how unhappy I truly was.

"Well, perhaps then we have nothing to discuss." Her eyes darkened. My nonchalance had angered her. Or maybe she'd thought she had more power to manipulate me with Aidan in her possession.

I wasn't too sure what to say. Should I beg for his freedom? Or just leave? What was the worst that could happen anyway? Aidan would just be out of my life forever. Again. Not something I wasn't used to. He'd betrayed me, lied to me. I shouldn't really give a damn what happened to him.

My silence filled the hall. All I heard was my hushed breathing and the nervous flutter of the wings at my back. Freya glared, and I felt an enormous pressure to speak. "What do you want? In return for Aidan?" My voice rang out, each syllable echoing around the hall like little explosions.

She smiled, satisfied. I knew I'd given in. Even gritted my teeth for backing down. But I didn't care. She wanted something and I was damned if I couldn't figure out what it was.

"Well, Brunhilde. You still have the same spirit." She nodded to herself.

"My name is Bryn. I'm not Brunhilde." The words spewed out before I could stop them, but it only amused the goddess. She laughed and the eerie peal of distant bells echoed.

"Ah, my child. Whether you accept the truth now or later in life, it shall not change who and what you are." Her eyes narrowed. "Are the dreams not enough confirmation?"

She saw the shock in my face and smiled, satisfied she was right.

"Never mind that," she said. "What is important is what you can do to obtain your lover's freedom." She walked to me so smoothly, as if she floated just above the ground. "I believe you do not know this, but you have something that belongs to me."

She towered over me again, and this time she reached for the pendant and grasped the amber orb, closing her eyes. Pure bliss radiated from her face. When she opened her eyes, both orbs glowed an amber that mirrored the pendant.

"Brisingamen!" She sang the word, a sweet joy emanating from her voice.

Although startled, recalling my earlier conversation with Sigrun, I kept my silence. I wanted to know more.

"If it is true you cannot remember the first time you lived, Brynhildr, then I will have to tell you something." Her voice deepened, intensified. "A long, long time ago, I lost a precious treasure. Something so close to my heart that I withstood the terrible things spoken about me, just to keep it safe. It was Brisingamen. The Circle of Suns. Called this because of the amber gems set in gold. The most beautiful treasure in all the world."

She began to pace as she told the story. "I chose the best Valkyrie I could find, the bravest, the most courageous. Brunhilde." Her eyes bored into mine. "I asked that she find Brisingamen for me," Freya continued, "and she took that vow, pledging to search the ends of the earth to find it. But she never came back. It was much later that we discovered she had been killed. Now, do you not think it is a strange coincidence to find this pendant on your neck?"

"This pendant?" I was flustered. The words came out shaky and confused.

"This pendant you are wearing is the main jewel of the Brisingamen. Where did you find it? Who gave this to you?" I couldn't understand the pent up emotion I sensed within her words. Was it a furious rage that she held at bay?

"It was sent to me by father's trustees," I said.

"Trustees?"

"My father died in an . . . accident when I was thirteen. The lawyers were instructed to send this to me when I turned sixteen, but I moved around a lot and I only received it just before I came to Asgard."

"Where did your father . . . ah, I see. He no doubt found Brisingamen where he found Brunhilde's body. I have heard the tale of Brunhilde's remains being unearthed, and how that discovery resulted in you." She turned on her heel, triumphant in her deduction and seemingly more confident now. "That must mean he knew where to find my precious Brisingamen. And that means you will find it for me."

I didn't follow the logic, but I said nothing.

"So, if you want your Aidan back, then find me the remaining jewels of Brisingamen, put them together, and bring it to me."

I raised my hand to unhook the pendant from my neck. She said, "No, keep it. It will keep you safe while you search, and it will help you find the rest. The amber jewels talk to each other. Now go. And do not come back without it."

I hesitated, then turned to leave the room. Under different circumstances, I'm sure I would have bowed and made vocal promises, but seeing as this mission wasn't my choice I didn't feel much like thanking her or bowing and scraping.

My hand pressed against the door when she called out, "Oh, and Brynhildr?" I turned. "Don't forget to take your lover with you."

I swallowed my gasp, but my expression of surprise was harder to contain. She'd just said I wouldn't get him back unless I got Brisingamen for her.

"Aidan will accompany you on your journey," Freya said. "I believe you may need his knowledge to retrieve my special jewel. Of course, it is not as simple as just walking out of Asgard again, my dear. Aidan shall be cursed."

She lifted her chin; her eyes, now molten gold, pierced mine, triumphant. "The moment he sets foot out of Asgard, he will begin to die. Each day away will take a little bit of life out of him, returning him to the corpse he was before he entered Odin's holy city. The longer you take to return, the further he will disintegrate. If you take more than a week to return Brisingamen, I will not be able to remove the curse."

I was somewhere between thrilled and horrified. Aidan would be released from his tenure with Freya temporarily, but if we didn't find Brisingamen and return in time, I would have sentenced him to death. A thousand troubled thoughts whirled in my brain, and I closed my eyes. When I opened them, intending to ask Freya if I could talk to Aidan first, the goddess had vanished.

I stood there in the silent hall, listening to the shadows laugh at my predicament.

Aidan's life was now well and truly at stake.

CHAPTER 31

As I turned to leave, dejected, disappointed and deathly afraid, the flapping of wings caught my attention. One of Odin's ravens flew at me. My hand shot up instinctively to protect my face, in case the bird was bent on clawing my eyes out.

It landed on my arm. Then, with another flutter, it jumped onto my shoulder. Craning my neck around, I stared the bird in the eye. If I shooed it away, would it decide it was now time to peck out my eyes? The raven tilted its head back and returned the stare.

An impasse, it seemed. Perplexed I looked around. We were not alone. Odin, in the shape of the old, hooded man, sat within his great throne.

Damn it. Do you guys have to keep appearing and vanishing all the time? Someone ought to tie little bells around your necks so we can hear you coming!

I smothered my thoughts, crossing my fingers and hoping the gods didn't have mind-reading powers.

Odin smiled and said, "He is my gift to you on your journey. He will be your guide and he will warn you of danger." Then Odin looked away, as if his thoughts were elsewhere. "His name is Hugin. Bring him back safely, Brynhildr."

I nodded then gave a deep bow. When I rose, Odin waved me away and I left in silence, the raven still perched on my shoulder.

I wasn't sure where to go then. Back to my room to dwell on my fears? To Valhalla to talk to Aidan? To find Sigrun or Fen? To the pet store, if Asgard had one, to buy whatever pet ravens ate?

"Do you talk, like a parrot?" I asked the bird. The raven blinked but said nothing.

I found myself walking along the path. Perched on my shoulder, Hugin drew stares, but I hardly noticed. Trusting my feet, I fell into thinking about Freya and her mission. How well she'd arranged the situation so I'd have everything to lose by taking the mission.

The amber was warm, but of no comfort. The jewel had lost its power to give me strength and solace when I'd discovered it belonged to Freya. Just something about her made my skin crawl, and now, so did the jewel. I wanted to rip the thing from my neck but was deathly afraid that even the smallest thing I did wrong might endanger Aidan's life further.

The raven shifted its weight, as if disturbed by my inner turmoil. His talons poked through the chainmail and touched my skin, but since they didn't hurt I didn't need to swat him away.

Soon I found myself before Njall's door, heat lapping at my face. Pushing the door in, I searched the darkness for the smith. He appeared like a troll or an ogre, back lit by the blazing fire, a huge misshapen monstrosity.

Then his face emerged from the darkness and he smiled that big welcoming smile I didn't even know I'd been looking for. His grin widened when he saw the raven on my shoulder. "Hugin!" he exclaimed. "Odin has honored you, Brynhildr. How may I be of service?"

After I explained my mission, we spent an hour picking out small weapons that Aidan and I could easily conceal on our bodies when we returned home. And talking. Soon I forgot the purpose of my visit and just enjoyed the company and the warmth of the fire.

THIS TIME my trip to Valhalla was totally legitimate. The doors even opened for me as I passed the golden tree. Inside, the hall was alive with people, so unlike the night Sigrun and I had snuck in. All the newly retrieved Warriors looked well, though Aidan was still relegated to the recuperation area.

"Bryn! What are you doing here?" His eyes goggled at the sight of Hugin on my shoulder, and he wasn't the only one. Guess it wasn't every day that Hugin left his post at the All-Father's shoulder to take up residence on another's. *Must mean I'm special.* My presence drew attention, but nobody ran at us with swords to drive me away. I relaxed and so did Aidan.

"I need to talk to you about Freya," I said.

"Sure, come have a drink." We chose a seat at the end of a long table filled with boisterous men. With the surrounding racket, I was fairly certain we could speak privately. Well, almost privately. I glanced again at Hugin and wondered how much he understood.

Aidan coughed, prompting me to say, "Freya made a deal."

"A deal?" He reached for two goblets on a tray, brought by a young girl who bore an uncanny resemblance to Turi.

I waited until she was out of earshot, then touched my pendant. "She said this jewel is from a necklace that belongs to her. It's called Brisingamen."

Aidan nodded. "I've heard of it."

"She also said I have to find it and return it to her."

"Why would she want you to do that?"

"Because it was the Valkyrie Brunhilde's task to find Brisingamen and return it to Freya all those years ago. And she thinks Brunhilde found the necklace. But she was killed before she could return it."

Aidan bent forward and lifted the warm gem off my neck. Hugin ruffled his wings and I tensed for a moment, hoping he wouldn't peck at Aidan's hand. Aidan frowned and said, "I've seen this before. Or something like it."

"Where? Aidan, I really need to find this necklace. And I need your help to do it. If you know anything, please, tell me." I shivered. I really didn't want to tell him about Freya's curse on him. I ignored it for now. "I need to leave as soon as possible," I said. "I've got one week to find it and be back here or I'm so dead."

Aidan stared at me. I could almost see his mind turning my

words over, analyzing them before deciding what his next option was.

"Will you come with me?" I whispered as another serving girl walked by, tray laden with food.

He fidgeted, picking at a hangnail. Finally he said, "Sure. Probably need the change of scenery right now. I still have no idea what the hell I'm doing here."

We hadn't had a proper chance to talk since he arrived. I wasn't sure if he'd had anyone clue him in on what a Warrior's roles and responsibilities were. I reached across the table for his hand. "What do you know so far? About why you are here?"

"We had one of the Warriors come talk to us. Tell us all about the *einherjar* and the Valkyries. Valhalla." Aidan laughed. "None of this is supposed to be real, you know."

I withdrew my hand. "Really? Is that why your decision to terminate was negative?" It was nasty to throw this in his face right now, when I needed his help so much, but hurt overruled a commonsense sales pitch.

He flushed, taking a drink from his goblet to hide his reaction. "Guess you studied the book."

"Yeah. It was certainly interesting reading," I said, my vocal chords strained. Then I thought of something. "Did you leave it behind on purpose?"

He stared at me, eyes clear, and amidst the testosterone-induced din surrounding us, I felt the magnetic pull between us. Felt the attraction that had made me throw caution to the air and open my heart to a guy for the first time. It had only gotten me betrayal and heartache, but here it was again.

He ignored my question and asked one of his own: "When do

we leave?" Startled, I glanced at his face, checking if he was serious. Was he really choosing to come with me?

He half-sighed, half-laughed at my reaction. "Don't look at me like that," he said. "What did you think? I'd leave you to go back and find the necklace without me? I have access to records, names of the people involved in the dig, lists of items retrieved. You name it, I can probably access it. You'd be lost without me."

Suddenly it clicked. "Your father?"

Aidan nodded, his face darkening, as if the mere mention of his father pulled a cloud over his emotions.

"Okay," I said. "Let me check with Fen to see how we can arrange this. I'll get a message to you as soon as I know what the deal is."

As I rose from the seat and turned to leave, Aidan grabbed my hand. I ignored the spike of heat that rippled up my arm and the shifting of Hugin's weight on my shoulder, and raised a questioning eyebrow.

"Thank you," said Aidan.

"What for?" I asked, puzzled.

"For retrieving me. It seems right . . . that you were the one to bring me here."

Guilt welled in my throat. Not only had I brought him here to serve the gods, disturbing his rest, but now I was lying to him. Convincing him to come with me to find the necklace without revealing one crucial fact.

Aidan's life hung by the filigree thread of a goddess's trinket.

CHAPTER 32

The jump from Asgard to Craven only took a few seconds, though still accompanied by the usual nauseous twisting in my belly. We materialized in bright moonlight and kept to the shadows as we walked up Elm Wood. The last thing we needed was for Ms. Custer to switch the veranda lights on and for Anna's nosy mother to see us enter the house this late. Who knew what the gossip would be then?

Aidan waited beside the bushes in front of the veranda in full view of the front door. The position was convenient. The veranda light would reach the shadow of the tree and only she would see us.

I ran to the door, stabbed the doorbell with one stiffened finger and sprang back to the shadow of the tree. Inside the darkened house the doorbell chimed, a hollow echo that was a bit on the spooky side. Soon Ms. Custer cracked open the door, staring outside, bleary-eyed and perplexed.

"Mom," I whispered, drawing her attention. Her eyes

widened as she saw me, and a smile stretched across her face. A smile that died a quick death. At first, I assumed it was Hugin she'd seen. I'd gotten used to the constant weight of the bird on my shoulder. But her eyes settled instead on Aidan beside me. Concern wrinkled her face. I nodded toward the side of the house, pointing a curved hand in the direction of the backyard. She silently mouthed the word "okay" and closed the door, flicking the light off.

We shuffled in the shadows, keeping to the edges of the house, and made it around to the back without incident. The door opened to reveal Ms. Custer, broom in hand, looking very much like my own personal avenging angel. She stared Aidan down. He hesitated then entered, passing her slowly, having the grace to flush a decent shade of red.

She didn't switch on any lights. Just put the kettle on and drew out cups and plates for tea and cake. The light from the street lamp outside cast a yellow glow through the large windows, enough light for us to get by. The cups and spoons clanked and clattered softly until at last Ms. Custer sat before us, staring from my face to Aidan's.

"What's going on?" she asked, her voice steady. Too steady. Her eyes flicked toward the raven and then back to me.

"We need a place to stay," I said.

"How long?"

Aidan answered, and I wished he hadn't. "Just tonight. We'll be gone tomorrow," he said. The look Ms. Custer sent him was blistering enough to fry an egg on his forehead.

"You have a lot of explaining to do, young man." She was angry but she still kept her voice low, controlled.

"I'm sorry, Ms. Custer. I know I deceived you. All of you." He looked at me, apologetic, shame-faced, still flushing.

I held my tongue, knowing if I spoke, all that would come out of my mouth was snark. I did plan to tell him how I felt. Soon. But now, sitting in the dark at Ms. Custer's kitchen table, whispering secrets about places and people that just shouldn't exist . . . well, now was not the best time.

I turned to Ms. Custer, who was the one who really needed an explanation. Unsure of how much I should say, I glanced at Hugin, wondering if I should ask his advice, but he avoided my eyes and just stared at Ms. Custer, a message to say I was on my own. Probably not a big enough issue for him to assist with. I decided winging it was my only option.

I took a deep breath and quickly ran through what happened since I'd left her more than a week ago: how Aidan had been left for dead by the stream and how I'd retrieved him, and how we'd been sent back to find the rest of the necklace. I left out the part in which the unpredictable goddess Freya had given me a deadline and Aidan's life hung in the balance.

"Okay." She sipped her tea and stared at its contents as if about to read tealeaves.

The silence was potentially damning.

"If I didn't trust you, Bryn, and if you didn't have a big ol' raven on your shoulder, I'm not sure I'd believe any of this," she said at last. "As long as you stay and leave without drawing attention to yourselves, it's fine by me. But remember, either of you do anything to endanger my kids, and you are out. They don't need any more upsets."

My heart tightened and I asked softly, "How are they?"

"They miss all three of you."

"I wish it could have been different," I said.

And it was the truth. It had been so easy to crave a new life, but when you're handed one straight from ancient mythology, it's a lot harder than just saying thank you and moving on. But given the chance to have things back to the way they were before, I would refuse. New possibilities had opened up for me. The hole left inside me after Joshua's death was easier to bear knowing he was still alive and meant for better things. Meant to make a difference to Midgard in the end. Brody and Aimee too. The part of me that had suffered in enforced silence ever since I'd begun to see the auras, no longer suffered. I no longer felt guilty for being unable to stop all those people from dying.

"At least you're still alive." Ms. Custer smiled brightly, clearly searching for the silver lining in our dark and crazy story. I couldn't respond to her without wanting to cry.

Aidan's days were numbered and he didn't know it. And who knew whether Freya would be happy with just taking his life as punishment if I didn't bring her Brisingamen?

"Well, you can have your old rooms back, just keep the blinds down and drapes closed." With that, she rose, rinsed her cup and saucer and placed them on the draining board. She stared out the window at the waning moon, just days past full. Did she see a parallel between that bright white disk and our farfetched tale? She sighed, then said goodnight and went up to bed.

The kitchen door swung back and forth, and I watched her retreating figure through the gap each time it swung into the dining room beyond. At last the door stilled and I looked back at the shining moon. I had a week. That moon's progress would mark the number of days left before I had to return with the necklace. The number of days left of Aidan's life.

UNEASY DREAMS HAUNTED MY SLEEP, and from the looks of Aidan the following morning, he'd been doomed to a similar fate. Dark bruises curved beneath red-rimmed eyes. I'd waited to rise until Izzy and Simon had left for school. It didn't seem right to disturb their routine when I planned on heading out this very morning. Unsure of when we would return, I didn't want to excite the kids, get them thinking we might be sticking around.

Aidan's actions mirrored mine, but he had no idea of the real urgency of this mission. We had breakfast in the kitchen, with Ms. Custer bustling about and serving pancakes and coffee. Hugin perched atop an empty chair while I ate. It was strange. I hadn't spent long in Asgard and yet I'd gotten so used to the routine of the day. Even pancakes tasted different. And Aidan's expression said he'd noticed it too.

"You will want your book then?" Ms. Custer asked. I looked up, expecting her to be speaking to Aidan, but my eyes met hers as she deliberately ignored his right of possession.

I nodded and followed her, grabbing the last pancake from my plate, trailing her upstairs to her nightstand. She fiddled with a small panel, then pulled it forward to reveal a secret drawer. The hiding place was so ingenious that the investigators had missed it when they'd searched the house. She placed it in my hands.

"I read some of it," she said, surprising me "You've inherited a bit of a job, my dear." Then she hugged me tight, and I held on as hard as I could. "Be safe, Bryn. Don't do anything stupid, okay?"

Soon after, we said goodbye and headed out the back way, taking the tree-lined pathways behind the houses and into the woods. Hugin returned to my shoulder, his weight now comfortable and familiar. Hidden beneath the trees, we paused to get our bearings. On the other side of the hill stood a small group of shops—a tourist stop for hunters and trampers on their way into the mountains.

"I'll go down," Aidan said. "Buy a cell phone. Should take me ten minutes tops. Stay right here."

I bristled. He seemed to think he was in charge. But just when I was ready to tell him where to get off, guilt raised its ugly head again and laughed at me. And I shut my mouth. It didn't matter. Let him take the lead. I owed him that much. Besides, we were most certainly not in a battle of wills. I had nothing to prove. Aidan, on the other hand, still had to prove his loyalty.

I stood in the shadow of a large tree and watched him slide down the steep incline toward the road. He crossed to the curio shop and emerged minutes later bearing a small bag. The trip up the hillside took twice as long, and only when he was standing beside me, tearing the plastic off a disposable cellphone, did I let go of my breath.

He rang the bus company, checking to see if we were near any bus routes. We had to avoid public places, where Aidan would be spotted, a dead man still alive, or where I'd be seen, probably with that APB still out on me. A shoulder-borne raven would no doubt attract unwelcome attention, too. Unfortunately, the nearest route went right through the center of the town, so we had to scratch the bus idea.

"Too bad you can't fly," Aidan quipped. His eyes darted to Hugin and back, then widened. "Can you fly?"

"No. I haven't learned that yet, and I'm not so sure I want to. Besides, we would draw a certain amount of attention, you know —a winged woman flying through the air carrying a guy."

Aidan grinned, and in that second I was reminded why I'd let him into my heart so quickly. That cheeky grin and those smiling eyes. I smiled back, and for that moment, everything was right with the world. It would all work out. I had absolutely nothing to worry about. Until he blinked and I blinked and the moment was gone.

"What do we do now?" I said.

"We need a ride out of this town. And a ride under the radar." When I frowned, he added, "We can't be traced. They'll be watching Craven for any suspicious activity in the area, so we can't make a move while it's light."

"Guess we have a good wait ahead of us, then?" The sun threw tepid warmth on our heads. I raised an eyebrow, wondering where we could possibly hide until nightfall.

"Yes, ma'am. Let me lead you to your lodgings." Aidan beckoned me with a flourish of his hand, leading me into a dense stand of trees. In this isolated part of town we were pretty safe, so I settled on the ground, my seat a cushion of thick autumn leaves.

Along with the cellphone, Aidan had bought a tiny bag of Doritos. He popped the bag and took a handful, then tossed the rest to me. "*Bon appétit.*"

To pass the time, I pulled the leather volume out of my bag.

Aidan didn't react. I ignored him, reading and snacking until he fell into a deep sleep. The sun dropped behind the trees, and darkness drew long shadows over the sleepy town. I let him rest, wondering how long it would take for Freya's curse to begin to wear him down.

He woke after midnight to the metallic tune of the alarm on his cellphone. Guess he had the forethought to set an alarm. He cleared his throat. "We'd better see about a car, then."

"So how do we get—" I started to say. Then an idea struck me. One that filled me with guilt, but ultimately it was our best option. The thought of doing something illegal appalled me, but this did count as desperate times.

"Bryn?" Aidan nudged me.

"Lots of kids in the area have cars or bikes they don't use too often."

He chuckled. "My, my, Bryn. That's not the most legal thought you've ever had, is it?"

I flushed, still shocked and now embarrassed. Hugin shifted his feet, as if sharing my unease.

"Not a bad idea though," Aidan said. "It might be our ticket out of Craven."

"Or we could ask Ms. Custer for her car?" I backed away from the thought of stealing a vehicle, wishing I'd never even mentioned it.

"No, they'd be watching her car. We want to avoid drawing any attention to Ms. Custer. Wait here. Watch for me." He pointed down at the roadside.

I knew he was going to jack a car. It had been my idea, and though I was relieved he wanted to spare me the experience, I couldn't let him go alone. This was my burden to bear and he was just caught up in Freya's little power play.

I called after him, whispering as loud as I could, "Wait. Aidan, hold on."

He turned and watched me catch up with a frown furrowing his clean brow. A memory of the bullet wound that had blasted his forehead open and marred that perfect skin triggered a shudder.

"I'm coming with you," I said. "This is my problem too."

"Be my guest. I just thought I'd save you the trouble."

I got you into this mess, no way am I letting you shoulder all the responsibility.

We fell into step beside each other and walked back to the suburb, silence hanging over us. Voices traveled farther at night, and we couldn't trust that we were passing through the area unobserved. Two a.m. in the morning and the homes were all dark. Aidan made a move to walk down the first driveway.

"No. That's Mr. Ralston's property," I whispered. "He's got one of those really vicious dogs. Rottweiler or something."

"Good thing you came along, then." He smiled. "So who doesn't have vicious, man-eating dogs?"

I nodded at a house across the road. Pete's house. Certainly would be fitting if it were his vehicle we jacked. We crept round back, keeping to the shadows again. Thankfully, huge, leafy trees filled Pete's garden and yard. The garage door was unlocked. I eased it open, and a strip of moonlight lit the inside of the garage, reaching silvery fingers as far as the driver's side of Pete's classic Lincoln Continental. Most of the kids in Craven had classics, probably handed down through the decades.

But my thoughts weren't on the beautiful car. My mind raced back among the shadows on the frozen path, with my cheek on fire and my abdomen in agony. My jaw was rigid. Images of Pete's attack ran through my head. All I could think about was lashing out at something, and the car seemed the most suitable option.

Aidan's voice and a soft squawk from Hugin broke the trance.

"You okay? You look upset. And about to punch something." His words held a smile, which oddly enough didn't anger me. It lightened my mood a bit. I unclenched my fist and leaned into the open window, scrabbling around the ignition for keys. Nothing.

"Looking for this?" Aidan indicated a rack of keys. He fished through them and withdrew one. I hoped it was the right one. We'd rather not wake Pete's family, so we'd have to roll the car out onto the drive and then onto the road before starting the engine.

The garage door was an ancient one: two large doors, which opened wide. I hadn't thought about what we'd do if it had been an automatic door. Way too noisy. We would have had to look for an easier car to steal.

I unhitched the door and eased one side open, going slowly and hoping it didn't creak. It didn't. Relieved, I kicked a brick in front of it and did the same with the other door.

Aidan got in, set the gear to neutral and got back out, holding onto the door, ready to push. "Get behind," he whispered.

I wondered who died and made Aidan the boss. Then I wanted to giggle. *He'd* died and I'd made him the boss. The joke was on me.

I did as he asked, and pushed.

The car rolled smoothly forward. We steered to the end of the drive, turned into the road and pushed it all the way to the corner, three houses from Pete's.

I thought about the garage door standing wide open like a gaping jaw. Pete was in for a surprise tomorrow morning. I'd never pegged myself as vindictive, and my little trip to Asgard had almost made me forget Pete's attack. But back here in Craven, staring at his car, the memory of that day seeped into my mind, crawling all the way into my bones. Shivers rippled through me. I jumped into the car.

Hugin flapped wildly, in such a crazed frenzy that I was afraid he'd either peck out my eye or scratch me with his sharp little talons. I let him fly out and watched as he ascended and circled above the car. Shaking my head, I shut the door as quietly as I could. The click of the lock echoed up and down the empty street. I shuddered, sure the cops would be on our tail in the next ten seconds.

Aidan jumped in and stabbed the key into the ignition. I held a breath and sent a prayer up to Odin. I breathed again only when the engine turned. It growled loudly and then settled into a low purr, waiting for Aidan to set it in motion. We drove off, leaving the sleeping neighborhood behind while I enjoyed imagining Pete's reaction when he discovered his car was gone.

CHAPTER 33

"So what's the plan? Where are we going?" The cracked blue leather squeaked with every move we made. Pete didn't take good care of his leather seats. The interior of the Lincoln was otherwise immaculate, even though it was probably made in the late sixties. They made cars well in the old days.

"Washington," said Aidan, tracing the soft blue leather of the huge steering wheel.

"State or DC?" I asked the dumb question even though it was clear we were on the old Route 66, heading east.

He raised an eyebrow. "DC. Rockville, Maryland, to be specific. The national hub of human gene research. We need to make a quick stop at the institute on the way to New York."

"The institute?"

My unhappy expression elicited a gravelly laugh. "Marlowe Institute of Genetic Science," he said.

I got the impression he'd said the full name just for effect. I shivered, remembering the Institute's emblem imprinted on the lab reports. The place where both our fathers had worked, competed and apparently hated each other enough for one of them to try to kill the other's daughter.

"I thought you said we have to stay under the radar? I'm not sure going into the lion's den is the best course of action when the point is to avoid said lion," I said dryly, staring straight ahead to study the dark Missouri night. I tried to stick my elbow on the low armrest, unsuccessfully.

"They have important records stored in their system. We'll have to risk it."

"How will we get in?" I stretched out, enjoying the legroom and marveling at my lack of tiredness. The chainmail chinked as I moved, reminding me that we were still clothed in our Asgard getup.

"I have a security pass."

I snorted. "You've been dead for a while. Don't you think they'd have deactivated your card by now?"

"I have my father's card."

"Oh." I looked at him, unsettled by the deadness of his voice, by the shadow that crossed his face. He'd been doing his father's bidding when he came to Craven, but the coldness in his voice when he mentioned his father sent a creeping shudder up my spine. "Well, I guess that will help. So, he's a genetic scientist, huh? Small world, hey? What exactly does he do at the institute?"

"He's in charge. Took over your father's role when he passed away." Aidan threw me a quick, apologetic glance before concentrating on the road again. Not that he needed to concentrate all that much. The road ahead was easy, just point and drive.

"Hey," Aidan said, "can that bird of yours keep up with us?" He squinted up at the sky.

Way to go on the swift change of subject, Biker-Dude. I rolled my eyes, shook my head, didn't bother to force the issue. Not yet.

Leaning forward I peered up at Hugin as he swooped in a circle, high above the car. I caught a glimpse of the raven when he crossed in front of the white-faced moon, bemused at the simple beauty of the bird, backlit by the pale moon.

But Aidan had a point. *Could* Hugin keep up with a car? He was no ordinary bird; he belonged to Odin, after all. And he'd made it pretty clear that he wasn't particularly fond of the Lincoln; he couldn't fly off fast enough. I shrugged. Nothing we could do now. We couldn't walk all the way to Maryland. Surely Hugin would keep up. We had to get to the institute, fast. Every minute wasted was a minute of Aidan's life gone, a minute closer to his last breath.

"So your dad's the boss now, huh?" I asked, determined to get my answers. "That's how he got his hands on those old reports."

"Yeah, he suspected your father was doing something odd right from the start."

I bristled, remembering that *I* was the thing he'd been suspicious of doing.

The road straightened, and Aidan gunned the engine. "After the DNA results came back negative, everything should have gone back to normal, but your father's investigations continued and my father became increasingly suspicious, so he looked at the files," he said. He paused, as if choosing his words carefully. "At that time, he couldn't find anything conclusive, but when your father passed away, he left a considerable amount of paperwork at the lab.

Incriminating paperwork." A bitter tone laced Aidan's voice. "He'd done blood tests on you when you were born. To investigate the level of nonhuman DNA in your blood at different stages of your life. Only three of them were ever performed."

"I still don't see the need to go right into the institute," I protested, glaring at him. "What's so all-fired important to risk our lives to go there?" The ticking time bomb that was Aidan's life filled my mind.

Aidan's hands gripped the steering wheel, tension radiating from him. "There are still vials of your blood stored in the lab freezer. Those vials are evidence of your existence, and I intend to remove them. No way am I leaving them any ammunition to use against you again."

"Oh," I said quietly.

He looked at me, his eyes pools of blackness in the night's shadows. When I said nothing and turned to stare at the blacktop racing at us from up ahead, he continued. "My father looked for you for a long time. The problem was you disappeared into the system when your father died, and he didn't have the connections to find out where you were. And when he eventually found out, it was always after the fact. You moved often enough to keep him just one step behind you."

I nodded. That's why the pendant had taken so long to find me, too.

Gazing outside, I watched Hugin as he flew above us. Apparently he could keep up just fine. Our very own sentinel. Just his presence up there made me feel safe.

"I'd always been interested in Norse mythology and my father had arranged for me to go to summer digs around the world,"

Aidan said. "I've been to the dig site where Brunhilde was unearthed. There's nothing there now. Everything was taken to New York, to the Neilsson Museum of Ancient History. That's our next stop after the institute."

"Don't tell me you worked for them, too?" I asked dryly.

"Actually I still work there. Well, until I died anyway." A self-deprecating and sad smile curved on his lips. "It'll take a while to get used to the whole being-dead-but-not-really-dead thing."

I wasn't sure what to say to that. I guessed it would be a bad time to remind him that the whole walking dead thing also applied to zombies. I bit back a smile, silently admonishing myself for those insensitive thoughts, and gazed out the passenger-side window. The silence felt endless. How do you make someone feel better about being dead?

A mile marker sign whisked by on my right. Then another. When I couldn't take the silence anymore, I asked, "What were you doing for the museum?"

He rubbed his eyes, then returned his hand to the steering wheel. "I was transcribing, and translating. That book you found? Many old books were found at the dig site. The book I had was a copy of one written by a Scottish professor of archaeology who'd gotten quite far with his translations. I was trying to do more of them, using scripts taken from the dig site."

My thoughts flicked to the back seat where my bag sat. Buried inside was the topic of this discussion. And although Ms. Custer had returned it to me, I hadn't given it back to Aidan yet. I needed more time. I still felt connected to the book, perhaps because it held within it a painting of me. A painting done hundreds of years before I'd even been born.

Neither had I told him that I'd completed the translations. I didn't want to tell him. Not yet. I felt like I'd negate all his hard work by admitting it took me only a couple of days to translate the whole thing, and correct his translations where he'd gone wrong.

It all made sense now, where the knowledge had come from.

Another long silence fell as the miles flew by and the milky moon slipped behind a cloud. "So how did you end up in Craven?" I finally got the nerve to ask.

"My father. He told me it was high time I proved myself. That I needed to make a decision as to which direction I was going with my studies. He showed me the reports and implied that if I were to be the one who discovered the existence of a real living Valkyrie I would gain international recognition and I would have my pick of Universities."

He sighed and glanced at me, his eyes apologetic and shadowed by . . . what? Regret? "I'm not proud of that lapse in judgment," he said. "My selfishness came to the fore. But the temptation to be the one to make that discovery . . . well, I took his offer. Then he sent me to Craven. All he wanted was someone who'd be able to fit in, at the foster home, at the school."

A quiver of anguish edged his voice, as if behind the pain a memory had come loose, fallen into the pool of his mind, causing rippling waves. I stayed silent. As much as I wanted to know more, I was tired and just a bit shell-shocked.

The ride seemed endless and felt like such a waste of all our precious minutes. I wished we'd had a plane or faster transport. I just wanted this whole escapade over and done with. We'd have to ditch the Lincoln soon, probably steal another one.

The hours slipped by and soon we'd traveled the whole night. I kept expecting sirens. The one time we heard them, I tensed and watched the rearview mirror until a police car passed us by and skidded onto a side road. By now, Pete would know his car was gone, but the Craven police chief would first want to rule out pranksters. We were already miles away, somewhere in south Illinois.

BEFORE MORNING HIT the horizon we slid off the highway into a nameless road and ditched Pete's car behind a dilapidated shed. It would have been so easy to dump it in the middle of a cornfield. Wrong season. Surrounding us were remnants of snow covered dark, furrowed soil, the land bare and waiting for the spring sowing. We borrowed another car from a nearby farmhouse. And got out of town.

Before we'd left Craven, Ms. Custer had handed me money. Which I refused to take until she explained it was mine. The trust had begun to execute my father's instructions, providing me with a monthly allowance, sent to Ms. Custer at my last known address. She alone knew where I'd gone, and she'd kept every cent in case I returned. *Thank you, Ms. Custer!*

At least we were now able to eat. And though we didn't need to stop to rest, common sense and a good dose of paranoia urged us to lie low during the day.

We spent the first day sleeping like the dead in a decrepit motel I was sure was the set of a bad horror movie. The sign outside proclaiming the hotel name was missing a few important bulbs, so the name was now *la Hell Motel* instead of Black Shell.

Threadbare brown-and-gold seventies carpets, intricately gouged furniture and a TV set bolted to the floor decorated the room. The shower stall looked clean, and I used it to get the grime off. The grime of lies and theft, of dishonesty and guilt, which seemed to have seeped into my pores beyond reach of scrubbing and soap.

Before I jumped into bed I nudged the curtains open a crack and spotted Hugin on a branch in a tree beside the parking lot. Good. I could cross "apologize to Odin for losing his raven" off my list of worries.

I dived under the covers, too afraid to inspect them, preferring to think positive. I plunged straight into a dreamless sleep, waking in the late afternoon as Aidan moved around the room trying not to wake me up. So much for stealth.

"We need food, for now and for the road," he said. "I'll go get something, you get ready."

I nodded, heading into the shower again, wondering when we'd fallen into the comfortable couple routine.

We ate an afternoon breakfast of bland chicken salad sandwiches and brown swill masquerading as coffee. Asgard's attempt to keep up with the influx of more modern Warriors by providing coffee had turned out better than what the real world had to offer. Unsatisfied but replete, we took to the road again right after sunset, the darkness hiding what scenery we could have enjoyed, but keeping us relatively safe. After a quick stop at a gas station, we were on the move again, night sky and stars watching our every move.

The roads were quiet, with only one other car behind us, a dark SUV, headlights low, keeping pace, seemingly heading east like us. A few hours later, our two-car caravan still sped toward Kentucky, the steady headlights behind us drawing closer. Too close.

A trucker zoomed by, way over the speed limit, advertising the latest technology in whitening toothpaste. Our stolen car rattled, and I gripped the armrest until the truck roared ahead. I checked the mirror and saw our SUV shadow had dropped back, put some distance between us. So I relaxed.

AGAIN, we didn't stop until dusk. The next motel was equally drab, equally depressing, somewhere off the expressway in West Virginia. Aidan stashed the car behind the motel, while I grabbed my bag and headed off to get us a room. As the gum-chewing, pink-haired, bored-out-of-her-mind clerk handed over the keys and mumbled about ice and keeping the noise down, Aidan moved past me and booked a second, adjoining room.

At first I felt hurt, my teen blood boiling at the insult, but my Valkyrie instinct reined me in. Something was up. A glance from Aidan confirmed my suspicions. He looked worried.

I left the office quietly and waited. Aidan popped out seconds later, a relaxed smile on his face that would have fooled anyone besides me.

We walked to the first room and entered in silence, with Hugin making a last minute landing on my shoulder. Puzzled, I watched as Aidan pointed to an inner door that led to the next room. He fiddled with the lock and it clicked open; then he hustled me into the other room, taking our bags with us, leaving the connecting door wide open.

Grabbing a notepad from the nightstand he scribbled a few lines, then handed it to me.

We've been followed. Will stay here. Return to other room, act normal, shower, change, etc. Leave bathroom window open, make them think we escaped the back way.

Icy hot chills ran up and down my spine. How did they find us? I ached to ask Aidan how he knew, but I bit my tongue as he beckoned me to go back to the other room. Hugin stayed behind, perched on the back of a chair. He twitched his head, agitated, as if sensing something was going on. But I couldn't tell him, and I was pretty sure he couldn't read Aidan's note, so I just hoped he'd behave.

We went about our normal routine, showered, then fluffed up the beds and rolled and stuffed a couple of rugs beneath the covers. I turned out the light and Aidan chained the door as well. Then he removed the light bulbs from the nightstand and the overhead lamp, to buy us time. Anyone breaking in would have to wait for their eyes to adjust to the darkness and shadows.

We ducked back into the other room, locked the inner door and left the lights off. The day was threatening to arrive full force, sunny but with a winter bite. The brighter it got the more dangerous it would be for our stalkers to act.

"They'll come soon," Aidan whispered. "Be ready." I nodded.

We didn't have to wait too long. Within ten minutes, a light scratching sound seeped through the door as they picked the lock. I picked Hugin up and set him on my shoulder again. We stood at the door to our second room, waiting for them to enter the first.

What if there weren't only two of them? What if only one of the thugs went into the room and the other saw us leave? My wings shivered behind me, invisible but still very much there. We'd have to take the risk and hope for the best.

They entered without speaking, pausing only to crowbar the safety chain. Two sets of footsteps, and a snick as they closed the door quietly behind them. Aidan cracked our room door open, nodded that the coast was clear. Hugin launched off my shoulder and soared over the parking lot. Aidan and I ran after him, dodging between cars and trucks until we reached the last line of parked cars.

Aidan tugged at door handles until one clicked open. We slid in. Before we closed the door, we heard shouting. They had discovered we'd gone. We watched through the car window as Worthington and his partner ran around the motel, searching the lot behind the building, cursing at each other.

"Get down," Aidan warned.

The two goons jumped into their SUV and swung around the back, following a small dirt road.

"How the hell did they find us?" I whispered, although I no longer needed to.

Aidan reached under the dashboard to hotwire the small Mazda we'd hidden in. The engine sputtered to life. "Don't know," he said. "Probably had someone watching Ms. Custer's place." Aidan's face was dark with fury and with something else. A certain hollowness. The sight threw reality into my face in one icy splash. He had started weakening. I'd have to keep a closer eye on him.

WE DIDN'T GO FAR. Just a couple of motels down the road, where we slept the day away, alternating shifts, constantly checking the window.

Back on the road, we took turns driving while Hugin kept pace high above us. The institute, which had seemed too far away when we left Craven, drifted closer and closer by the mile. By the time we reached the city, we were on to our third stolen car and our third day.

And Aidan had begun to show signs of fatigue. We stopped outside Rockville and I got Aidan to down a bit of Mead. The golden liquid rejuvenated him quickly enough, and though my mouth watered for a taste, the fear that we might run out of the precious liquid stopped me from drinking any.

We ditched the Mazda near a junkyard and walked through a deserted part of the town. A short while later we grabbed a bus into the central city, leaving the stolen car far behind.

So far we'd obeyed Fenrir's instructions not to remove any of our armor, but I just couldn't bear the thought of wearing my helmet wherever I went. I kept it with me, tucked safely within my bag. Fenrir had claimed the glamor that disguised us was foolproof, but he wasn't with us on this mission. Better safe than sorry. So we made a short detour, stopping to buy ankle-length coats, and boots to cover our leather-strapped feet. Our swords still hung from our hips, invisible beneath the glamor and our coats, ready to draw at the tiniest hint of trouble.

We needed a few more things. A quick visit to the convenience store and we left with the necessities: flashlights, gloves, flash drives, disposable cameras. Aidan bought a small cooler and fresh ice. Must be for the blood samples we were to retrieve.

Then we hid out at another motel, resting while the day passed. We'd have no chance in hell of escaping notice if we barged into the facility in broad daylight.

CHAPTER 34

ater that night, we hopped on a bus, got off a mile from the institute, and walked into the parking lot under cover of the darkness, breathing hard against the freezing December air.

Three stories of imposing red brick loomed ahead, its walls eerily lit by small spotlights hidden within the surrounding plant beds. Wings fluttered as Hugin flew down toward us. He'd followed the bus on an air current high overhead.

He landed on my shoulder and I shook him off. "Better for you to stay outside. In case we want to make a quick getaway. You're a bit heavy on a girl's shoulder, you know." He found a perch on a nearby sill, cocked his head and gave me a glassy-eyed blink.

We snuck around back, blood thundering in my ears as Aidan swiped his card. Images flew through my mind: alarms sounding, police swooping in, spotlights and helicopters. But nothing happened. Just the annoyed buzzing of a suicidal bug as it repeatedly flew into the dinner plate-sized light in the flowerbed nearest to us.

The little light in the security panel went from red to green and the door swished open. A darkened stairwell greeted us; emergency signs threw weak light onto the concrete stairs. I followed Aidan up to the third floor, and held my breath again as we left the stairwell and crept along a dark passage. The carpet absorbed the sound of our progress, but the various security cameras strategically placed along the way would be recording our progress for posterity. Or for Aidan's father.

We kept our heads down. I hoped our glamor was good enough to fool the cameras in case our entry was discovered and someone tried to identify the intruders. I trailed Aidan through a warren of passages until he paused at a set of double doors and swiped the card to release them.

Inside, the room was dark. We left it that way, using our flashlights to get around.

Aidan knew exactly where to go. He booted up the nearest workstation, keying in a password. While he waited, he went to a set of fridges at the back of the room, punched in another code and stared into the frigid interior, scanning row after row of labeled tubes of blood samples. At last he withdrew four tubes, shut the fridge and deposited them into the little cooler bag we'd bought.

"What are you going to do with them?"

"Get them out of here."

"I'd like to have them destroyed or thrown into the garbage," I said; the idea of my blood samples hanging around just creeped me out.

He nodded, but still sat the bag with the glass vials carefully on the floor. Why would he be so careful with it? The way he held the bag you'd think it contained some kind of lethal airborne virus or something. I snorted in silence as he returned to the computer. I leaned against a counter filled with vials and strange machines. With our flashlights switched off, darkness still shrouded most of the room, just the glare from the monitor and dials of various machines providing minimal light.

Among the deeper shadows of the room, in the far corner of the lab, a red spot glowed. It reminded me of a cigar. The spicy aroma teased my nostrils. I squinted. A shadow moved, ever so slightly. Instinct said scream but common sense countered with silence.

"I wouldn't scream if I were you," a man said, almost as if he could read my mind, and far too nonchalant for my liking.

Aidan's seat went rolling across the tiled floor, and he stood by my side in two seconds, staring at the shadow. "Who's there?"

"Oh, don't get your knickers in a knot." And he stepped from the shadows. He smiled. A mischievous smile, bordering on charming. An oily, practiced, all too self-aware charming.

"Who are you? How did you get in?" Aidan demanded. He'd locked the door behind us when we entered, a small precaution. Not wanting the open door to attract a curious late-night staffer. No other doors or windows offered entry. It seemed impossible that the intruder had been hiding in here in the shadows all along. Watching us.

"I can go where I wish, when I wish." He left the shadows, strolled toward us and had the audacity to blow cigar smoke at our faces and smile serenely. His bright blue eyes sparkled and white blond hairs stuck up in a multitude of angles at the top of his head. Broad-shouldered, tall and entirely too good looking to be trustworthy. His demeanor was designed to put us at ease, but I wasn't buying it. And it seemed, neither was Aidan. He tensed beside me.

"Who are you? And what do you want?" Anger edged Aidan's voice. Anger at this man who'd followed us here and who'd no doubt get us caught.

"Don't worry, my dears, I'm only here to help you." He affected a quick bow. "My name is Loki."

"Loki?" I blinked, first shocked then dismayed to discover who our stalker was. Even I knew the stories of Loki and all the nonsense he got up to. Aidan's hands curled into fists. I could almost feel the energy flow off his body.

"Don't look so excited to see me, Brynhildr." Loki seemed put out by my lack of enthusiasm.

"My name's Bryn," I shot back. "So how do you plan on helping us? And why?"

"I have an item which might be of interest to you." His eyes glittered.

The more he talked, the more the gem at my throat warmed beyond its usual comforting heat. Much like when I'd been close to Freya herself. I watched Loki, eyes narrowed, as he withdrew a small cloth package from his pocket.

He unfolded it, his hands graceful, mimicking those of a magician, as if mere gestures would throw us at his mercy. But what he unwrapped was the last thing I expected. An amber stone lay in the middle of the silky black cloth, so similar to mine it was undoubtedly part of a set or part of something bigger.

Loki held a piece of Brisingamen in his hand.

BOTH AMBER jewels glowed as if each sensed the nearness of the other piece. I imagined Brisingamen, once put together, would be a sight beyond beautiful. But as much as I wanted to reach for it, I didn't trust Loki. The God of Mischief, the god not known for playing fair. Something about his eyes gave me visions of Shylock, demanding his pound of flesh. Or my heart on a silver platter.

I held back, but Aidan reached for the gem, holding it in his palm as if it were a fragile seashell, as if it would disintegrate if you even breathed on it. "Where did you get this?" Aidan asked, his voice harsh. No respect for this god.

"Well, boy. That counts as information, doesn't it?" Loki grinned.

I had no patience for his fun and games. "What do you want? You bring part of Brisingamen to us and then tease us with it? That doesn't sound much like help to me."

"Oh no. Now don't you go making me out to be the bad guy here. I'm not the one who sent you on this near impossible mission, am I?" Loki wagged a finger at me, teeth gleaming in the dim light. But his eyes glowed, bitter black coals. Funny, I could have sworn they'd been an icy blue when he'd first emerged from the shadows. "I want to help you. Because I'm such a nice guy."

How was it that Loki spoke with such a modern accent? Perhaps he had spent a few years in Midgard then. I didn't really care to waste time thinking about it. I asked, "And in return?"

"Nothing. I don't want payment for helping you. It's time Freya got her damned jewels back. She's had to live without them for far too long. Takes the fun out of teasing her, you know."

"So where did you find this?"

"It was given to me by someone. As a gift."

"Who is this *someone*?" Aidan bit out the question, impatient with Loki as he drew out each answer.

"His name is Nidhogg, and—"

"And he lives in the frigging Underworld!" Aidan spat. I was grateful he, at least, knew his Norse mythology well. "How do you propose we get there?"

"Oh, I can help you get there if you agree to go." Loki leaned against a table and withdrew a slim metal knife to clean his fingernails, while he puffed away at his cigar. He had no problem making himself comfortable.

"On one condition," Aidan said. I scowled, annoyed he'd made the decision without consulting me. Annoyed in spite of knowing I would have agreed myself.

"Well, boy, let's hear your condition, then." Loki cleaned the tiny blade, inspected the grit he'd removed, then flicked it away, not caring where it would land. I cringed, disgusted, and watched the swirling blue cigar smoke snake around the room, wondering if it would set the fire alarm off.

Aidan raised his chin with attitude. "Give us three days. Then we'll agree to go."

"Why not go now?" Loki's eyes narrowed, now simmering a catlike green.

"Because I only just got out of Asgard. That's why. I'd rather not go running back there just yet." Aidan shrugged, appearing nonchalant, buying time with the only excuse that might sound believable to a god who hadn't exactly had fun in Asgard.

"Ah, the Warrior doesn't like his new accommodation. If you must know, Freya's place isn't much better, although it's not much worse. But then, you probably won't go there either way." Loki looked at me, held my gaze and grinned. Not a hint of maliciousness in his cheerful smile, but I could feel his meaning reaching out to me from his eyes.

He knew.

"We'll go back as soon as we find Brisingamen," I said. "But we need the three days. There are a few things we need to do first. Going back is really a one way trip for both of us." I pretended I'd missed his underlying malevolence, smiling coyly as I spoke.

"Very well. Three days. Don't worry, I'll find you, kiddos."

We blinked and he was gone.

AIDAN HANDED ME THE PENDANT, and I frowned, turning the piece over and over in my hand. Unlike my stone, this pendant had no silver filigree around it and I guess that perhaps it had been treated differently from the main stone. I untied the cord around my neck and slipped Loki's gift beside it's sister. Together the two stones glowed like a pair of shimmering suns.

We completed gathering information, or rather Aidan did, as he knew what he was looking for and how to retrieve it. I felt unnecessary, wondering for a few minutes why I'd even come along.

Then I thought about Loki and his intentions. The god gave me the creeps, and I was grateful Aidan had the presence of mind to hold him off for a few days. My stomach did a trio of flip-flops when I recalled his subtle threat. Somehow, he knew that Aidan was ignorant of Freya's curse on his health. I battled my demons, waiting for Aidan.

A few minutes later, he powered the workstation down, and I grabbed the icebox. We left the building the same way we entered, joined Hugin outside and returned to the motel at the outskirts of the city. Hugin flew through the open door, right before I closed it. I sneaked a look up and down the passage, pretty sure the motel owners didn't allow pets, furred, feathered or otherwise.

We swallowed a dinner of burgers and fries. Still not as satisfying as Asgard's dinners but it filled the hole inside me, at least for a short while. I sprinkled a few fries onto the nightstand and beckoned Hugin, but he just thanked me with his usual glossy stare and didn't move. I studied Aidan as he munched. It made sense that we shared a room. Safety, company and planning dictated it was the best option. Not to mention dollars. Although I had money, it wouldn't last long if we were careless.

We sat on our beds, facing each other, eating and talking, coats discarded and armor glinting in the mean light of the motel room. It was so easy to forget we still wore the armor. The beauty of their construction was that although they were solid, impenetrable metal, they molded to the skin and adapted to the temperature of the wearer's body so well that soon you forgot you were even wearing cold metal. Amazing.

I watched Aidan, still a little annoyed that he'd made the

decisions for both of us. I wanted to know why. "Now what? Why'd you buy time?" I asked.

"I wanted to make sure we had as much information as possible. We need to go to the museum too, retrieve those records." He glanced at the thumb drive on the bed, now filled with data from the lab's computers.

"Why bother when Loki said Brisingamen is with this Nidi person?"

"Because Loki is a liar and because Nidhogg is a dragon, for God's sake." Aidan sighed, exasperated, and challenged me with one raised eyebrow.

"A dragon? Wow, I thought those were purely imaginary creatures." I glanced at Hugin who perched on top of the TV set. He inclined his head as if in agreement with Aidan. Well.

Aidan snorted. "Clearly they're not. We've just had the reality of Asgard, Valhalla, Valkyries and Freya shoved down our throats."

"Not to mention Fenrir," I added.

"Fenrir? What do you mean?" Aidan's eyes widened.

"You've met him. Fen. Fenrir." What did I have to do? Spell it out to him?

"*That* was Fenrir? *The* Fenrir?" He rubbed his hair, tossing curls every which way and still managing to make it look like it was meant to be that way.

"Yes, Fenrir. How many Fens do you know of?" I was starting to get annoyed with him. "Why the hell is this bugging you so much?"

"Well, if he really is Fenrir, he's also a *wolf*." I raised both eyebrows, as if to say *duh*. Aidan blushed. "So you know that too," he said. "Do you know he's supposed to cause Odin's demise in the Great War? And what the hell is he doing in Asgard anyway? He's supposed to be in chains."

"He pledged his services to Odin. He's vowed he has no intention of killing Odin, and that's how he ended up training the Warriors and the Valkyries."

"Okay, this just keeps getting better." Aidan rubbed a hand through his hair and shook his head, clearly bewildered by this strange twist to the original myth. I decided to throw him another one.

"He also trains his entire army of Ulfr, who are all based in Asgard too." I paused. "They will fight for Odin."

Aidan's jaw dropped. "Why didn't I get to see that before we left?"

"Because you were still in recovery." I popped the last fry into my mouth, squashed the wrappings into a ball and threw it in the wastebasket beside the TV. Neither of us was remotely interested in the television. The drama of our immediate life was much more invigorating than watching some reality show.

"Bet Loki loves that," Aidan muttered.

"Why?"

"Because Fenrir is his son," said Aidan with about the same emotion as if he'd just said the Earth was round.

"What?" I shook my head. Fenrir and Loki? Unbelievable. "I swear, if this is all a dream and I wake up back in Craven, I promise I'll study harder at Norse mythology. Any mythology, in fact."

Aidan laughed.

I lay back, staring at the ceiling, tracing the water stains that spread across it, marking irregular circles in a pattern from the doorway toward the bare light at the middle of the room. My eyes drifted closed and I was almost asleep, breathing so even. . . .

"What was it like?" Aidan's voice entered my sleep haze.

"What was what like?" I mumbled, turning to him, pulling the covers over me.

"Seeing me dead by the stream."

Damn you, Aidan!

I was just about asleep, and he had to go and ask me a question of paramount proportion. I sat up and looked straight at him. He lay on his stomach, propping his head onto folded arms. His eyes said the question was serious. Not a joke. Not a test.

I swallowed a sad and weary sigh. "It was a shock. I was so angry with you, first for leaving and then for coming back with your mob-men. But one look at your body and I forgot I was there to retrieve you. Forgot you would be okay. Fenrir had to give me a good shake and remind me what I was there to do."

"Fenrir came with you?"

I nodded. "Every Valkyrie has an Ulfr to accompany her. It was too soon for me to have trained with one. So, as the General, and as my trainer, Fenrir came with me." I lay back against my pillow. "I went to see Ms. Custer first. She told me you'd called and said you were coming, but you never arrived. I guess I found out why."

"I remember being hit in the head. Then nothing."

"They would've had to knock you out. You didn't look like you put up much of a fight either."

"So how did they kill me? I definitely remember pain in my head when I woke up in Valhalla." Aidan fingered his forehead.

A frigid wave of shock washed through my blood. Aidan had no idea how he'd died. I wasn't sure how to tell him. I decided to tell the whole story. He was a Warrior, after all. He could handle it.

"You were lying beneath the old bridge in the reserve behind the park. You had one foot in the stream and your eyes were open." I swallowed as tears gathered in my throat. "You still had your black leather jacket on, but it was stained with mud and probably blood, too. I think I recognized it, but I didn't pay any attention to it at first. Only when I got real close. They executed you, Aidan. A bullet in the middle of your forehead at close range."

The tears fell and neither of us moved.

Aidan's fingers still traced his forehead, now wrinkled with a frown, darkened with anger. He was so silent for a while I thought he wasn't going to talk about it anymore. That the thought of his violent death was too difficult for him. But when he responded I was surprised.

"I'm sorry you had to go through that," he said. "You know it was probably worse for you than for me. I felt nothing more than a thump on my head and then it was lights out for me. No pain. Nothing. Next thing I knew I was waking up in Valhalla. Feeling as if I'd drunk a whole bottle of whiskey."

He rose, as if he was about to get up and come to me. Just the thought of him offering me comfort made me want to bawl my eyes out. I rolled over, turned my back to him, and burrowed under the covers. To hide the tears that slipped so quickly down my cheeks, hide the ripe emotion in my eyes.

I lay there, listening to him listening to me. It took us both forever to fall asleep. Much later, I heard the fluttering of wings and the rustle of the curtain as Hugin flew from the TV stand to the window, looking outside at who knows what.

When I finally slept, I dreamed of Loki and cruel laughter, and bright colored eyes. Of dead eyes and icy blood coating my hands. And of Freya, standing beautiful, perfect with her glowing circle of suns around her graceful neck.

CHAPTER 35

The next afternoon Aidan rose from a fitful sleep, with purpling bruises beneath his eyes and a tired, strained look pulling his face tight. But it was the faint bruise in the middle of his forehead that made my heart slam against my ribs. I contemplated telling him about the curse right then and there, before he could commit himself any further. But it wouldn't be worth it. He'd just be forced to come with me, if only to save his own life. And he would hate me for it.

I gave him half a glass of Mead.

"Wow. Whatever is in this drink is potent."

I glanced up at him as I zipped up my boots. "You feeling better, then?" I tightened the belt around my waist and slung the pack over my shoulder. Thankfully, with the wintry weather we didn't stand out too much, all dark coats and boots.

"Absolutely. I feel brand new." Aidan's eyes shone. I silently kicked myself, certain I must have given him too much. The last thing we needed right now was for Aidan to be high on Mead.

"Come on then, Mr. Brand Spanking New. We have a museum to visit." I grabbed his arm and pushed him out the door, smiling as he chuckled and made his way out.

We checked out, grabbed a bus into the city center, then another into New York. The rest had done us well. In body, if not in mind.

WE LURKED AROUND the park across the street from the museum until well after closing. I studied the old building, with its towering columns guarding the museum's entrance, an impressive structure, built to awe those who passed over its threshold. Old stone meshed with modern architecture and landed on perfect.

Again, the back entrance was our route, and Aidan's access cards still worked. The museum no doubt had no idea he'd "died." We slipped into the darkened building, bypassing the alarmed museum area, making our way upstairs to the offices and cataloging rooms. We passed standard issue offices ensconced amid intricate architrave work, and beautiful old prints on the walls. Aidan knew his way around and led us to a room in the far corner of the floor.

Aidan made himself comfortable before the closest workstation, tapping away at the keyboard. Soon, a printer hummed in a corner by the window, and I went to gather the papers for him, stuffing them into a large plastic envelope.

The air conditioner would have shut off hours ago and the

room was stuffy. I stood by the window, looking out at the thick darkness of the park, at the slight movement in the branches of the nearest tree where Hugin waited.

It was so dark outside that the window reflected my face back at me. A young woman stared back, one who looked unaffected by the trauma and the stress, and the guilt of the last few weeks. Was it the Valkyrie blood that made me this way? Strong in the face of adversity. Eyes still bright and alive, hair as hideously red as ever.

Aidan's voice broke through my thoughts. "Right, got everything."

"So what were you looking for?"

He rustled the envelope in his hand. "A report listing all the items found at the original dig site and another one, which is a catalog of everything the museum has in its collection."

"So what happens if the rest of the necklace isn't there?"

"Then we come back and have a look at another catalog."

I folded my arms and frowned. "Isn't that a bit of a risk, Aidan? Coming back here again? What if your access card has some kind of trigger to it and makes them keep an eye out for you, or it locks you out? You don't know who your father knows here at the museum."

"That's it!" He waved a finger at me and tapped the keyboard some more.

"What's *it*?"

He didn't answer, merely scribbled furiously on a piece of paper. He rose and stuffed the paper into his pocket, logged off the system and shut it down. "Come, we're done here."

We headed out into the frigid night. And I breathed a sigh of relief. Every minute inside the museum had ticked by with the constant fear of being discovered.

WE GRABBED SOME TAKEOUT, another tasteless meal in a long string of tasteless meals. We found a motel, much the same as the last one, and hunkered down for the night, eager to study the information Aidan had printed.

"So what were you looking for?" I asked, my voice a tad too sharp. I was annoyed with him for keeping his hunches close to his chest, like the information he'd scribbled on the piece of paper. He still hadn't told me what that was.

"I needed a catalog of every item found at the dig where Brunhilde was uncovered," he said. "And an inventory of the museum's collection of artifacts from the burial site. Now all we need to do is check through the two lists, tick off what's duplicated, and find what's missing. The rest of the necklace must have been found in the grave. It must be where your father found your pendant."

I thought it was unlikely the reports would say: *Brisingamen found. Brisingamen lost.* But I paid attention. He began to read off items off one list, while I ticked them off on the other. A long, tedious process, and a necessary one. I crossed off lines that sounded insignificant, like feather and stones and shards of pottery.

At last, he stopped calling out items and we had a small list of unmatched jewelry, adornments, clothing and weapons. We completed the checks and found what we were looking for.

Two neckpieces.

They were listed in the catalog, each marked with a note indicating they were no longer part of the collection. Aidan and I looked at each other, pretty satisfied with this development.

"Well, we know your dad had one. Now, to figure out who has the other item."

"Do you think it could be the one Loki gave us?" I asked.

"No, I don't. Unless the other piece was given to him by the museum or whoever had it in their possession."

"Who do you think has it, then? What about the archaeologist who supervised the dig?"

"Exactly who I was thinking of." Aidan nodded, then jumped off the bed to dig around in the pocket of his coat. He waved the paper at me and said, "This number should lead us directly to the Professor."

I sighed. Relieved that we were making headway with our search. "You're ringing her now? It's almost three in the morning."

But he was already picking up the phone and dialing, giving his head a tight shake as if a three a.m. phone call wouldn't piss a sleepy Professor off. When his face crumpled I knew we'd hit a snag. "It's a message. She's on a dig in Greenland."

"I don't suppose the message said how long she will be away?" I should have known it was too good to be true.

"Her message said to ring her service and they will get in touch with her. But what the hell do I say to her to get her to ring me back?"

"Give me the phone. I have an idea," I said.

I dialed the service and left my message. "Dr. Wayne, this is Bryn Halbrook, I need to talk to you about Brisingamen. This is extremely important—life and death."

I cut the call and prepared to wait for a response. It would still be daylight for her in Greenland. The chances were slim that she would ring back in the next few hours. So I was shocked when the phone rang only two hours later as we were both finally falling asleep. I scrambled to answer it.

"Hello," I said. I didn't say my name. Things had become radically crazy in the last few weeks and the knowledge that we'd already been followed was never far from my mind. Aidan's dad's thugs could be tracking us right now.

The voice was female, with a clipped American accent. "Bryn Halbrook?"

"This is she."

"This is Professor Wayne here. You left a message with my service?"

"Yes, I needed to speak to you, but it's not something I can discuss over the phone."

"I can understand that. But I can't exactly take a cab to meet you. Can you charter a plane to get you here? I can't leave the dig site. Part of the glacier has shifted and opened up a burial site. I can't leave until the entire site has been processed."

"I'm sorry, but we don't have that kind of money." I was appalled that she'd thought we could afford such an extravagance.

Her next words astonished me. "Sure you do, girl. You are Geoffrey's daughter, are you not?"

"Yes, but—"

"Okay, I'll arrange the flight for you. The charter will ring with the details. How long do you have?" She was all business, and yet a little vibration in her voice matched the shiver of fear running down my own back.

"Not much—a few days," I answered, knowing she'd have no idea what the reason for the deadline was.

"That's cutting it pretty close, but get here and we'll see what we can do."

We said our goodbyes and I hung up. I stared at the phone, aware that everything had just gone haywire. A charter plane to Greenland!

Hugin fluttered his dark wings and flew toward me. At first, I'd been uncomfortable with the bird, especially when he flew right at me to land on my shoulder. Now, all I did was watch him until he settled. He cocked his head and stared at me.

"What is it?" I asked.

For the first time, the enigmatic black bird spoke to me. I almost jumped out of my skin. "*There is a way for you to get there without using a mechanical transport,*" he said, his sensual baritone so unsuited to his placid eyes. Such sexy tones didn't mesh well with the black-feathered raven.

"Which is?"

"*The same method that you used to move from Asgard to your town of Craven.*"

CHAPTER 36

 idan stared at me and it took me few seconds to figure out he hadn't heard a thing. *So only I could hear the bird speak? Just great.*

I repeated Hugin's suggestion to Aidan and we exchanged doubtful glances.

"Hugin, I have no idea how to do that. I've had someone from Asgard with me each time."

Hugin cocked his head, his glassy eye staring straight at me. *"There are different worlds that exist. I believe you refer to them as dimensions. We can travel through these worlds too, using the Bifrost."*

"Bifrost?" I asked, frowning.

"Yes, the Bifrost. It is the Rainbow of the Gods. The bridge between the worlds."

"The room in Odin's palace?"

"That is one of the locations where the Bifrost sets down."

"What are these locations then?"

"Places where the walls between the worlds are thinner and easier to traverse, where the bridge can reach through the worlds."

I raised my eyebrows, then filled Aidan in. "Right then, what do I need to do?" I asked.

"Wait for me. I shall search out the nearest location and take you to it."

Hugin flew into the bathroom and pecked at the window. I rushed to open it for him, and out he went in a rush of flapping feathers.

A rainbow bridge between the worlds.

I wasn't sure I wanted to believe such a farfetched concept, but the chink of chain armor reminded me that I was living in the middle of an ancient Norse myth. It was crazy and interesting and unbelievable all at the same time.

Hugin came back within a short space of time and beckoned us to follow. "It can't be far since he got back so quickly. I'll go with him," I said, wanting Aidan to rest.

"No way I'm letting you go anywhere without me, especially at this hour." He sat up, more pale and drained that he'd been yesterday morning. The curse was sapping more and more energy as the days went by. For a moment, he teetered on wobbly legs, then he slumped back onto the bed. "Okay, seems I don't have the energy at the moment. Why can't you wait until tomorrow?"

"We need to check it out as soon as possible, so we can plan our next move. I'll be fine. Hugin will warn me of any danger and Fen's trained me practically to death. I can take care of myself, you know."

Aidan muttered and scowled, upset with me for going and

with himself for being too weak to join me. I hoped he'd get over it.

Outside, the darkness fled from the sky as sunlight struggled to make its way through thick, angry snow clouds. I followed Hugin a few blocks into a dark alley. He came to rest on the edge of a putrid sky-blue dumpster and waited for me to catch up.

"This is it?" I asked the bird.

"*Yes. What did you expect it to be?*"

The Rainbow of the Gods touched down right beside a stinking dumpster. I wondered where it would land on the other side of our trip. Let's hope we didn't find ourselves trapped beneath frozen glaciers. We left the alley and went back to fetch Aidan.

The early morning air was icy cold and my breath circled my head, a white frozen mist. My footsteps echoed around the empty street. Soon the sound of a second set echoed in tandem to mine. I sped up and so did my stalker. Pausing, pretending to inspect the contents of a darkened pawnshop storefront, I scoped out the shape and size of my tail from the corner of my eye. The best way to deal with a stalker was direct confrontation—best performed when you have a sword strapped to your waist, of course.

I rounded on the person, coming up right in front of his face, only to discover it was a girl. Low-cut blouse, a skirt so short it might as well have been a pair of hot pants. *How come she wasn't freezing to death?* I wanted to ask.

Aloud, I asked the more important question instead. "Why are you following me?"

"I'm not following you." The woman's eyes rounded, shocked

at my confrontation, but I didn't buy it. Something just didn't sit right with this girl.

"What do you want?" She'd definitely been following me, and I intended to find out why. Too many things could go wrong. Who knew what Freya was up to, or whether she would send someone to keep an eye on us, to protect her investment? Everything about this girl looked ordinary at a glance. Pretty skin, dark hair, young enough for me to wonder if she was still in school. But I found it odd when she didn't even shiver in the frigid weather. The edges of my eyes hazed, and for a moment my vision blurred.

The girl's eyes swirled with color, an entrancing blue. Not your average eye color. Now where had I seen that before? My own eyes narrowed, studying her face, and I decided to go with my gut.

"Loki? What do you want?" I kept my voice raised, projecting confident knowledge where I was just guessing. But it was not just my confidence that destroyed his ruse. In that same instant Hugin cawed above me, flapping his wings and landing with a shudder on my shoulder.

"Hugin? What—" Loki stumbled backward, teetering on three-inch heels. Then the air changed, thickened. The girl slowly dissolved and disappeared. In her place, a pitch-black raven clawed the cold bare concrete.

Hugin cawed again from my shoulder. Clearly unhappy. "*Loki!*"

The Loki-raven disappeared in a puff of smoky shadows, and now a man stood before me. Not the visitor we'd received in the lab, though. This Loki was taller, more muscle-bound, almost wrestler material. Square jawed with large bright green eyes, he grinned from ear to ear.

"Mighty astute of you, my dear. For a girl," Loki said. And he did look surprised. So what had he been used to, then—dimwitted, Mead-bearing subservients?

I looked askance at Hugin. "You could have been a little more help, you know."

The darned bird just stared back at me, unperturbed.

"So, I see you have dear Hugin as a companion. A nice loan from Odin." Loki nodded, but I could almost hear his mind working as he tried to figure out why I deserved the company of one of Odin's precious birds.

"Yeah. He's good company most of the time," I said." Now what do you want? We still have three days left before we have to give you an answer."

"Yes, yes. I know that." Loki's eyes brushed my response away, but his annoyance was visible in the tight line of his mouth and the rigid set of his shoulders. "I've just popped in to make sure you're both making some headway."

"So, you mean you're spying on us?" I raised an eyebrow. "Are you sure Freya didn't send you?"

Loki's eyes swirled a liquid gold.

"Three days, Loki, that's all we asked for. Now, if there's nothing specific you want, I need to get back to Aidan." I turned on my heel and began to walk away, not daring to release my pent-up breath. Loki would pounce on the first sign of weakness.

"Have you told him yet?" Loki's disembodied voice hovered before me, accompanied in a rush by the rest of his bulk, to successfully block my escape. I wasn't sure what the punishment was for knocking out a god, so I flared my fingers and held my hand stiffly by my side. At last he'd revealed what he'd really come for. To prey on my guilt.

I frowned, hoping to pull off a credible puzzled expression; I was never a good actor. "Told who what?"

"Don't pretend, my dear. Have you told your boyfriend that his life will soon begin to slip away, and that unless you accept my help this whole mission will take far too long and he may just die in the process?" Loki smirked.

Pure anger rose within me, heating my blood. It was a battle to hold onto my urge to hit him. I'd never been a violent person. Never had the slightest urge to raise my hand and hit or hurt someone just because of how I felt. But looking at Loki and his gleaming eyes, a fury burned inside of me the likes of which I'd never known.

"We said we needed three days and we still do. Come back when the time is up and we'll probably take up your offer. For now, please leave us alone." We could do without this sort of distraction, without Loki haunting me with his insinuations.

"Three days." Loki flashed pearly white teeth that were no doubt some kind of mirage. His once-blue eyes shifted to a startling shade of green. "And if you don't agree to take my offer, then I'll be forced to tell your beloved the truth about the limited extent of his life."

I glared at Loki, whose eyes were now solid black, probably reflecting the color of his putrid soul.

"Three days and I will tell Aidan he is soon going to die," he repeated.

As if he needed to speak twice.

I SHIVERED as I shut the door on both the bone-chilling cold and Loki's words. But the cold was easy to shut out. Not so with Loki. His threat rang inside my skull, sharp and insistent. Aidan looked up as I entered and frowned at the worried creases in my brow. I'd need to be more careful with my fears.

"What happened?" he asked.

"Nothing, it's just freezing outside and it looks like snow. Hugin showed me the place, so we can leave as soon as you're ready." I didn't need to fake the shiver that ran through me.

"We should cancel the charter first, though."

"We can't sit around and wait for them to call. I was hoping we could leave now." I was eager to be out of there, as far from Loki as possible.

"Yeah. You're right. The charter wouldn't be able to reach us to confirm anything. Besides, we'll get to Professor Wayne in no time. She could cancel the charter when we get there."

I nodded, gathering our stuff and scanning the room, wondering if we were about to shock the life out of the poor professor. She didn't sound like the wilting wallflower type, but she would have a lot of questions for us.

And boy did we have some myth-busting answers for her.

CHAPTER 37

We checked out and set off for the stinking alley, our boots killing the beautiful, fluffy snowflakes littering the sidewalk. Soon the pristine white would be transformed into a wet, black sludge.

Aidan walked silently beside me, while I searched the streets for any sign of Loki.

"Are you okay?" I asked, concerned about his silence.

He grumbled. "Couldn't Hugin have told us about this magic bridge back in Missouri, and saved us three days of driving? Not to mention several felonies." His eyes scanned the gray sky for the raven. Hugin circled high above us, out of earshot.

"Maybe we had to prove ourselves first," I said. "Or maybe the Bridge doesn't connect to DC." Aidan shrugged. He stopped a moment, closed his eyes and massaged his temples.

"Aidan!" I touched his shoulder. "Are you okay, really?"

"Yeah, just tired. Not sure what's up. Maybe it's coming back to Midgard. Yikes, I can never get used to calling our world

Midgard." Aidan shook his head, black curls bouncing. They'd grown, just brushing his shoulders.

I handed him one of the small leather pouches of Mead that Sigrun had packed. Suddenly I longed to see my friend again. I hadn't had this experience before, missing a living person so deeply. I'd ached for Joshua's presence after he'd died. And for Aidan, I'd keened inside, my grief both for my broken and my betrayed heart. But now, I just missed Sigrun as you'd miss a friend and confidante. I held the thought close to me.

Aidan slugged, then returned the pouch. Almost reluctantly. I watched his face. Saw the pleasure there. And I worried. Feared he would get addicted. He'd need the drink more and more over the next few days. I had to preserve our stash and decided to keep a better eye on the Mead from that moment on. The longer we remained here the more we'd need the Mead.

We reached the alley, Hugin leading. It stank. Urine, garbage and heaven knew what else. Hugin flew down and perched on my shoulder, like an ever-present, overbearing conscience. We stood, almost hidden from the street by the incongruously cheerful blue dumpster.

"*Stand together, side by side and be calm,*" he said.

I repeated his words to Aidan, who raised a questioning eyebrow. He also raised one offended nostril, as if asking me if this could seriously be the location of the Bridge. I shrugged and tried clear my thoughts.

"*Think of Greenland and your professor,*" Hugin's sultry baritone spoke in my ear.

"Er, I don't really know much about either of them," I

admitted, unsure how I'd get there if I hadn't met the archaeologist or ever been to Greenland.

"That is not a problem. Just think of both her name and the place you intend to go to. The Bridge knows what's in your mind. It will connect you to her. That is why you need to clear your mind of other thoughts or you might end up going somewhere else."

Again, I relayed Hugin's comments to Aidan. At first, I felt slightly ridiculous, standing in a dark, dank, dead-end alley, facing a mold-ridden brick wall beside a foul-smelling dumpster. But once I settled my mind and concentrated, I forgot about our location. My mind focused elsewhere. I felt light-headed.

Pain spliced my ribs, agony spread white-hot fingers into my flesh. Was this right? I gasped, thrown back by the momentum of the pain, disoriented and confused. What had Hugin done to me?

"Bryn? What's the matter?" Aidan's voice swam down to me, distorted as if we were conversing underwater. His hands went around me to support me as I began to fall to the ground. His touch sent blinding shafts of pain into my side. I sagged against the dumpster and grunted in agony, but I refused to be a wuss and scream.

"Don't touch me," I tried to say, but all that left my mouth was hysterical groaning.

"Shit!" Aidan's hand came away from my side. Though my eyes were heavy-lidded with pain, I watched him gape at his hand, now coated thickly in ripe, red blood.

Hugin fluttered around, the speed of his wings amplified by his anxiety.

"What happened?" Aidan shouted. He opened my coat and

found the glamor hiding my Valkyrie attire had disappeared. Blood saturated the chainmail, seeping through the fine bronze links, with a perfect red circle at the center of the leaking wound. "You've been shot, Bryn."

He reached for my hems, both chainmail and dress, lifting carefully until he reached the wound. I didn't care that my thighs were bared, or that my entire midriff was open to view. The pain wiped out every bit of modesty I had left. Aidan inspected the entrance of the wound with tender fingers, then slipped his hand beneath my back, checking for an exit wound. Alarm filled his eyes. His fingers found the ridges of the open wound, coming away moist and red.

He covered me up, then, an expression of poisonous anger on his face. When he peeked around the edge of the dumpster to search for the sniper, he almost received a bullet to his face for his troubles. It plunged into the brick on the wall behind him, sending a silent shower of dust floating to the grime-coated alley floor.

Fear sluiced through my veins so fast my hands and knees shook. My vision had cleared, although it took far too long for my liking. I struggled to sit up higher, knowing we needed to hurry to get out of this place. Funny, but I did prefer to be as far away from snipers as possible, considering my current condition.

"Aidan?"

A stricken look haunted his face—no surprise after having almost met a bullet in the face twice in so many weeks. "Yes, I'm here. What do you need?"

"The Bifrost. It's our only way out."

He nodded and looked at Hugin. "Alright, Blackbird. Let's get out of here."

I desperately wanted to laugh as Aidan helped me get back on my feet, imagining what Hugin would think of his new nickname. The world spun around me and all I could think of was Mead.

"I think I need some Mead before we use the Bifrost. Who knows how the traveling will affect me."

Aidan obliged and I soon downed half a bag of Mead. Some part of my consciousness screamed at me not to drink too much. Aidan would need the rest. I tried to think. How many had he used, how many had we brought? My head hurt. Too hard to think.

A few moments later, I felt better, breathed easier. Even the world righted itself a little. I let go of Aidan's arm, and stood on quivering legs.

"Can we go now?" I asked.

Aidan choked back a laugh. Another bullet ricocheted off the wall. "Yes, ma'am," he said.

We stayed within the shadows of the dumpster. Aidan wouldn't dare to risk his life again by checking who had shot at us. We both concentrated hard, thinking of Greenland and the Professor.

Then we stepped forward, knowing they would see us once we moved out of the shadows. Why did the entrance to the Bridge have to be out in the open? Especially when somewhere out there Worthington and his partner were trying to terminate us.

We held our breaths and prayed. Everything slowed down, to the point that I heard the pop of the bullets disengaging from the barrels, the whoosh as they sped through the air, heading straight toward us.

A low hum surrounded us, and I was pulled forward, sucked into a strange vortex of air currents.

CHAPTER 38

I stumbled as my feet hit solid ground again. I whirled and turned, panicked when I couldn't see Aidan. But the thwack of his heels hitting the ground beside me was a comforting sound.

I looked around, absorbing the biting air as it fought its way into my skin, right into my bones. I shook with the cold, despite my armor still maintaining the warm temperature of my body. Aidan shivered beside me. Thank heaven we hadn't ended up standing in the icy snow or on a lonely glacier out in the white wilderness. No. I thought. *Thank you, Bifrost.*

Each trip on the Bifrost was slightly different. My trips with Fen were blink-and-you're-there, yet this one felt like a ride on a little tornado. Tornado! In that pain-filled moment I recalled my first trip on the Bifrost. From Ms. Custer's front yard. Had there really been an entrance to the Bridge right on my doorstep all this time?

A violent shiver pulled me out of my thoughts. We stood in

the middle of a passage marked with sealed doors at regular intervals. A metal door, set with a large window, guarded the end of the passage. Beyond the door snow swirled, so thick it was impossible to say if it was twilight or high noon.

Biting agony forced its way into every conscious brain cell. The pain hadn't worsened, but it hadn't lightened either. I hoped the Mead had done some good. My palm went to my ribs, where heat radiated out of my body like flames in an overactive furnace. My hand came away with blood. Not the thick, pulsing surge it had been beside the dumpster, rather a steady dribble that, hopefully, meant I was on the mend.

Wings flapped and fluttered, and Hugin made an appearance, for once not the picture of calm. Black feathers fluttered to the floor as he landed on Aidan's shoulder. Shocked, Aidan almost dusted him off, but caught his hand at the last minute. He stared at the bird out of the corner of his eye, standing stiff and uncomfortable with his new burden.

"You okay?" I asked the perturbed creature.

"*Yes, although it is not every day I get shot at,*" he answered.

"Yes, I agree. Not a usual occurrence for us either." I forced the words out as adrenaline vacated my body in one sweeping rush.

I staggered against the wall, sliding slowly to the ground, unable to stop my descent. Aidan crouched beside me, pulling my coat forward to look at the wound. Soon, I found the half-pouch of Mead stuck in my face. I drank, again filled with guilt. As yet, I hadn't felt a significant change to my condition other than the halting of the bleeding.

I handed the pouch back to Aidan, experiencing a moment of

clarity in which his pale skin shone bloodless and blue-veined, in which purple and blue blotches riddled the center of his forehead, forming a neat circular pattern around the bullet hole that had killed him. The slope of his shoulders screamed out the true state of his weakness.

Soon, I was well enough to rise. I felt as if the rest had done more than the Mead, and I was beginning to wonder at its effectiveness. Better keep a closer eye on Aidan, just in case. I teetered on numbed legs, holding on to Aidan until the dizziness vanished.

I figured we'd start at the first door on our right, and I grabbed the handle.

"Be careful. We have no idea if we're even in the right place. Let's have a peek first before we go barging into a room full of murderers," Aidan said. He grinned, knowing he sounded severely paranoid, but he had a point.

I placed my ear against the door, but it was well insulated against the cold and thus against sound too. I opened the door and allowed it to move toward me, leaving it slightly ajar. Voices filtered toward us. Two speakers. A woman and a man. I looked at Aidan.

"Does it sound like her?" I whispered.

He nodded. We slipped into the room and the door closed behind us in a soft whoosh. Hugin took off, leaving Aidan's shoulder as he walked over to a desk overflowing with papers and photographs and maps. The bird landed on the top of the nearest cabinet.

The two occupants, deep within their conversation, faced a

white board filled with notations and plastered with a number of maps. They were discussing ice shelves and separations.

"Professor Wayne?" Aidan spoke.

She turned, eyes reluctant to leave the board, auburn hair flickering in the crude fluorescent light. When her glance came to rest on Aidan, her eyes widened. "Aidan? What are you doing here?"

My eyes narrowed as I turned my own gaze on him. Seems I'd missed the part where Aidan mentioned he and the Professor knew each other personally. Probably met at one of the many digs he'd been on.

"I know we're interrupting, but I have to speak to you," Aidan said. "It's very important."

The man scowled. "Elisabeth, this ice shelf isn't going to wait while we babysit a bunch of kids." The tone of his voice matched the frigid weather, and he stared at us as if teens were freaky, yet-to-be-understood creatures. His forehead was a mass of creases, a stark contrast to the smoothly combed hair sitting on his head like a skullcap. A cold impatience gleamed in his black eyes and I could almost read his mind. How long would it take him to have security throw us out into the snow?

"Never mind, Henri. I can handle this. I'm sure it won't take long, and please let me know if the ice shelf should move in the next ten minutes, will you?" The Professor smiled, dismissing him smoothly. Henri left the room in a huff, not bothering to look at us as he shoved his way through the door. Unfortunately for him, he couldn't slam the vacuum lock door.

"Sorry, Aidan, Henri believes he's on a tight deadline." Her smile was affectionate and I understood in that moment that she had no idea Aidan had been killed.

Aidan shrugged. I moved to stand beside him, and the Professor's eyes widened. From the shock in her eyes and the flush on her cheeks, it was supremely clear that she recognized me. But who did she recognize? Dr. Halbrook's progeny or the Valkyrie they'd unearthed?

"Who's your friend, Aidan?" she asked, cautiously, as if one breath in my direction would cause me to disappear in a puff of snow.

"Professor Wayne, this is Bryn Halbrook."

She blinked and frowned. "But, I just spoke to you on the phone a couple of hours ago. I haven't even called the charter yet." She walked back and forth, not quite wringing her hands, but it was close enough. Surely, this was the part where a normal human being would faint or cry or throw a hysterical fit at the unreality of it all. She approached Aidan and asked, "How the hell did you get here this fast?"

Aidan shrugged his shoulders again, pursed his lips and said, with an Oscar-winning air of nonchalance, "We used the Bifrost."

"You used what?" Her eyes narrowed.

"The Bifrost, the Rainbow of the Gods. The bridge between worlds," I answered.

She opened her mouth. Closed it. Then she looked from him to me and her eyes narrowed. "Is this some kind of prank?"

"No. No, I'm really sorry. Aidan's not telling you everything." I gave Aidan a nasty look. We didn't have time to waste with dodging reality. "I know what my father did. With the DNA from the dig site."

Her mouth formed a silent "O" and she sat down slowly. It was a risk to mention it, but how many people knew about what my father had done? If Aidan's father had found out, how did I know who else knew?

Her next words just confirmed my fears. "You know about that?" She whispered the question in a voice so small it bordered on a squeak.

I nodded.

"Who told you?"

"You won't believe me even if I told you." My response was dry.

"Young lady, I don't have time to mess around. If you expect my help, you need to be straight with me." Suitably chastised, I nodded.

I took a step back, opened my coat and allowed the glamor to fall away.

Professor Wayne rose to her feet. Her face was strained as she whispered a name.

"Brunhilde!"

"Dear Lord, is this real?" She looked at Aidan and promptly sat back in her chair, so shocked her legs folded, unable to hold her weight. My wings glimmered and fluttered at my back.

But not before she saw the blood.

"What happened to you?" She rose, surprising me with the speed with which she reached me.

"It's okay. We were shot at when we used the Bifrost to get here." I waved her off.

"You need a doctor. I can get a medic to see to you, patch you up."

I shook my head, desperate to change the topic. "I'm fine, it's healing. The bullet went right through and the bleeding stopped ages ago."

I'd tried to make her feel better but it seemed I'd done the opposite by revealing my apparent mortality. I dropped the glamor back, more adept and comfortable with the skill now. I pulled my coat closed.

But the professor was no longer looking at me. She stared, shocked, at Aidan instead. She'd seen Aidan in his battle gear when I dropped the glamor.

I sympathized with the Professor. Although she'd spent her lifetime chasing after artifacts, it would be hard to find an archaeologist who truly expects a mythology to be real. Everyone knows myths are called myths because of the very nature of the stories. Farfetched, sketchy, too magical for the modern techno-kid to accept.

"Professor? You okay?" Aidan went closer to her, and she flinched, staring at his chest.

"What are you wearing?" she asked, her hands and voice shaking.

"He is *einherjar*. It's his armor," I answered. Aidan looked helplessly at me. Things had gotten pretty out of hand in the past few minutes.

The Professor took a deep breath, gripping her hands together in a twisted fist, taking a few staggered breaths. "Both of you, sit." She was one cool, professional woman and I decided I could learn a lot from her. "Coffee? Chocolate?"

"Anything." We answered in unison, both not caring very much what we drank as long as it was warm.

She rang for coffee and steepled her fingers, looking over at us, eyes still wrinkled with worry. And waiting. "Right," she said. "Start from the beginning."

Aidan cleared his throat and began to tell his tale, from his mission to find Halbrook's mutant child to discovering me alive and well in Craven.

"Bryn wasn't an animal to be terminated," he said, the skin on his face tight.

The heat pump sputtered weakly, reminding me of the cold blanket of air that hugged me tightly.

"Terminated? What do you mean?"

"My father wanted me to infiltrate the foster home and determine the extent of Bryn's mutation, and to recommend termination if it was true she was part Valkyrie. He believed it was a threat to humanity if she was allowed to live." Aidan paused and threw a warm glance in my direction. "I didn't agree with him. I admit I went to Craven under his instruction, but I'd only paid half an ear. For me it was an opportunity to get away from him. To be able to study the book without his constant interference."

"What book?"

I fished in my satchel and handed her the leather-bound volume. She nodded. "Ah yes. I understood that your father had procured a copy of this volume."

"I was also worried for Bryn's safety," Aidan said. "Something strange was happening to her." He paused, and only continued when she raised a questioning brow. "Bryn can tell you."

I cleared my throat. "I was about five years old when I began to see people who glowed. A strange golden aura around them. I spent most of my childhood seeing a psychiatrist who made it his life's work to rid me of my psychosis. When I moved to Craven, I discovered that the glow really meant the person was going to die. Aidan was there when one of my little foster brothers died. I was helpless, distraught. But after Aidan left, something weird happened." I didn't miss the look of remonstration she threw him. "I was taken to . . . a strange place."

"You were abducted?" Twin spots of pink appeared on her cheeks as she leaned forward, outraged.

"Not exactly." I hesitated, unsure of what she'd say, whether she'd think I belonged in a loony bin. "I was in Asgard. I received my wings in the Hall of Odin, during the Rite of the Valkyrie."

The Professor blanched. But she remained silent. The conversation paused as a man entered, bringing with him three cups of steaming hot coffee. I sipped mine gratefully, eager to relieve the tightness in my throat. I waited for him to leave before I spoke again.

"When the time came for my first Retrieval I went back to Craven. My foster mom told me Aidan had called and said he was coming to see her. He had something really important to tell her. She was very worried, as he hadn't arrived. After speaking with my foster mother, I was taken to perform my Retrieval and it—"

The Professor interrupted. "Sorry, what is Retrieval?"

"It's when the Valkyries bring home their chosen Warrior."

Her nod was tight and she said nothing. I had to hand it to her. She was taking it pretty well since her initial shock. I liked her.

"My Retrieval, the Warrior I was meant to take back to Valhalla, had been murdered and left beside a stream in Craven. He'd been shot in the forehead at pointblank range and would have been lying there for a week at least." I swallowed hard, fighting memories of icy water running over my foot, of Aidan's weightless body and the putrid odor from his long-dead flesh. "It was Aidan."

"What?" She looked at Aidan and then back at me. "Okay. This is getting a bit much, Bryn. Do you really expect me to believe that Aidan is dead when he's standing in front of me, breathing and alive?"

"I showed you what we look like in true form. Surely you understand. An *einherjar* can only become a Warrior of Odin in death. It was a horrible shock for me, too. I'm sorry you had to find this out so suddenly. But we need your help. We need more information on Brisingamen. It would help if you could tell us anything about any pieces of jewelry taken from the collection of artifacts uncovered in the burial." I sipped the coffee again, my throat dry from a frigid mix of cold, revelation and memories.

"How do you know about Brisingamen?" the Professor asked, the air of skepticism slowly receding.

"From its owner. The goddess Freya wants us to find it for her. If we fail, we pay with our lives."

"The catalog indicated two pieces of amber jewelry that were found. We know where one of the pieces is, but we haven't found the other item," said Aidan.

"Well," she said, shifting in her seat, "I removed the necklaces from the museum catalog collection for further study. It matched a carving we found at the site of a full necklace, but we were only able to find two pieces. They seemed to have been removed from the necklace and fashioned into two pendants. I see you've received the one I gave to your father."

Her eyes narrowed on the pendant around my neck.

My ears rang. "*You* gave it to him?"

"Yes, I was furious when I discovered he'd lied about the DNA results. I went to visit him in the Hamptons. You were a baby, about a year old, I believe. He was so afraid I would call the cavalry on him. But angry as I was that he'd thwarted my accolades for being the first and only archaeologist to ever uncover a real mythological creature, I wasn't inhuman." She shook her head, and the soft curly hair jittered. A look of intense sadness flitted across her face. "The life of a little child hung in the balance. If I'd outed him, you would've been taken from your parents. I didn't have the heart to leave you at the mercy of modern science on the off-chance that you *could* be part Valkyrie. I gave him the necklace to keep until you were sixteen. He promised to give it to you, and I'm glad he upheld his end of the bargain."

I looked away. *Thanks, Dad.* Seemed a waste of effort to get the darned necklace to me just so it could get me into more trouble than it was worth. "Do you have any idea where the other piece is? We need to retrieve the entire necklace and return it within the next week or we're toast."

The Professor nodded, reached for her keys at her waist. They jangled as she flicked through the bunch. She handed me a small silver key. "It's the key to my safe deposit box in New York. Your name is the password, current spelling. The key will open the box itself. There is a drawing of the necklace as it should look if all the pieces were intact." She paused and I wondered why she would freely give this to me. "There used to be a time when glory was something I wanted, but knowing that I found Brunhilde was enough for me. In the end, I wasn't even angry with Geoffrey. Perhaps I was even thankful he'd denied the authenticity of the body as a Valkyrie. It would have opened up a whole new can of worms. And I'm not sure the world was ready to know she existed."

Personally, I didn't think the world was ready to know that *mythology* was actually real.

WE LEFT with a sad farewell to the Professor. She'd looked after my interests when I was a baby, and now she helped us so willingly. And I'd always be thankful for that. It didn't stop me from being bitter though, or furious at a father whose death saved him from explaining what the hell he'd been thinking.

We stood out in the cold passageway, making way for Henri to stride past us. The glare he threw us was enough to freeze any melting iceberg.

I worried about the effect our travels on the Bridge of the Gods would do to both my wounds and Aidan's all-round health. I worried about arriving beside the dumpster and being shot straight through the heart. What if they were still waiting for us?

My heart thumped a dull beat beneath my ribs.

"Hugin?" The bird had flown out of Professor Wayne's office

and landed on Aidan's shoulder again. When I spoke, he turned a liquid eye to me. "You know another way back to Midgard? If we waltz back the same way we left, we'll be eating bullets."

The bird nodded. All we could do was trust him. And follow him.

CHAPTER 39

The landing hurt more than the actual traveling. Although it was just a case of disappear and appear, both Aidan and I stumbled, disoriented, on arrival; we ended up walking right into each other. We hadn't been that close since our encounter in Valhalla. I'd been careful to skirt any personal space infringements. They usually went hand-in-hand with the high guilt factor.

We stared at each other, a moment lost in emotion, free from betrayal, anger and guilt. A moment that lasted too few seconds and ended way too quickly.

We'd arrived on the outskirts of Central Park in the guarding shadows of a huge elm, crunching snow beneath the soles of our boots. Funny how the Bifrost always touched ground in a secure area.

On our way to the bank, we passed Rockefeller Center and paused to admire the beauty of the gigantic tree. I wondered then if Asgard had a similar tradition. I would miss Christmas. It was my most favorite time of the year.

At the bank, the manager ushered us through mahogany lined halls. We signed various papers in a large, hushed room while the haughty manager looked down his nose at us, dusting non-existent specks off his expensive suit. At last we collected the Professor's necklace without incident. We exited the steel vault, drawing strange stares from the stiff, stern-faced bank employees. Along with the necklace, we'd taken the pencil sketch of the necklace, which showed us what Brisingamen would have looked like if the entire piece were intact.

Trudging through the snow, we passed shop windows fitted out for Christmas, all red holly and deep green trees. The cheer of the holidays was lost on Aidan and me as we found another nondescript motel in another nondescript part of town to hunker down in, where the Christmas spirit was dusty and torn, old and broken.

We'd been elated with our find at first, entranced by the third glowing pendant; the set of three shimmered against the skin around my throat. But we came crashing back down when we examined the drawing in detail. The complete necklace was a series of smaller pendants, each holding a large amber gem in its center. In total, nine individual gems would circle the wearer's neck in a garland of little gleaming suns. Three down, six to go.

"Now what?" Aidan looked at me, eyebrows heavy and shoulders drooping as he sat on the sagging, pumpkin-orange bedcover. His skin was pallid, slowly drained of his blood. The faint outline of the bullet hole-sized bruise in his forehead was more prominent than ever. The Mead had hidden it for the short time we were with the Professor, but it had returned with a vengeance when we crossed the Bifrost.

I dug out a pouch of Mead and poured a glass for each of us. "Now, we wait for Loki," I said.

"Oh. Yeah. Forgot about him."

ANOTHER RESTLESS NIGHT PASSED, while I pondered the wisdom of accepting Loki's offer. I was pretty certain Aidan worried about the same thing. He grew weaker by the day, believing it was Midgard that drained his energies, while I wallowed in my own special brand of guilt.

We ate breakfast at a rundown diner around the corner from the motel. Bad coffee, worse food. Dull chrome and ripped leather. A man sat two booths down from us, watching us over an untouched cup of coffee. He smiled, showing white teeth, tanned skin and hair that seemed darker than Aidan's even in the weak morning light.

"He's here," I hissed. Aidan frowned and turned to look at Mr. Mysterious.

"Loki?"

I nodded. Then raised my own coffee cup in salute to the god. Loki's eyes swirled a bronze-gold hue, and he rose, bringing his cup with him. I shifted and he sat beside me. Aidan stared at this new version of Loki and shook his head.

"So, what's the deal? How do we find Nidhogg?" I asked. Something about Loki made my skin crawl. Just his presence sent shivers up and down my spine.

The bell over the door jangled and the only other customer walked out, head bent low, wrapping his scarf against the blast of Arctic air. Right before the door swung shut, Hugin flew in through the open crack. I glanced at the waitress. Thank heaven she was busy clearing a table and didn't notice. I hoped nobody else would.

Hugin landed on my shoulder. I should have considered it significant that he chose the shoulder farthest from the god, but I was merely grateful for his presence. He felt like living protection.

"*Take care what you promise Loki and what promises you extract from him. He is not the most trustworthy of gods.*" Hugin's baritone soothed my nerves and calmed me.

"You're ready to play at last?" The smug smile on Loki's face made me want to draw my sword and dice him into small pieces. Instead, I gritted my teeth and smiled.

"This isn't a game to us," I answered. Loki knew Aidan's life was at stake, but he continued to treat this as a sport. He was beginning to piss me off. "Now, how do we get to this Nidhogg?"

"The Rainbow of the Gods," said Loki.

"The what?" Aidan asked. An expression of confusion flickered over his features.

Apparently, Aidan didn't trust the god either and I intended to play along. The less Loki knew about our travels, or the extent of our knowledge, the better.

"Also known as the Bifrost. It's the method the gods use to travel between the Nine Worlds," Loki said, impatience furrowing his brow. "You'll need to find the nearest location and use it to travel to Muspell. Muspell is the Realm of Fire."

I didn't need to feign ignorance here. But Aidan didn't look in the least confused.

"The Great Nidhogg resides within the Realm of Fire. It is he whom Loki wishes you to seek. But beware, for he is a trickster." Hugin's honeyed voice sounded in my ear.

I rolled my eyes. Tell me something I don't know.

Loki looked at me and smiled his cheerful, cloying grin. "Do you know how to find the Bifrost?"

"No, but I'm sure Hugin can help us. So how did Nidhogg end up with the rest of the necklace, and why can't you go there and take it from him yourself?" I snapped, unafraid to reveal my impatience with the god.

I'd begun to wonder if this was all a setup. One huge ruse to ensure Brunhilde the Ancient was well and truly punished for her failure to fulfill her original pledge to Freya. Maybe the goddess was just a vindictive bitch and was, right now, laughing at my predicament.

The hopelessness of the whole situation was getting to me. Or maybe it was seeing Aidan get more and more ill every day, or the recent bullet to the ribs I'd received. The Mead seemed to have done nothing to help the healing, and I wondered whether it worked at all to help Aidan.

I was also curious why Loki wanted us to do his dirty work for him. I doubted he really wanted us to give the necklace back to Freya.

Loki picked up a menu and scanned it, a bored look on his face. "As you know, a gem of Brisingamen will glow when it detects the presence of the other gems," he said. "Using that piece of the necklace, I was able to track down the rest of the pieces. But I cannot enter Muspell. Therefore, I cannot retrieve the rest of the necklace and return it to Freya." He tossed down the menu, smiled and shook his head, sadness fairly oozing from his pores. But the aqua swirl of his eyes held a malevolent gleam.

"You've been stealing Brisingamen from Freya for centuries. Why should we believe that you want to return it to her now?" Aidan asked.

Loki pouted. "It's no fun when I can't steal the necklace because it's lost. I want to give it back to her so I can see her face when I steal it from her again."

His eyes glittered and although I believed his reasoning, my gut said that the whole necklace issue went deeper than just giving it back so the trickster god could steal it again. But it didn't matter to me what happened to the necklace once Freya had it in her possession. Loki could steal it a hundred times over for all I cared. As long as I returned it in time to save Aidan's life I'd be happy.

But I remembered Hugin's words of warning.

"We'll find this Nidhogg and get the necklace back to Freya. But what do you want in return?" I asked Loki, sure he had a price to extract from this bargain.

"Who, me?" Loki's attempt at looking offended was a rip-roaring success. Except for his eyes. They turned a flat icy blue, revealing an ancient evil rather than mere mischief. "I don't want anything. You just find the necklace and return it to her Majesty. That is reward enough for me."

He wasn't budging. By now, I'd tired of the additional energy required to keep up the pleasantries with the odious god, tired of the agony of my wound, weighed down with worry of how fast time was running out. I wanted very much for this conversation to be over.

The weak light of the morning had dissipated and bright sunlight now streamed into the overly warm diner. The buttery aroma of waffles and fried eggs rode the air, and the rich bitterness of cheap coffee reeked. The doorbell jingled a few times. More voices encircled our booth, more ignorant people living day-to-day lives I would give my right arm to live now. So far, no one had noticed Hugin. Aidan's face looked paler in the brighter light, dark purple smudges encircled his eyes and the veins in his face and hands were clearly visible through his thinned skin.

I sighed and turned to Loki, unsure how to get rid of him.

He was gone.

Aidan raised an eyebrow and sighed. "So, let's get our stuff sorted and head to the Bridge, then. The sooner we get this done the sooner we can go home."

And that was when it hit me like a two-by-four to the skull; Asgard was home to both of us. Our lives in Midgard had reached a clear and conclusive end.

"Do we use the Central Park Bridge?" I asked Hugin, hoping for something closer to our motel.

My heart sank when the bird nodded.

WE ARRIVED in Muspell in a rush of heat scalding enough to burn the eyebrows off our faces. Quite a change from Greenland

and New York at Christmastime. We both smiled, happy to have survived another journey on the Rainbow of the Gods.

"Right, we get in, get the necklace and get the hell outta here," Aidan said, punctuating the sentence with a few dry coughs.

Hugin scrabbled on my shoulder and put his beak to my ear. "What is it, Hugin?"

"*Once you enter Muspell there is no way out. The Nidhogg will have to release you from the bindings of this world or you may never leave.*"

"Can't you just be straight with us for once?" I bit back, fuming.

"*What do you mean, Brynhildr?*"

"You could have told us that sooner." I gritted my teeth, steeling myself against swatting the daft bird up the side of his head. We were stuck here, whether I skewered the bird with my sword or not.

CHAPTER 40

"What?" Aidan almost shouted the question when I relayed Hugin's news. "That was information we could have used *before* we decided to come here!"

As much as I was angry with Hugin, I understood exactly where we stood. "We would've come whether or not we knew about it. We have no choice but to follow every lead. If Nidhogg has the necklace, we do whatever we have to to get it. And get out of here." I swallowed my outrage at Freya, who'd put me in this position.

My hurt and anger at Aidan had faded, replaced with a little understanding and a dash of forgiveness. Time heals wounds, true, but time also seemed to have cleared my vision of the haze of self-pity, too. I could see how Aidan had come to Craven, doing the job his father requested. I'd have done the same for my father.

Worse was his father's betrayal, sending his thugs out to kill his own son. I couldn't fathom how a father could possibly do such a thing to a son.

Aidan paced around, as if looking for something to kick in frustration. "This is ridiculous. We could be stuck here forever. We could very well die here. Damn that stupid bird!"

"Stop it, Aidan! It's not Hugin's fault. Damn it, it's not even your fault. It's all mine." I stood at the edge of my abyss again. Held back only by the unraveling tendrils of truth.

"Don't be stupid. It's not your fault. It's Freya's pathetic scheming. You'd think gods would be benevolent, kind beings, but no. They're just a bunch of manipulative, cruel users."

Aidan's anger seemed to aggravate the decline in his health. He skin looked so pale and thin I feared he'd rupture the surface with the slightest movement. The bruise from the bullet hole purpled his forehead, ridged in the middle of the wound so much like the day we'd found him beside the stream. Tears filled my eyes as I saw just how ill he really was. I blinked them away angrily.

"No, it's my fault you are here with me," I said.

"Look, Bryn, I wanted to come with you. You needed me to help find the necklace." Aidan placed his hands on my shoulders, locking me in place.

"No," I whispered, looking everywhere else but at his face. "You needed me more."

"What the hell are you talking about?" He shook me slightly, his patience wearing as thin as the skin on his body.

"Freya put a curse on you. A curse to force me to take you on the quest. I would've refused, would've just given her the pendant and been done with it, but she pulled you into the bargain." I pulled away, but distance from him was little consolation.

"What are you talking about?" His voice lowered, dark and dangerous.

"Freya put a curse on your life. She gave you one week from the day we left Asgard. Every day we spend outside Asgard takes one day from your life, brings you closer and closer to death. If we don't get back to Asgard, by tonight, with the necklace, you'll die. Again. Forever, this time."

Silence hung in the air, dark and heavy, and it scared me. I saw all sorts of things inside that silence. Anger and hatred and blame all rolled into one vacuum of sound.

"When were you planning on telling me this?" His face was ashen.

"I don't know. I meant to. I just couldn't bring myself to tell you. Especially when you insisted you'd come with me. Freya instructed me to take you with, and she was right. Most of what we found so far was only because you had access to the right information." As I spoke, I was shocked by the realization that Aidan's presence and his gradual decline had hindered me, too, delaying me as I cared for him. Guess it didn't matter now. I continued, "And then we were here. And then . . . it was too late."

Aidan stared at my face, and I could see he was trying to either find something to say or trying to stop himself from saying something. Either way, I think I preferred the silence more.

He turned and stomped off, despite not knowing in which direction we were meant to go. Hugin caught up with him, and I breathed a sigh of relief, since Aidan could easily lose himself here in the bowels of this hellish world.

I trailed behind them in a self-pitying silence. What could have been was way too far in the past to concentrate on right now. I had to look ahead to finding a way to get out of this place alive.

Especially now, after Hugin's revelation. How do we steal something from Nidhogg and then ask him to allow us to leave?

The tunnels we walked through were so hot that hot was probably too mild a description. The heat parched my throat and dotted my forehead with beads of perspiration.

Great, the sauna of the underworld?

Thankfully, we had Hugin to guide us through the darkened passageways, lit by thin streams of red hot lava, which ran in thin gutters on either side of the rock floor.

Minutes later, I was grateful he'd headed Aidan off.

The passage widened before us, almost as large as a basketball court. But I paid very little attention to the decor of the cave. My eyes were stuck on the monstrous creature that stood between us and our route to Nidhogg.

THE GIANT STOOD NO LESS than ten feet tall, with muscles that bulged larger than our heads, and hair that stood out in every direction as if permanently electrified. One slam of a meaty fist and it would be goodnight for us. He could have been any giant, even Jack's beanstalk climbing giant, except for his beard of living flame. And his eyes. Twin flaming orbs that twisted and crackled within his skull.

He wore flaming armor too, with huge bracers protecting his hands and manacles of fire at his ankles. I shivered despite the constant bombardment of sweat-wringing heat.

"What is that?" I whispered to Hugin.

"*That is a Surt, one of the Giant Race, who guards the land of Muspell from intruders.*"

"And we're the intruders." I sighed, resigned to one more thing we didn't know. "Why didn't you tell us about him, Hugin? We would have at least been prepared."

"*You did not ask me, Brynhildr. And it is unlikely that foreknowledge would have been sufficient to prepare you for this battle.*" He reared his head, unperturbed by the raw fury boiling in my veins.

Wiseass, I thought.

I turned to Aidan, hoping he was up to the challenge of a battle with the brute. "Hankering for a good fight with a Fire Giant?"

"Can I check my calendar and get back to you?" He smiled, and I saw a glimpse of the old Aidan, despite the tightness around his eyes.

"Nope, now's the time for action," I said. My hand went to my sword and Aidan followed suit. I tilted my head at Hugin. "Okay, Blackbird, anything we should know, any tips on defeating this monster?"

"*I am afraid I cannot assist you, Brynhildr. A battle with a Guardian of a Realm is a battle only you can fight. To breach the borders of a realm one must win the opportunity to enter using one's strength, agility and intelligence.*" With that, the raven took flight, finding a small ledge along the cave wall, well out of range of any danger.

Bloody great. So much for the purpose of the damned raven.

I stared at the giant, meeting his gaze head on, hoping I projected a confidence and strength that would have him turn and run with his fiery tail between his legs. If he had a tail. When he didn't flee, I sighed in silence and brandished my sword. The shiiing of the blade leaving the scabbard was calming. And right now I needed calm.

My heart thudded, knocking painfully against my ribs, sweat beading my face. Aidan matched my pose beside me, but my confidence slipped at the sag to his sword and the tired hunch of his shoulders. We should have paused for a drink of Mead when we arrived. Too late now.

I bounced on lowered knees, waiting to see what the giant might do. I saw the swirling ball of fire almost too late. It zinged past my abdomen, singeing the bronze of my armor as it made a full circle. The giant growled again, air pushing at the curtain of his mustache, and grabbed hold of the fireball. The flames died, revealing a ball and chain. Deadly enough in its own right, but a pure menace with all those flames.

Aidan crouched beside me as the giant stepped forward. The ground reverberated when his foot hit the stone floor. It was a waltz, a fiery dance with three participants. We avoided one strike after another from Surt's ball and chain, and his sword. Though we began to tire, Surt himself seemed filled to overflowing with energy as he continued his relentless onslaught.

I moved away from Aidan, trying to draw the giant's attention from him. But it didn't work. Surt swung his fiery ball and hurled it at Aidan, and he did something he hadn't done since we began our little battle. He let go of the chain, allowing the ball to fly at Aidan, with the chain trailing behind its round, fiery body like a comet's tail.

I watched in pure horror as the ball hit Aidan at the top of his shoulder, the tail swinging around to whip hard against his other shoulder and curl across his chest. Flames blazed bright orange against his armor and then fizzled out. Aidan sagged forward, falling to his knees, literally bowing to the power of the fire giant. He grunted as he crumpled to the stone floor, the ball and chain clanking as it rolled away from its victim.

I retraced my steps and circled around Aidan. The giant roared his victory and stamped his foot, slapping his meaty thigh. He was laughing at us.

That's it, no more Miss Nice Guy!

I picked up the ball and chain, expecting it to be way too heavy to lift, considering the ball itself was larger than my entire head. But my own strength surprised me, and I wondered if the power came with being a Valkyrie.

I held it close. An idea began to form.

Circling Surt again, I stepped away from Aidan, who still lay stunned on the ground. The giant drew his sword and thrust it at me. I jumped back, hoping he wouldn't catch me against the stone wall with nowhere to go. A trail of heat slid by my abdomen as he missed. He brought the sword back to him with an angry flick. He tried again, and again, and each time I avoided the sword's heat and bite by a mere hair's breadth.

Surt howled his frustration. I threw the ball at his fist, knocking the sword from his hand. The weapon tumbled to the ground, losing its living flame to reveal a plain, ugly steel blade. He stared at his empty fist and then at my face; angry confusion darkened his face. Surt did not like defeat.

His eyes flamed, swirling orange and red, much like Loki's multihued eyes. When he ran at me, I swung the ball and chain again, catching him at the ankles. The ball curved around both his ankles, tying them together like a trussed chicken. Surt tilted, falling to the ground. He landed with a thunderous thud. Rocks, loosened from the impact, fell from above our heads and I ducked.

Aidan sat up, eyes dazed and filled with pain. I went to him, a bit fearful he would push me away, but he didn't resist. We skirted the unconscious giant, not daring to spend any time studying him.

We crossed the large cavern, hurrying to the passageway, as fast as we could with Aidan almost passing out on my shoulder. Hugin fluttered down from his safe perch in a blur of black, flying ahead of us. I kept the ball and chain, figuring I might need it. In a land as unusual as Muspell, it no doubt helped to have unusual weapons on hand.

As soon as we thought we were safe from the fiery, angry giant, we stopped to rest. Both Aidan and I benefited from sitting down, and a good old slug of Mead put a zing in our veins. My bullet wound had closed but was still incredibly painful to touch.

When I tried to check Aidan for broken bones or other injuries beneath his armor, he batted my hands away and rose to his feet. Then he set a pace that began to worry me. Sure, he would want to get Brisingamen and get out of here, but not at the expense of his health. I'd have no hope of saving him if he killed himself before we got back to Asgard.

CHAPTER 41

The journey seemed endless; and with no daylight to tell us the hour, I was unable to guess how long we had left. I tried to think of other things, or to concentrate on following Hugin. I even replayed my fight with Surt in my mind to see if I could learn anything from it. Nothing worked. I was tired, drained of emotional and physical energy, and just a little drained of faith.

When I was absolutely sure I could go no further, that one more step would just about kill me, Hugin slowed down.

We approached a ledge, overlooking a large canyon. Aidan stuck a hand out to prevent me from stepping straight into the void and tumbling to my death. A ledge, carved out of the solid rock, curved around the canyon, descending all the way to the ground. A part of my brain thought it looked strangely like a wheelchair ramp. Go Muspell for full compliance with disability access laws.

A thunderous, deep-throated growl stopped us in our tracks.

We peered over the edge and stared in abject horror at the creature moving around at the base of the canyon. It glinted, gold and fiery within the dark shadows at the base of the cavern.

"He is the Nidhogg. He is the leader of the Race of Nidhogg," said Hugin.

I tried to calm my nerves, but breathing exercises didn't help at all. In the end, I just relayed Hugin's revelation.

"Well, could you ever say that life was boring?" asked Aidan.

"Nope, negotiating the release of a mythical necklace, with a bloody real-live dragon is all part of day's work where I come from," I answered, not sounding in the least bit overjoyed at the prospect.

Aidan chuckled tiredly, then shuffled to the ramp. I got the message—make it out of here in one piece. I followed, descending into the dragon's lair, resigning myself to a Warrior's death.

I sighed silently, listening to the hollow popping in my ears as we dropped, finally reaching the bottom. Aidan could barely stand upright. We'd come this far, and turning back was not an option, especially when the route back was most definitely cut off.

A blast of heat singed us, hotter and angrier than the temperature of the passageways. The dragon hulked before us, his rippling golden scales reflected the meager light. He exhaled fire-flecked puffs of air high above us. The pads of his feet ended in curved golden claws as large as each of my legs.

I shook my head. This was impossible. How did we expect to fight this golden beast?

The dragon had a wingspan greater than that of a small plane. In fact, the creature was larger than a Cessna, towering over us. If it hadn't been for Aidan, I would have turned and ran. I gripped my sword and my stolen ball and chain, more for comfort than intention to use them. What good were they against so fierce a creature?

He stared at us with eyes so reminiscent of the amber gems of Brisingamen that I had to blink a few times before I was convinced I wasn't seeing things.

He didn't wait too long to strike. We were trespassers, interlopers on his territory. And what would a dragon do but defend his turf? I circled him, leaving Aidan propped against a wall. He was in no shape to be fighting, and I felt a pang of fear. How much time did he really have left? A twisting in my belly hinted that our time was almost up.

The golden wings spread out, and the dragon roared; streams of liquid fire spewed from his open jaws. His mouth, lined with people-sized teeth, clamped shut just inches from my face. I swung my sword around my head, threatening, but not yet ready to move in.

He swiped at me with one of his unusually short hands. Or were they technically legs? His blow connected with my chest, sending me flying into the rough rock face behind me. Armor crunched between my body and the unforgiving rock.

I pulled a golden scale the size of a dinner plate from my armor. I might take that with me as a souvenir if I lived through this battle. It was all so surreal. A scale made of pure gold, a beard of pure fire. I sighed.

Dragons and fire giants. Why am I not surprised?

He waited for me to rise, circling me, golden orbs watching with interest. I lunged, felt the sword connect and then needed to stop my ears against the incredible roar of pain. But I couldn't afford to let go of my weapon. I watched as he limped, retreating for a second. But his dragon anger or dragon pride didn't allow him to back down.

He charged at me again. I mimicked Surt's throw and flung the ball and chain at the dragon's forelegs. The ball hit his left leg, the chain spinning around and tightening over both his ankles as his momentum kept him moving forward. Unable to prevent it, he fell face first, in much the same way as Surt did—the same bone-crunching thud into the ground followed by similar mini-avalanches of rock from the upper regions of the rock faces.

The dragon groaned. Breathed a few weak puffs of fire, and collapsed onto the ground, his huge pink tongue lolling out of his mouth. His golden eyelids shut over his large eyes.

I leaned over, breathing hard, reveling in my victory. I should have kept a close eye on his tail. Should not have taken my attention off such a powerful weapon.

It might have been the smile that did it. I was a bit proud of my victory. A tiny female and I'd taken down a humungous dragon. I didn't see his tail spin around, didn't see the tip of it, as large as a bed, come flying through the air at me.

I felt it, though. A rush of air alerted me, but it was too late. Too late to move, I could only watch as it bore down on me.

Then I went flying through the air, hitting the ground, striking my elbow against the stone floor, sending stars flying through my head. But the impact was smaller than what I'd expected. I looked up, and caught the perplexed expression on the dragon's face as he twisted his upper body around. He was staring now at Aidan, who stood glaring at the beast, his sword dripping great big drops of golden blood.

I watched in amazement as the dragon blinked, looked slightly cross-eyed and crumpled to the ground again.

I caught my breath. Aidan limped toward me.

"Good job there, Valkyrie."

"Back atcha, Warrior."

He pulled me up, propped me against him and began to dig into the bag for the Mead.

"No, I'm fine." I shook my head, listening to the deep huffing sound of the dragon's unconscious breathing. "You drink it. You need it way more than me."

"You're kidding me, right?" he said, shock on his face. "You look like you're halfway to the grave."

"*You* need to last until we get back to Asgard. The Mead gives you strength. I can manage without it, but you need it to survive."

THE SILENCE PRICKED MY AWARENESS. The dragon no longer emitted those small, spark-filled puffs of breath. We looked around for the Nidhogg but the canyon was now strangely silent. How could such a huge creature slink away without us noticing? Impossible. Yet somehow he'd magically puffed into thin air.

"Great timing. Where the hell did he go?" Aidan asked under his breath.

I nudged him in the ribs, forgetting for an instant that his body was failing him.

A step up led to a stone platform, remarkably similar to Odin's dais in his Great Hall. A large stone throne took up the center of the platform, intricately carved with images of trees and fire and dragons. The throne lay empty. A man stood to the right of it. He held a swatch of fabric against his forearm, and his large golden eyes fixed onto Aidan and me as we stood staring back at him.

He looked ordinary enough. Golden-haired and large, though not in a brutish sort of way. But one thing screamed that he was far from your usual good-looking blond hunk.

The tiny scales of his golden reptilian skin glittered as he moved toward us.

"Please don't tell me *he* is the dragon," Aidan whispered beside me.

"Er, pretty sure he is."

The Nidhogg moved closer. He didn't walk or stride. It was more of a smooth glide. I looked at his feet and yes, he had two of them.

"A Valkyrie and a Warrior. I am well and truly defeated." He bowed, and even his voice sounded rich and smooth.

"I apologize for fighting with you," I said, more hesitant and flustered than I'd ever been before. I flushed. "We're in need of a favor. Many lives depend on it."

I wiped my brow and succeeded in only spreading soot over my moist face and arms.

"It was a fair fight, my dear. And you won. I see you have met Bal." He nodded so slightly that I almost missed it.

"Bal?" I asked, confused.

"Bal, the fire giant whose weapon you now hold in your hand."

"I thought his name was Surt."

"No, he is a Surt, a fire giant. But his name is Bal." The dragon-man smiled benevolently then walked to his throne and seated himself. "Very well then, you may tell me what it is that you wish me to do for you."

"I—we have been searching for Brisingamen," I said. "And we have been told that you have it. Or most of it anyway." Aidan shifted from one foot to another beside me.

I was amazed the dragon-man allowed me to finish. He fairly vibrated with raw rage.

"Who told you that?" he roared. Chunks of rock fell from the sides of the cavern, crashing down around us in great heaps of splintered rock and dust.

I decided it was best to go with the truth. "Loki told us you had Brisingamen, and he was unable to come to Muspell to retrieve it."

His expression changed at once. Now the cavern shook with roaring laughter. Were dragons slightly psychotic? Or just this dragon?

"Loki told you that? Oh, my." The Nidhogg wiped golden tears from his eyes and tried to regain some semblance of control over his hilarity. "Oh, my dear Valkyrie. Loki is never to be trusted."

"Yeah, we figured that pretty much the first time we met him," Aidan said. "So why can't he come here, then? I thought all the gods could move between all the Worlds."

"Loki can too, although technically he is a Jötunn, a frost giant, supposed to be imprisoned until the Great War, but Odin has a heart that is too good. The All-Father allows Loki to roam free as long as he behaves. But it looks as if he has already begun his mischief." The dragon-man shook his head, his lip curling in disgust. "And as to why he cannot enter Muspell, it is because he tried to steal a Nidhogg treasure, and my father fortified the wall around Muspell to ensure it did not allow the god Loki to enter. I do not understand how it works, but I believe he used a hair from the trickster god's head."

I smiled. "I suspected as much. He can't enter Muspell, and he's using us to do his dirty work. What does he want with Brisingamen?"

"What he has always wanted. To gain sway over Freya. His jealousy clouds his judgment. Jealousy of power. And his ever-increasing nastiness. It used be fun. All those tricks he played on the gods and on people. Used to be funny. But something changed inside him and the funny evolved into meaner, nastier stuff. From making people laugh, he began to hurt people. It is sad, of course. But it means one needs to keep an ever-watchful eye on him."

I tightened my grip on my sword. "But we have to take Brisingamen to Freya before sunrise." Just saying those words aloud made the reality of the danger to Aidan more tangible. "How do we evade Loki and succeed when he is so determined to keep an eye on us? He's been following us everywhere."

I paused, suddenly cautious, suspicious. The dragon-man hadn't said he would help at all, hadn't even confirmed he had the necklace. Was I assuming he would help just because he was easy on the eye?

"What will happen if you don't hand over the necklace?" he asked, a lazy grin gleaming on his face.

"Aidan will die." Each word fell from my lips like rocks, dark and heavy and filled with pain.

I looked at Aidan. The raw agony of seeing him lying dead beside the freezing stream still made me ache. "I wish I could trade places with him, but Freya is determined to get the necklace back in one piece. And she is happy to use Aidan to get what she wants."

"And if I do give you Brisingamen, what do I get in return?" His eyes glittered, but I felt no malevolence in them.

"I'm not sure what I can trade with." At a loss, I could see the chances of saving Aidan quickly disappearing. I met the dragon-man's eyes. "Well, I have my armor and my weapons."

"And in the bag?" He nodded toward the battered leather bag Sigrun had given me.

"Mead. We have the Mead to sustain Aidan."

A satisfied glint entered his eye. "I will have the Mead in exchange for Brisingamen. It is a small price to pay for taking away such a coveted treasure."

I hesitated. "Can we keep a little, in case Aidan needs it before we get back to Asgard?"

He shook his head, "You will go straight to Asgard. I want all of it. Every drop is important."

I nodded. The trade made sense if we could go straight into Asgard from here. Then we'd go right to Freya with the necklace.

Nidhogg disappeared in a shower of golden dust. He wasn't gone long though, back within seconds with rest of the necklace in his hand. He headed to a table at the side of the dais where Aidan and I joined him. Laying the piece down carefully, he nodded at my neck where the other three pieces glowed brighter than ever before. So bright, I couldn't stand to look at them.

I removed the three pendants from my neck, slipping the one my father had bequeathed me off the leather thong it shared with the golden Glasir leaf. Reluctance slowed my hand. I didn't want to part with the one source of comfort I'd depended upon for the last five months. The pendant and its smaller sisters lay in my quivering palm. And when the dragon-man took the pieces away I felt bereft, serenity ripped from within my clenched fingers.

If he had noticed my discomfort he ignored it, and I was silently grateful.

"I see this piece of Brisingamen has been set in silver." Nidhogg noted with a frown.

I shrugged. "That's how I received it." I stared at my pendant, more worried now that he wouldn't help me because the pendant had been re-set. "Is that going to be a problem?"

"Not really." He said with the merest of nods. He ran his thumb over the fine network of silver that encased the pendant, and solid metal melted into nothing. Then the dragon man smiled.

He set about arranging the pieces; long, tapered and elegant fingers worked effortlessly to bind each gem together, restoring the necklace to its former glory. At last, he touched his finger to the broken links and joined them together one at a time. Leaning forward, I studied the links. Perfect, even if I had to shade my eyes from the glare.

The necklace shone like the circle of suns it was known to be. "There you have it. Brisingamen." He held it up to me. "You should wear it until you get back to Asgard. Do not part with it for anyone."

I nodded as he fitted it around my neck and stepped away from me. I arranged my hair to cover most of the glowing jewels and turned to Aidan, who now leaned against a nearby wall, his eyes half-closed. Nidhogg seemed in no need of chairs for unexpected guests. Aidan looked ready for the grave, eyes black and hollowed, cheekbones poking from beneath thinned blue-tinged skin.

"Thank you. Thank you so much," I said to Nidhogg, smiling brighter than I'd smiled in a long time.

"It was a good trade. I will show you the way."

He turned to the rock face at our right. The black rock softened, liquefied and swirled like a whirlpool. Then it evaporated and a doorway appeared. He stepped into a dark passageway, a carbon copy of the ones we'd used to get to Nidhogg.

He beckoned, and I held on to Aidan, supporting him as we followed our dragon-man through a series of tunnels. Wings flapped in the darkness above me, and Hugin rejoined our little procession.

After a few minutes, the passageway ended in a small cave. We stopped. Nidhogg stood in the center of the cave and waved his hand. A shimmering circle of rainbow-speckled mist grew, and I wondered why Muspell had such beautiful entrances to the Bifrost whereas even Asgard's entrance was plain and seemingly invisible.

"The Rainbow of the Gods," he said with an elegant flourish of his hand.

"Thank you, Nidhogg." I wasn't sure how else I could express my gratitude except for words. A hug would probably seem too forward and might get me in more trouble than I could afford right now.

His laughter took me by surprise.

"I am *the* Nidhogg. The Master of the Nidhogg, the race of dragons who live within Muspell. Did Hugin not tell you this?" He cast a disparaging eye at the raven on my shoulder.

"Hugin has an interesting method of imparting information," I said with a wry smile.

"My name is Steinn and I am a Nidhogg." He smiled, unaffected by my ignorance. I released a tense breath, freeing the pent-up fear that I'd just offended him.

I returned his wave as we stepped into the swirling entrance to the Bifrost. We huddled through and walked straight into the transfer room in Asgard.

CHAPTER 42

I studied Aidan; my first concern was how he'd fared after our journey on the Bridge. His pallor had worsened, and he leaned more of his weight on me as we regained our footing on Asgard ground. He really did look like the walking dead.

Then a spike of exhilaration replaced the turmoil in my stomach. We had won! My arms stayed where they were, tight around his waist, while his fingers moved from my shoulder to the curve of my neck. Pulling me close, keeping me close. The nature of the air changed; electricity rippled around us, between our bodies, which were so close hardly a breadth of air could pass between us.

I forgot to breath, just absorbed Aidan into my pores. It wasn't as if either of us had much of a choice. An inexplicable force pulled us together, body seeking body, skin needing skin. Breath breathing breath. Our lips met in an explosion of honeyed heat, building to a frenzied crescendo that threatened to consume us both whole.

The door slammed open, iron handle crashing into the wall. Sigrun entered, a smile brightening her face as she ran forward and threw her arms around me. I blinked, still awash with heat and an emotion I'd never felt before. I tugged at Sigrun's arms, putting much needed space between us.

"Oh my. I am so very happy you are back! Freya arrived in Asgard two days ago, in case you arrived early. Did you find it?" Her eyes gleamed with happiness as she waited for my answer.

I nodded and smiled, glad she was the first person I saw. And yet, something felt off. I brushed it off as tiredness. My wounds hadn't fully healed and I suspected the bullet had pulverized my rib on its journey through my torso.

She grabbed me and hugged me again. I winced and swallowed a gasp of dizzying agony. Sigrun was a wonderful friend, and terribly kind too, but she wasn't the over-effusive, touchy-feely type. She must really have missed me. "So where is it?" she asked. "Can I see Brisingamen?"

"I have it here." I pointed at my neck, where the necklace peeked out from under the collar of my coat. I was vaguely aware that we'd arrived still wearing our Midgard clothing. "I'm going to take it straight to Freya."

"Please, Brynhildr, could I see it? Once you give it to Freya she will be gone, and we seldom get to see Brisingamen. And never up close." Sigrun smiled.

I opened the top button of my coat and allowed her to get a good look. If Brisingamen was this much of a renowned object, it was no surprise that anyone would want to get a look up close.

"Brynhildr, do you think you could let me wear it? Just for the tiniest second? Please. It would mean the world to me." Sigrun clasped her fingers together beneath her chin and pleaded, her eyes filled with pure expectation.

"Sure." I started to hand it over to my friend, until the tight grasp of Aidan's fingers on my forearm stopped me.

"Bryn, remember what Steinn said." Aidan's weak voice brought me back to reality. *"Don't part with it for anyone. We should be going."*

I glanced at Sigrun, apologetically and maybe a little suspiciously. Why would she have made such a request? But it was her reaction that was more befuddling. Her eyes glowered, her fury so palpable it fairly twisted her face with red rage. I retreated, worried and upset. I'd never seen Sigrun this angry before, and I was torn between hurrying to Freya and comforting my friend.

But we had no time to waste. Aidan looked ready to fall apart. I grabbed his hand and pulled it around my neck, slipping my arm around his waist. I'd carry him if I could, but Aidan would never allow such a thing, so I didn't bother to offer. Didn't want to offend his male ego.

We left the room, entering the darkened hallway. We cast strange and ghoulish shadows as we trudged along; torch lights flickered wildly on the walls. Sigrun's low scream of frustration followed us, evolving into a guttural growl that raised the hair on the back of my neck. My feet dragged and I stopped, the warmth in my blood slowly eking out.

We turned to face the growling monster standing behind us, cloaked in shadows, eyes glowing so much like the amber necklace encircling my neck. She . . . no, *he* snarled, yellow teeth bared to black-mottled gums, saliva glistening in anticipation of the taste of our flesh. The amber eyes swirled and an arctic fist rammed into my gut.

Loki.

He padded toward us, and instinct bade me move in front of Aidan. No way was I allowing him to play big strong protector when he damned well needed the protection himself. Thankfully, Aidan didn't put up a fight.

The massive wolf lowered his bristling body almost to the floor, then launched off his hind legs with all the force of godly power within those muscles. He flew at me, aiming his front paws at my chest, but I backpedaled further down the passage and away from Aidan.

Loki landed on the cold stone, skittering, claws scrabbling for footing. He growled, and goose bumps rippled on my skin. This was Loki, a powerful god. I had no business fighting him. But he wanted Brisingamen. How he intended to remove the necklace from my neck with those gleaming claws was a mystery to me, but that was beside the point. Aidan had so little time left.

Even now, my heart did that funny little jumping dance when I remembered our recent kiss. It had been so long since we'd been so close. It sucked that Loki had to come by at just the right time to spoil my fun.

The hulking beast growled again; his thick black pelt shivered as he sprang again. This time I waited, drawing my sword from the leather scabbard in pained silence. He was almost on me. I brought my sword around in a wide arc, slamming the hilt into his skull with all the force I could muster. The animal fell to the ground beside me, disappearing into a shower of black smoke and puffs of glimmering light too pretty to be connected to this sneaky god.

The dense smoke spread, thicker, larger, until Loki in human guise stood before me, shaking with fury. He ran at me, smashing me into the wall, his forearm pressed into my throat, cutting off my circulation. I pushed, frantic to get him off me and away from the necklace, but no amount of strength could move him. My vision grew dark and heavy at the edges, until I almost passed out. All I could think of was Aidan at the mercy of this vindictive monster.

Then I was free, gasping for breath, rubbing my throat.

Aidan grunted. I looked up to see him and Loki embroiled in a fierce struggle, faces red and veined. Aidan had Loki around the neck, struggling to land a blow to the god's gut. Loki fended off Aidan's hand. Aidan's breath came in short, tired bursts and my heart sank.

I pushed off the wall and grabbed at Loki. Aidan's strength had waned and he was unable to hold on to the god. Loki whirled, daring to bare his back at me, and slammed his fist into Aidan's midriff. All I heard was a desperately anguished groan as the blow landed.

Loki spun toward me, a triumphant sneer on his face, eyes honing in on my neck, where the necklace blazed in tandem with his fury. His face, blood-filled, feral, reduced my knees to Jell-O. So much for being a warrior maiden. I couldn't decide if my best choice was to run, or lash out at him.

Then we both were struck down, pain splicing my cheekbone as I fell to the cold stone. Loki fell with me, surprise, frustration and fury melding into an almost comical grimace.

Fenrir.

He fell upon Loki, trussing him up so fast I barely saw his hands move, and almost missed the glowing chain of gold he withdrew from his belt to wind around the tricky god's hands. The second Fen's eyes met mine, I registered the irony. Fenrir had just captured the god Loki, trickster and troublemaker of the Aesir, who also happened to be his father.

A WARM HAND grasped my arm. I turned to stare into Sigrun's worried eyes. She glanced back at Fen as he drew the bristling Loki to his feet and marched him past us.

"What happened? Are you alright? Is Aidan alright?" Sigrun stared me up and down and did the same for Aidan. Her face fell at his condition. "The Mead?"

The torchlight nearest to her flickered as if in worried agreement with her. It hit me then that the clues had been there in the fake Sigrun. Those hugs, her overly effusive personality, even how she'd called me Brynhildr. Sigrun had stopped calling me that ages ago.

"It helped a little," I said. I was in shock, post-Loki shock.

He'd almost killed me. But I was still standing and I had Fen to thank. And Aidan. He hunched over beside me, his weight leaning more onto me than ever. The necklace was white hot around my neck and all I wanted was to rip it off. The thing had almost cost me Aidan's life. And mine.

We followed Fen as he led Loki to Odin's Hall. The backs of both men were rigid with two different brands of pure rage.

I walked behind them, supporting Aidan with one arm until we neared the entrance.

"I will bring him, you go on," Sigrun said, her voice hushed.

I shrugged the long coat off my shoulders, revealing Brisingamen shining at my neck. The necklace burned hot against my skin, sending sparks of fire into my flesh, hotter and hotter as we neared the hall, as we neared its mistress. My heart thumped within my chest. I hoped the return of her precious treasure would appease her. Aidan's life depended on it.

CHAPTER 43

Our footsteps echoed as we entered Odin's Hall, which thankfully was empty except for Freya, Astrid and Odin. And Hugin, who flew to his master and reclaimed his position on Odin's shoulder.

Despite Loki's intervention, we'd fulfilled our end of the bargain, bringing Brisingamen with us. Elation built within me with each slow step toward the throne. Aidan walked at my side, pushing Sigrun off, demanding to stand alone despite the weakness in his stride and the deathly white pallor of his skin. Odin turned and sent me a pride-filled glance. A burst of emotion flooded my body. Tears dammed hot behind my eyes and the urge to shed them was so strong I almost lost control of that potential flood.

Freya stood to Odin's right, her eyes alight as they settled on my neck. Her delight to see her long-lost necklace echoed in the golden glow shining from her face and body. Her pure happiness revealed her unparalleled beauty as the Goddess of Love.

Beside Freya, Astrid glared at me, cold fury shining from her face, the feathers of her white wings shivering behind her.

I moved forward, smiling.

Freya stepped off the dais, her golden chain-armor shimmering over a dress of spun gold. She seemed to me a stunning vision, and yet I knew the depth of her cruelty. At this point, though, I didn't mind ignoring the way she'd used us. It was done. Over.

She drew close. The fragrance of jasmine flowers drifted to me. I tilted my head, fiddled with the clasp and removed the shining neck piece. Freya snatched it from me, barely waiting for me to hand it over. She stared at the gleaming ring of amber and let out a peal of joyous laughter. Her smile was infectious, her laughter so happy that even I lost the edge to my anger with the goddess.

"My dear Brynhildr. You have succeeded in fulfilling my deepest desire," Freya said, her eyes still fixed on her prized necklace. "To be honest, I didn't expect you to succeed."

There it was. The vein of venom beneath the golden aura of this goddess. Aidan had almost died in the quest to return her precious trinket and she didn't care one bit. No surprise there.

With an ominous edge in her voice, Freya said, "Of course, you shall receive your reward, my dear."

My heart tripped, and I wondered if she meant to renege on her promise to remove the curse from Aidan. I almost stepped in front of him, the need to protect him still my highest priority, but I controlled my instinct. Such an insult to the goddess in Odin's own hall would not be tolerated. I had to force myself to trust her.

For now. He needed to be free from her curse. Free from her hold again.

Freya stood close to Aidan, close enough to place a gentle kiss on his lips. A wave of jealous anger crashed into me. Surely she was able to remove the darned curse without making out with him. At first, wrapped up in the green folds of my jealousy, I didn't see the wisps of golden breath that wafted from her mouth. I stifled a gasp as a snaking coil of golden mist swirled and danced before Aidan's lips.

It entered his mouth.

I shuddered. Freya's magic was beautiful and disgusting at the same time. I wanted to close my eyes, to avoid seeing Freya kissing Aidan. But I remained transfixed, fascinated. A matching twist of mist erupted from Aidan's mouth, only his was a foul mix of green and purplish smoke.

Freya's golden coil pulled the poisonous smoke into it, enveloping it, swirling and twisting around until the green and purple mist was swallowed whole. Not a trace of the poison remained. I sighed, relieved, shaking, and still a little jealous. As she stepped away, I wondered how such a beautiful goddess could instill so deep a hatred within a mere mortal.

Freya returned to the dais, but my attention turned to Loki as he struggled to free himself from his son's bonds. Odin watched, his lone eye burning with fury, a living flame twisting violently within his gaze.

"Take him away, Fenrir." Odin's voice boomed, more suited to his giant presence than the old stooped man. "I will deal with him later." A deep sadness filled his eyes as son led father out of the gigantic hall.

"Thank you." Aidan whispered the words into my ear, color slowly returning to his pale face. "For forgiving me. For saving me."

My heart sang, joyful at the prospect of our future, at grabbing the time we had together with both hands. We'd fought so hard for this—for the chance to be together again.

"You're not so bad yourself." I smiled back at him.

Aidan reached out a hand, tenderly tracing my cheek—and then he groaned. His warm fingers slipped from my face and his shoulders hunched over. Agony streaked across his stricken face as he slumped slowly to the floor. I tried to grab him. But his dead weight pulled me along and I ended up kneeling beside him, struggling to prop him up.

Freya!

I glared up at her, unable to hide my hatred. Had she tricked us into believing that Aidan was cured? But the furrows of concern on her face forced me to stop and think, to temper my fury.

She rushed forward. "Lay him down, let me check him," she said.

I tilted Aidan onto his back, taking his weight on my hands, to lay him gently on the ground. His pallor had worsened so quickly. I couldn't understand why, just moments ago, he'd seemed to be recovering. I parted his coat to free him of his sword—and let out a small cry of horror.

His simple white t-shirt glistened bright red, still wet with fresh blood.

Freya knelt beside us, lifting Aidan's sodden shirt to inspect a vicious open wound. "How old is this wound?" she asked.

I shook my head, unable to answer, my voice choked off by vicious fingers of terror.

"Speak, girl! This is no time for hysterics."

Freya's voice brought me back from my hell, and I cleared my throat. "He didn't have any such injury when we arrived. And the only fighting he did was with Loki."

As I spoke the trickster's name, I turned to the doorway, slowly replaying the fight. Loki'd had so many opportunities to stab Aidan. My gaze followed as Fen and Loki reached the threshold. Then the trickster turned and met my eyes, an evil, triumphant gleam sparkling within those bright green orbs. He smirked at me.

I shivered and broke the gaze.

Freya still sat bent over Aidan, eyes closed as if in deep meditation. I risked disturbing her. "Can you make him better?" I pleaded with her, praying she could heal his wounds, even while dread filled my veins and entwined my soul like vicious creeping vines.

Freya shook her head and sighed. "No. I can do nothing for him. The wound is not the problem. It is the poison in his wound that is killing him."

"Poison?" My voice shattered as I spoke the word.

Odin had moved to Aidan's side. "It is the poison of Skadi's venomous serpent," he explained. "Loki has used this venom before, using the very means of punishment the goddess Skadi used on him."

I knew the myth of Loki's punishment, but couldn't squeeze out a drop of sympathy for whatever agony he may have undergone. I stroked Aidan's hair, my voice sinking to a whisper as I asked, "So . . . Aidan will die?"

"It is possible. But—" Odin and Freya shared a glance. At her tiny nod, he continued. "There is one place where the poison will cease to work."

I grasped at the hope in his words. "Where? We have to take him there if it will save him."

I rose to my knees, reaching again for Aidan, but Freya held my arm and said, "I will take him. There is nothing you can do for him. But I shall try to find a cure."

"Where are you taking him? Can I come and see him?"

"I will take him with me to Hel. Hel is the only place in the world where any poison, not of my creation, becomes useless. You may visit, of course. But, I fear you may be rather occupied." Freya rose slowly, golden silk shimmering with her movements.

My heart sank. I knew then that I wouldn't see Aidan for a while, that I wouldn't be able to make him better after all.

What a viciously beautiful irony.

We'd come all this way, succeeded in returning Brisingamen to Freya, even succeeded in getting Loki incarcerated again, and it was all for nothing. Aidan was still going to die. I wasn't sure I believed that Hel was the best place for him. But I had to trust Odin's advice. It didn't mean I had to trust Freya, though. Not by a long shot.

Aidan now lay so still I could have sworn he was dead. His

skin had turned alabaster, his lips so blue they appeared black. I touched his cheek and was relieved to find it still held a hint of warmth. The muscles in my jaw tightened. *I will save you, whatever it takes*, I thought. Turning my head, I brushed a tear from my cheek and sat up, away from him, stiff-backed and stiff-lipped.

Freya held my gaze, a silent question simmering in the golden depths of her eyes. I nodded.

She leaned over Aidan, touched the tip of her finger to his skin. They both disappeared, the shapes of their bodies shimmering, smoky and ethereal, until they were gone and Odin and I were alone.

"He will be well, Brynhildr. Freya will find a way to heal him. Do not fear. And do not grieve. There is much to do, child. You will have need of your strength and your courage." Odin's voice, though soft, echoed around the hall, and within my head. I nodded, unable to speak. If I so much as opened my mouth, I knew I'd burst into tears.

The god retreated into the shadows of the Hall. Hugin fluttered after Odin as he walked away, leaving me alone with my thoughts.

I sat motionless on the cool marble, admiring the pure white tiles, admiring the bright red of Aidan's blood where grotesque color marred pristine beauty. A wash of grief flowed through me, tears filling my eyes, blurring my vision. I raised my hand to wipe the rivulets of moisture from my eyes and cheeks.

A strange, sticky warmth kissed the soft skin of my face.

I froze, snatching my hand away, my throat cutting off a gasp as I stared at my quivering palms.

Aidan's blood soaked my hands; deepest ruby covered every inch of skin. And, as I studied Aidan's blood on my palms, the sound of Loki's laughter drifted toward me from the open doorway.

THE STORY CONTINUES IN
Dead Embers

The Valkyrie Series
Dead Radiance
Dead Embers
Dead Chaos
Dead Wrath
Dead Silence

TEE AYER

DEAD EMBERS

THE VALKYRIE NOVELS

Book 2

CHAPTER 1

Cold burrowed into my knees, digging icy claws deep into bone. Despite the pain, I didn't move. I just knelt there on the white marble floor of Odin's Hall, time suspended in a maelstrom of seconds and minutes and unshed tears.

Bright red blood, Aidan's blood, dripped from my quivering hands, warm and sticky like honey. Yet there was nothing sweet or pleasant about having the warm ruby liquid seep into the whorls of my fingers and stain my hands and my clothing.

I blinked.

The sounds of the Great Hall simmered around me, fading into the shadows of my despair. Only the rabid cackle of Loki's laughter filtered through my sorrow. The rattle of his chains echoed in my ears as Fenrir dragged him away.

Loki's treachery should not have taken us by surprise at all. I'd never trusted him, not for a minute. Neither had Aidan. We'd expected Loki to show his hand at some point. But when he finally made his move, we never saw it coming. In the end he'd driven his poisoned dagger deep into Aidan's flesh. And now Aidan's blood marred the bold purity of the white tiles, while I sat bereft, haunted by a god's callous laughter and my own pathetic tears, which refused to fall.

I exhaled, a sobbing, shuddering sound that felt too loud and yet not loud enough. I wanted someone to make it all right, or to just make everything go away.

I wanted to curl into a ball and tell everyone to just shut up and leave me the hell alone.

Grief and anger and guilt warred inside me, and I clenched my fingers. The darkening blood beneath my nails glared at me, mocking my grief. A desperate urge engulfed me, a need to scrub the flesh of my fingers raw, to get every last spot of blood out, to erase the rosy tint from my skin.

Soon.

My vision dimmed, eyes unfocused, time passing unnoticed.

Someone touched my shoulder, and I flinched, hand flying to my sword. My knuckles tightened on the hilt beneath my fingers. But when I looked up, it was only Joshua, his brow wrinkled with concern. And Aimee, who stood behind him, gazing at me with watery eyes.

"Bryn," Joshua said, crouching beside me, the heat of his hand warm on my shoulder. "There's nothing more you can do here."

I tried to focus, tried to tell him to leave me be, but instead I said nothing, just let him help me to my feet, let them lead me away to the deafening silence of my room. A pitcher of water sat waiting for me, the people around me preempting my needs. I should have been grateful, should have said thank you.

I said nothing.

Just rubbed the rose-petal-encrusted soap bar all over my fingers and grabbed a little brush, whose intricate dragon carvings barely made any impression on my blurring vision. Rubbing and scrubbing, I was lost in a desperate need to get the blood off my hands, and off my skin.

And my soul.

I was lost. Until Aimee's warm hands grasped mine, tugging the brush from my deadened fingers, rubbing them dry with a clean washcloth. Aimee handed me a clean dress and shooed Joshua out. He threw me a sad, apologetic grin, and all I managed in the way of thanks was a weak smile before Aimee shut the door in his face.

Changing into the fresh garment, I kicked the bloodstained clothes away from me. They landed a bit too close to the fire. Fitting, really. They deserved to burn.

I sat on the bed, and the wool-filled mattress sank as Aimee plopped beside me, giving my arm a sisterly squeeze. I guess I was projecting my mood pretty well because she just sat with me, saying nothing. I was grateful for her silence, and even more for the fact that she wasn't Sigrun, thank goodness.

I wasn't ready to face Sigrun yet.

In my room, I sat unmoving on the fur-laden bed and glared at the red and yellow flames of the fire as it crackled merrily and tried its best to warm me. But my heart remained a blackened, useless lump of ice. I could think of nothing but Aidan— unconscious, abandoned in Hel, alone.

The memories of everything we'd been through together burned like accusatory flames. We'd fulfilled the goddess Freya's demands; we'd found her precious necklace. But in the end it had been for nothing.

In the end, I'd still lost Aidan.

A large part of me blamed Asgard for Aidan's predicament, along with everyone who had anything to do with the realm of Odin. Another part of me blamed my father for messing with DNA and inadvertently creating a Valkyrie. A tiny part of me blamed myself for not paying enough attention to spot Loki's treachery.

So many places where I could lay the blame.

But it was Asgard itself that I now hated with a violent, visceral passion. Asgard had called Aidan to Valhalla, to serve Odin as his Warrior. A goddess of Asgard had played with him, and with me, as if we were just pieces on a chessboard: used, manipulated, then discarded.

And a god of Asgard had poisoned him.

I blinked, and the memory of Odin's face wavered before me, his words echoing in my mind. Soothing, reassuring words. About how I'd had no choice and how Aidan was better off in Hel. But who was Odin kidding? Seriously, there was no friggin' way I could ever agree that Aidan was better off in Hel. How could that possibly be a good thing? And Freya? What sane part of me could ever believe her promise to try her best to help him? I didn't trust her, not by a long shot.

I lay back on the bed, bone-weary. But when my lids finally closed, rest was the last thing I got. Loki's evil snarls and visions of Aidan twisting in his poisoned coma plagued my dreams. Better to stay awake.

For three days, I shut them all out and tried to forget. And at night, while the palace slept, I found solace in the lights of the aurora borealis. Iridescent lights—emerald, mauve, pink and yellow—shimmered across a black night.

I trudged to the rise just beyond the Hall of Valhalla, wrapped tightly in furs to keep out the winter freeze. There I stood, mesmerized by the Northern Lights, as the dark winter's night slid by.

In Asgard they believed the lights marked the passage of the new Warriors into their new life in service to Odin, risen from the dead to fight in the Great War. To die for a greater reason. The lights grounded me with the knowledge that the world turned. No matter my great and insurmountable grief, no matter Aidan's seemingly helpless situation.

Life went on.

When the pale fingers of weak morning light began to steal away the brightness of the aurora, I hurried back to my room before I bumped into anyone and was forced to make small talk.

But my solitude didn't last long. A knock on the door jolted me from my thoughts. "Brynhildr?" A soft, unfamiliar voice filtered through the thick wooden door. "You are summoned. The All-Father awaits your presence."

I closed my eyes a moment and pictured Aidan. Lying asleep, waiting for me. Maybe my pity party had lasted long enough.

During the last few days I'd cried enough tears, then dried them all. Now I reached for the door and yanked it open, fast enough to startle the young Valkyrie in the hall.

"I'm ready," I said.

CHAPTER 2

The soft murmuring in the Great Hall fell silent as I entered. I avoided the eyes of the assembled Warriors and Valkyries and strode toward the shadowed figure on the raised dais.

Odin leaned forward on his seat, his expression softer than I'd expected. The kindness in his smile hurt my heart, and brought burning tears to my eyes.

A wild flutter of black wings in the air caught my attention, and soon a sooty raven landed on my shoulder. Hugin. Odin had given me his favorite raven, Hugin—the legendary Bird of Thought—as a guide when Aidan and I had gone back home to find Freya's beloved necklace, Brisingamen.

The bird weighed next to nothing as he perched on my shoulder. I tilted my head to stare at him, eye to eye; emerald to gleaming obsidian. He bent to my ear and whispered, *"The time spent within the arms of Grief is only worth it if you have a reason to live. Take heed, Brynhildr. You have strength and courage. Use them to free your beloved."*

His ultra-sultry tones were hard for me to process. Every time he spoke, I wondered if he'd gone and swallowed Barry White.

Hugin's advice sounded heartfelt, but I didn't reply. I was still pretty annoyed with the little cat-and-mouse game he'd played on our last mission. The annoying clump of feathers had fed me information one little crumb at a time. Too many times he'd held back crucial information that would've helped us get back home to Asgard sooner.

Hugin tipped his head and pierced me with a knowing, contemplative stare, as if he knew I wasn't his greatest fan, as if that knowledge disappointed him.

I shrugged, not caring that my movement forced Hugin to shuffle to regain his balance.

Well, too bad, Blackbird. In the end, despite your advice, the gods got what they wanted, and Aidan still ended up in Hel with Freya.

Odin crooked a gnarled finger at me. "Come closer, Brynhildr." His patched eye hid within shadows cast by a black, floppy-brimmed hat, the little accessory giving the powerful god a decidedly approachable mien.

I hesitated for an instant, then walked to the beckoning god, leather-sandaled feet making no sound on the marble floor. The links in my chainmail clinked against my sword, the echo slowly fading into the far corners of the hall.

Odin scrutinized me, his single grey eye gleaming with life and with a certain sparkle of cheer.

What did he have to be cheerful about?

I took care to school my features to a more neutral and

acceptable respectfulness. After all, I stood before Odin, God of War, the All-Father.

"My lord." I bowed my head, standing still in front of the seated god.

"Child, I know you have grieved. And I do know you feel you are to blame. But you must release yourself from such a punishment. None of what happened is your fault."

So, time for my telling off at last. A few days hiding in my quarters must have gotten tongues wagging and a whole heap of people worried if the Supreme Father of the Norse Pantheon was so concerned for the well-being of a nobody like me.

"I understand, my lord."

Odin nodded at my words, but I wasn't finished, and I hadn't intended to just agree with him. I couldn't agree. Tears rose and singed my throat, and I added, "But I should really have paid closer attention to Loki, and to Aidan. Aidan was my responsibility. And no matter how I look at it, I failed."

Odin's mouth twitched, and his one-eyed expression shifted from pleasant to scowling. His eyebrows, thick and wiry, almost met at the middle of his forehead. I glared back without flinching. Somehow, I had no fear of this great god. Not that I lacked respect for him or his almighty power. I knew he cared about me, and something told me he would never harm me.

But I was still mad at him.

A soft rumbling like distant thunder sounded as Odin cleared his throat. "Come now, Brynhildr. You must pull yourself out of this grief and self-blame. It is time to move ahead. Time to act instead of feeling sorry for yourself." Odin paused, and a flush spread across his pale cheeks; whatever he'd been thinking had just angered him. When he spoke again, he raised his voice. "Life is moving along without you, and I can no longer allow you to wallow in self-pity. I need you on the front lines."

Something about the urgency in his words piqued my curiosity. "What's going on?" My forehead creased as I looked around the room at the gathered troops, then back at Odin.

Odin's gaze shifted to something behind me, just for an instant, and then his eyes met mine again with a fierce intensity. "We have assembled the scout teams," the All-Father said. "And Fenrir needs to train and dispatch the teams. We need you, Brynhildr, and we cannot wait."

Bootsteps scruffed the marble behind me, the sound making me glance over my shoulder, just as a new voice spoke.

"Well, I thought I would have to come and drag you out of your room by your lovely red hair, Bryn!" Fen's voice rang through the hall as he strode toward the dais.

His teasing brought a small smile to my lips. As much as I'd stubbornly denied it all this time, I now had to admit I had a certain fondness for Fenrir, despite the unfortunate fact that he happened to be the son of the god who'd stabbed Aidan. Or the fact that he also just happened to be a living, breathing, super-strong werewolf. He grinned at me and slapped my shoulder as he stopped beside me.

"What say you, Bryn, are you ready to return to Midgard? We have a fair amount of trouble to attend to," Fen said.

"What do you mean?" My eyes flicked from Fen to Odin. "What's going on?"

"Mimir has spoken," Odin said, his voice booming. "The Vanir have placed their spies in Midgard. People in strategic and important positions. Positions that will be sure to undermine the power of the gods."

I still didn't understand what this had to do with me. Had the god Mimir seen something in my future? I cast a glance at Fen, but his eyes were on Odin, waiting for the Father of the Gods to finish.

"Brynhildr, we have to increase our effort to gather more Warriors. We are no longer in a position to wait. We are creating an elite scout team, one that will do both Search and Retrieval, and do it in double or triple the volume of the old teams. And we will be including the Warriors, too."

This news startled me enough that I risked interrupting. "But I thought the scout teams were always Valkyrie and Ulfr?"

Odin's scowl darkened, tracking deeply above his eyebrows. "Yes, they are, and always have been," he said. "But things are different now. Our army of Warriors has been depleted over time. Retrievals are occurring less and less often. Our army is no longer at a capacity that will ensure our success at Ragnarok."

Fen grumbled, "We need more Warriors, and we are just not getting them anymore."

"Why aren't we getting new Warriors?" I blinked. Confusion clouded my brain as a dull headache set in. I was starting to think I should have stayed in my room.

"That is what we need to find out," answered Fen. "And that is why we need a skilled, strong and courageous team." He gripped my shoulder and gave it a light shake.

"So who's on the team?" I asked.

"Joshua, Aimee and Sigrun, plus our Ulfr."

"Joshua and Aimee?" My jaw dropped. "But they aren't even

trained properly." As soon as I spoke I regretted my outburst. Who was I to judge, when I'd been so deeply immersed in self-blame and self-pity. Fen's next words confirmed my thoughts.

"Bryn, the whole Nine Realms did not stop when you went to find Brisingamen. Nor did it stop when Aidan was poisoned." He smiled a little, perhaps to take the edge off his words.

Too right. It was just my world that had ground to a halt.

Fen jabbed his hand toward the back of the hall, where my two friends from Craven stood among the crowd. "Joshua and Aimee have trained long and hard these past few weeks, and from their progress they are ready enough to take on this mission."

Aimee grinned at me, and Joshua flashed a thumbs-up. My heart warmed at the sight of them, and I gave them a small, happy wave. Adrenaline surged through me at the very thought of working again, of training again, and for a brief moment I forgot the steady ache in my heart. It had taken me far too long to embrace who and what I was: a real, living, breathing Valkyrie—and the only one in the history of Asgard born as a Valkyrie. Accepting that news would've been hard had it not been for my friends. And now I had the opportunity to work beside them.

I grinned at Fen. "So when do we leave?"

"Patience, Brynhildr." Fen's dark eyes narrowed to lupine slits, and my grin dissolved. He hadn't called me anything but Bryn in a long while now, and he knew the full name irked me. But I let it slide.

"You have a few things to learn," he said.

I crossed my arms, my tense shoulders no doubt revealing my stubborn streak. I didn't want to be held back any longer. I'd beaten a fire giant for heaven's sake . . . what more did they expect me to learn?

Fen's eyebrows rose an inch, his eyes gleaming in amusement. My wings fluttered in nervous response as he fixed his stare upon them. I opened my mouth, but Fen's next words startled me into silence, forcing me to swallow whatever smartass quip hovered on my tongue.

"Those things are useless until you actually learn how to use them, you know?"

For the first time since I'd scrubbed Aidan's blood from my hands, a thrill of excitement coursed through me—sweet and hot and filled with delight.

I was going to learn how to fly!

THE STORY CONTINUES IN
Dead Embers

The Valkyrie Series
Dead Radiance
Dead Embers
Dead Chaos
Dead Wrath
Dead Silence

Valkyrie-in-training Bryn Halbrook just can't catch a break.

With her boyfriend stuck in Hel and the taunting laughter of Loki still ringing in her ears, she struggles to concentrate on her training and duties in Odin's realm. The last thing she expects-- or wants--is more adventure!

But then, treachery, a shocking abduction, and a chilling discovery, send her forth on another perilous, globe-hopping mission. As the ultimate battle, Ragnarok, draws closer, it's a race against time for Bryn, Fenrir and their team, to discover who kidnapped her foster brother and what's causing the mysterious deaths of so many of Odin's chosen warriors.

Bryn encounters dwarfs and dragons, new friends and old foes -- but the worst enemy of all may be the person she trusts most.

TEE AYER

FIRE & SHADOW

A HAND OF KALI NOVEL BOOK ONE

CHAPTER 1

Maya flinched. A thousand tiny knives of white-hot pain splintered through her skin. Her teacher's knuckles crunched against her cheekbone and she spared a fleeting thought for the beautiful bruise sure to flower across the side of her face by the next morning.

It was her own fault. Her attention had strayed. Again. Not that she was very good at any form of martial arts anyway.

But she did try.

She should have tried harder.

If she had, she wouldn't be lying flat on her back with the whole room spinning around her. She wouldn't be lying so close to the gym mat that she had to wonder if the odd smell came from the plastic or from the hundreds of sweaty fighting bodies traveling over it every day.

Neither would she be cursing the fact that she'd be sporting this hideous bruise all the way until prom.

Darn it.

"Honey, are you okay?" Leela Rao hurried to her daughter's

side, her dark hair escaping from the knot at the top of her head. She knelt and threw a narrow-eyed glance at Maya's teacher.

At least Mom cares enough to check if I'm still alive.

Maya groaned as her mom's fingers probed her cheekbone, only causing further pain. And maybe even breaking off splintered bone.

Her mom tucked a stray strand of Maya's black hair behind her ear and sat on her heels. "It's fine, nothing broken. But you will have a lovely black eye for the next few days."

"Yeah, let's see what Child Services says," Maya muttered.

She was prone to opening her mouth and spewing out words without thinking. It's what usually got her in trouble. She immediately regretted the comment and hoped her mom hadn't heard.

One look at her mom's face told her otherwise. Leela frowned and shook her head, as if wanting to scold, but knowing the time and the place was entirely wrong for disciplining her daughter. Still, Maya had no intention of apologizing.

"Come on. If you're fine enough to be a smart-ass then you're fine to get back up and practice."

Her Kung Fu teacher smiled, all teeth, and stuck his hand in front of Maya's face. She glared at the hand. She really had no choice so she took it and allowed him to lift her back to her feet in one fluid move.

"No pain, no gain, hey Maya?"

She dusted herself off despite knowing full well no dust clung to her. She kept her eyes on the floor, not daring to look around. How many of the other students had witnessed her embarrassing knockout?

Nik was there too, somewhere within the broiling group greeting their instructors and filing out of the studio. Nik who always seemed to be around, ever since his arrival three months ago. If they didn't happen to run in the same social circles, Maya would have suspected him of stalking.

But no, they went to the same school, and within days of Nik's arrival they'd shared the same martial arts class, even had a few short and awkward conversations when she'd caught him watching her and he hadn't been able to flee easily.

Nik Lucas, with his dark curling hair, strong chiseled features and deep black eyes.

Nik Lucas.

The forbidden fruit.

Nope, only nice Indian boys need apply. Besides, if she'd heard it once, she'd heard it a thousand times - when she was ready for boys then she was ready for marriage. Nik remained off-limits.

Too white.

Not Indian enough.

Whatever.

Maya couldn't even allow herself the pleasure of daydreams. She'd be setting her heart up for the inevitable break.

Maya tried to stop thinking of Nik, tried to convince herself he'd probably missed the whole debacle. She resumed her position, wide stance, bent knees, weight on the balls of her feet.

Her cheek stung, a reminder to keep her eyes on her teacher's hands, or rather her Sifu. She had to call him Sifu during her lessons.

Them's the rules.

She really wanted to grit her teeth but the blow to her cheekbone still bled icy pain into her jaw.

Maya blocked her instructor's first strike with an effortless snap of her wrist. He was going easy on her. Which meant he'd bring out the big guns soon enough. She tested her jaw, moving it side to side as she circled him.

Eye to eye.

Hand to hand.

She hoped eating wouldn't be a problem.

Two lightning fast moves later, she froze nose to skin with his fist. He'd spared her the full impact of the punch. And he wasn't usually that generous. Maya blinked, staring at his golden-brown eyes over the edges of his knuckles.

Nope, not a hint of sympathy.

Nothing.

She sank into her stance again and knew it would inevitably end in trouble. This time he used a smooth roundhouse kick, and whacked her feet from under her.

The bone-shattering impact with the ground left Maya in stunned agony. Way worse after the blow to her cheekbone. Way worse when her head hit the floor so hard she almost passed out.

"Dad!" Maya cried, her voice filled with unshed tears and pain.

"Sorry, honey. Are you okay?" He peered at her, a cheeky grin pasted on his face.

It wasn't fair when he did that. In fact, he got away with everything because of that stupid, lopsided grin. He pushed wet strands of hair from her cheeks, his fingers moving to her neck to check her pulse.

"Maybe we should call it a day, okay?"

Er . . . like I'm going to actually say no? Really Dad? She nodded, and allowed him to help her to her feet. When her knees buckled he swung her smoothly into his arms.

So embarrassing.

Sixteen years old, and her father still carried her as if she weighed the same as she had ten years ago. But she let him, and just rested her head on his chest.

This time she refused to fight him.

Teacher or not, next time he'd better watch out.

Maya's mom fluffed up her pillows and smiled down at her daughter. "You'll be happy to know this injury will get you out of going to temple this week."

"Why is that? Wouldn't it be better to go and show all your friends you're bringing up your daughter the traditional, well-disciplined way?" The words were out and there was nothing she could do to take them back.

"Maya," her mom gasped. But the shock melted from her face as she sat on the edge of Maya's bed. "Honey, you know we haven't brought you up in the 'traditional' way. You wouldn't be learning to fight if we did."

"So why am I? You and dad can both see how terrible I am? Why don't you let me give it up?"

Maya pouted, glad they'd moved on to another topic, a safe distance from her insults to her parents..

Her mom tucked her hair behind her ear; she'd always said Maya shouldn't hide her pretty face behind her hair. "Because you must learn to protect yourself. We need to know that you have at least some ability to defend yourself. Just in case."

"In case of what? Somerville's probably the safest suburb in the state of California. Maybe even the whole of the western seaboard," Maya grumbled.

Grabbing a cushion from beside her, she began to pull at the beaded tassels. She'd been training under her dad's tutelage since she was six years old. He'd been running the school ever since her parents arrived in America when Maya was just a baby.

"Well, you just never know-" a note of hesitation in her mom's voice drew Maya's gaze.

Her mom opened her mouth to say something, but a moment later the urge seemed to subside and she went silent.

Then she sighed and said, "You should send up a prayer or two." Maya stared as her mom pointed a finger to the ceiling. "You probably need all the help you can get especially with a black eye that bad."

"Mom," Maya scolded, shocked she'd suggest such a thing. "You know what I think."

"Yes, honey. I know you don't believe now. But someday soon, you may no longer have a choice. Now, get some rest."

Her mom stood, gently patted Maya's cheek before leaning over to kiss her forehead. Her waist length hair, so like Maya's, swayed as she walked out of the room.

At the doorway she turned and winked at her daughter. "If

you don't want the gods to help you, then you'd better be prepared to help yourself."

The door closed with a snick just as the cushion Maya had been playing with hit it. Maya shook her head, chuckling. Her mom always had a way with words.

Although her parents had accepted she didn't fully believe in the theology of Hinduism, her mom never failed to try her luck at convincing her every so often.

Still, she was thankful they didn't force her to perform all the rituals and customs. They were less orthodox than the other parents in the community, like her friend Ria's father. But they still maintained their belief in the gods.

It's merely mythology.

Not actually real.

But when her mother looked at her that way, Maya had to wonder what it really took to believe.

The Hand of Kali Series

Fire & Shadow

Blood & Gold

Time & Fate

Fury & Virtue

Spirit & Soul

Demigod

After a thousand years, things are beginning to fall apart for angel Evangeline. Her mentor is near death. Her new boss, Marcellus, is obsessed with bronze disks and dead demons. And Evie is feeling guilty having just wiped another demon off the face of the earth. So Evie does what Evie does best.

And when an enigmatic albino demon with dreadlocks and a potent angel allergy reveals the true nature of the disks, Evie must do everything in her power to keep Marcellus away from them. It should be simple. But as usual, everything is not as it seems, and Evie is thrust headlong into a race against time; to save her own life and that of the uber-hot Julian; current ruler of Hades. And everything hangs in the balance; her life, her destiny, and her dreams.

Eighteen-year-old Gray McAllister flees from a dangerous past and attempts to start anew. Her path crosses with Thane Blackwell, leading to an intense attraction.

As Thane recovers from surgery in Gray's apartment, they struggle to control their feelings.

With high stakes, secrets, and lies threatening their relationship, it's uncertain if Gray's past or Thane's secrets will disrupt their lives first.

My name's Ella Raimi.

Until last week, my life was pretty normal for a sixteen-year-old. Until I spent that awful night trapped in the janitor's closet in utter darkness. Until the dreams began—suffocating, panic-filled dreams. My best friend Kyla stays with me, but the dreams still continue.

And I wake each morning with cuts & burns on my skin. I don't recall inflicting them. And then there is the blood on my hands and my sheets when I wake up. I'm afraid of myself.

I'm afraid I am a killer.

ACKNOWLEDGEMENTS

To Dharshini and Dhivya – for tiptoeing and whispering, for random cups of tea and for your unfailing belief in your mom – Best Daughters Ever.

To Patti Larsen, writing partner, mentor, and friend – for keeping me sane.

To Cassie Hart – who forced me to churn out pages just so she could know what happens next.

To Natasha Pillay – an incredible friend and soul sister.

To my Beta readers Courtney McDonald, Mina Witteman, Rachna Chhabria, Kimberly Kinrade, Dharsh and Patti – for loving this book even when it was a grubby first draft.

To my editor Eric Pinder, rock star of editors – for all-nighters and bleary eyes, for knowing what needed fixing without me having to explain.

To Valerie Bellamy, print designer and mind-reader – for somehow knowing exactly what I want and for your eternal patience.

To Eduardo Priego, super-talented cover artist – for bringing to life the cover I thought would only exist in my imagination.

And to you, the reader – you are the reason I write.

ALSO BY TEE AYER

Young Adult Paranormal

THE VALKYRIE SERIES

Dead Radiance

Dead Embers

Dead Chaos

Dead Wrath

Dead Silence

Joshua - Dead Radiance

Joshua II - Dead Embers

THE HAND OF KALI SERIES

Fire & Shadow

Blood & Gold

Time & Fate

Fury & Virtue

Spirit & Soul

Demigod

<u>***Adult Urban Fantasy***</u>

THE DARKWORLD SKINWALKER SERIES

Skin Deep

Lost Soul

Last Chance

Blood Promise

Scorched Fury

Fate's Edge

Grave Debt

Oath Bound

Rebel Heart

Veiled Curse

Dark Hunt

THE DARKWORLD ORIGINS

Pyros (Logan)

Ailuros (Kailin)

Join my Newsletter

Keep up to date on all the newest releases, giveaways and news when you subscribe to my newsletter.

ABOUT THE AUTHOR

Tee's passion for strong females and ability to spin a fairly decent sentence, has resulted in over 60 published titles spanning 3 pen names and over 7 genres.

Tee's alter ego, Toni Vallan, writes Psychological Horror and Suspense.

Writing since 2010, Tee currently lives in Middle Earth. She is a proudly #AfricanAuthor, and in South Africa will her roots remain. Her heart still longs for the endless beaches and the smell of moist soil after a summer downpour.

She loves the beach, and her readers, is an artist, a nerd, and a geek, hates crowds, and sings like Adele (only in her head). If she could grow up to be Wonder Woman she'd die happy.

Most days, Tee can be found typing away at her laptop, creating more words.

Stalk Tee here:

www.teeayer.com

tee@teeayer.com

facebook.com/TeeAyerAuthor

amazon.com/author/teeayer

instagram.com/tee.ayer